THE PRODIGAL APPRENTICE

Other Victor Books by George MacDonald

A Quiet Neighborhood
The Seaboard Parish
The Vicar's Daughter
The Shopkeeper's Daughter
The Last Castle

George MacDonald

Edited by
Dan Hamilton

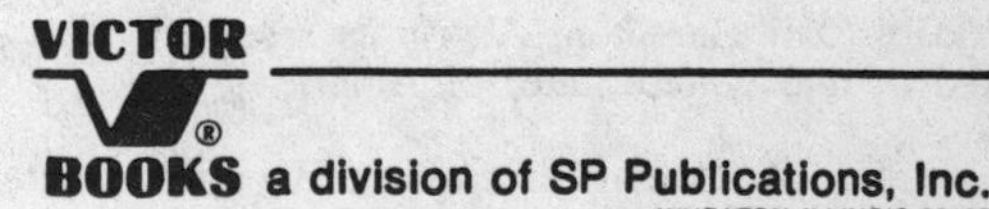

a division of SP Publications, Inc.
WHEATON, ILLINOIS 60187

Offices also in
Whitby, Ontario, Canada
Amersham-on-the-Hill, Bucks, England

The Prodigal Apprentice was first published in 1867 in England, under the title of *Guild Court*.

Library of Congress Catalog Card Number: 85-62713
ISBN: 0-89693-151-X

Printed in the United States of America

VICTOR BOOKS
A division of SP Publications, Inc.
Wheaton, Illinois 60187

TABLE OF CONTENTS

Editor's Foreword

The Prodigal Apprentice is the sixth George MacDonald novel from Victor Books. Originally published in 1867 as *Guild Court,* this is one of MacDonald's few tales located primarily in a large city; as such, the book places MacDonald beside Dickens as a perceptive and able chronicler of Victorian London. MacDonald describes the wretched side of London street life without descending to the intermittent mawkishness of Dickens'; he also rises above Dickens by his constant and acute awareness of the certain life that lies beyond what we now know.

One of MacDonald's favorite themes is woven into this story. He maintained that a knowledge of "correct doctrine" (emphasized throughout his strict religious upbringing) was not enough; that a man's spiritual standing depended largely upon whether he was moving closer to God or farther away from Him. Therefore, he frequently portrayed some of the supposed "elect" as spiritually dead people who were becoming less and less godly as they grew older and colder—usually in contrast to a character who made no obvious claim to Christian belief, but who was all the time moving closer to God in action, understanding, and agreement. MacDonald held that doctrine was useless until it was *done*—that it was a mere empty parroting of memorized words unless action transformed the words in the mind into meaning in the heart. And *The Prodigal Apprentice is* a novel of decisions, actions, consequences, and motion both toward and away from God. Seldom does any book—and especially any fiction—so consistently and accurately document and display the process of sin, conviction, repentance, confession, forgiveness, and reconciliation. Such a work is a glimpse into the kingdom of heaven being hammered out on earth.

All of MacDonald's work is well worth the reading. Unfortunately, only his children's fantasy works (*At the Back of the North Wind, The Princess and The Goblin, The Princess and Curdie,* and others) have been widely available since his death; this has given the world a somewhat distorted impression of his interests, talents, and works. He was much more than a fantasist and writer of juveniles, but his novels, poetry, and sermons have not been reprinted in their entirety since the early years of this century. The current series of edited novels from Victor Books should help to fill that gap, and is intended to make MacDonald's "forgotten" works available and affordable for a new generation.

There are certain economic and editorial necessities involved in republishing MacDonald—including some trimming of the original voluminous manuscripts. *The Prodigal Apprentice* is no exception. MacDonald told a good story, but (like many other Victorian writers) he used more words than necessary to tell the tale, and frequently allowed the narrative to wander off in unrelated directions. I have trimmed away the tedious and awkward passages which do so little either to advance the story line or to grant us MacDonald's unique insight into God and man. For the story in all its slow richness, with all its curious tangents and minor asides, the reader will have to turn to one of the original editions.

I do not represent this edited version as any *better* than the original—merely more affordable and more appealing to the readers of our time. I sincerely hope that the recent success of edited MacDonald novels, which has reawakened interest in MacDonald himself, will eventually create a demand for his republished works in their unaltered form. Until such time, these condensed editions will continue to provide MacDonald's essence, flavor, and message.

Dan Hamilton
Indianapolis, Indiana
February 1986

INTRODUCTION

George MacDonald (1824-1905), a Scottish preacher, poet, novelist, fantasist, expositor, and public figure, is most well known today for his children's books—*At the Back of the North Wind, The Princess and the Goblin, The Princess and Curdie,* and his fantasies *Lilith* and *Phantastes.*

But his fame is based on far more than his fantasies. His lifetime output of more than fifty popular books placed him in the same literary realm as Charles Dickens, Wilkie Collins, William Thackeray, and Thomas Carlyle. He numbered among his friends and acquaintances Lewis Carroll, Mark Twain, Lady Byron, and John Ruskin.

Among his later admirers were G.K. Chesterton, W.H. Auden, and C.S. Lewis. MacDonald's fantasy *Phantastes* was a turning point in Lewis' conversion; Lewis acknowledged MacDonald as his spiritual master, and declared that he had never written a book without quoting from MacDonald.

1. The Countinghouse

On an unusually grand November morning, young Thomas Worboise was walking from Highbury to the City. There was a lofty blue sky overhead, with multitudes of great clouds half-way to the earth, among which a glad west wind was reveling.

Although Thomas enjoyed the wind on his right cheek as he walked down High Street, he was largely depressed, and his look was down at his light trousers or his enameled boots, and never rose higher than the shop windows.

As he turned into the churchyard to go eastward, he was joined by Charles Wither, an acquaintance and workmate a few years older than himself.

"Jolly morning, ain't it, Tom?" Charles said.

"Ye-es," answered Tom, with a fashionable drawl, and in the doubtful tone of one who will be careful how he praises or condemns anything. "It almost makes one feel young again."

"Ha! How long is it since you enjoyed that pleasing sensation?"

"None of your chaff, now, Charles."

"Well, if you don't like chaff, you put yourself at the wrong end of the winnower. But I can afford to stand your chaff, for I feel as young as the day I was born. If you were a fast fellow, now, I shouldn't wonder. But for one like you that teaches in the Sunday School and all that, I am ashamed of you, talking like that. Confess now, you don't believe a word of what you cram the goslings with."

"Charles, you may make game of me as you like, but I won't let you say a word against religion in my presence. You may despise me if you please, and think it very spoony of me to teach in the Sunday School, but—"

"You know as well as I do, old fellow, that you don't believe a word of it. I don't mean you want to cheat me or anyone else. You're above that, but you do cheat yourself. What's the good of it all when you don't feel half as merry as I do on a bright morning like this? I never trouble my head about that rubbish. Here am I, as happy as I care to be—for today, at least—and 'sufficient unto the day . . .' you know."

Thomas might have replied, had he been capable, that although the evil is sufficient for the day, the good may not be. But he said something very different, although with a solemnity fit for an archbishop.

"There's a day coming, Charles, when the evil will be more than sufficient. I want to save my soul. You have a soul to save too."

"Possibly," answered Charles, with more carelessness than he felt, for he could not help being struck with the tone of the reply, if not with its meaning. "But if your soul be safe," he continued, "why should you be so gloomy?"

"Are there no souls to save but mine? There's yours now."

"Is that why you put on your shiny trot boxes and your lavender trousers, old fellow? Come, don't be stuck-up. I can't stand it."

"As you please, Charles. I like you too much to mind your making game of me."

"Come now," said Charles, "speak right out. You seem to know something I don't. You might convert me and save my soul that you make such a fuss about. For my part, I haven't found out that I have a soul yet. What am I to do before I know I've got it? But that's not the point. It's the trousers. When I feel miserable about myself—"

"Nonsense, Charles! You never do."

"But I do, though. I want something I haven't got often enough. And, for the life of me, I don't know what it is. Sometimes I think it's a wife. Sometimes I think it's freedom to do whatever I please. Sometimes I think it's a bottle of claret and a jolly good laugh. But to return to the trousers."

"Now leave my trousers alone. It's quite disgusting to treat serious things after such a fashion."

"I didn't know trousers were serious things. And I was talking about my own trousers, not yours."

"I see nothing particular about yours."

"That's because I am neither glad nor sorry. When I am in such a serious and foggy mood as yours, I never dream of putting on lavender trousers."

So talking, they soon reached Bunhill Fields and the countinghouse, the scene of their daily labor. The long, narrow room was rather dark, and situated in a narrow street that opened off one of the principal city thoroughfares.

As the young men entered, they were greeted with a low growl from the principal clerk, Mr. Stopper—a black-browed, long-nosed man. Two other clerks looked up with a "Good morning" and an odd expression in their eyes. Some remarks had apparently been made about the most recent arrivals, and now a voice came from the depths of the room.

"Tom, I want you."

Tom disposed of his hat and gloves with some care.

"You hear the governor, Mr. Worboise?" growled Mr. Stopper.

"Yes, I hear him," answered Tom with nonchalance—some real and some assumed.

Mr. Richard Boxall, the governor, could be seen at his writing-table behind a glass partition which crossed the whole room. He had a high forehead, a commonplace countenance, and hair finely tonsured by the scythe of time into an iron-gray corona.

When he was quite ready, Tom walked into the inner room.

"Tom, my boy, you are late," said Mr. Boxall. There was great brilliance in his deep-set eyes, and a certain touch of merriment about the mouth.

"Not very late, I believe, Sir," answered Thomas. "My watch must have misled me."

"Pull out your watch, my boy, and let us see."

Thomas obeyed.

"By your own watch, it is a quarter past," said Mr. Boxall.

"I have been here five minutes."

"I will not do you the discredit of noting you have spent that time in taking off your hat and gloves. Your watch is five minutes slower than mine," continued Mr. Boxall, pulling out a saucepan of silver, "and mine is five minutes slower than the Exchange. You are nearly half an hour late. You will never get on if you are not punctual. It's an old-fashioned virtue, I know, but first at the office is first in the race. You'll never make money if you're late."

"I have no particular wish to make money," said Thomas.

"But I do," rejoined Mr. Boxall, good-naturedly, "and you are my servant and must do your part."

Thomas bridled visibly.

"Ah! I see," resumed the merchant. "You don't like the word. I will change it. There are no masters or servants nowadays; they are all governors and employees. What they gain by the alteration, I don't know."

"Mr. Wither was late as well, Sir. Why should I always be pulled up, and nobody else?"

"Mr. Wither is very seldom late, and you are often late, my boy. Besides, your father is a friend of mine, and I want to do my duty by him. I want you to get on."

"My father is very much obliged to you, Sir."

"So he tells me," returned Mr. Boxall, with remarkable good humor. "We expect you to dine with us tomorrow, mind."

"Thank you, but I have another engagement," answered Thomas, with supposed dignity.

Mr. Boxall's brow fell, but he looked more disappointed than angry.

"I am sorry for that, Tom. I wish you could have dined with us. I won't detain you longer. Mind you don't ink your trousers."

Was Thomas never to hear the last of the trousers? He began to wish he had worn something else. He made his bow, and withdrew in chagrin, considering himself disgraced before his fellows. But his heart smote him—gently, it must be confessed—for having refused the kindness of Mr. Boxall, and showing so much resentment where the governor was quite right.

Mr. Boxall was a man who had made his money without losing his money's worth. Nobody could accuse him of having ever done a mean or dishonest thing, yet he was well recognized as a sharp man of business, and any Exchange jobber knew it useless to dream of getting an advantage over Mr. Boxall. He was keen as an eagle on his own side, yet thoroughly just on the other, and driven by no uncertainty to give the other side anything more than was just right. Yet Mr. Boxall knew how to be generous upon occasion, both in time and money. His chief fault was too great a respect for success. He had risen himself by honest diligence, and he thought when a man could not rise it must be either from the want of either diligence or honesty. Hence he was perhaps too ready to trust the successful man. Part of his success was his family of three daughters, two of whom were near Thomas' age, and the other but a child.

Thomas Worboise's father, a lawyer, had been a friend of Boxall's for many years, at least so far as the relation could be called friendship. It consisted of meeting in business, dining together two or three times in the course of the year, and keeping an open door to each other's family. Thomas was an only son, with one sister, and his father would gladly have brought him up to the legal profession. But as Thomas showed considerable disinclination to the necessary studies, he had placed him with hope in Mr. Boxall's countinghouse.

Tom's mother was a woman of weak health and intellect, but strong character. She was very religious, and had great influence over her son, who was far more attached to her than he was to his father. Tom's sister Amy, on the other hand, leaned more to her father, an arrangement not uncommon in families.

Either father would have gladly seen Thomas engaged to one of the Boxall daughters. They were both men of considerable property, and thought that this would be a pleasant way of securing the future of their possessions. At the same time Mr. Boxall was not quite satisfied with Tom's business character. However, since there had been no signs of interest between him and either of the older girls, there was no cause to be particularly anxious about the matter.

2. At Home

Office hours were long over before Tom appeared at home that night. He went into his mother's room, and found her, as usual, reclining on her pillowed couch. Her face, perhaps in consequence of her never desiring sympathy, was hard and unnaturally still. When her son entered, a gentle shimmer of love shone out of her troubled blue eyes, but her words did not correspond to the shine. She was one of those who think God jealous of the amount of love bestowed upon other human beings, even by their own parents, and therefore struggle to keep down their deepest and holiest emotions, regarding them not merely as a weakness but as positive sin.

"Well, Thomas," said his mother, "what has kept you?"

"Oh, I waited and walked home with Charles Wither. He had some extra business to finish."

However, it was business of his own, not office business; and Tom, finding out that he would be walking home a couple of hours later, had arranged to join him that he might have this account to give of himself.

"I do not like that young man," she continued. "He is not religious, but quite worldly. Does he ever go to church?"

"I don't know, Mother. He's not a bad sort of fellow."

"He *is* a bad sort of fellow, and the less you are with him the better."

"I can't help being with him in the office, you know, Mother."

"You need not be with him after office hours."

"Well, no, perhaps not. But it would look strange to avoid him."

"I thought you had more strength of character, Thomas."

"I—I spoke very seriously to him this morning, Mother."

"Ah! That alters the case, if you have courage to speak the truth to him."

The door opened, and the young curate of St. Solomon's was announced. Mrs. Worboise was always at home to him, and he called frequently, both because she was too great an invalid to go to church, and because they supposed (by using the same religious phrases in their conversation) that they understood each other. With him the profession had become everything, for humanity never had been anything. He walked through the crowded streets in the neighborhood with hurried steps, eyes fixed on the ground, his pale face rarely brightening with recognition, for he seldom saw any passing acquaintance. When he did, he greeted him with a voice that seemed to come from far-off shores, but came really from a bloodless, nerveless chest that had nothing to do with life, save to yield up the ghost in eternal security and send it safe out of it. He would not have hurt a fly, and he would have died to save a malefactor from the gallows, that he might give him another chance of repentance. But mere human aid he had none to bestow—no warmth, no heartening, no hope.

Mr. Simon bowed solemnly and shook hands with Mrs. Worboise.

"How are you tonight, Mrs. Worboise?" he said, glancing round the room. The only sign of humanity about him was a certain weak admiration of Amy Worboise, a merry girl who made great sport of "the little church mouse."

Mrs. Worboise did not reply to this question, which she always treated as irrelevant. Mr. Simon then shook hands with Thomas.

"Any good signs in your church class, Mr. Thomas?" he asked.

The question irritated Tom. He had entered upon another phase of experience since he saw the curate last, and the Sunday School was a little distasteful to him at the moment.

"No," he answered, with either weariness or indifference.

The clergyman thought it the latter, and proceeded to justify his question, addressing his words to the mother.

"Your son thinks me too anxious about the fruits of his labor, Mrs. Worboise. But when we think of the briefness of life, how soon the night cometh when no man can work, I do not think we can be too earnest to win souls for our crown of rejoicing, when He cometh with the holy angels. There are so many souls that might be saved, and so few years to do it in."

"That is too true," responded the lady.

"I try to do my best," said Thomas, in a tone of apology, and with a lingering doubt whether he was really speaking the absolute truth. But he comforted himself with saying to himself, "I only said, 'I try to do my best'; I did not say, 'I try my best to do my best.' "

"I have no reason to doubt it, my young friend," returned the curate, who was not ten years older than Tom. "I only fancied that you did not respond quite so heartily as usual to my question."

The mother's eyes were anxiously fixed on her son during the conversation, for her instincts told her that he was not quite at ease. She had never given him any scope, never trusted him, or trained him to freedom; but, herself a prisoner to her drawing room and bedroom, sought to keep and strengthen the invisible cable by which she held him, even when he was out of her sight.

Mr. Simon changed the subject. "Have you much pain tonight, Mrs. Worboise?"

"I can bear it," she answered. "It will not last forever."

"You find comfort in looking to the rest that remaineth," responded Mr. Simon. "It is the truest comfort. Still, your friends would gladly see you enjoy a little more of the present dispensation."

"The love of this world bringeth a snare," suggested Mrs. Worboise, believing that she quoted Scripture.

Thomas rose and left the room, and did not return till the curate had taken his leave. As soon as he entered he felt her anxious, pale-blue eyes upon him.

"Why did you leave, Thomas?" she asked, her face twinging from sharper pain than ordinary. "You must listen to him. He is a man whose conversation is in heaven."

"I thought you would like to have your private talk with him. But," he continued, "I wanted to speak to you about something. You mustn't mind my being late once or twice a week now, for I am going in for German. A very good master lives a few doors from the countinghouse, and if I take lessons in the evening at his lodgings, he charges much less. And it is such an advantage nowadays for anyone who wants to get on in business to know German!"

"I will speak to your father about it," she answered.

This was as Thomas hoped, for he had no fear of his father making any objection. He kissed his mother on the cheek, and they parted for the night.

3. The Boxalls' Dinner

Thomas descended to breakfast, feeling fresh and hopeful. It was a clear frosty morning, and the cold, blue cloudless sky and cold, gray leafless earth reflected each other's winter attributes. Thomas stood up with his back to the blazing fire, and through the window saw his father coming in from the garden. Father and son did not shake hands or wish each other a good-morning, but they nodded and smiled, and took their seats at the table.

Mr. Worboise smoothed the two long side-tresses of his thin hair, trained like creepers over the bald top of his head. His eyebrows were very dark, straight, and bushy; his eyes a keen hazel; his nose straight on the ridge, but angled at the point; his mouth drawn upward by the corners when he smiled, which gave him the appearance of laughing down at everything. No one ever saw his teeth, though to judge from his table performance they were in serviceable condition. He was tall, shapeless, and wore black clothes.

"You're dining at the Boxalls tonight, I believe, Tom. Mr. Boxall asked me, but I can't go. I am busy with a case, so I accepted for you and declined for myself."

"No, Father. I don't mean to go," said Tom.

"Why not?" asked Mr. Worboise with some surprise, and more than a hint of dissatisfaction.

"Well, sir, to tell the truth, I don't think he behaved quite well to me yesterday. I happened to be a few minutes late, and—"

"And Boxall blew you up, and this is how you show your dignified resentment. Bah!"

"He ought to behave to me like a gentleman."

"But how can he, if he isn't a gentleman? He hasn't had your upbringing, but he's a good honest fellow, and says what he means."

"That is just what *I* did, Sir. And you have always told me that honesty is the best policy."

"Yes, but that is not exactly the kind of honesty I mean," returned Mr. Worboise, with a fishy smile. "The idea of good old Boxall insulting a son of mine is too absurd, Tom. You must remember you are his servant."

"So he told me," said Tom, with reviving indignation.

"And that, I suppose, is what you call an insult, eh? A disagreeable fact. Come, come, my boy. Better men than you will ever be have begun by sweeping out their master's office, but no reference is made to the fact when they call the office their own. You go and tell Mr. Boxall that you will be happy to dine with him tonight if he will allow you to change your mind."

"But I told him I was engaged."

"Tell him the engagement is put off, and you are at his service."

"But—" began Tom, and stopped. He was going to say the engagement was not put off. "But I don't like to do it," he continued. "He will take it for giving in and wanting to make up."

"Leave it to me, then, my boy," returned his father, kindly. "My business is not so very pressing but that I can go if I choose. I will write and say that a change in my plans has put it in my power to be his guest, after all, and that I have persuaded you to put off your engagement and come with me."

"But that wouldn't be true."

"Pooh, pooh! I'll take the responsibility of that. Besides, it *is* true. Your mother will make a perfect spoon of you, with the help of good little Master Simon. Can't I change my plans if I like? We must *not* offend Boxall. And he *is* your governor. He is a man of mark—and warm, quite warm!"

What he really meant was that Mr. Boxall had not only money but two daughters of age, to one of whom it was possible that his son might take a fancy.

"Very well, Sir. I suppose I must leave it to you," answered Tom. They finished their breakfast without returning to the subject.

When he reached the countinghouse, Tom went at once to Mr. Boxall, and made his apologies for being late again, on the ground that his father had detained him while he wrote the letter he now handed to him. Mr. Boxall glanced at the note.

"I am very glad, Tom, that both your father and you have thought better of it. Be punctual at seven."

Tom and his father arrived that evening at the Boxalls', an old-fashioned house in Hackney with great rooms and a large garden.

The dinner was good, well-contrived, and rather antiquated. But Tom abused the whole affair within himself as nothing but a shop dinner, for there was Mr. Stopper, the head clerk, looking as sour as a summons, and Mr. Wither, a good enough fellow, but still of the shop. Mr. Boxall had invited him out of mere good nature, for he did not care much about introducing him to his family, although his conduct in the countinghouse was irreproachable.

Tom sat a little way from his father, with Mary Boxall beside him, and many were the under-browed glances which the bald Mr. Stopper shot across the dishes at the couple.

Mary was a very pretty, brown-haired, white-skinned, blue-eyed damsel, whose charms lay in her pleasing color and general roundness, the smallness of her extremities, and her simple kindheartedness. Tom could not help being pleased at having her beside him. She was not difficult to entertain, for she was willing to be interested in anything, and while Tom was telling her a story about a young lad in his class at the Sunday School, whom he had gone to see at his wretched home, those sweet eyes filled with tears. Mr. Stopper saw it and choked in his glass of sherry.

Charles Wither, on the opposite side of the table was being attentive to Jane Boxall, a fine-featured, dark-skinned young woman. They were watched with stolen glances of some anxiety from both ends of the table, for neither parent cared much for Charles Wither.

After the ladies retired, the talk was about politics, the

money market, and other subjects quite uninteresting to Tom. Being a reader of Byron, he had little sympathy with human pursuits unless they included piracy or the like. So he stole away from the table to join the ladies before the others rose from their wine, not, however, before he had himself drunk more than his gravity of demeanor was quite able to ballast. He found Mary turning over some music, and as he drew near he saw her laying aside a song of Byron's.

"Oh, do you sing that song, Miss Mary?" he asked eagerly.

"I have," she answered, "but I am afraid I cannot sing it well enough to please you. Are you fond of the song?"

"I know the words, and should like to hear you sing it."

He put the music on the piano as he spoke. Mary adjusted her white skirts and her white shoulders, and began to sing with taste and simplicity. Her voice was very pleasant and moving to Thomas, and the signs of his emotion would have been plainly seen had not the rest of the company been employed with Jane's portfolio of drawings. All the time Tom had his eyes upon Mary; stooping to turn the last leaf from behind her, he kissed her white shoulder lightly. At the same moment the door opened, and Mr. Stopper entered. Mary ceased singing, and rose with a face of crimson and the timidest, slightest glance at Tom, whose face flushed up in response.

None of the parents would have been displeased had they seen what had passed between the young people. Nor was Mary offended. While she sat singing, she knew that the face bending over her was handsome, of almost pure Greek outline, with a high forehead, and dark eyes with a yet darker fringe. Tom had nothing yet that could be called character, and his face could express only his feeling. When Mary felt the kiss and glanced at his face, she read more than there was in it to read, and the touch of his lips went deeper than her white shoulder.

As the dinner party dissolved, Mr. Boxall went with Mr. Worboise and Tom to let them out at a door in the garden wall, which would save them a few hundred yards in going to the North London Railway. As he returned he heard a rustle among the lilacs that crowded about a side walk, and thought he saw the shimmer of a white dress. When he entered the drawing room, his daughter Jane entered from the opposite door. He glanced round the room; Mr. Wither was gone. This made Mr. Boxall suspicious and restless, for he was convinced that Mr. Wither, though punctual and attentive to business, was inclined to be a fast man.

The evening wind was cold and grateful upon Tom's brow, for the immediate influence of the wine he had drunk had worn off. Now he wondered if he had got himself into a scrape with Mary Boxall. He had *said* nothing to her, and had not committed himself to anything, but a glow of pleasure warmed him as he recalled her blush, and the glance she had so timidly lifted toward his lordly face. That was something to be proud of! Certainly he must be one whom women were ready to fall in love with. Proud position! Enviable destiny! He resolved to be careful how he behaved to Mary Boxall; but he hugged his own handsome idea in the thought that she felt his presence, and was just a little in love with him.

4. Lucy and Grannie

Mr. Boxall's office was closed and the shutters were up. The narrow street looked very dreary, for most of its windows were similarly covered. It was a blowing night with intermittent showers; the shutters and pavements shone and darkened by fits, and everything wet reflected the gas lights. Great masses of gray went sweeping over the sky. One moment the moon gleamed out, and the next was swallowed by floating rain.

Fighting now with a fierce gust, and now limping along in comparative quiet, with a cotton umbrella for a staff, an old woman passed the office, glanced up at the shuttered windows, and turned into a paved archway. Going along a narrow passage, she reached the small paved square called Guild Court. Here she took from her pocket a key, opened a door, and ascended a broad staircase dimly lit by a tallow candle. When she reached the first floor, she went to the end of a passage and opened a door. A cheerful fire burned at the far end of a large room. By the side of the fire sat a girl, gazing so intently into the glowing coals that she seemed unaware of the old woman's entrance.

"So you're home, Lucy, and searching the fire for a wishing cap!" said the old lady cheerily. The girl did not reply, so she resumed, with a little change of tone, "I do declare, Child, I'll never let him cross the door again, if he drives you into the dumps that way. Take heart, my girl—you're good enough for him any day. Though he be a fine gentleman, he's no better gentleman than my son."

With a light sigh Lucy moved across the room to a chest of drawers. In doing so she turned her back on the old woman, and only then replied, in a low voice which wavered a little, as if a good cry were not far off. "I'm sure, Grannie, you're always kind to him when he comes."

"I'm civil to him, Child. Who could help it? Such a fine handsome fellow! And very winning ways too! That's the mischief of it! I always had a soft heart to a frank face. A body would think I wasn't a bit wiser than the day I was born."

And she laughed a pleasant old laugh. By this time she had her black bonnet off, revealing a widow's cap, with gray hair neatly arranged down the sides of a very wrinkled old face. Yet there was not one deep rut in her forehead or cheek, for care seemed to have had nothing at all to do with her wrinkles.

"Well, Grannie, why should you be so cross with me for liking him, when you like him just as much yourself?" said Lucy, archly.

"Cross with you, Child! I'm not cross with you, and couldn't be even if I should. But I *am* cross with him, for he can't be behaving right to you when your sweet face looks like that."

"Now don't say a word against him, Grannie, or you and I shall quarrel, and that would break my heart."

"Bless the child! I'm not saying a word against him, only I'm afraid you're a great deal too fond of him, Lucy. What hold have you of him now?"

"What hold, Grannie!" exclaimed Lucy, indignantly. "Do you think if I were going to be married to him tomorrow, and he never came to the church—do you think I would lift my bonnet to hold him to it? Indeed, then, I wouldn't."

Lucy did not cry, but she turned her back on her grandmother as if she would rather her face should not be seen.

"What makes you so out of sorts tonight, then, Lovey?"

Lucy made no reply, but she moved hastily to the window, for she heard a footstep which she knew. She made the smallest possible chink between the blind and the window frame, peeped into the court, and then glided like a ghost out of the room.

"I wonder when it will come to an end," the old lady murmured to herself. "Always the same thing over again, I suppose, to the last of the world. It's no use telling them what *we* know. It won't make one of them young things the wiser. The first man that looks at them turns their head. But if I was young again myself, and hearkening for my John's foot in the court, pretty fast I'd hobble down the stairs to open the door for him. But then John was a good one, and there's few o' them like him now, I doubt."

Lucy entered with Thomas Worboise. Her face was shining like a summer morning now, and a conscious pride sat on the forehead of the young man. The last of a sentence came into the room with him. "—so you see, Lucy, I could not help it. My father—How do you do, Mrs. Boxall? What a blowy night it is, but you have a warm nest here, for hardly a breath gets into the court, when our windows down below in the countinghouse are shaking themselves to bits."

Thomas carried a chair to the fire, and put his feet on the broad-barred, bright kitchen fender in front of it.

"Are your feet wet, Thomas?" asked Lucy, with some gentle anxiety, and a tremor upon his name, as if she had not yet grown used to omitting the *Mr.* before it.

"Oh no, thank you. I don't mind a little wet. Hark how the wind blows in the old chimney up there! It'll be an awkward night on the west coast, this. I wonder what it feels like to be driving right on the rocks at Land's End, or some such place."

"Don't talk of such things. You make my blood run cold," said Mrs. Boxall.

"He doesn't mean it, you know, Grannie," said Lucy, mediating.

"I should like to know how it feels," persisted Thomas, "with the very shrouds taut as steel bars, blowing out in the hiss of the nor'wester."

"Yes, I daresay!" returned the old lady, with some indignation. "You would like to know how it felt so long as your muddy boots was on my clean fender!"

Thomas did not realize that she had lost one son at sea, and had another as the captain of a sailing vessel, or he would not have spoken as he did. But he never could bear anyone to be displeased with him except he were angry himself, and his countenance fell. He instantly removed his feet from the fender, pulled his handkerchief from his pocket, and began to restore the brightness of the desecrated iron. This went at once to the old lady's heart, and she snatched the handkerchief out of his hand.

"Come, come, Mr. Thomas. Don't ye mind an old woman!"

Thomas looked up in surprise. "I didn't think of your fender," he said.

"Oh, drat the fender!" exclaimed Mrs. Boxall, with more energy than refinement.

And so the matter was dropped, and all sat silent for a few moments, Mrs. Boxall with her knitting, and Tom and Lucy beside each other with their thoughts.

Lucy presently returned to their talk on the staircase. "You were out at dinner on Wednesday?"

"Yes. It was a great bore, but I had to go. And I didn't mean that Mr. Boxall was a bore, though he is a little particular, but it was a bore to go there when I wanted to come here."

"Is my cousin Mary *very* pretty?" asked Lucy.

Thomas could not help blushing, and she could not help seeing, for she had eyes, very large ones, and at least as loving as they were large.

"Yes, she is very pretty," answered Thomas, "but not nearly so pretty as you, Lucy."

Thomas was not stupid, although he was weak enough. Lucy was more than half satisfied, though she did not like that blush. But Thomas himself did not like either the blush or its cause.

He did not stay more than half an hour. When he left, instead of walking straight out of Guild Court by the narrow paved passage, he crossed to the opposite side of the court and entered another ancient house. Reappearing after about two minutes, he walked home to Highbury, and told his mother that he had come straight from his German master.

5. Guild Court

Mrs. Boxall was Richard Boxall's mother. Her husband, John, had owned a small farm on which they brought up a family of three sons and one daughter, of whom Richard was the eldest, and the daughter, Lucy, the youngest. However, none of the sons showed the least inclination to follow the plough. When manifested by Richard, this occasioned his father considerable annoyance, but he did not oppose his son's desire to go into business instead of farming, for he had perpetuated in his sons a certain family doggedness.

He yielded to the inevitable, and placed him in a merchant's office in London, where Richard soon made himself of importance. When his second son showed the same dislike to farming, old John Boxall was still more troubled, but gave his reluctant consent. His cheerful wife was a great support to him under what he felt as a slight to himself and the whole race of Boxalls.

He began to look upon his beloved fields with a jaundiced eye, and the older he grew the more they reminded him of the degenerate tastes and heartlessness of his boys. And a few years later, when Lucy had pledged herself to a music master from the next town, he flew into a terrible rage, which was not appeased by the girl's elopement and marriage. He never saw her again, though it was to her that Edward, the youngest son, fled after a quarrel with his father, whose temper had now become violent as well as morose. He followed his second brother's example, and went to sea.

The mother was still cheerful for she had no reason to be ashamed of her children. None of them had done anything to be ashamed of, and why should she be vexed? And John, a third mate already, and Lucy's husband, Cecil Burton, sought after in London for lessons as if he were one of the old masters!

Yet the wind blew harder for her at night since Edward went to sea, for a boy was in more danger than a grown man like John. And so it proved, for one night when the wind blew a new hayrick of his father's across three parishes, it blew Edward's body ashore on the west coast.

Soon after this, a neighboring earl enlarged his borders, and John Boxall was willing enough to part with his small patrimony, provided he had a good sum of ready money, and the house secured to him for his own life and that of his wife.

When he died within a year, his wife went up to London to her son Richard, who was by this time the chief manager of the business of Messrs. Blunt and Baker. To him she handed over her money to use for the advantage of both. Paying her a handsome percentage, he invested it in a partnership in the firm, and soon became the principal man in the company. The two other partners were both old men; in the course of a few years, they, speaking commercially, fell asleep, and in the course of a few more, departed this life, commercially and otherwise. It was somewhat strange, however, that all this time Richard Boxall had given his mother no written acknowledgment of the money she had lent him, and which had been the foundation of his fortune.

When his mother first came to London, he had taken her into his home. But Mrs. Boxall senior would not consent to be the permanent guest of Mrs. Boxall junior, and insisted on taking a lodging in the neighborhood. It was not long, however, before she left the first for a second, nor long again before she left the second for a third. Mrs. Boxall was quite unfitted for living with another household, and her changes of residence were frequent.

Up to the time when he became a sleeping partner, Mr. Blunt had resided in Guild Court. As soon as mother and son heard that Mr. Blunt had bought a house in the country, the same thought arose in the mind of each—to install her in his vacated quarters. The house belonged to the firm, and a door by which Mr. Blunt passed immediately from the glass-partitioned part of the countinghouse to the foot of the oak staircase. The countinghouse also used two of the rooms in the house as places of deposit for old books, letters, and papers. So Mrs. Boxall made haste to take up her abode in the habitable region, relying upon the ministrations of a charwoman. The door between the house and the countinghouse was now locked, and its key seldom taken from the drawer of Mr. Boxall.

After that, her daughter Lucy's husband died. They had lived from hand to mouth as so many families of uncertain income are compelled to do, and his unexpected death left his wife and child in need. Mr. Boxall had never regarded his sister's match with a music master as other than a degradation to the family. When she was compelled, upon the death of her husband, to accept Richard's kindness in the shape of money, it was with a bitterness of feeling which showed itself plainly enough to wound the self-love of the consciously benevolent man of business.

Two years after the death of Cecil Burton, his wife followed him, and Mrs. Boxall took her grandchild Lucy home to Guild Court. Even a severe mother can become an indulgent grandmother—and such might have been the case with Mrs. Boxall and Lucy, had Lucy been of a more spoilable nature. There was a certain wonderful moral discrimination about her, a sense of what was becoming as well as of what was right, which resulted in a freedom the legalist would have called boldness, and in a restraint which the same judge would have called fastidiousness; for Lucy's ways could not but be different from the ways of one who feared and obeyed.

She was not clever, but neither did she think she was, and therefore it was of no consequence; for she was not dependent upon her intellect for those judgments which alone are of importance in the reality of things, and in which clever people are just as likely to go wrong as any. She had a great gift in music, a gift which Thomas Worboise had not yet discovered.

Lucy's Uncle Richard, though incapable of being other than satisfied that the orphan should be an inmate of the house in

Guild Court, could not, or at least did not, forget the mildly defiant look with which she retreated from his outstretched hand and took her place beside her mother, on the sole occasion on which he had called upon his sister after her husband's death. Lucy had not seen her cousins for years, but had only heard remarks from her mother. Hence she had not once, since she had taken up her abode with her grandmother, been invited to visit her cousins; there was no affectation, but only a little anxiety, in the question she asked Thomas about Mary Boxall's beauty.

But Lucy was not dependent upon her uncle, and scarcely on her grandmother. Even before her mother's death she had begun to give lessons in music to a child younger than herself, the daughter of one of her father's favorite pupils. The Morgenstern family lived in one of the wealthier, older quarters of the west end of London, and paid Lucy handsomely. Every week morning except Saturday, she went by the underground railway to give an hour's lesson to Miriam Morgenstern.

6. Mattie and Her Mother

Lucy left one morning to go to her pupil, and entered the flagged passage which led from the court through the archway. There she met Mattie Kitely, an eight-year-old girl of her acquaintance who was very small for her age. Her neatly parted hair brushed on each side of a large smooth forehead projected out over quiet eyes of blue, made yet quieter by the shadow of those brows. The rest of her face was very diminutive and sober. She looked as if she had pondered life and its goal, and had made up her little mind to meet its troubles with patience. She was dressed in a cotton frock printed with blue rosebuds, faded by many washings.

"Well, Mattie," said Lucy, "how are you this morning?"

"I am quite well, thank you, Miss," answered Mattie, "but I don't call this *morning.* The church clock struck eleven five minutes ago." This was uttered with a smile which seemed to say, "I know you want to have a little fun with me, but I can enjoy the joke of it."

Lucy smiled too, but not much, for she knew the child. "What do you call the morning, then, Mattie?" she asked.

"Well, I call it morning before the sun is up."

"But how do you know when the sun is up? London is so foggy."

"Is it? I didn't know. Are there places of another sort, Miss?"

"Oh, yes, many."

"Well, about the sun. I always know what *he's* about, Miss.

I've got an almanac."

"But you don't understand the almanac, do you?"

"Well, I don't mean to say I understand all about it, but I always know what time the sun rises and goes to bed, you know."

"But how is it that we don't see him today, if he gets up when the almanac says, Mattie?"

"Well, Miss, he sleeps in a crib. And the sides of it are houses and churches, and St. Paulses, and the likes of that. And I daresay he's cross some mornings, and keeps the blankets about him after he's got his head up."

The child laughed, and it was impossible for Lucy to tell whether those were her real ideas about the sunrise.

"How is Mr. Kitely?" Lucy asked next.

"My father is quite well, thank God," the child answered, "and so is my mother. There he is, looking down at us."

"Whom do you mean, Mattie?" asked Lucy, now bewildered, for she knew that the child's mother had died two or three years ago.

"Well, my *mother*," answered Mattie, with an odd smile.

Lucy looked up from the flagged passage. The archway from Bagot Street into this passage was tunneled through a house facing the street, and from this house a wall, stretching inward to the first house in the court, formed one side of the passage. At the middle, this wall broke into two small and strange workshops. From top to bottom of the nine-foot wall, glass divided in the middle formed two windows, one above the other. On the right side of the glass were two doors or hatches, one above the other. The small tenement room had been divided into two horizontally, by a floor in the middle. The two cells thus formed could not have been more than five feet by four, and four feet in height. In this under cell a cobbler sat, hammering away at his lapstone—a little man, else he could hardly have worked there. Every now and then he glanced up at Lucy and Mattie, but never omitted a blow in consequence.

On the thin floor over his head sat a still smaller man, cross-legged like a Turk, busily plying his needle and thread. His hair stood straight up (which gave a look of terror to his thin, pale countenance) and almost touched the roof. As plants run to seed, he seemed to have run to hair. A calm keen eye underneath its towering forest revealed observation and peacefulness. He might be forty, or fifty, or sixty.

Lucy said, "That is Mr. Spelt, not your mother."

"Well, but I call him my mother. I can't have two fathers, you know, so I call Mr. Spelt my mother." She looked up and smiled knowingly at the little tailor, who leaned forward to the window and nodded.

As soon as Lucy had disappeared beyond the archway, Mattie turned toward the workshops. Mr. Spelt stretched down his arms to lift her across the shoemaking region into his own more celestial realm of tailoring. In a moment she was sitting in the farthest and snuggest corner, with her feet invisible in a heap of cuttings, from which she was choosing what she would for the dressing of a doll Mr. Spelt had given her. As often happened, Mattie and the tailor sat for nearly an hour without a word passing between them beyond what sprung from the constructive needs of the child. Neither of them was given to much utterance, and they would sit together sometimes for half a day without saying a word.

Mattie heard a footstep pass below. She was too far back in the cell to see who it was, and so did not lift her eyes from her work. "Wasn't that Mr. Worboise that just passed? Mr. Boxall must be out. But he needn't go there, for Miss Burton's always out this time o' day."

"What do you mean, Mattie?" again asked the tailor.

"Well, perhaps you don't understand such things, Mr. Spelt, not being a married man."

Poor Mr. Spelt had had a wife who had killed herself by drinking all his earnings, but Mattie knew nothing about that. "No more I am. You must explain it to me."

"Well, you see, young people will be young people. Old Mrs. Boxall says so. And that's why Mr. Worboise goes to see Miss Burton."

Thomas returned, bearing a huge ledger under his arm, for which Mr. Stopper had sent him round to the court. However, had Lucy been at home, he would have laid a few minutes more to the account of the errand.

After a long pause the child spoke again. "Is God good to you today, Mother?"

"Yes, Mattie. God is always good to us."

"But He's better some days than others, isn't He?"

To this question the tailor did not know what to reply, and therefore, like a wise man, did not make the attempt. He asked her instead (as he often did with Mattie) what she meant.

"Don't you know God's better to us some days than others? And He's better to some people than He is to others."

"I am sure He's always good to you and me, Mattie."

"Well, yes—generally."

"Why don't you say always?"

"Because I'm not sure about it. Today it's all very well, but yesterday the sun shone in at the window a whole hour." Then she added, doubtfully, "He could make the sun shine every day, if He liked. I suppose He could."

"I don't think we should like it, if He did," returned Mr. Spelt. "The drain down below smells in the hot weather."

"But the rain might come at night and wash it all out. Mightn't it, Mother?"

"Yes, but the heat makes people ill. And if you had such hot weather as they have in some parts, as I am told, you would be glad enough of a day like this."

"Well, why haven't they a day like this when they want it?"

"God knows," said Mr. Spelt, whose ammunition was nearly exhausted, with the enemy pressing on vigorously.

"Well, that's what I say. God knows, and why doesn't He help it?"

And Mr. Spelt surrendered, if silence is surrender, but only for a moment. "I fancy, perhaps, Mattie, He leaves something for us to do. You know they cut out some of this work at the big shop, but I can't do much more with that but put the pieces together. But when a repairing job comes in, I can contrive a bit then, and I like that better."

Mr. Spelt's words involved the shadow of a great truth—that all the discords of the universe are God's trumpets, sounding to the sleeping human will that it must work with His will to make all things pure and healthy and bright. Until a man learns to be happy without the sunshine, and therein becomes capable of enjoying it perfectly, it is well that the shine and the shadow should be mingled, so as God only knows how to mingle them. To effect the blessedness for which God made him, man must become a fellow worker with God.

After a little while Mattie resumed operations. "But you can't say, Mother, that God isn't better to some people than to other people. He's surely gooder to you and me than He is to Poppie."

"Who's Poppie?" asked Mr. Spelt, sending out a flag of negotiation.

"Her down in the gutter, as usual," answered Mattie, without lifting her eyes.

That tailor peeped out of his window, and saw a barefoot child in the court below. Just then the sound of sharp tapping nails came from a window just over the archway, at right angles to Mr. Spelt's workshop. It was very dingy with dust and smoke, allowing only the outline of a man's figure to be seen from the court. Poppie thought the tapping was intended for her, and so fled from the court on soundless feet.

But Mattie rose at once from her corner, laid aside cuttings and doll, and said, "That's my father wanting me. I'm sure I don't know how he would get on without *me*, poor man! He misses my mother more than I do, I believe."

The tailor eased her down to the pavement below, stretching his arms like a bird of prey with a lamb in its talons.

She spoke from the ground, her head thrown back that she might look the tailor in the face, who was stooping over her like an angel from a cloud in the family Bible. "Well, I'll see you again in the afternoon, or about the same hour tomorrow."

"Very well, Mattie," returned Mr. Spelt. "You know your own corner well enough by this time, I should think."

He drew himself carefully into his shell, and a soft smile glimmered on his face. Although he was used to Mattie's old-fashioned ways, the questions that she raised were food for his meditation all day long.

Though Mr. Spelt never went to church, he did read his New Testament. He was one of those few who seem to be born with a certain law of order in themselves, a certain tidiness of mind which would gladly see all the rooms or regions of thought swept and arranged. Such a one not only makes them orderly, but searches after the order of the universe.

Mattie soon reappeared beneath the archway. "Father sends his compliments," she said, "and will you come and take a dish of tea this afternoon?"

"Yes, Mattie, if you will fetch me when the tea's ready."

"You just keep your eye on St. Jacob's clock, Mr. Spelt, and at five o'clock, when it has struck two of them, you get down and come in, and you'll find your tea a-waiting of you. There!"

Mattie turned and walked back through the archway. She never ran, still less skipped as most children do, but held her head up like an older lady, and gave it an occasional conceited toss.

7. Mattie's Father

When two strokes of the five had sounded, Mr. Spelt laid his work aside, took his tall hat from one of the corners where it hung on a peg, leaped lightly from his perch into the court, shut his half of the door, and told the shoemaker below that he was going to Mr. Kitely's to tea, if anyone should want him.

There was a door to Mr. Kitely's house under the archway, but the tailor preferred going round the corner to the shop door in Bagot Street. The shop was a labyrinth of bookshelves, those in front filled with decently if not elegantly bound books, and those behind with innumerable books in all conditions of dinginess, mustiness, and general shabbiness. Jacob Kitely spent his time patching and mending these, and drawing up catalogs of them. He was not one of those booksellers who are so fond of their books that they cannot bear to part with them and therefore, when they are fortunate enough to lay their hands upon a rare volume (the highest pleasure they know in life), justify themselves in keeping it by laying a manuscript price upon it, and considering it so much actual property. Such men, perhaps, know something about the contents of their wares; but while few surpassed Jacob in a knowledge of the outsides of books, from the proper treatment of dilapidated covers, and of leaves when water-stained or mildewed or dry-rotted, he seldom advanced beyond the title page. The rate at which he sold was determined entirely by the rate at which he bought. Hence he sold his books cheaper than any other bookseller in London, contenting himself with a profit proportioned to his expenditure, and taking his pleasure in the rapidity with which the stream of books flowed through his shop.

Mr. Spelt made his way through the maze of books into the back shop, and found Mr. Kitely busy over his next catalog.

"How are you, Spelt?" he said in a vigorous voice. "Just in time, I believe. My little woman has been busy in the parlor for the last hour, and I can depend upon her to the minute. Step in."

"Don't let me interrupt you," suggested Mr. Spelt, meekly, reverentially even, for he thought Mr. Kitely must be a very learned man indeed to write so much about books. He had at home a collection of Kitely's catalogs, complete from the year when he had first occupied the nest in the passage from Mr. Kitely.

"Not at all," returned Mr. Kitely. "I'm very happy to see you, Spelt. You're very kind to my Mattie, and it pleases both of us to have you to tea in our humble way." His humble way was a very grand way indeed to poor Spelt—and Mr. Kitely knew that.

The tailor and the book dealer stepped into the parlor, beyond the back shop, and Mr. Spelt found himself in an enchanted region. A most respectable fire burned in the grate, and a consequential cat lay on the hearth rug. A great black oak cabinet stood at the end of the room. And a number of birds hung around it in cages of all sizes and shapes, most of them covered up now so that they might go to sleep.

Mattie took the brown teapot from the hob, the muffins from the oven, and three herrings from a pan and placed them on the table. Then she placed chairs for them all, and after having her chair gallantly held for her by Mr. Spelt, Mattie sat enthroned to pour the tea. On opposite sides of the table sat the meek tailor and the hawk-faced bookseller. The latter had a broad forehead and large clear light eyes. He wore no beard, and bore his face in front of him like a banner. Plenty of clear-voiced speech, with a breezy defiance of nonsense in every tone, bore in it as well as a certain cold but fierce friendliness, which would show no mercy to any weakness you might vaunt, but would drag none to the light you abstained from parading. Opposite him sat the thoughtful thin-visaged small man, with his hair on end, and between them the staid old-maidenly child, with her hair in bands on each side of her face.

"Well, how's the world behaving to you, Spelt?" asked the bookseller.

"The world has never behaved ill to me, thank God," answered the tailor.

"You've got nobody to thank but yourself."

"But I like to thank God," said Mr. Spelt, apologetically. "I forgot that you wouldn't like it."

"Pshaw, pshaw! I don't mind it from you, for I believe you're fool enough to mean what you say. But tell me this, Spelt—did you thank God when your wife died?"

"I tried hard not to. I'm afraid I did though," answered Spelt, staring like one who has confessed and awaits his penance.

The bookseller burst into a loud laugh, and slapped his hand on his leg. "You have me there, I grant, Spelt."

"She was a splendid woman," said the tailor. "She weighed twice what I do, and her fist—" Here he doubled up his own slender hand, laid it on the table, and stared at it, with his mouth full of muffin. Then, with a sigh, he added, "She was rather too much for me, sometimes. She was a splendid woman, though, when she was sober."

"And what was she when she was drunk?"

This grated a little on the tailor's feelings, and he answered with spirit, "A match for you or any man, Mr. Kitely."

The bookseller replied, "Bravo, Spelt!" and said no more.

They went on with their tea for some moments in silence. Then Mr. Kitely said, "Tell me honestly, Spelt, do you believe there is a God?"

"I don't doubt it."

"And I do. If there was a God, would He have a fool like that Mr. Potter in the church over the way there, to do nothing but read the service, and a sermon he bought for eighteenpence, and—"

"From you?" asked Spelt, with increased interest.

"No, no. I was too near the church for that. But he bought it of Spelman, in Holywell Street. Well, what was I saying? Don't tell me there's a God, when He puts a man like that in the pulpit!"

Spelt was no logician, but something better. He was not one of those who stop to answer arguments against going home, instead of making haste to kiss their wives and children.

"I've read somewhere—in a book I dare say you mayn't have in your collection, Mr. Kitely—they call it the New Testament." There was not an atom of conscious humor in the tailor as he said this. He really thought Mr. Kitely might have conscientious scruples as to favoring the sale of the New Testament. Kitely smiled, but said nothing.

"I've read," the tailor went on, "that God winked at some people's ignorance. I dare say He may wink at Mr. Potter's."

"Anyhow, I wouldn't like to be Mr. Potter," said the bookseller.

"No, nor I," returned Spelt. "But just as I let that poor creature, Dolman, cobble away in my ground floor—though he has never paid me more than half his rent since he took the place—"

"What a fool you are then, Spelt, to—"

"Mr. Kitely," interposed the tailor, with dignity, "do I pay your rent?"

"You have my receipts," answered the bookseller, offended in his turn.

"Then I may make a fool of myself as I please," returned Spelt with a smile which took all offense out of the remark. "I only wanted to say that perhaps God lets Mr. Potter hold the living of St. Jacob's in something of the same way that I let poor Dolman cobble in my ground floor."

"You're a good-natured, honest fellow, Spelt. Half a herring more?"

"No more, thank you. But all the clergy ain't like Mr. Potter. Perhaps he talks such nonsense because there's nobody there to hear it."

"There's plenty not there to do something for, for his money," said Kitely.

"That's true," returned the tailor. "But seeing I don't go to church myself, I've no right to complain. Do you go to church, Mr. Kitely?"

"I should think *not,*" said the bookseller. "Pardon me, there's someone in the shop."

He disappeared, and presently voices were heard, if not in

dispute, yet in difference.

"You won't oblige me so far as that, Mr. Kitely?"

"No, I won't. I never pledge myself. I've been too often taken in for a man goes away and forgets. No offense. Send or bring the money and the book is yours. I daresay it won't be gone tomorrow, but I won't promise to keep it."

"Very well, I won't trouble you again in a hurry."

"That is as you please, Sir," said the bookseller, and no reply followed.

"I don't like that young Mr. Worboise," said Kitely, reentering. "He's a humbug."

"Miss Burton does not think so," said Mattie, quietly.

"You don't give credit, Mr. Kitely?" said the tailor.

"No, not to my own father. I don't know though, if I had the old boy back again, now he's dead. I didn't behave over well to him, I'm afraid. I wonder if he's on the moon, or where he is. I should like to believe in God now, if it were only for the chance of saying to my father, 'I'm sorry I said so-and-so to you.' Do you think he'll have got over it by this time, Spelt? You know all about those things. But I won't have a book engaged and left and not paid for. If young Worboise wants the book, he may come for it tomorrow."

8. Adventure in the Snow

Thomas Worboise made no further opportunities of going to the Boxall's, but the relations of the families rendered it impossible for him to avoid seeing Mary sometimes. He made no great effort to evade such meetings, and it was with a glow of inward satisfaction that he saw her confusion and the rosy tinge that spread over her face when they met. But he could not keep an outward appearance of coolness correspondent to the real coldness of his selfish heart, and the confusion which was only a dim reflection of her own was sufficient to make soft-hearted, impressible Mary suppose that similar feelings were at work in the handsome youth. Why he did not *say* anything to her had not yet begun to trouble her, and her love was as yet satisfied with the ethereal luxuries of dreaming and building castles.

Amy Worboise and the Boxall girls had arranged between them that if Christmas Day were fine, they would persuade their fathers to go with them to Hampstead Heath in the morning. Some of this arrangement was perhaps a sly suggestion on the part of Mary in the hope of seeing Tom, though Jane did contrive that Charles Wither should have a hint of the possibility. The plan was accepted, and the two families—with the exception of Mrs. Boxall and the invalid Mrs. Worboise—found themselves, after morning service, on the platform of the Highbury railway station, whence they soon reached Hampstead.

The walk from the station up the hill to the top of the heath was delightful. It was a clear day, with the sun shining overhead and the ground sparkling with frost under their feet. The keen, healthy air brought color to the cheeks and light to the eyes of all the party, possibly with the sole exception of Mr. Worboise who, able to walk uncovered in the keenest weather, was impervious to all the gentler influences of nature. He was not a disbeliever in nature, for he had not the smallest idea that she had any existence beyond an allegorical one. What he did believe in was the law—not the Mosaic or the Christian, nor the law of love or the law of right—but the law of England, as practiced in her courts of justice. Therefore, he was not a very interesting person to spend a Christmas morning with, and he and Mr. Boxall—an equal believer in commerce—were left to entertain themselves.

Mary Boxall was especially merry, Amy Worboise roguish as usual, and Jane Boxall rather silent, but still bright-eyed, for who could tell whom she might meet on the heath? And with three such girls Tom could be no other than merry, if not brilliant.

They reached the flagstaff. The sun was getting low, a wind was blowing from the northwest, and all London lay south and east in wonderful clearness. Then a vapor slowly melted away the dome of St. Paul's until all was a gray cloud. The young people felt their spirits affected, and set off to walk briskly to the pines above the "Spaniards." They had not gone far before they met Charles Wither sauntering carelessly along—at least, he seemed much surprised to see them. He turned and walked between Jane and Amy, and Mary and Tom dropped behind. Quite unintentionally on Tom's part, the distance between the two parties increased, and when he and Mary reached the pines, the rest of the party had vanished. They had, in fact, gone down into the Vale of Health, to be out of the wind, and to return by the hollow, at the suggestion of Charles Wither, who wished thus to avoid being seen by Mr. Boxall.

Charles took his leave of them just as they came in sight of the flagstaff, where Mr. Worboise and Mr. Boxall had appointed to meet them on their return from the pines. Jane begged Amy to say nothing about having met him.

"Oh!" said Amy, with sudden and painful illumination. "I am so sorry to have been in the way."

"On the contrary, dear Amy. I should not have known what to say to Papa, except you had been with me. I am *so* obliged to you."

Meanwhile, the two gentlemen had gone to have a glass of wine together, and while they were seated together before a good fire, it seemed to Mr. Boxall a suitable opportunity for a matter of business.

"What will you say to me, Worboise, when I tell you that I have never yet made a will?"

"I needn't tell you what I think, Boxall. You know well enough. Very foolish of you, and very imprudent—although I suspected it, for you would hardly have asked anyone else to draw up your will but your old friend. So I came to the conclusion that, not being unkind or suspicious, you must be dilatory, and, in this sole point, foolish."

"I grant the worst you can say. But you shall say it only till tomorrow—that is, if you will draw up the will, and have it ready for me to sign."

"I can't undertake it by tomorrow, but it shall be ready by the next day at twelve o'clock."

"That will do perfectly. I must remain 'a foolish man' for twenty-four hours longer—that is all."

"You won't be much the worse for that. May I ask, as part of the instructions, how much you have to leave?"

"Oh! About thirty thousand. It isn't much, but I hope to double it in the course of a few years, if things go on as they are doing."

Mr. Worboise had not known quite so much about his friend's affairs as he had pretended to his son. He uttered a slight "Whew!" before asking, "And how do you want the sum divided?"

"I don't want it divided at all. There's no occasion whatever to mention the sum. The books will show my property. I want my wife, in the case of her surviving me, to have the whole of it."

"And failing her?"

"My daughters, of course—equally divided. If my wife lives, there is no occasion to mention them. I want them to be dependent upon her as long as she lives, and so hold the family together as long as possible. She knows my wishes about them in everything. I have no secrets from her."

"Suppose your daughters wish to marry?"

"I leave all that to their mother, as I said. They must be their own mistresses someday."

"Well, call on me the day after tomorrow, and I shall have the draft ready."

So when the two girls reached the flagstaff, the fathers were not there. Jane was glad, for it precluded questioning. As they stood waiting, large snowflakes began to fall and the wind rose. But they had not waited long before the gentlemen made their appearance, conversing so busily that they joined the girls and walked away without asking after Mary and Thomas. Not until they reached the railway station did Mr. Boxall become aware that they were missing.

"Why, Jane, where's Mary? And Tom?"

"Somewhere about the pines. They should have been back long ago."

The two fathers looked at each other knowingly.

"Well," said Mr. Worboise, "they're old enough to take care of themselves. I vote we don't wait for them."

"Serves them right," said Mr. Boxall.

"Oh, don't, Papa," interposed Jane.

"Well, Jane, will you wait for them?" said her father. But a sudden light flashed into Jane's eyes, and the suspicion of Charles Wither suddenly rose in his mind. "Come along," he said. "Let them take care of themselves."

The suspicion had troubled him more than once that Mr. Wither and Jane had contrived to meet without his knowledge, and the thought made him writhe with jealousy. He was jealous of every man of whom his wife or daughters spoke well—that is, until he began to like him himself, when the jealousy vanished. But it was not jealousy alone that distressed him, but the the anxiety of real love as well.

When Tom and Mary arrived at the pines, the rest of their party had gone.

"Oh, never mind," said Mary, merrily. "Let us wait in the hollow till they come back."

Partly from false gallantry, partly from inclination, Thomas agreed. They descended the opposite direction from that actually taken by Jane and her companions, and wandered down along the heath. By this time, the sky was all gray and white, and long masses of vapor were driving overhead.

But down in the hollows of the heath all was still, and they two wandered on for some time without heeding the coming storm. They talked about nothing worthy of record, although every word that Thomas uttered seemed to Mary to have some hidden meaning she would gladly hear more of. At length, something cold fell on her face. She looked up—the sky was one mass of heavy vapor, and great downy snowflakes were settling slowly to the earth.

In a moment they were clasped hand in hand. The pleasure of the snow, the excitement of being shut out from the visible (or rather seeing) world, wrapped in the skirts of a storm with a pretty girl for his sole companion, wrought deeply upon Thomas, who loved to be moved and hated to will. He forgot Lucy and stood in delight, gazing at the falling snow but holding Mary's hand tightly in his own. She crept closer to him, for a little gentle fear added to her pleasure, and in a moment more his arm was about her—to protect her, he said to himself.

He had sense enough to turn to lead her back toward the road. But this was already a matter of difficulty, for there was no path here, and the darkness and snow already hid the high road across the heath, so that the first question was in what direction to go to find it. They kept moving. Mary leaned a good deal on Tom's arm, and grew more and more frightened. Tom did his best to comfort her, but soon found that at the suspicion of actual danger the romance of the situation had vanished. And now as the snow fell rapidly the wind blew it sharply in their faces and blinded them with both its sting and its darkness.

After wandering for more than an hour, Mary burst out crying, and said she could not walk a step farther. With the kindest encouragement (though he was really downhearted himself) he persuaded her to struggle up a little height nearby. From the top they saw a light, descended the opposite side of the hill, and found a road where an empty cab stood by the door of a public house. Mary refused any refreshment within, and Tom had the cab man drive them to the station. In the railway carriage, Mary lay like one dead, and although he took off both his coats to wrap about her, she seemed quite unconscious of the attention. With great difficulty they reached her home, for there was no cab at the Hackney station, and the snow was by now a foot deep.

Thomas was not sorry to give her up to her mother, who immediately began to scold him. Then Mary spoke for the first time, saying, with an effort, "Don't, Mother. If it hadn't been for Thomas, I should have been dead long ago. He could not help it. Good night, Tom."

And she feebly held up her face to kiss him. Tom stooped to meet it, and went away feeling tolerably miserable. He was wet and cold, his momentary fancy for Mary was quite gone, and he could not help seeing that now he had kissed her before her mother he was in a scrape.

Before morning Mary had a high fever.

9. POPPIE

Thomas woke the next morning with a well-deserved sense of something troubling him. This was Boxing Day, but he did not feel in a holiday mood. It was not from any fear that Mary might be the worse for her exposure, nor was it from regret for his conduct toward her. What made him uncomfortable was the feeling that her mother now had an advantage over him, and was not likely to neglect the advantage. Nor did it console him to imagine what Lucy would do if she should chance to hear of yesterday's affair.

He had arranged to meet Lucy at the Marble Arch, and take her to that frightful reservoir of amusement, Madame Tussaud's. Her usual morning engagement led her to that neighborhood, and it was a safe place to meet, far from Highbury, Hackney, and Bagot Street.

The snow was very deep, and old Mrs. Boxall tried to persuade Lucy not to go. But where birds can pass lovers can pass, and she was just finishing her lesson to resplendent little Miriam as Thomas got out of an omnibus at Park Street to saunter up to the Marble Arch.

Hyde Park was wrapped in a grotesque beauty such as rarely meets the eye of a Londoner. Even while waiting for a lovely girl, Thomas could not help taking notice of the trees—every bough, branch, twig, and shoot supported a ghost of itself.

Thomas had not sauntered and gazed for more than five

minutes before he saw Lucy coming down Great Cumberland Street. He stood and watched her approach, for she looked so picturesque flitting over the spotless white in her violet dress, her red cloak, and her grebe-feather muff. Her dainty morocco boots made little holes in the snow all across Oxford Street, and Thomas stood filled more with pride in the lovely figure that was coming to *him* than with love of her.

"Have I kept you waiting long, Thomas?" said Lucy, with the sweetest of smiles.

"Oh! About ten minutes," answered Thomas. "What a cold morning it is!"

"I don't feel it much," returned Lucy. "I came away the first moment I could. I am sorry I kept you waiting."

"I should be only too happy to wait for you as long every morning," said Thomas, gallantly, though not tenderly.

Lucy did not relish the tone, but a tone is one of the most difficult things to fix a complaint upon. Besides, she was not in a humor to complain of anything. And she was a little afraid of offending Thomas, for she looked up to him ten times more than he deserved.

"How lovely your red cloak looked crossing the snow. Quite a splendor!" he continued.

Lucy received this as a compliment to herself, and smiled again. "What a delightful morning it is!" she said. "Oh! Do look at the bars of the railing."

"How can you look at such vulgar things as iron stanchions when you have such a fairy forest as that before you?"

"But just look here," insisted Lucy, drawing him closer to the fence. "It is snow on one side of the bars, but not on the other. Look at the lovely crystals."

On the eastern quarter of each upright bar the snow had stuck fast to the depth of an inch. Exactly opposite was a half-inch growth of slender crystals standing out from the bar like a fantastic little forest of ice.

"I do not care about such microscopic beauties," said Thomas, a little annoyed that she whom he thought unpoetical could find out something lovely sooner than he could. "Those trees are much more to my mind now."

"Ah, but I do not love the trees less. Come into the park, and then we can see them from all sides."

"The snow is too deep. There is no path there."

"I don't mind it. My boots are very thick."

"No, no, come along. We shall get to Madame Tussaud's before there are many people there. It will be so much nicer."

"I should like much better to stay here awhile," said Lucy, half-vexed and a little offended.

But Thomas did not heed her, and only led the way up Oxford Street. She dropped his arm, and now walked by his side. He was not so bad as this always, or even gentle-tempered Lucy would have quarreled with him. The weight of yesterday was upon him, and while they were walking up the street, as handsome and fresh a couple as you would find in all London, Mary was lying in her bed talking wildly about Thomas.

Having thus left the truths of nature behind them for the horrible art of Madame Tussaud's ahead, Thomas became aware from Lucy's silence that he had not been behaving well to her. He therefore set about being more agreeable, and before they reached Baker Street she had his arm again, and they were talking and laughing gaily enough.

Behind them, at some distance, trotted a small apparition.

It was a little girl, perhaps ten years old, looking as wild as any forest savage. Her face was pretty, as far as could be judged through the dirt. Her eyes were black and restless. Her dress was a frock of some indeterminate stuff, scarcely reaching below her knees, and rent upwards into an irregular fringe of ribbons that frostily fanned her little legs. Her shoes were much too large for her, and had already worn such holes as to afford more refuge for the snow than for her feet. Her little knees were very black, and her poor legs were caked and streaked with dirt, their delicate skin thickened and cracked with frost, and east winds, and neglect! Her hair was black, mingled with a reddish tinge from exposure to the hot sun of the preceding summer. It hung in tangled locks about her face, which peeped out with the wild innocence of a gentle and shy—but brave—little animal of the forest.

This was not the first time she had followed Lucy; like a lost pup she would go after someone for a whole day from place to place, obedient to some hidden drawing of the heart. She had often seen Lucy start from Guild Court, and had followed her to the railway; and, at length, by watching first one station and then another, she had found out where she went each morning. But she had never seen Lucy with a gentleman before.

This was the little girl whom Mattie patronized, although Poppie was at least two years older. Poppie had no other name, for no one knew where she had come from, or who her parents were, and she herself cared as little about the matter as anybody.

Thomas and Lucy were some distance ahead of her when they entered the passage leading to the wax works. The instant she lost sight of them, Poppie started in pursuit, and lost one of her great shoes. Instead of turning to pick it up, she kicked the other after it and scampered barefooted over the snow.

Poppie never thought about *might* or *might not,* but only about *could* or *could not.* So she darted in to see whether she could not get another peep of the couple. Thomas was paying admission at the turnstile. As the man admitted them, he turned away from his post, and Poppie crept through underneath in an instant. She dodged after them, taking care not to let them see her.

Poppie had seen more than one dead man carried home upon a stretcher. And she had seen the miserable funerals of the poor, and the desolate coffins put in the earth. But she knew that grand and wealthy people lived in great houses, from which they were carried away in splendid black carriages, drawn by ever so many horses with great black feathers growing out of their heads. What became of them after that she had not the smallest idea. When she entered the wax works exhibition the question was solved: this was one of the places to which they carried the grand people after they were dead, and set them up dressed in their very best. She did not much like the appearance of the dead people, and thought it better to put them in the earth and have done with them, for they looked as if they did not altogether like the affair themselves. And when one of them stared at her, she dodged its eyes; for though Poppie was not afraid of anybody, she knew that it was better to keep out of some people's way.

Poppie followed her friend till the couple went into the Chamber of Horrors. Then, seeing a large party arrive, she looked about for a place of refuge. In the art of vanishing she was adept, with an extraordinary proclivity toward holes and corners.

There was a couch in a nearby recess, and on this couch lay a man. He did not look like the rest of the dead people, for his eyes were closed. Then the dead people *did* sleep sometimes. Happy dead people, in a bed like this! For there was a black velvet cover thrown over him so that nothing but his face was visible, and to Poppie this pall looked so soft, so comfortable, so enticing! Poppie sprang into the recess, crept under the cover like a hunted mouse, and lay still, the bedfellow of no less illustrious a personage than the Duke of Wellington. Cold as he was, Poppie found him warmer than her own legs, and the place quite comfortable. It was a rare sensation to be warm, and she found it delightful. Every now and then she peeped from under the cover to see whether Thomas and Lucy were coming.

But at length she fell fast asleep, until she was suddenly aroused by a rough hand and a rough cursing voice. Poppie was used to curses, and did not mind them a bit—somehow they never hurt her—but she was a little frightened at the face of indignant surprise and wrath she saw bending over her when she awoke. It was one of the attendants with a policeman beside him. It was well for Ruth there were no police when she slept in Boaz's barn—still better that some of the clergymen who serve God by reading her story on Sunday were not magistrates before whom the police carried her. With a tight grasp on her arm, Poppie was walked away in an uncomfortable manner to what she had learned to call *the jug*, namely, the police prison. But Poppie did not mind it much. In such weather the jug was very cold, but she had the warm memories of the near past to comfort her. When she fell asleep on the hard floor, she dreamed that she was dead and buried, and trying to be warm and comfortable as she ought to be in her grave, but the wind *would* blow through the chinks of her pauper's coffin, and she wished she had been a duke or a great person to be so grandly buried in the cemetery in Baker Street.

Poppie heard a good many bad words and horrid speeches in the jug, but her own language was not the very pink of propriety. How could it be? The vocabulary in the houses she knew had ten vulgar words in it to one that Mattie might hear. But Poppie, when speaking the worst language that ever crossed her lips, was not lower, morally and spiritually, than the young lord in the nursery, who, speaking with clear-cut articulation and in proper language, refuses his brother a share of his tart and gobbles it up himself. If Poppie could swear, she could at least share.

Of course she was liberated in the morning, and was only reprimanded for being where she had no business to be, and sent away. But now she knew Thomas again whenever she saw him, and would even trot after him for the length of a street or so. But he never noticed her.

10. Mr. Simon

The next day the sun shone brilliantly on the snow as Thomas walked to the countinghouse. He was full of pleasant thoughts, though they were crossed and shadowed by a few of a different kind. The sense of having a secret which must get him into trouble if it were discovered (and discovered it must be someday) could not fail to give him uneasiness. However, nothing (as it seemed to him) could be done, for he was never ready to do anything to which he was neither led nor driven.

He reached Bagot Street, and sought out Mr. Boxall, whose face bore an unaccustomed look of anxiety.

"I hope Miss Mary. . . " Thomas began, with a little hesitation.

"She's very ill," said her father. "Very ill, indeed. It was enough to be the death of her. Excessively imprudent."

Now Mary was as much to blame as Thomas, if there was any blame at all, but he had enough generosity not to say so to her father. He was only selfish, not mean. "I am very sorry," he said. "We were caught in the snow, and lost our way."

"Yes, yes, I know. I oughtn't to be too hard on young people," returned Mr. Boxall, remembering perhaps his share of the blame in leaving them to themselves. "I only hope she may get through it. But she's in a bad way. She was quite delirious last night."

Thomas was really concerned for a moment, and looked so. Mr. Boxall saw it, and spoke more kindly. "There is no immediate danger, but it's no use you coming to see her, for she can't see anybody but the doctor."

This was a relief to Thomas, but it was rather alarming to find that Mr. Boxall clearly expected him to want to see her. "I am very sorry," he said again, and that was all he could find to say.

"Well, well," returned his master, accepting the words as if they had been an apology. "We must do our work, anyhow. Business is the first thing, you know."

Thomas took this as a dismissal, and retired to the outer office, in a mood considerably different from that which Mr. Boxall attributed to him.

A clerk's duty is a hard one. He has no personal interest in the result of his special labor, nor can this labor have much interest of its own beyond what comes of getting things square, and the sense of satisfaction that springs from activity and the success of completion. A man must do his duty, if he would be a free man, whether he likes it or not, and whether it is appreciated or not. But if he can regard it as the will of God, the work not fallen upon him by chance, but *given* him to do—understanding that everything well done belongs to His kingdom, and everything ill done belongs to the kingdom of darkness—surely even the irksomeness of his work will be no longer insuperable. But Thomas had never been taught this, and he did not know that his day's work had anything to do with his soul.

Hence Thomas regarded his work only as drudgery; he considered it beneath him; he judged himself fitter for the army, and had hankerings after gold decorations. He dabbled with the fancy that there was a serious mistake somewhere in the arrangement of mundane affairs; for was he not fitted by nature to move in some showy orbit, instead of being doomed to rise in Highbury, shine in Bagot Street, and set yet again in Highbury? And so, though he did not absolutely neglect his work (for he hated to be found fault with) he just *did* it, not entering into it with any spirit. And as he was clever enough, things went on with tolerable smoothness.

That same evening when he went home from his German lesson of a quarter-of-an-hour, and his time with Lucy of an hour-and-a-quarter, he found Mr. Simon with his mother.

Thomas would have left the room, for his conscience now made him wish to avoid Mr. Simon—who had pressed him so hard with the stamp of religion that the place was painful, although the impression was fast disappearing.

"Thomas," said his mother, with even more than her usual solemnity, "come here. We want to have some conversation with you."

Thomas obeyed, and threw himself nonchalantly into a chair.

"Thomas, my friend," began Mr. Simon, with the tone which corresponds to the long face some religious people assume the moment the conversation turns towards sacred things, "I am uneasy about you. Do not think me interfering, for I watch your soul as one that must give an account. I have to give an account of you, for at one time you were the most promising seal of my ministry. But your zeal has grown cold; you are unfaithful to your first love; and when the Lord cometh as a thief in the night, you will be to Him as one of the lukewarm, neither hot nor cold, my poor friend. He will spew you out of His mouth. And I may to be blame for this, though at present I know not how. Ah, Thomas! Do not let me have shame of you at His appearing. The years are fleeting fast, and although He delay His coming, yet He *will* come; and He will slay His enemies with the two-edged sword that proceedeth out of His mouth."

Mr. Simon knew nothing of human nature, and the gulf had widened between him and Thomas till his poor feeble influences could no longer reach across it. Thomas had transferred his growing contempt for the clergyman to the religion of which he was such a poor representative. Mr. Simon had not the shadow of a chance of making him confess. How could Thomas tell such a man that he was in love with one beautiful girl, and had foolishly gotten himself entangled with another?

By this direct attack on him in the presence of his mother, the clergyman lost the very last remnant of his influence over Thomas.

"Why do you not speak, Thomas?" said his mother, gently.

"What do you want me to say, Mother?" asked Thomas in return, with rising anger.

"Say what you ought to say," returned Mrs. Worboise, more severely.

"What ought I to say, Mr. Simon?" said Thomas, with a tone of mock submission.

"Say, my young friend, that you will carry the matter to the throne of grace, and ask the aid—" And so the flow of sacred words continued for a time.

Thomas, however, was not yet so much of a hypocrite as his training had hitherto tended to make him, and he sat silent for a few minutes. Then he spoke, anxious to get rid of the whole unpleasant affair.

"I will promise to think of what you have said, Mr. Simon."

"Yes, Thomas, but *how* will you think of it?" said his mother.

Mr. Simon, however, glad to have gained so much of a concession, spoke more genially. He would not drive the matter further at present. "Do, dear friend, and may He guide you into the truth. Remember, Thomas, the world and the things of the world are passing away. You are a child no longer, and are herewith called upon to take your part, for God or against Him—" and so on, till Thomas grew weary as well as annoyed.

"Will you tell me what fault you have to find with me?" he said at last. "I am regular at the Sunday School, I am sure."

"Yes, that we must allow, and heartily," answered Mr. Simon, turning to Mrs. Worboise as if to give her the initiative, for he thought her rather hard on her son. "Only I would suggest to you, Mr. Thomas, the question whether your energy is equal to what it has been? Take care lest, while you teach others, you yourself should be a castaway. Remember that nothing but faith in the merits—" Thus started again, he went on, till Thomas was forced from all sympathy with things so unmercifully driven upon him, and vowed in his heart that he would stand it no longer.

Still speaking, Mr. Simon rose to take his leave. Thomas, naturally polite, and anxious to get out of the scrutiny of those cold blue eyes of his mother, went to open the door for him, and closed it behind him with a sigh of satisfaction. Then he went to his own room, feeling wrong, and yet knowing quite well that he was going on to be and do wrong.

The next morning mother and pastor held a long and dreary consultation over Thomas. If Mr. Worboise had overheard it, he would have laughed, not heartily, but with a perfection of contempt, for he despised all these things.

The sole result was that his mother watched Thomas with yet greater diligence, and Thomas began to feel that her eyes were never off him. He felt them behind his back, and disliked them because he feared them. They haunted him in Bagot Street. Even with Lucy, those eyes followed him, as if searching to find out his secret. A vague fear kept growing that his discovery was at hand, and hence he became more and more cunning to conceal his visits.

One good thing only came out of it all: he grew more and more enamored of Lucy, and almost came to love her.

11. Business

After some days Mr. Boxall called upon Mr. Worboise.

"Ah, Boxall! Glad to see you! What a man you are to make an appointment with!" So saying, he went to a drawer to get out the will.

"The fact is," Mr. Boxall said, "I have been so uneasy about Mary—"

"Why? What's the matter?" interrupted Mr. Worboise, stopping on his way across the room.

"Don't you know?" returned Mr. Boxall, in some surprise. "She's never gotten over that Hampstead Heath affair. She's been in bed since."

"God bless me!" exclaimed the other. "I never heard a word of it. What was it?"

So Mr. Boxall told him the story.

"Never heard a word of it!" repeated the lawyer.

The statement made Mr. Boxall more uneasy than he cared to show. "But I must be going," he said, "so let's have this troublesome will signed and done with."

"Not in the least a troublesome one, I assure you. Rather too simple, I think. Here it is."

And Mr. Worboise began to read it over point by point to his client.

"All right," said the latter. "Mrs. Boxall to have everything to do with as she pleases. Failing your wife, your daughters. And who comes next?"

"Nobody. Whom do you think?"

"It's rather short—not quite businesslike. Put in anybody just for the chance."

"Stick yourself in then, old fellow. It won't do you any good, but it'll be an expression of my long esteem and friendship for you."

"Thank you, old friend," said Mr. Worboise quietly, and entered his own name in succession.

The will was soon finished, signed, and witnessed by two of Mr. Worboise's clerks, and the long-neglected matter put right and done with.

"By the way," asked Mr. Worboise, "how is that son of mine getting on?"

"Oh, pretty well. He's regular enough, and I hear no complaints of him from Stopper, and *he's* sharp enough, I assure you."

"But you're not oversatisfied with him yourself, eh?"

"Well, between you and me, I don't think he's cut out for the business."

"That's to say he's of no use for business of any sort."

"I don't know. He does his work fairly well, but he doesn't seem to have any heart in it."

"Well, what do you think he *is* fit for now?"

"Well, you could easily make a fine gentleman of him."

Mr. Boxall spoke rather bitterly, for he already had doubts whether Tom had been behaving well to Mary. It had become very evident since her illness that she was most in love with Tom, and that Tom should be a hairbreadth less in love with her was offense enough to rouse the indignation of a man like Boxall, good-natured as he was; and that Tom had never thought it worthwhile even to mention the fact of her illness to his father was strange to a degree.

"But I can't afford to make a fine gentleman of him. I've got his sister to provide for, as well. I don't mean to say that I could not leave him as much, perhaps more, than you can to *each* of your daughters, but girls are so different from boys. Girls can live on anything, fine gentlemen can't."

"Well, it's no business of mine," said Mr. Boxall. "If there's anything I can do for him, of course, for your sake, Worboise—"

"The rascal has offended him somehow," said Mr. Worboise to himself. "It's that Hampstead Heath business."

"Have patience with the young dog," he said aloud. "That's all I ask you to do for him. Who knows what may come out of him yet?"

"That's easy to do. As I tell you, there's no fault to find with him," answered Mr. Boxall, afraid that he had exposed some hidden feeling. "Only one must speak the truth."

With these words Mr. Boxall took his leave.

Mr. Worboise sat and cogitated. "There's something in that rascal's head, now," he said to himself. "His mother and that Simon will make a spoon of him. I want to get some sense out of him before he's translated to kingdom come. But how the deuce to get any sense out when there's so precious little in! I found seventeen volumes of Byron on his bookshelves last night."

To her husband Mrs. Worboise always wore a resigned air, believing herself unequally yoked to an unbeliever with a bond she was not at liberty to break, because it was enjoined upon her to win her husband by her chaste conversation coupled with fear. Therefore, when he went into her room that evening, she received him as usual with a look that might easily have been mistaken, and not much mistaken, either—as expressive of a sense of injury.

"Well, my dear," her husband began, in a conciliatory, yet complaining tone, "do you know what this precious son of ours has been about? Killing Mary Boxall in a snowstorm, and never telling me a word about it. I suppose you know the whole story, though? You *might* have told me!"

"Indeed, Mr. Worboise, I am sorry to say I know nothing about Thomas these days. I can't understand him. He's quite changed. But if I were not laid on a couch of suffering—not that I complain of that—*I* should not come to *you* to ask what he was about. I should find out for myself."

Her husband's communication made her still more anxious about Thomas, and certain suspicions she had begun to entertain about the German master became more decided. In her last interview with Mr. Simon, she had hinted to him that Thomas ought to be watched, that they might know whether he really went to his German lesson. But Mr. Simon was too much of a gentleman not to recoil from the idea, and Mrs. Worboise did not venture to press it. When she saw him again, however, she suggested her fears that the German master had been mingling German theology with his lessons, and so corrupting the soundness of his faith. This seemed to Mr. Simon very possible indeed, for he knew how insidious the teachers of such doctrines are; and, glad to do something definite for his suffering friend, he offered to call upon the man and see what sort of person he was. This offer Mrs. Worboise gladly accepted, without thinking that of all men to find out any insidious person, Mr. Simon, in his simplicity, was the least likely.

But they knew neither his name nor where he lived, and they could not ask Thomas about him. So Mr. Simon inquired in the neighborhood of Bagot Street.

"My friend," he said, stepping the next morning into Mr. Kitely's shop—he had a way of calling everybody his friend, thinking so to recommend the Gospel.

"At your service, Sir," returned Mr. Kitely, brusquely.

"I only wanted to ask you," drawled Mr. Simon, in a drawl both of earnestness and unconscious affectation, "whether you happen to know of a German master somewhere in this neighborhood."

"Well, I don't know," returned Mr. Kitely, for he always liked to know why one asked a question, before he cared to answer it. "I don't know as I could recommend one over another. I know at least six of them near. What's the name you want, Sir?"

"That I cannot tell you."

"He must want Mr. Moloch, Father," said a voice from somewhere near the floor, "the foreign gentleman that Mr. Worboise goes to see up the court."

"That's the very man, my child," responded Mr. Simon. "Thank you very much. Where shall I find him?"

"I'll show you," returned Mattie.

"Why couldn't he have said so before?" remarked Mr. Kitely to himself with indignation. "But it's just like them." By *them* he meant clergymen in general.

"What a fearful name—*Moloch,*" reflected Mr. Simon, as he followed Mattie up the court. He would have judged it a name of bad omen, had he not thought *omen* rather a wicked word.

The fact was, the German's name was Molken, a very innocent one, far too innocent for its owner, for it only means *whey*.

Herr Molken was a ne'er-do-well student of Heidelburg, a clever fellow if not a scholar, whose bad habits came to be too well known at home for him to indulge them there any longer, and who had taken refuge in London. Thomas had as yet spent so little time in his company, never giving more than a quarter of an hour or so to his lesson, that Molken had had no opportunity of influencing him in any way. But he was one of those who, the moment they make a new acquaintance, begin examining him for the sake of discovering his weak points, that they may get some hold of him. Of all dupes, one with some intellect and no principle, weakened by the trammels of a religious system with which he is at odds, is the most thorough prey to the pigeon-plucker, for such a one has no recuperative power, and the misery of his conscience makes him abject. Molken saw that Tom was clever, and that he seemed to have some money.

The next lesson fell on the evening after Mr. Simon's visit to Guild Court, and Mr. Molken gave Thomas a full account of the "beseek" he had had from "one soft ghostly" who wanted to find out something about Thomas, and how he had told him that Mr. Worboise was a most excellent and religious young man, that he worked very hard at his German, and that he never spent less (here Mr. Molken winked at Thomas) than an hour and a half over Krummacher or some other religious writer.

All this Mr. Simon had faithfully reported to Mrs. Worboise, never questioning what Mr. Molken told him. For Mr. Molken was a small wiry man, about thirty, with brows overhanging his eyes like the eaves of a Swiss cottage, and rendering those black and wicked luminaries blacker and more wicked still. His hair was black, his beard was black, his skin was swarthy, his forehead was large, and his nose looked as if if had been made of putty and dabbed on after the rest of the face was finished. Yet he could make himself so agreeable, and had such a winning carriage and dignified deference, that he soon disarmed the suspicion caused by his appearance. He had many accomplishments, and seemed to know everything—at least to a lad like Thomas, who could not detect the assumption which not unfrequently took the place of knowledge. He manifested also a genuine appreciation of his country's poetry, and even the short lessons to which Thomas submitted had been enlivened by Herr Molken's enthusiasm for Goethe.

Now he believed he had got by Mr. Simon's aid the hold that he wanted. His one wink revealed to Thomas that he was a master of his secret, and Thomas felt that he was, to a considerable degree, in his hands. This, however, caused him no apprehension.

His mother, although in a measure relieved, still cherished suspicions of German theology. So when Thomas came into her room that evening, she said, "Mr. Simon has been making some friendly inquiries about you, Thomas. He was in the neighborhood, and thought he might call on Mr. Moloch—what a dreadful name! Why do you say nothing to me of your studies? Mr. Simon says you are getting quite a scholar in German. But it is a dangerous language, Thomas, and full of errors. Beware of yielding too ready an ear to the seductions of human philosophy, and the undermining attacks of will-worship."

Mrs. Worboise went on in this unintelligible strain for at least five minutes, having not the vaguest notion of what she meant by German theology. Thomas did not interrupt her once; by allowing the lies of the German master to pass thus uncontradicted, he took another long stride down the plane of deceit.

After this he became naturally more familiar with Mr. Molken, who abandoned books and began to teach him fencing, talking to him in German all the while, and thus certainly increasing his knowledge, though not in the direction of mastery of commercial correspondence.

12. Mother and Daughter

Mr. Boxall, with some reluctance and difficulty, made his wife acquainted with his annoyance over the discovery that Tom Worboise had not even told his father that Mary was ill.

"I'm convinced," he said, "that the young rascal has only been flirting."

"I'm none so sure as that, Richard," answered his wife. "You leave him to me."

"Now, my dear, I won't have you throwing our Mary in any fool's face. It's bad enough as it is. I would rather see her in her grave than scorned by any man."

"You may see her there before long," answered his wife, with a sigh.

"Eh? What? She's not worse, is she?"

"No, but she hasn't much life left in her. I'm afraid it's settling on her lungs. Her cough is something dreadful to hear, and tears her to pieces."

"It's milder weather, though, now, and that will make a difference before long. Now, I know what you're thinking of, my dear, and I won't have it. I told the fellow she wasn't fit to see anybody."

"Were you always ready to talk about me to everyone that came in your way, Richard?" asked his wife, with a good-humored smile.

"I don't call a lad's father and mother in the way—though, I daresay, fathers and mothers are in the way sometimes," he added, with a slight sigh.

"Would you have talked about me to your own father, Richard?"

"Well, you see, I wasn't in his neighborhood. But my father was a stiff kind of man to deal with."

"Not worse than Mr. Worboise, depend upon it, my dear."

"But Worboise would like well enough to have our Mary for a daughter-in-law."

"I daresay. But that mightn't make it easier to talk to him about her—for Tom, I mean. For my part, I never did see two such parents as poor Tom has. It's quite a shame to sit upon that amiable young lad as they do. He can hardly call his nose his own. I wouldn't trust Mr. Worboise if I was drowning.

"And that mother of his! Her religion freezes the life out of you the moment you come near her. How a young fellow could talk about a sweetheart to either of them is more than I can understand. So don't look so righteous over it."

Mrs. Boxall's good-natured audacity generally carried everything before it, even with more dangerous persons than her own husband. He could not help trying to smile, and though the smile was rather a failure, Mrs. Boxall chose to take it for a smile. Indeed, she generally put her husband into good humor by treating him as if he were in a far better humor than he really was.

A few days later, Mrs. Boxall wrote to Tom.

"My dear Mr. Thomas,

Mary is much better, and you need not be at all uneasy about the consequences of your Christmas expedition to the North Pole. I am very sorry I was so cross when you brought her home. Indeed, I believe I ought to beg your pardon. If you don't come to see us soon, I shall fancy that I have seriously offended you. But I knew she never could stand exposure to the weather, and I suppose that was what upset my temper. Mary will be pleased to see you.

I am ever yours sincerely,

Mrs. Richard Boxall."

Tom received this letter before he left for town in the morning. What was he to do? Of course, he must go and *call* there, but he pronounced it a great bore. He was glad the poor girl was better, but had no fancy for being hunted up after that fashion. What made him yet more savage was that Mr. Boxall was absolutely surly when he went into his room upon some message from Stopper. He did not call that day nor the next.

On the third evening he went, but the embarrassment of feeling that he ought to have gone before was added to the dislike of going at all, and he was in no enviable condition of mind. An unrelenting east wind was blowing, and Tom felt more like a man going to the scaffold than one going to visit a convalescent girl.

There was something soothing, however, in the glow of warmth and comfort which the opening door revealed. The large hall carpeted throughout, the stove burning in it most benevolently, the brightness of the thick stair rods, like veins of gold in the broad crimson carpeting of the wide staircase. Mrs. Boxall was one of those nice, stout, kindly, middle-aged women who have a positive genius for comfort, and one felt it the moment one entered her house.

It was with a certain tremor that Tom approached Mary's room. And what a change from the Mary of the snowstorm! She lay on a couch near the fire, pale and delicate, with thin white hands. Thomas felt that she was far lovelier than before, and approached her with some emotion. There was no light in the room but that of the fire, and it lightened and gloomed over her still face, as the clouds and the sun do over a landscape. In the shadow Thomas could not tell whether she was looking at him or not, but Mary was reading his face like a book in a hard language. Very little was said between them, for Mary was sad and weak, and Thomas was sorrowful and perplexed.

She had been reckoning on this first visit from Thomas ever since she had recovered enough to choose what she would think about, and now it was turning out all so different from what she had pictured. Her poor heart sank away somewhere and left a hollow place behind. Thomas sat there, but there was a chasm between them that she no longer sought to cross. She wished he would go. A few more commonplaces were exchanged, the glimmering fire sank into a sullen gloom, and the face of neither was visible to the other. Then Thomas rose with the effort of one in a nightmare. Mary held out her hand to him, and he took it in his, cold to the heart. The fire gave out one flame which flickered and died. In that light she looked at him—was it reproachfully? He thought so, and felt that her eyes were like those of one trying to see something at a great distance. One pressure of her hand, and he left her. "Good-bye, Thomas," "Good-bye, Mary," were the last words that passed between them. Outside the room he found Mrs. Boxall.

"Are you going already, Mr. Thomas?" she said, in an uncertain tone.

"Yes, Mrs. Boxall," was all Tom replied with.

Mrs. Boxall went into her daughter's room, and shut the door. Thomas let himself out and walked away.

She found Mary staring at the fire, with great dry eyes, lips pressed close together, and face even whiter than before.

"My darling child!" said the mother.

"It's no matter, Mother. It's all my own foolish fault. Only bed again will be so dreary now. No, Mother, don't say a word. I'm a good deal wiser already than I used to be. If I get better, I shall live for you and Papa." A dreadful fit of coughing interrupted her. "Don't fancy I'm going to die for love," she said, with a faint attempt at a smile. "I'm not one of that sort. If I die, it'll be of a good honest cough, that's all."

Thomas never more crossed that threshold. And ever after, Mr. Boxall spoke to him as a paid clerk and nothing more. Mr. Stopper either knew something, or merely followed the tone of his principal. Even Charles Wither was short with him after a word from Jane. So Tom had no friend left but Lucy, and was driven nearer to Mr. Molken. He still contrived to keep his visits to Lucy a secret at home, but Mr. Stopper had begun to suspect.

As the spring drew on, Mary grew a little better. With the first roses, Uncle John Boxall came home from the Chinese Sea, and took up his residence for six weeks or so with his brother. Mary was fond of Uncle John, and improved rapidly at his appearance. He gave himself up almost to the invalid, and as she was already getting over her fancy for Tom, her love for her uncle came in to aid her recovery.

"It's the smell of the salt water," he said, when they remarked how much good he had done for her, "and more of it would do her more good yet."

13. Mattie's World

One bright spring morning, Mattie was seated with Mr. Spelt in his workshop. She was not dressing a doll now, for Lucy had set her to work upon some garments for the poor.

"I wonder how ever God made me," she said. "Did He cut me out of something else, and join me up, do you think? If He did, where did He get the stuff? And if He didn't, how did He do it?"

"Well, my Dear, it would puzzle a wiser head then mine to answer that question," said Mr. Spelt, who plainly judged ignorance a safer refuge from Mattie than any knowledge he possessed upon the subject. Her question, however, occasioned the return of an old suspicion that Mrs. Spelt had once had a baby; yet, somehow, he never knew what had come of it. She had recovered from her "illness," and yet the baby was nowhere.

"I wish I had thought to watch while God was making me, and then I should have remembered how He did it," Mattie resumed. "Ah! But I couldn't," she added, checking herself, "for I wasn't made till I was finished, and so I couldn't remember."

This was rather too profound for Mr. Spelt. Mattie, however, seemed bent on forcing conversation, and presently tried another vein.

"Do you remember a talk we had, in this very place, about God being kinder to some people than to other people?" she asked.

"Yes, I do," answered Mr. Spelt, who had been thinking about the matter a good deal since. "Are you of the same mind still, Mattie?"

"Well, yes and no," answered Mattie. "I can't quite get to the bottom of it. Do you know, Mother, that when I was a little girl I envied Poppie? Now, wherever was there a child that had more of the blessings of childhood than me?"

"What made you envy Poppie, then, Mattie?"

"Well, my father's shop was a rather awful place, sometimes. I never told you, Mother, what gained me the pleasure of your acquaintance. I used to grow frightened at father's books. Sometimes, you know, they were all quiet enough—you would generally expect books to be quiet, now wouldn't you? But other times they wouldn't be quiet. They kept thinking about me till my poor head couldn't bear it any longer.

"Even yet I have not got over my fancies about the books. Very often, as I am falling asleep, I hear them all thinking—they can hardly help it, you know, with so much to think about inside them. The one thinks into the other's thinks, and they blot each other out, and there is nothing but a confused kind of a jumble in my head till I fall asleep. Well, it was one day very like this day—wasn't it, Mother? I was standing at the window over there, and Poppie was playing down in the court. And I thought what a happy little girl she was, to go where she pleased in the sunshine, and not need to put on any shoes. Father wouldn't let me go where I liked, and there was nothing but books everywhere. My nursery was all round with books, and some of them had dreadful pictures in them. All at once the books began talking so loud as I had never heard them talk before. And I thought with myself, 'I won't stand this any longer. I will go away with Poppie.' So I ran out, but Poppie was gone, and then . . . what next, Mother?"

"Then my thread knotted, and that always puts me out of temper, because it stops my work. And I looked down into the court, and there I saw a tiny maiden staring all about her as if she had lost somebody, and her face looked as if she was just going to cry. And I knew who she was, for I had seen her in the shop before. And so I asked her what was the matter."

"And I said, 'It's the books that will keep talking.' "

"And I took you up beside me. But you were very ill after

that, and it was long before you came back again."

This story had been gone over and over again between the pair every time that Mattie wanted to rehearse the one adventure of her life.

"Well, where was I?" asked Mattie after a pause, laying her hands on her lap.

"I'm sure I don't know, Mattie."

"I was thinking, you know, that perhaps Poppie has her share of what's going, after all."

"And don't you think," suggested her friend, "that perhaps God doesn't want to keep all the good-doing to Himself, but leaves room for us to have a share in it? It's very nice work that you're at now, isn't it, Mattie?"

"Well, it is."

"As good as dressing dolls?"

"Better, because the dolls don't feel a bit better for it, you know. And them that'll wear that flannel petticoat will feel better for it, won't they?"

"But suppose everybody in the world was as well off as you and me, Mattie. If everybody had a father like yours that spoiled them, you wouldn't have any such clothes to make, and you would be forced to go back to your dolls as have no father or mother, and come across the sea in boxes."

"Well, I suppose I must allow that it is good of God to give us a share in making people comfortable; but you'll allow it does seem rather hard that I should have this to do now, and there's Poppie hasn't either the clothes to wear or to make."

"Can you do something for Poppie, then?"

"Well, I'll think about it, and see what I can do."

Mattie laid aside her work, crept on all fours to the door, and peeped over into the passage below.

"Well, Poppie, how do *you* do?" she began, in a condescending tone.

Poppie heard the voice and looked all round, but not seeing where it came from, turned and scudded away under the arch. Though Mattie knew Poppie, Poppie did not know Mattie, or at least did not know her voice. Poppie was not exactly frightened, but she was given to scudding when anything happened she did not precisely know what to do with. However, she did not run far this time. As soon as she reached the shelter of the arch, she turned and peeped back towards the court.

At that moment Lucy came out of the house and down the passage. She saw Mattie still leaning over the threshold of the workshop, and stopped. Thereupon Poppie came out and slowly approached.

"Are you getting on with that petticoat, Mattie?" said Lucy.

"Yes, Miss, I am. Only I'm afraid you won't like the stitch."

"Never mind—it will be a curiosity, that's all. But what do you think, Mattie! The kind lady, who gives us this work to do for the poor people, has invited all of us to go and spend a day with her."

Mattie did not answer. Lucy supposed she did not care to go, but she wanted very much to take her. She continued, "She has such a beautiful garden, Mattie! And she's *so* kind."

Still Mattie made no reply. Lucy would try again. "And it's such a beautiful house too, Mattie! I'm sure you would like to see it. "And," she added, almost reduced to her last resource, "she would give us such a nice dinner, I know."

This at length burst the silence, but not as Lucy expected.

"Now that's just what I will *not* stand," said the little maid.

"What *do* you mean, Mattie?" exclaimed Lucy, surprised and bewildered.

"Well, it's all very kind of Mrs. Morgingturn to ask you and me, what are well-to-do people, and in comfortable circumstances, to go and spend this day or that with her. Mr. Spelt," and here Mattie drew herself up and turned from Lucy to the tailor, "this kind lady, who gives me petticoats to make instead of dolls trousers, is doing the very thing you read about last night of the New Testament before I went to bed."

"What did Mr. Spelt read to you, Mattie?" asked Lucy.

"He read about *Somebody*—"

It was very remarkable how Mattie would use the name of God, never certainly with irreverence, but with a freedom that seemed to indicate that to her He was chiefly if not solely an object of metaphysical speculation or, possibly, of investigation, yet she hardly ever uttered the name of the Saviour, but spoke of Him as *Somebody*.

"He read about *Somebody* saying you shouldn't ask your friends and neighbors who could do the same for you again, but you should ask them that couldn't, because they hadn't a house to ask you to, like Poppie there."

Lucy looked round her and saw the most tattered little scarecrow. She had a vague impression that she had seen the child before, and could not help thinking of the contrast between the magnificent abode of the Morgensterns and the lip of the nest from which Mattie preached down into the world.

Lucy told the whole story to Mrs. Morgenstern, who heartily enjoyed it. Nor was Lucy in the least deterred from speaking of *Somebody* by the fact that Mrs. Morgenstern did not receive Him as the Messiah of her nation. If He did not hesitate to show Himself where He knew He would not be accepted, why should Lucy hesitate to speak His name? And why should His name not be mentioned to those who, although they had often been persecuted in His name by those who did not understand His mind, might well be proud that the Man who was conquering the world was a Jew?

When Mrs. Boxall senior heard of Mrs. Morgenstern's invitation, she resolved that Lucy should go. So the good old lady set herself to feel better in order that she might be better, and by the time Lucy awoke, she was prepared to persuade her that she was quite well enough to let her have a holiday.

"But how am I to leave you all alone, Grannie?" objected Lucy.

"Oh! I daresay that little Mattie of yours will come in and keep me company. Make haste and get your clothes on, and go and see."

Lucy went round the corner and entered Mr. Kitely's wilderness of books. She saw no one, but peeping round one of the many screens, she spied Mattie sitting with her back toward her, and her head bent downward. Looking over her shoulder, she saw that she had a book with a large folding plate of the funeral of Lord Nelson open before her, and was studying the black shapes and horrible plumes with unaccountable absorption.

"What *have* you got there, Mattie?" asked Lucy.

"Well, I don't ezackly know, Miss," answered the child, looking up, very white-faced and serious.

"Put the book away, and come and see Grannie. She wants you to take care of her today while I go out."

"Well, Miss, I would with pleasure, but Father is gone out,

and has left me to take care of the shop."

"But he won't be gone a great while, will he?"

"No, Miss. He knows I don't like to be left too long with the books. He'll be back before St. Jacob strikes nine—that I know."

"Well, then, I'll go and get Grannie quite comfortable, and if you don't come to me by half past nine, I'll come after you again."

"Do, Miss, please, for if Father ain't come by that time—my poor head—"

"You must put that ugly book away," said Lucy, "and take a better one."

"Well, Miss, I know I oughtn't to have taken this book, for there's no summer in it, and it talks like the wind at night."

"Why did you take it then?"

"Because Syne told me to take it. But that's just why I oughtn't to ha' taken it." And she rose and put the book on the shelf.

Lucy watched her uneasily. "What do you mean by saying that Syne told you?" she asked. "Who is Syne?"

"Don't you know Syne, Miss? Syne is—but it's all nonsense, when you're standing there. There isn't no such person as Syne, when you're there. But when you're gone away—I don't know. I think he's upstairs in the nursery now," she said, putting her hand to her big forehead. "No, no, there's no such person." And Mattie tried to laugh outright, but failed in the attempt, and the tears rose in her eyes.

"You've got a headache, Dear," said Lucy.

"Well, no," answered Mattie, "not just a headache, you know. But it does buzz a little. I hope Mr. Kitely won't be long now."

"I don't like leaving you, Mattie, but I must go to my grandmother," said Lucy, with reluctance.

"Never mind me, Miss. I'm used to it. I used to be afraid of Lord Syne, for he watched me, ready to pounce out upon me with all his men at his back, and he laughed so loud to see me run. But I know better now, and never run from him. I always frown at him, and take my own time, and do as I like. I don't want him to see that I'm afraid, you know. And I do think I have taught him a lesson. Besides, if he's very troublesome,

Miss, I can run to Mr. Spelt. But I never talk to him about Syne, because when I do he always looks so mournful. Perhaps he thinks it is wicked. He is so good himself; he has no idea how wicked a body can be."

Just then Mr. Kitely came in. Lucy repeated her request about Mattie, and he granted it cordially.

"I'm afraid, Mr. Kitely," said Lucy, "the darling is not well. She has such strange fancies."

"Oh, I don't know," returned the bookseller, with mingled concern at the suggestion and refusal to entertain it. "She's always been a curious child. Her mother was like that, you see, and she takes after her. Perhaps she does want a little more change. I don't think she's been out of this street now all her life. But she'll shake it off as she gets older."

So saying, he turned into his shop, and Lucy went home. In half an hour she went back for Mattie, and soon set out herself for the west end, where Mrs. Morgenstern was anxiously hoping for her appearance and her assistance.

14. Mrs. Morgenstern

Mrs. Morgenstern looked splendid as she moved among the hothouse plants, arranging them in the hall, on the stairs, and in the drawing rooms. She judged and rightly that she ought to be more anxious to show honor to poor neighbors by putting on her best attire, than to ordinary guests of her own rank. Therefore, although it was still the morning, she had put on a dress of green silk, trimmed with brown silk and rows of garnet buttons which set off her dark complexion and her rich black hair. She was half a head taller than Lucy, who was by no means short.

Lucy was as dark-haired and dark-eyed as Mrs. Morgenstern, but had a smaller face and regular features. Her high, close-fitting dress of black silk, with a plain linen collar and cuffs, left her loveliness all to itself. Lucy was neither strikingly beautiful nor remarkably intellectual.

While they were thus busy with the flowers, Miriam joined them, wearing a frock of dark red, with a band of gold in her rich dusky hair. Her splendid eyes, olive complexion, and rounded cheeks would make her a glory some day. She flitted into the room, and flew from flower to flower like one of those black and red butterflies that Scotch children call witches. The sight of her brought to Lucy's mind by contrast the pale face and troubled brow of Mattie, and she told Mrs. Morgenstern about her endeavor to persuade the child to come and how and why she had failed.

"Oh, do go and bring little Mattie," said Miriam. "I will be very kind to her. I will give her my doll's house, for I shall be too big for it next year."

"But I left her taking care of my grandmother," said Lucy, "and if she were to come I must stay at home, and besides, she would not want to come without me."

"Couldn't you bring the little Poppie she talks about?" asked Mrs. Morgenstern. "I should like to show Mattie that we're not quite so hard as she thinks us."

Lucy had been making inquiries in the neighborhood, and though she had not traced the child to headquarters anywhere, everybody in the poor places in which she had sought information knew something about her, though all they knew put together did not come to much. She slept at the top of a stair here, in the bottom of a cupboard there, but no one could say where her home was, or indeed if she had any one.

"If you would really like to have her," said Lucy, "I will go try to find her."

"You shall have the brougham."

"No, no," interrupted Lucy. "Go in a brougham to look for Poppie? Besides, I should not like the probable consequences of seating her in your carriage. But I should like to see how that wild little savage would do in such a place as this."

"Oh, do go," cried Miriam, clapping her hands. "It will be *such* fun."

Now Lucy had recently seen Poppie between Guild Court and Staines Court in the neighborhood of Shoreditch, but she did not know that it was because she was there that Poppie was there.

Nor did she know that Poppie had followed her almost to Mrs. Morgenstern's door that very morning. Poppie had then found a penny in the gutter, bought a fresh roll with it, given the half of it to a child younger than herself, whom she met at the back of the Marylebone police station. After contemplating the neighboring churchyard through the railings while they ate their roll together, and comparing this resting place of the dead with the grand Baker Street Cemetery, she had judged it time to scamper back to the neighborhood of Wyvil Place, that she might have a chance of seeing the beautiful lady as she came out again. As she turned the corner, she saw Lucy walking away towards the station, and after following her till she entered it, scudded off for the city, and arrived in the neighborhood of Guild Court before the third train reached nearby Farringdon Street.

Lucy looked in on her grandmother, and then set off for Staines Court, where she was glad of the opportunity of doing some loving-kindness while seeking Poppie. The first house she entered was dreadfully neglected. There were hardly more balustrades in the stairs than served to keep the filthy handrail in its place; and doubtless they too would follow the rest as firewood. The cupboard doors of the room into which Lucy entered had vanished, along with some of the flooring, revealing the joists and the ceiling of the room below. All this dilapidation did not matter much in summer weather, but when the winter came, the residents would just go on making larger and larger holes to let in the wind, and fight the cold by burning their protection against it.

In this room there was nobody. Something shining in a dingy sunbeam that fell upon one of the holes in the floor caught Lucy's eye. She stooped, and putting in her hand, drew out a bottle. Then someone spoke, and she started and let it fall back into the hole.

"Don't touch Mrs. Flanagan's gin bottle, Lady. She's a good 'un to swear, as you'd be frightened to hear her. She gives *me* the creepers sometimes, and I'm used to her. She says it's all she's got in the world, and she's ready to die for the old bottle."

It was Poppie speaking, and her pretty but dirty face and her wild black eyes that looked round the doorpost.

Lucy felt considerably relieved. She replaced the bottle carefully, saying as she rose, "I didn't mean to steal it, Poppie. I only saw it shining, and wanted to know what it was. Suppose I push it farther in that the sun mayn't be able to see it."

Poppie thought this was fun and showed her white teeth.

"But it was you I was looking for," added Lucy. "Will you come with me?"

"Yes, Lady," answered Poppie, looking as if she would bolt in a moment.

"Come, then," said Lucy, approaching her where she stood in the doorway.

But before she reached her, Poppie scudded to the bottom of the stair. Lucy saw at once that it would not do to make persistent advances, or show the least desire to get hold of her. Careful as one who fears to startle a half-tamed creature with wings, Lucy again approached her—but she vanished again, and Lucy saw no more of her till she was at the mouth of the court. She seemed to divine where Lucy was going, and with endless evanishments still reappeared in front of her, till she reached the railway station. And there Poppie was not to be seen.

Lucy was dreadfully disappointed. She had not yet a chance of trying her powers of persuasion upon the child—had not even been within arm's length of her. So she stood at the station door, hot and tired, with all the holiday feeling gone out of her.

Poppie had left her only because she had no access to the subterranean regions of the guarded railway. She turned away, but at that very moment her eye fell on something in the gutter—a bit of red glass. Now Poppie delighted in colored glass. She darted at the red shine, wiped it on her frock, sucked it clean in her mouth, and polished it up with her hands, scudding all the time in the hope that Lucy might still be at the station. Poppie wanted to give Lucy her treasure trove, for she never doubted that what was valuable to her would be valuable to a beautiful lady.

Lucy was sitting in the open waiting room, so weary and disappointed that little would have made her cry. She had let one train go on the vague chance that the erratic little maiden might yet show herself, but her last hope was almost gone when, to her great delight, she spied the odd creature peeping round the door. She had presence of mind not to rise, and instead made her a sign to come to her. This being just what Poppie wished at the moment, she obeyed. She darted up to Lucy, put the piece of glass into her hand, and would have been off again like a low-flying swallow, had not Lucy caught her by the arm. Once caught, Poppie never attempted to struggle. On this occasion she only showed her teeth in a rather constrained smile, and stood still. Lucy, however, did not take her hand from her arm, for she felt that the little phenomenon would disappear at once if she did.

"Poppie," she said, "I want you to come with me."

Poppie only grinned again. So Lucy rose, still holding her by the arm, and bought two second-class tickets. Poppie went on grinning, and accompanied her quietly down the stairs.

When they were fairly seated in the carriage, and there was no longer any danger of her prisoner endeavoring to escape, Lucy thought of the something Poppie had given her, at which she had not even looked, so anxious was she to secure her bird. When she saw it, she comprehended it at once—the sign of love, the appeal of a half-savage sister to one of her own kind, the richest human gift, simple love, unsought, unbought. Thus a fragment picked up out of the gutter by a beggar girl, who had never yet thought whether she had a father or a mother, became in that same girl's hands a something which the Lord Himself would have recognized as partaking of the character of His own eucharist. And as such, though without thinking of it after that fashion, it was received by the beautiful lady. The tears came into Lucy's eyes. Poppie thought she had offended or disappointed her, and looked very grave. Lucy saw Poppie misunderstood her, and so stooped and kissed her. Then the same tears came into Poppie's eyes.

Then the train moved off. Although the child by no remark and no motion showed astonishment any more than fear, she watched everything with the intensity of an animal which in new circumstances cannot afford to lose one moment of circumspection, since a true knowledge of the whole may be indispensable to the preservation of its liberty; and before they reached King's Cross, her eyes were clear, and only a channel on each cheek (ending in a little mudbank) showed where two tears had flowed and dried undisturbed.

When they reached Baker Street station, Lucy again took her charge by the hand along to Mrs. Morgenstern's door. Lucy's weariness had quite left her, and her eyes shone with triumph.

They made a strange couple, that graceful lady and that ragged, bizarre child—who would, however, have shown herself lovely to any eyes keen enough to see through the dirt which came and went according to laws as unknown to Poppie as the London fog.

The door was opened by a huge porter in rich livery and shoulder knots. He stared, but stood aside to let them enter with all the respect he ever condescended to show to those who, like Miss Burton, came to instruct Miss Morgenstern, and gave him (so much their superior) the trouble of opening the door to them. Lucy, however, cared as little for this form of contempt as did impervious little Poppie by her side, who trotted as unconcerned over the black and white lozenges of the marble floor as over the round stones of Staines Court. She strode through the grand house as though it were only Mistress Flanagan's hovel, and through a glass door at the back to a lawn behind, such as few London dwellings have to show.

Mrs. Morgenstern, in a little company of her friends, was standing in the middle of the lawn, while many of her neighbors were wandering about the place enjoying the flowers and fresh air, when Lucy came out with the dirty bare-legged child in hand.

Lucy had the bit of red glass in her mind, and led Poppie straight toward a lovely rose tree that stood in full blossom on one side of the lawn. How cool that kindly humble grass must have felt to the hot feet of the darling, but she had no time to think about it, for as she drew near the rose tree, her gaze became more and more fixed upon it. When she stood before it and beheld it in all its glory, she burst into a very passion of weeping. The eyes of the daughter of man became rivers and her head a fountain of waters, filled and glorified by the presence of a rose tree. All that were near gathered about, until Lucy, Poppie, and the rose tree were the center of a group. Lucy made no attempt to stay the flow of Poppie's tears, for her own heart swelled at the sight of the child's feelings. Surely it was the presence of God that so moved her; if ever bush burned with fire and was not consumed, that rose tree burned with the presence of God.

Poppie had no handkerchief, but she did not even put her hands to her face to hide her emotion. She let her tears run down her stained cheeks, and let sob follow sob unchecked, gazing ever through the storm of her little world at the marvel in front of her. She had seen a rose before, but had never seen a tree of roses. At last Lucy drew her handkerchief from her pocket, and for the first time in her life Poppie had tears wiped from her face by a loving hand.

The only man in the company—Mr. Sargent, a young barrister—was the first to speak. He drew near to Lucy and inquired in a half whisper, "Where did you find the little creature, Miss Burton?"

"That would be hard to say," answered Lucy, with a smile. "Isn't she a darling?"

"You are a darling, anyhow," said Mr. Sargent, but only to himself. He had been like one of the family for many years, for his father and Mr. Morgenstern had been close. He had admired Lucy ever since she went first to the house, but he had never seen her look so lovely as she looked that morning.

Little Miriam pulled at her mamma's skirt. "Somebody has lost that one," she said, pointing shyly to Poppie.

"Perhaps," said her mother.

But the answer did not satisfy Miriam. "You told me you had lost a little girl once," she said.

Mrs. Morgenstern had never yet uttered the word *death* in Miriam's hearing, but had said only that she had lost a child, and Miriam had interpreted the phrase for herself.

"Don't you think, Mamma," pursued Miriam, with the tears rising in her great black eyes, "that that's my little sister?"

Mrs. Morgenstern had the tenderest memories of her lost darling, and turned away to hide her feelings. Meantime, a little conversation had arisen in the group. Lucy had let go her hold of Poppie, whose tears had now ceased. Miriam drew near shyly and possessed herself of the hand of the vagrant. Her mother turned and saw her, and motherhood spoke aloud in her heart.

"What shall we do with her, Miriam?" she said.

"Ask nurse to wash her in the bath, and put one of my frocks on her."

The wild-eyed Poppie snatched her hand from Miriam's and began to search after a hole to run into. Mrs. Morgenstern turned away to Lucy who was on the other side of the rose-bush, talking to Mr. Sargent.

"Couldn't we do something to make the child tidy, Lucy?" she said.

Lucy gave her shoulders a little shrug, as much as to say she feared it would not be of much use. She was wrong there, for if the child should ever be clean again in her life, no one could tell how the growth of moral feeling might be aided in her by her once knowing what it was to have a clean skin and clean garments. But although Lucy did not see much use in washing her, she could not help wondering what she would look like if she were clean, and therefore proceeded to carry out her friend's wishes.

Poppie was getting bored already with the unrealized world of grandeur around her, and was only looking out for a chance to escape. Yet when Lucy spoke to her she willingly yielded her hand, perhaps in the hope that she was, like Peter's angel, about to open the prison doors and lead her out of the prison.

Lucy later gave an amusing account of how Poppie looked askance, with a mingling of terror and repugnance, at the great bath half full of water, into which she was about to be plunged. But the door was shut, and she submitted. Lucy found that she had undertaken a far more difficult task than she had expected—especially when it came to her hair. It was nearly two hours before she was able to produce the little savage on whom she had been bestowing this baptism of love.

When she came down at last, the company was seated at luncheon in the large dining room. Poppie was dressed in an old summer frock of Miriam's, and her hair was reduced to order, but she had begun to cry so piteously when Lucy began to put stockings on her that she gave up at once, and her legs were still bare. But nice and clean as she looked, she certainly had lost something by her decent garments. Poppie must have been made for rags and rags for Poppie—they went so admirably together. And there is nothing wicked in rags or poverty. It is possible to go in rags and keep the Ten Commandments, and it is possible to ride in purple and fine linen and break every one of them. Nothing, however, could hide the wildness of those furtive eyes.

Seated beside Lucy at the table, Poppie darted her eyes from one to another of the company with the scared expression of a creature caught in a trap. Lucy tried hard to make her eat, but she sat and stared, and would touch nothing. Her plate, with the wing of a chicken on it, stood before her unregarded. But all at once she darted out her hand like the paw of a wild beast, caught something, slipped from her chair, and disappeared under the table. Peeping down after her, Lucy saw her seated on the floor devouring the roll which had been by the side of her plate. Judging it best not to disturb her, she took no more notice of her for some time, during which Poppie, having discovered a long row of resplendent buttons down the front of her dress, twisted them all off. When the company rose from their seats, she crawled out from under the table and ran to Miriam, holding out both her hands. Miriam held out her hands to meet Poppie's, and received them full of the buttons off her own old frock.

"Oh! You naughty Poppie!" said Lucy, who had watched her. "Why did you pull off the buttons? Don't you like them?"

"Oh, don't I just! And so does *she*." Poppie had no idea she had done anything improper. It was not as buttons, but as pretty things, that she admired the knobs, and therefore she gave them to Miriam. Having said thus, she caught at another roll, dived under the table again, and devoured it at her ease—keeping, however, a sharp eye upon her opportunity. Finding one when Lucy's attention was elsewhere, she crawled out at the door, and with her hand on the ponderous lock of the street door, found herself seized from behind by the porter. She had been too long a pupil of the London streets not to know the real position of the liveried in the social scale, and for them she had as little respect as any of her tribe. She therefore assailed him with such a torrent of bad language, scarcely und erstanding a word that she used, that he declared it made his "'air stand on end," although he was tolerably familiar with such at thc Spotted Dog round the corner.

Finding, however, that this discharge of cuttlefish ink had no effect upon the enemy, she tried another mode—and with a yell of pain, the man fell back shaking his hand, which bore the marks of four sharp incisors. And Poppie was free and scudding, her introduction to civilized life at an end.

Poppie had not found it nice. She preferred all London to the biggest house and garden in it. True, there *was* that marvelous rose tree, but freeborn creatures cannot live upon the contemplation of roses. After all, the things she had been brought up to, the streets, the kennels, with their occasional crusts, pennies, and bits of glass, the holes to creep into, and the endless room for scudding, were better. And her unsuitable dress—seldom seen in connection with bare hair and legs—would soon accommodate itself to circumstances, taking the form of rags before a week would be over. For like the birds of the air and the lilies of the field, she had no care.

At the porter's cry, Lucy started, and found to her dismay that her charge was gone. She could not, however, help a certain somewhat malicious pleasure at the man's discomfiture, and the babylike way in which he lamented over his bitten hand. Both Mrs. Morgenstern and Lucy, after the first disappointment and vexation were over, laughed heartily at the affair. Even Miriam was worked up to a smile at last, though she continued very mournful over the loss of her "sister."

Mr. Sargent did his best to enliven the party. He was a man of good feeling, and of more than ordinary love for the right. From a dread, however, of what he would have called *sentimentality,* he persisted in regarding his feeling as a mere peculiarity, and possibly as a weakness. If he made up his mind to help anyone who was wronged (for which, it must be confessed, he devoted more time than he would have cared to acknowledge) he would say that the case involved points of interest which he was willing to see settled. He never said that he wanted to see right done; that would have been enthusiastic, and unworthy of the cold dignity of a lawyer. So he was one of those few men who represent themselves as inferior to what they are.

And Lucy was pleased with him. She never thought of comparing him with Thomas, which was well for Thomas. But she did think he was a very clever, gentlemanly fellow, who knew how to make himself agreeable.

Though he offered to see her home, she declined, and did not even permit him to walk her to the railway.

15. Conversations

Lucy found the two "old women" seated together at their tea. Not a ray of the afternoon sun could find its way into the room. It was dusky and sultry, with smell of roses.

"Well, Miss Burton, here you are at last!" said Mattie.

"Yes, Mattie, here I am. Has Grandmother been good to you?"

"Of course she has—very good. Everybody is good to *me*. I am a very fortunate child, as my father says, though he never seems to mean it."

"And how do you think your patient is?" asked Lucy, while Mrs. Boxall sat silent, careful not to obstruct the amusement.

"Well, I do not think Mrs. Boxall is worse. She has been very good, and has done everything I found myself obliged to recommend. I would not let her get up so soon as she wanted to."

"And what did you do to keep her in bed?" asked Lucy.

"Well, I could not think of a story to tell her just then, so I got the big Bible out of the bookcase, and began to show her the pictures. But she did not care about that. I think it was my fault, though, because I was not able to hold the book so that she could see them properly. So I read a story to her, but I do not think I chose a very nice one. It was an ugly trick of that woman to serve a person that never did *her* any harm, and I wonder at two sensible women like Mrs. Boxall and Deborah sticking up for her."

"Is it Jael she means, Grannie?" asked Lucy very softly.

"Yes, it is Jael she means," answered Mattie for herself, with some defiance in her tone. "For my part," she continued, "I think it was just like one of Syne's tricks."

"Have you seen Mr. Spelt today, Mattie?" asked Lucy, desirous of changing the subject.

"Well, I haven't," answered Mattie, "but I will go and see now whether he's gone or not."

Mattie bade them good-night with an expression of hauteur and marched solemnly down the stairs, holding carefully by the balusters, for she was too small to use the handrail comfortably.

Mr. Spelt's roost was shut up for the night; he had gone home, and Mattie turned toward her father's shop.

In the archway she collided with Thomas, so that he had to clasp her to prevent her from falling.

"Well, you needn't be in such a hurry, Mr. Thomas, though she *is* a-waiting for you. She won't go till you come, I know."

"You're a cheeky little monkey," said Thomas, good-naturedly. Mattie, feeling her dignity invaded, walked into the shop with her chin projecting.

"Come, my princess," said her father, seating himself in an old chair and taking the child on his knee. "I haven't seen my princess all day. How's your royal highness this night?"

Mattie laid her head on his shoulder and burst into tears.

"What's the matter with my pet?" said her father with much concern. "Has anybody been unkind to you?"

"No," said the child, "but I feel so lonely! I wish you would read to me a bit, for Mr. Spelt ain't there, and I read something in the Bible this morning that ain't done me no good."

"You shouldn't read such things, Mattie," said the bookseller. "They ain't no good. I'll go and get a candle."

"Don't leave me here—I don't like the books. Carry me with you."

The father took his child on his arm, got a candle from the back room, and sat down with Mattie in a part of the shop which was screened from the door, where he could yet hear every footstep that passed.

"What shall I read now, my precious?" he asked.

"Well, I don't think I care for anything but the New Testament tonight, Father."

"Why, you've just been saying it disagreed with you this very morning," objected Mr. Kitely.

"No, father, it was near the beginning, and told all about a horrid murder. I do believe," she added, reflectively, "that that Book grows better as it gets older—younger, I mean."

The poor child wanted someone to help her out of the Bible difficulties, and her father certainly was not the man to do so, for he believed nothing about or in it. She was laboring under the misery of the fancy that everything related in the Old Testament without remark is sanctioned by the divine will. If parents do not encourage their children to speak their minds about what they read generally, and especially in the Bible, they will one day be dismayed to find that they have not merely the strangest but the most deadly notions of what is contained in that Book, as, for instance, that God approved of all the sly tricks of Jacob—for was not he the religious one of the brothers, and did not all his tricks succeed? Children are not able without help to regard the history broadly, and see that just because of this bad that was in him, he had to pass through a life of varied and severe suffering, and he punished in the vices which his children inherited from him, in order that the noble part of his nature might be burned clean of the filth that clung to it.

But such was Mr. Kitely's tenderness over his daughter, increased by some signs of the return of the brain fever from which he had nearly lost her some years before, that he made no further opposition. He rose again, brought an old Breeches Bible from a shelf, and taking her once more on his knee, supported her with one hand and held the Book with the other.

"Well, I don't know one chapter from another," reflected Mr. Kitely aloud. "I'm sure I can't tell what to read."

"Read about *Somebody,*" said Mattie.

He opened the Gospel part of the book at random and began to read.

He read the story of the Transfiguration, to which Mattie listened without a word or motion. He then went on to the following story of the lunatic and apparently epileptic boy. As soon as he began to read the account of how the child was vexed, Mattie said conclusively, "That was Syne. *I* know him. He's been at it for a long time."

" 'And Jesus rebuked the devil, and he departed out of him; and the child was cured from that very hour,' " the bookseller continued in a very subdued voice.

But the moment he read those words, Mattie cried, "There! I knew it! I knew that Somebody would let him mind what he was about—I did. I wonder if He let a flash of that light out on him that He had just shut up inside Him again. I shouldn't wonder if that was it. I know Syne couldn't stand that—no, not for a moment. I think I can go to bed now."

Meanwhile, Richard and John Boxall had been talking after their dinner.

"I tell you what, Brother," said the captain, "you're addling good brains with overwork. You won't make half so much money if you're too greedy after it. You don't look the same fellow you used to be."

"I hope I'm not too greedy after money, John. But it's my business, as yours is to sail your ship."

"Yes, yes. I can't sail my ship too well, nor you attend to your business too well. But if I was to sail two ships instead of one, or if I was to be on the deck instead of down at my dinner when she was going before the wind in the middle of the Atlantic, I shouldn't do my best when it came on to blow hard in the night."

"That's all very true, but I never miss my dinner by any chance."

"You know what I mean well enough. But I've got a proposal to make—the jolliest in the world."

"Go on. I'm listening."

"Mary ain't quite so well now, is she?"

"Well, I don't think she's been getting on so fast, and I'm sometimes rather uneasy about her."

"And there's Jane. She don't look at home, somehow."

For some time Richard had been growing more and more uneasy as the evidence of his daughter's attachment to Charles Wither became plainer. Both he and his wife did the best they could to prevent their meetings; but having learned a little wisdom, and knowing well the hastiness of his own temper, he had as yet managed to avoid any open conflict with his daughter, who he knew had inherited his own stubbornness.

"And there's your wife," continued the captain. "She's had

a headache almost every day since I came to the house. You must all make this next voyage in my clipper. It'll do you all a world o' good, and me too."

"Nonsense, John," said Richard, feeling, however, that a faint light dawned through the proposal.

"Don't call it nonsense till you've slept on it, Dick. You'll have to pay a little passage money, just to keep me right with the rest of the owners, but that won't be much. Anyway, I believe it's not the money so much as the making of it that fills your head."

"Still, you wouldn't have me let the business go to the dogs?"

"No fear of that, with Stopper at the head of affairs. You must take him in."

"Into partnership, do you mean?" said Richard, expressing no surprise, for he had thought of this before.

"You'll have to do it someday, and the sooner the better. If you don't, you'll lose him, and that won't be a mere loss. That man'll make a dangerous enemy. Where he bites he'll hold. And now's a good time to serve yourself and him too."

"Perhaps you're right, Brother," answered the merchant, "I certainly should not be sorry to have a short holiday. I haven't had one to speak of for nearly twenty years."

His wife was consulted. Although she shrank from the thought of a sea voyage, she yet saw in the proposal a way out of many difficulties. So between them the whole was arranged before any of the young people knew of it. Jane heard it with a rush of blood to her heart that left her dark face almost livid. Mary received the news gladly, even merrily, though a slight paleness followed, indicating that she regarded the journey as a symbol and sign of severed bonds. Julia, a plump child of six, danced with joy at the idea of going in Uncle John's ship. And Mr. Stopper threw no difficulty in the way of accepting a partnership.

A short time after, the *Ningpo* was ready to drop down with the next tide to Gravesend, where she was to take her passengers on board.

16. On the River

In spite of the good-humored answer Thomas had made to Mattie, her words had stuck to him, and still occasioned him a little discomfort. For if the bookseller's daughter, whose shop lay between the countinghouse and the court, knew so well of his visits to Lucy, how could he hope that they would long remain concealed from other and far more dangerous eyes? This thought oppressed him so much one evening that, instead of paying his usual visit to Mr. Molken, he went to Mrs. Boxall's at once. There, after greetings, he threw himself gloomily on the cushions of the old settle. Lucy looked at him with some concern, and Mrs. Boxall murmured something about his being in the doldrums.

"Let's go out, Lucy," said Thomas. "It is so sultry."

Lucy was quite ready to comply, for she wanted to talk to him. So she made the old woman comfortable in her armchair, and went out with Thomas.

The roar of the city had subsided. There was little smoke in the air, only enough to clothe the dome of St. Paul's in a faintly rosy garment. The sun was under a cloud, and a cooling wind was gathering to flow at sunset through the streets and lanes.

The two went down one of the lanes leading toward the river. Here they passed through a sultry region of aromatic fragrance, where the very hooks that hung from cranes in high doorways seemed to retain something of the odor of the bales they had lifted from the wagons below. By yet narrower alleys they went toward the river, descended a short wooden stair and a long wooden way, and came on a floating pier.

A boat was just starting up the river toward the light.

"Let's have a ride," said Thomas, and they went on board. The wheels churned the dark waters of the Thames into a white fury, as they moved upstream. They went forward into the bow of the boat to get clear of the smoke, and sat down. There were so few on board that they could talk without being overheard. But they sat silent for some time, for the stillness of the sky seemed to have sunk into their hearts. Its light and color illuminated the surface of the river, which was not yet so vile that it could not reflect the glory that fell upon its face. Lucy sat gazing at the ragged banks, where the mighty city had declined into a sordid, tattered fringe upon a rich garment. Then she turned her gaze down upon the dirty river, which crawled fiercely away to hide itself in the sea.

"How different things would be," she said, "if they were only clean!"

"Yes, indeed," returned Thomas. "Think what it would be like to see the fishes shooting about in clear water under us, like so many silver fishes in a crystal globe! If people were as fond of the cleanliness you want as they are of money, things would look very different indeed!"

As Thomas loved Lucy more and more, he had begun to find a poetic element in her, and he flattered himself that he had developed it. Men like women to reflect them, no doubt; but the woman who can only reflect a man, and is nothing in herself, will never be of much service to him. The woman who cannot stand alone is not likely to make either a good wife or mother. She may be a pleasant companion, but scarcely more.

"I wish the world were clean, Thomas, all through," said Lucy.

Thomas did not reply, for his heart smote him. Those few words went deeper than all Mr. Simon's sermons, public and private. For a long time he had not spoken a word about religion to Lucy. Nor had what he said ever taken any hold upon her intellect, although it had upon her conscience; for, not having been brought up to the vocabulary and jargon of his religion, it had been to her a vague sound, which yet she re ceived as a reminder of duty. Some healthy religious teaching would be of the greatest value to her, but Mr. Potter provided little that could be called food.

Finding that Thomas remained silent, Lucy looked into his face, and saw that he was troubled. This brought to the point of speech the dissatisfaction with himself which had long been moving restlessly and painfully in his heart, and of which the quiet and peace about him had made him more conscious than he had yet been.

"O Lucy," he said, "I wish you would help me to be good."

To Lucy only could he have said so. Before Lucy at this moment, he could be humble without humiliation, and could even enjoy the confession of weakness in his appeal for her aid.

She looked at him with a wise kind of wonder in her look."I do not know how I can help you, Thomas, for you know better about such things than I do. But there is one thing I want very much to speak to you about, because it makes me rather unhappy." She laid her hand upon his, and he looked at her lovingly. She was encouraged, and continued. "I don't like this way of going on, Thomas."

"What do you mean, Lucy?" asked Thomas, his heart beginning already to harden at the approach of definite blame. It was all very well for him to speak as if he might be improved; it was another thing for Lucy to do so.

"Do not be vexed with me, Thomas. I wish your mother knew all about us." And then her face flushed red as a sunset.

"She'll know all about it in good time," returned Thomas testily. "You do not know my mother, or you would not be so anxious for her to know all about it."

"Couldn't you get your father to tell her then?"

"My father," said Thomas coolly, "would turn me out of the house if I didn't give you up! And as I don't mean to do that, and don't want to be turned out of the house just at present, when I have nowhere else to go, I don't want to tell him."

"I *can't* go on in this way, then. Besides, they are sure to hear of it, somehow."

"Oh, no, they won't. Who's to tell them?"

"Don't suppose I've been eavesdropping, Tom," a new voice broke from behind them, "merely because I have heard your last words." It was Charles Wither. "I have been watching for an opportunity to tell you that Stopper is keeping far too sharp a lookout on you to mean you any good by it. I beg your pardon, Miss Burton," he resumed, taking off his hat. "I fear I have been rude, but as I say, I was anxious to tell Mr. Worboise to be cautious. I don't see why a fellow should get into a scrape for want of a hint."

Wither's manner made poor Lucy feel that there was not merely something unfitting, but something even disreputable, in the way her relation to Thomas was kept up. She grew pale, rose and turned to the side of the vessel, and drew her veil nervously over her face.

"It's no business of mine, of course, Tom. But what I tell you is true. Though, if you take my advice," said Wither, and here he dropped his voice to a whisper, "this connection is quite as fit to cut as the last one, and the sooner you do it the better, for it'll make an awful row with old Boxall. You ought to think of the girl, you know, though your governor's your own lookout."

He turned with a nod and went aft. The steamer drew into the pier, where he went ashore.

For a few minutes not a word passed between Thomas and Lucy. A sudden cloud had fallen upon them. They must not go on this way, but what other way were they to take? They stood side by side, looking into the water, Thomas humiliated and Lucy disgraced.

Lucy was the first to speak. "We must go ashore at the next pier."

"Very well," said Tom, as if he had been stunned into sullenness. "If you want to get rid of me because of what that fellow said—"

"O Tom!" said Lucy, and burst out crying.

"Well, what *do* you want, Lucy?"

"We must part, Tom," sobbed Lucy.

"Nonsense!" said Tom, as a great painful lump rose in his throat.

"We can love each other all the same," said Lucy, still sobbing, "only you must not come to see me anymore till you have told them all about it. I don't mean now, but sometime, you know. When will you be of age, Tom?"

"Oh, that makes no difference. As long as I'm dependent,

it's all the same. I wish I was my own master. I should soon let them see I didn't care what they said."

Silence again followed, during which Lucy tried in vain to stop her tears by wiping them away. A wretched feeling awoke in her that Thomas was not manly, that he could not help her when she would do the right thing. She would have borne anything rather than that, and it put her heart in a vise.

The boat stopped at Westminster Pier, and they went on shore. The sun was down, and the fresh breeze made Lucy shiver with cold, for loss had laid hold of her heart. As they walked up Parliament Street, Thomas felt that he must say something, but what he should say he could not think. He always thought what he should say—never what he should do.

"Lucy, dear," he said at last, "we won't make up our minds tonight. Wait till I see you next. I shall have time to think about it before then. I will be a match for that sneaking rascal, Stopper, yet."

Lucy felt that to sneak was no way to give sneaking its own, but she said neither that nor anything else.

They got into an omnibus at Charing Cross, and returned despondent into the city. They parted at Lucy's door, and Thomas went home, already much later than usual.

What should he do? He resolved upon nothing, and did the worst thing he could have done. He lied.

"You are very late tonight, Thomas," said his mother. "Have you been all this time with Mr. Moloch?"

"Yes, Mother," answered Thomas. And when he was in bed he consoled himself by saying that there was no such person as Mr. Moloch.

When Lucy went to bed, she prayed to God in sobs and cries of pain. Hitherto she had believed in Thomas without question, but now she had begun to doubt, and the very fact that she could doubt was enough to make her miserable. His beautiful face, pleasant manners, self-confidence, and, above all, her love, had blinded her to his faults. But once she had begun to suspect, she found enough ground for suspicion. She had never known grief before—not even when her mother died, for death had not done anything despicable, and Thomas had.

The words from Charles Wither were true enough. Mr. Stopper was after him. Ever since the dinner party at Mr.

Boxall's, Mr. Stopper had hated Tom, and he bided his time. Mr. Stopper was a man of forty, in whose pineapple whiskers and bristly hair the first white streaks of autumn had begun to show themselves. He had entered the service of Messrs. Blunt and Baker some twenty-five years before, and had gradually risen through all the intervening positions to his present post. Within the last year, moved by prudential considerations, he had begun to regard the daughters of his principal against the background of possible marriage. For the moment he saw Mary Boxall with this object in view, he fell in love with her after the fashion of such a man—beginning instantly to build not castles, but square houses in the air, in the rooms of which her form appeared in gorgeous and somewhat matronly garments amid ponderous mahogany, seated behind the obscurity of tropical plants. His indignation when he entered the drawing room after the Boxalls' dinner, and saw Thomas in the act of committing the indiscretion recorded, passed into silent hatred when he found that while his attentions were slighted, those of Thomas which had not even been offered, but only dropped at her feet in passing, were yet accepted.

Among men, Mr. Stopper was of the bulldog breed, sagacious, keen-scented, vulgar, and inexorable. And now one of his main objects was to catch some scent of Thomas' faults till he should have a chance of pulling him down at last. His first inclination toward this revenge was elevated into an imagined execution of justice when Mary fell ill, and it oozed out that her illness had not a little to do with some behavior of Thomas. Hence it came that Mr. Stopper was watching the unfortunate youth, though so cautious was Thomas that he had not yet discovered anything of which he could make a definite use. Nor did he want to interrupt Thomas' projects before they put him in his power.

The weak and conceited youth lay between the malign aspects of two opposite stars—watched, that is, and speculated upon by two able and unprincipled men: the one, Mr. Molken, searching him and ingratiating himself with him, to the end to govern him; the other, Mr. Stopper, watching not for the sake of procuring advantage to himself but injury to Thomas. And they soon began to play into each other's hands without knowing it.

17. The Tempter

The next day Thomas had made up his mind not to go near Guild Court; but in the afternoon Mr. Stopper himself sent him to bring an old ledger from the floor above old Mrs. Boxall's.

"There's no use in going round the long way," said Mr. Stopper. "Mr. Boxall's not in—you can go through his room. Here's the key of the door. Only mind you lock it when you come back."

The key had lain in Mr. Boxall's drawer, but now Mr. Stopper took it from his own. Thomas was not altogether pleased at the change of approach. He was, as it were, exposed upon the flank. Annoyance instantly clouded the expression of eagerness which he had not been able to conceal, and neither the light nor the following cloud escaped Mr. Stopper.

Thomas had nothing to do but take the key and go. He had now no opportunity of spending more than one minute with Lucy. When the distance was of some length, he could *cut* both ways, and pocket the time gained; now there was nothing to save upon. Nevertheless, he sped up the stairs as if he would overtake old Time himself.

He secured the ordered chaos of vellum before he knocked at Mrs. Boxall's door, which he then opened without waiting for the response to his appeal.

"Lucy! Lucy!" he said. "I have but half a minute, and hardly that."

Lucy appeared with the rim of a rainy sunset about her eyes. "If you have forgotten yesterday, Thomas, I have not," she said.

"Oh! Never mind yesterday," he returned. "I'm coming in tonight, and I can stay as long as I please. My father and mother have gone to Folkestone, and there's nobody to know when I go home. Isn't it jolly?"

And without waiting for an answer, he scudded like Poppie. As he reentered the countinghouse he was aware of the keen glance cast at him by Stopper, and he reddened. But he laid the ledger on the desk before him, and perched again with as much indifference as he could assume.

Wearily the hours passed. How could they pass otherwise with figures everywhere, Stopper right before him at the double desk, and Lucy one story removed and inaccessible? Some men would work all the better for knowing their treasure so near, but Thomas did not yet love Lucy well enough for that. People talk about loving too much, but most mischief comes of loving too little.

The dinner hour at length arrived. Thomas did not attempt to see Lucy then, but took himself to a court off Cornhill, and ascended to one of those eating houses where a man may generally dine well, and always at moderate expense.

Now this was one of the days on which Thomas usually visited Mr. Molken. But as he had missed two lessons, the spider had become a little anxious about his fly, and knowing that Thomas went to dine at this hour, and knowing also where he went, he was there before him. When Thomas entered, there he was signaling to him to take his place beside him. Thomas did not see that in the dark corner of an opposite box sat Mr. Stopper. He obeyed the signal, and a steak was presently broiling for him upon the gridiron at the other end of the room.

"Vy haff you not come for your lesson, Mr. Verbose?" asked Molken.

"I was otherwise engaged," answered Thomas carelessly. He had not yet made a confidant of Mr. Molken.

"Ah! Yes. Oddervise," said Molken, and he broke into a suppressed laugh.

"What is it you find so amusing, Mr. Molken?" Tom asked.

"I beg your pardon," returned Molken. "It vas very rude, but

I could not help it. I vill tell you von story I did see last night. I am a man of de vorld, as you know, Mr. Verbose, and I vas last night in von of dose shops vere dey have de gambling. I vas at de bar haffing a glass of Judenlip, ven down through de green door, vit a burst, comes a young man I know. He vas like yourself, Mr. Verbose, a clerk in a countinghouse."

Thomas winced, but said nothing. He regarded his business as he ought to have regarded himself—as something to be ashamed of.

" 'Herr Molken,' he says, 've are old friends. Vill you lend me a sovereign?' 'No,' I said, 'I never lend money for gambling. Get de man who von your last sovereign to lend you anodder.'

"He svore and turned avay. I hadn't a sovereign, but I vasn't going to tell him dat. But if I had had von, he should haff had it; for I can't forget de glorious excitement it used to be to see de gold lying like a yellow molehill on de table, and to think dat von fortunate turn might send it all into your own pockets.

"Now I had seen him fumbling about his vaistcoat as if he vould tear his heart out, and all at vonce dive two fingers into a little pocket dat vas meant to hold a vatch, only de vatch had gone long ago. 'By Jove!' he said, and then he rushed through de green door again. I followed him. He had found a sovereign in dat little pocket, and in haff an hour he had broken de bank. He svept his money into his pockets and vent. Now let me tell you a secret," continued Molken, leaning across the table, and speaking very low and impressively, "dat young man confessed to me dat ven I refused him the sovereign, he had just lost de last of two hundred pounds of his master's money. Today I hope he has replaced it honestly as he ought; for his vinnings dat night came to more dan seven hundred."

"But he was a thief," said Thomas bluntly.

"Vell, so he vas—but no more a thief dan many a respectable man who secures his own and goes on risking odder people's money. It's de vay of de vorld. There *vas* a time in my life ven I used to live by it."

"How did you manage that?"

"Dere are certain rules to be observed, dat's all. You must make up your mind neffer to lose more dan a certain fixed sum any night you play, and you vill find your vinnings alvays in excess of your losses. Everyting goes by laws, you know—aws dat cannot be found out except by experiment, and dat, as I say, is von of de laws of gambling."

All this time Mr. Stopper had been reading Mr. Molken's face. Suddenly Tom caught sight of his superior; Wither's warning rushed back on his mind, and he grew pale as death. Molken, perceiving the change, sought for its cause, but saw nothing save a stony gentleman in the opposite box sipping sherry.

"Don't look that way, Mr. Molken," said Tom, in an undertone. "That's our Mr. Stopper."

"Vell, haffen't ve as good a right to be here as Mr. Stopper?" returned Molken, in a voice equally inaudible beyond the table, but taking piercing eyeshots at the cause of Tom's discomposure.

The two men very soon had something like each other's measure. Each could understand his neighbor's rascality, while his own seemed only a law of Nature.

"He hates me," said Tom, "though why, I'm sure I don't know. I can only guess."

"Some girl, I suppose," said Molken, coolly.

Thomas felt too much flattered to endeavor even to dilute the insinuation, and Molken went on.

"Vell, but how can de fellow bear malice? Of course, he must haff seen from de first dat he had no chance vit you. I'll tell you vat, Verbose: I haff had a good deal of experience, and it is my conviction dat you are von of de lucky vons—von of de elect, you know, born to it, and can't help yourself."

"What do you mean?"

"Some men are born under a lucky star. Heaven must have some favorites, if only for de sake of wariety. At all events, dere is no denying dat some men are born to luck. Dey are lucky in everyting dey put der hands to. Did you ever try your luck at a lottery, now?"

"I did in a raffle, once, and won a picture."

"I told you so! And it vould be just de same vatever you tried. You haff de luck-mark on you. I vas sure of it."

"How can you tell that?" asked Tom, lingering like a fly over the sweet poison, and ready to swallow almost any absurdity that represented him as something different from the run of ordinary mortals.

"I haff experience, and your own Bacon says dat de laws of everyting are found out by observation and experiment. I haff observed, and I haff experimented, and I tell you you are a lucky von."

Tom stroked the faintest neutrality of a coming moustache, ponderingly and pleasedly, and said nothing.

"By de vay, are you coming to me tonight?" asked Molken.

"No," answered Tom, still stroking his upper lip with the thumb and forefinger of his left hand. "I think not."

"Den I needn't stop at home for you. By de vay, haff you a sovereign about you? I vouldn't trouble you, you know, only as I told you, I haffen't got von. I beliefe your quarter's tuition is due tonight."

"Oh, I beg your pardon; I ought to have thought of that. I have two half sovereigns in my pocket, no more, I am sorry to say. Will one of them do for tonight? You shall have more tomorrow."

"I *vill* take de ten shillings, for I vant to go out dis evening. Yes. Thank you. Never mind tomorrow, *except* it be convenient."

Tom settled the bill, and put the change of the other half sovereign in his pocket. When Molken left him at the door of the tavern and Tom went back to the countinghouse.

"Who was that with you at the Golden Fleece, Tom?" asked Mr. Stopper as he entered, for he took advantage of his position to be as rude as he found convenient.

Taken by surprise, Tom answered at once, "Mr. Molken."

"And who is he?" asked Stopper, again.

"My German master," answered Tom.

"He's got a hangdog face," said Mr. Stopper, as he plunged again into the business before him.

Tom's face flushed with wrath. "I'll thank you to be civil in your remarks on my friends, Mr. Stopper."

Mr. Stopper answered him with a small puff of a windy breath from distended lips. Tom felt his eyes waver, and he grew almost blind with rage. He was inclined to crack his ruler down on Stopper's head, and yet he did not, merely because of his incapacity for action of any sort.

18. Tom's Evening

When Tom left the office he walked into Mr. Kitely's shop, for he was afraid lest Mr. Stopper should see him turn into Guild Court. He had almost forgotten Mr. Kitely's behavior about the book he would not keep for him, and his resentment was quite gone. There was nobody in the shop but Mattie.

"Well, Chick," said Thomas, kindly, but more condescendingly than suited her tastes.

"Neither chick nor child," she answered promptly.

"What are you then? One of the fairies?"

"If I was, I know what I would do. I would turn your eyes into gooseberries, and your tongue into a bit of leather a foot long, and every time you tried to speak, your long tongue would slap your blind eyes and make you cry."

"What a terrible doom!" returned Thomas, offended but willing to see it through. "Why?"

"Because you made Miss Burton's eyes red, you naughty man! Nobody else could make her eyes red but you, and you go and do it."

Thomas's first movement was of anger, for he felt (as all who have concealments are ready to feel) that he was being uncomfortably exposed. He turned his back on the child, and proceeded to examine the books. While he was this engaged, Mr. Kitely entered.

"How do you do, Mr. Worboise?" he said. "I have another copy of that book you and I fell out about some time ago. I can let you have this one at half the price."

It was evident that the bookseller wanted to be conciliatory. Thomas, in his present mood, was inclined to repel his advances, but he shrunk from contention, and therefore said, "Thank you, I shall be glad to have it." Ashamed to appear again unable, even at the reduced price, to pay for it, he pulled out the last farthing of the money in his possession (which came to the exact sum required) and pocketed the volume.

As he counted the money, Mr. Kitely said, "I would give you a hint, Mr. Worboise, about that German up the court. He's a clever enough fellow, I daresay—perhaps too clever. Don't you have anything to do with him beyond the German. Take my advice. I don't sit here all day at the mouth of the court for nothing."

"What is there to say against him, Mr. Kitely? I haven't seen any harm in him."

"I'm not going to commit myself to warning you, Mr. Worboise; but look out, and don't let him lead you into mischief."

"I hope I am able to take care of myself, Mr. Kitely," said Thomas, with a touch of offense.

Just then Mr. Stopper passed the window. Thomas listened for the echo of his steps up the archway, and as none came, he knew that he had gone along the street. He waited, and then sped from the shop, round the corner, and up to Mrs. Boxall's door. The old lady herself opened for him, not looking as pleased as usual to see him. Mr. Molken was watching from the opposite ground-floor window. A few minutes after, Mr. Stopper repassed the window of Mr. Kitely's shop and went into the countinghouse.

Thomas rushed eagerly up the stairs and into the sitting room. Lucy, red-eyed, rose and held out her hand, but her manner was constrained, and her lips trembled as if she were going to cry. Thomas would have put his arm around her and drawn her to him, but she gently pushed him away, and he felt—as many a man has felt—that in the gentlest repulse of the woman he loves there is something terribly imperative and absolute.

"Why, Lucy!" he said, in a tone of hurt. "What have I done?"

"If you can forget so soon, Thomas," answered Lucy, "I cannot. Since yesterday I see things in a different light altogether. I cannot, for your sake any more than my own, allow things to go on in this doubtful way."

"Oh, but Lucy, I was taken unawares yesterday, and today, now that I have slept upon it, I don't see there is any such danger. I ought to be a match for that brute Stopper, anyhow."

"But that is not the question, Thomas. It is not right to go on like this. People's friends ought to know. I would not have done it if Grannie hadn't been to know. But then I ought to have thought of your friends as well as my own."

"But there would be no difficulty if I only had a grandmother," urged Thomas, "and one as good as yours. I shouldn't have thought of not telling then."

"I don't think the difficulty of doing right makes it unnecessary to do it," said Lucy.

"I think you might trust that to me, Lucy," said Thomas, falling back upon his old attempted relation of religious instructor to his friend.

Lucy knew that the time had come for altering their relative position, if not the relation itself. "No, Thomas," she said, "I must take my own duty into my own hands. I will not go on this way."

"Do you think then, Lucy, that in affairs of this kind the fellow ought to do just what his parents want?"

"No, Thomas. But I do think he ought not to keep such things a secret from them."

"Not even if they are unreasonable and tyrannical?"

"No. A man who will not take the consequences of loving cannot be much of a lover."

"Lucy!" cried Thomas, now stung to the heart.

"I can't help it, Thomas," said Lucy, bursting into tears. "I *must* speak the truth, and if you cannot bear it, the worse for me—and for you too, Thomas."

"Then you mean to give me up?" said Thomas, pathetically, but without any real fear of such an unthinkable catastrophe.

"If it be giving you up to say I will not marry a man who is too much afraid of his father and mother to let them know what he is about, then I do give you up. But it will be you who gives me up if you refuse to acknowledge me as you ought."

Lucy could not have talked like this ever before in her life, but she had gone through an eternity of suffering in the night. She was a woman now, and had been but a girl before. Now she stood high above Thomas, and was all at once old enough to be his mother. There was no escape from the course she must take; no dodging was possible. But she was and would be gentle with poor Thomas.

"You do not love me, Lucy," he cried.

"My poor Thomas, I do love you, so dearly that I trust and pray you may be worthy of my love. Go and do as you ought, and come back to me—like one of the old knights," she added, with the glimmer of a hopeful smile, "bringing victory to his lady."

"I will, I will," said Thomas, overcome by her solemn beauty and dignified words. It was as if she had cast off the husk of the girl and come out a saving angel. But the perception of this was little more to him yet than a poetic sense of painful pleasure. "But I cannot tonight, for my father and mother are at Folkestone. But I will write to them, that will be best."

"Any way you like, Thomas. I don't care how you do it, so it is done."

All this time the old lady had discreetly kept out of the way, for she knew that the quarrels of lovers are most easily settled between themselves. Thomas now considered it all over and done with, and Lucy, overjoyed at her victory, leaned into his arms, and let him kiss her ten times. She ought not to have allowed him to touch her till he had done what he had promised. To some people the promise is the difficult part, to others the performance. To Thomas, unhappily, the promising was easy.

They did not hear the door open, and the two were full in the light of the window, visible enough to the person who entered. He stood still for one moment, during which the lovers unwound their arms. Only when parting did they become aware that a man was in the room. Richard Boxall came forward with hasty step. Thomas looked about for his hat while Lucy stood firm and quiet, waiting.

"Lucy, where is your grandmother?" asked Richard.

"Upstairs, Uncle, I believe," answered Lucy.

"Is she aware of this fellow's presence?"

"You are not very polite, Uncle," said Lucy, with dignity. "This is my friend, Mr. Worboise, whom I believe you know. Of course, I do not receive visitors without my grandmother's knowledge."

Mr. Boxall choked an oath in his throat, or rather the oath nearly choked him. He turned and went down the stair again, but neither of them heard the outer door close. Thomas and Lucy stared at each other in dismay.

The *Ningpo* had dropped down to Gravesend, and the Boxalls had joined her there. But a day's delay had arisen, and Mr. Boxall had made use of the time to come up to town. And perhaps it was by the contrivance of Mr. Stopper, who had watched Tom and seen him go up the court, that he went through the door from his private room instead of going round, which would have given warning to the lovers. He had returned to see his mother; but after the discovery he made, avoided her partly because he was angry and would not quarrel with her the last thing before his voyage. And so he left for Gravesend again.

"Well, Thomas," said Lucy at last, with a sweet watery smile. She had her lover, but she had lost her idol. She had got behind the scenes, and could worship no more; but Thomas as her own was a fine idea, notwithstanding his fall, and if she could not set him up on his pedestal again, she would at least try to give him an armchair.

"Now he'll go and tell my father," said Tom, "and I wish you knew what a row he and my mother will make between them."

"But why, Tom? Have they any prejudice against me? Do they know there *is* such a person?"

"I don't know. They may have heard of you at your uncle's."

"Then why should they be so very angry?"

"My father because you have no money, and my mother because you have no grace."

"No grace, Tom! Am I so very clumsy?"

"I forgot," said Tom, bursting into a laugh. "You were not brought up to my mother's slang. She and her set use Bible words till they make you hate them."

"But you shouldn't hate them. They are good in themselves, though they be wrongly used."

"That's all very well. Only if you had been pestered with them as I have been, I am afraid you would hate them too, Lucy. I never did like that kind of slang. But what am I to do? Your Uncle Richard will be sure to write to my father before he sails."

"Well, but you will reach him first, and then it won't matter. You were going to do it at any rate, and the thing now is to have the start of him," said Lucy, perhaps not sorry to have the occurrence as an additional spur to prick the sides of Thomas' intent.

"Yes, yes, that's all very well," returned Thomas, dubiously.

"Now, dear Tom, do go home at once and write. You will make the last post if you do," said Lucy decidedly. She saw more and more the necessity of urging him to action.

"So, instead of giving me a happy evening, you are going to send me home to an empty house!"

"You see the thing must be done, or my uncle will be before you," said Lucy, beginning to be vexed with him for his utter want of decision, and with herself for pushing him toward such an act. Indeed, she felt all at once that perhaps she had been unmaidenly. But there was no choice except to do it, or break off their understanding.

Now whether it was that her irritation influenced her tone and infected Tom with like irritation, or that he could not bare being thus driven to do what he so much disliked, while on the whole he would have preferred that Mr. Boxall should tell his father and so save him from the immediate difficulty, the evil in him arose once more in rebellion.

"Lucy, I will not be badgered this way. If you can't trust me, you won't get anything out of me."

Lucy drew back a step and looked at him for one moment. Then she turned and left the room. Thomas, choosing to arouse a great sense of injury in his bosom, took his hat, and went out.

Just as he banged Lucy's door behind him, out came Mr. Molken from his. It was as if the devil had told a hawk to wait, and he would fetch him a pigeon.

"Coming to haff your lesson after all?" he asked.

"No, I don't feel inclined for a lesson tonight."

"Vere are you going, den?"

"Oh, I don't know," answered Tom, trying to look uninterested.

"Come along vit me, den. I'll show you someting of life after dark."

"But where are you going?"

"You'll see dat ven ve get dere. You're not afraid, are you?"

"Not I," answered Tom, "only a fellow likes to know he's going."

"Vell, vere vould you like to go? A young fellow like you really ought to know someting of de vorld."

"I don't care. It's nothing to me where I go. Only," Tom added, "I have no money in my pocket. I spent my last shilling on this copy of Goethe's poems."

"Ah! You never spent your money better! Dere's a man, now, dat never contented himself vit hearsay. He vould know all de vays of life for himself - else how vas he to judge of dem all? He vould taste of everyting, dat he might know de taste of it. Vy should a man be ignorant of anyting dat can be known? Come along. I vill take care of you."

"But you can't be going to London for nothing. And I tell you I haven't got a farthing in my purse."

"Never mind dat. It shan't cost you anyting. I vant to make an experiment vit you. I told you about it de odder day. You are von of dose fortunate mortals doomed to be lucky. Vy, I knew von man whose friends at last vould haff noting to do vit him vhere any chance vas concerned. If it vas only for a sixpenny, he von everyting."

"Then what do you want with me? Out with it."

"I only vant to back you. I haff plenty to spend." Here Molken pulled a few sovereigns from his pocket as he went on, and it never occurred to Tom to ask how he had gotten them since dinner.

All this time they had been walking along, and they entered a region of London entirely unknown to Tom. "But you haven't told me where you are going," he said.

"Here," answered Molken, pushing open the door of a public house.

The next morning Thomas made his appearance in the office at the usual hour, but his face was pale and his eyes were red. His shirt front was tumbled and dirty, and he had nearly forty shillings in his pocket. He never looked up from his work, and now and then he pressed his hand to his head.

All this Mr. Stopper saw and enjoyed.

19. Lucy's Evening

When Lucy left Tom alone in the room, her throat felt as if it would burst with the swelling of something like bodily grief. She did not know what it was, for she had never felt anything like it before. She thought she was going to die.

She went to her own room and threw herself on her bed, but started up again when she heard the door bang, flew to the window, and saw all that passed between Molken and Thomas till they left the court together. She had never seen Molken so full in the face before; she felt a dreadful repugnance to him from that moment, and became certain that he was trying in some way or other to make his own out of Thomas. With this new distress was mingled a self-reproach that she had driven him to it. Why should she not have borne with the poor boy who was worried to death by his father and mother and Mr. Stopper and that demon down there? He would be all right if they would only leave him alone. He was but a poor boy and, alas, she had driven him away from his only friend! She threw herself on her bed, but she could not rest. All the things in the room seemed pressing upon her as if they had staring eyes in their heads, and there was no heart anywhere.

"What's the matter, my pet?" asked her grandmother as she entered the room and found her lying on her bed. "You've quarrelled with that shilly-shally beau of yours, I suppose. Well, let him go. *He's* not much."

Lucy made no reply, but turned her face toward the wall. Grannie had learned a little wisdom in her long life, and left her. She would get a cup of tea ready, for she had great faith in bodily cures for mental aches.

Lucy could not rest. She tossed and turned. What could Thomas be about with that man? What mischief might he not take him into? Good women, in their supposed ignorance of men's wickedness, are not unfrequently like the angels, in that they understand it perfectly, without the knowledge soiling one feather of their wings. They see it clearly, even from afar.

She understood something of the kind of gulf into which a man like Molken might lead Thomas, and she could not bear the thoughts that sprang out of this understanding. She got up and put on her bonnet and shawl, and went downstairs, arriving before the tea was even in the teapot.

"Where on earth are you going, Lucy?" asked her grandmother.

Lucy did not know in the least what she meant to do. She had a vague notion of setting out to find and rescue Thomas from the grasp of Molken, but the moment her grandmother asked her the question, she saw how absurd it would be. Still she could not rest. So she invented an answer, and ordered her way according to her word.

"I'm going to see little Mattie," she said. "The child is lonely, and so am I. I will take her out for a walk."

"Do then, my dear. It will do you both good," said the grandmother. "Only you must have a cup of tea first."

Lucy drank her tea, and then went to the bookshop. Mr. Kitely was there alone.

"How's little Mattie tonight, Mr. Kitely? You wouldn't mind me taking her out for a little walk, would you?"

"Much obliged to you, Miss," returned the bookseller, heartily. "It's not much amusement the poor child has. I'm always meaning to do better for her, but I'm so tied with the shop that somehow we go on the old way. She'll be delighted."

Lucy went into the back parlor, and there Mattie sat, with her legs curled up beneath her on the windowsill.

"I want you to come out for a walk with me, Mattie," said Lucy. "You must put on your hat, and come out with me."

Wise Mattie glanced up in her face. She had recognized the sadness in her tone. "My bonnet, Miss. Hats are only fit for very little girls."

Lucy got Mattie's bonnet, and heedless of the remarks of the child, put it on her, and led her out. They had left Bagot Street, and were in one of the principal thoroughfares, before Lucy began to consider where they should go. When they came out into the wider street, the sun, now going down, was shining golden through a rosy fog. Long shadows lay or flitted about over the level street. Lucy had never before taken any notice of the long shadows of the evening, but now her sorrowful heart saw the sorrowfulness of the long shadows. The sight brought the tears again into her eyes, and yet soothed her.

From this moment Lucy began to see and feel things as she had never seen or felt them before. Her weeping had made a way for a deeper spring in her nature to flow—a gain far more than sufficient to repay the loss of such a lover as Thomas, if indeed she must lose him.

But Mattie saw the shadows too. "Well, Miss, who'd ha' thought of such a place!" she said. "I declare it bewilders my poor brain. I feel every time a horse puts his foot on my shadow as if I must cry out. Isn't it silly? It's all my big head—it's not me, you know, Miss."

To get out of the crowd on the pavement Lucy turned aside into a lane and was halfway down it before she discovered that it was one of those through which she had passed the night before with Thomas. She turned at once to leave it. As she turned, right before her stood an open church door. It was one of those sepulchral city churches where the voice of the clergyman sounds ghostly, and it seems as if the dead below are more real in their presence than the half-dozen worshippers scattered among the pews.

On this occasion, however, there were seven present when Lucy and Mattie entered. There was the housekeeper in a neighboring warehouse, who had been in a tumult all day, and at nightfall thought of the kine-browsed fields of her childhood, and went to church. There was an old man who had once been manager of a bank, and had managed it ill both for himself and his company. Having been dismissed in consequence, he had begun to lay up treasure in heaven. Then came a brother and two sisters, none of them under seventy. The former kept shifting his brown wig and taking snuff the whole of the service, and the latter two wiping with yellow silk handkerchiefs their brown faces inlaid with coal dust. These, with the beadle and his wife, and Lucy and Mattie, made up the congregation.

When they left the lane there was no sun to be seen, but when they entered the church, there he was—his last rays pouring in through a richly stained window, the only beauty of the building.

This change from the dark lane to the sunlit church laid hold of Lucy's feelings. It aroused her with some vague sense of that sphere of glory which enwraps all our lower spheres, and she bowed her knees and her head, and her being worshiped. The prayers had commenced, and as she kneeled, the words, "He pardoneth and absolveth," were the first that found luminous entrance into her soul. And with them came the picture of Thomas, as he left the court with the man of bad countenance. Of him, and what he might be about, her mind was full; but every now and then a flash of light, in the shape of words, broke through the mist of her troubled thoughts, till at length her mind was so far calmed that she became capable of listening a little to the discourse of the preacher, Mr. Fuller.

He was not like Mr. Potter of St. Jacob's, who considered himself possessed of worldly privileges in virtue of a heavenly office. Some people considered Mr. Fuller very silly for believing that he might do good in a church like this, and with a congregation like this, by speaking that which he knew, and testifying to that which he had seen. But he did actually believe it. Because he was so much in the habit of looking up to the Father, the prayers took hold of him every time he read them, and he so delighted in the truths he saw that he rejoiced to set them forth—was actually glad to *talk* about them to anyone who would listen.

He took for his text the words of our Lord; "Come unto Me, all ye that labor and are heavy-laden." He could not see the faces of the strangers, for they sat behind a pillar, and therefore he had no means of discovering that each of them had a heavy-laden heart; Lucy was not alone in trouble, for Syne had been hard on Mattie that day. Mr. Fuller addressed himself especially to the two old women before him, but the basin into which the fountain of his speech flowed was the heart of those girls.

No doubt presented itself as to the truth of what the preacher was saying, nor could either of them have given a single argument from history or criticism for the reality of the message upon which the preacher founded his exhortation. But the truth is not dependent upon proof for its working. Doubt must not be considered an unholy thing; on the contrary, a spiritual doubt is far more precious than intellectual conviction, for it springs from the awakening of a deeper necessity than any that can be satisfied from the region of logic. But when the truth has begun to work its own influence in any heart, that heart has begun to rise out of the region of doubt.

When they came from the church, Lucy hastened home with Mattie, anxious to be alone. She did not leave the child, however, before she had put her to bed. Once at home, she sat a few minutes with her grandmother, and then went to bed. As soon as she had closed her door, she knelt down by her bedside and prayed.

"O Jesus Christ, I come. Hear me now, for I am weary and heavy- laden. Give me rest. Help me to put on the yoke of Thy meekness and Thy lowliness of heart, which Thou sayest will give rest to our souls. I cannot do it without Thy help. Teach me. Give me Thy rest. How am I to begin? I am very troubled and vexed. Am I angry? Am I unforgiving? Poor Thomas! Lord Jesus, have mercy upon Thomas. He does not know what he is doing. I will be very patient. I will sit with my hands folded, and bear all my sorrow, and not vex Grannie with it; and I won't say an angry word to Thomas. But, O Lord, have mercy upon him, and make him meek and lowly of heart. I have not been sitting at Thy feet and learning of Thee. Thou canst take all my trouble away by making Thomas good. I ought to have tried hard to keep him in the way his mother taught him, and I have been idle and self-indulgent, and taken up with my music and dresses. I have not looked to my heart to see whether it was meek and lowly like Thine. O Lord, Thou hast given me everything, and I have not thought about Thee. I thank Thee that Thou hast made me miserable, for now I shall be Thy child. Thou canst bring Thomas home again to Thee. Thou canst make him meek and lowly of heart, and give rest to his soul. Amen."

Is it any wonder that she should rise from her knees comforted? She was already more meek and lowly; gentle and good she had always been. She had begun to regard this meekness as the yoke of Jesus and, therefore, to will it. Already, in a measure, she was a partaker of His peace.

Worn out by her suffering, and soothed by her prayer, she fell asleep the moment she laid her heau upon the pillow.

20. The Storm

Tom went home that night with a raging headache. Gladly would he have gone to Lucy for comfort, but he was too ashamed of his behavior to her, and too uneasy in his conscience. He was, indeed, in an abject condition of body, intellect, and morals. He went at once to his own room and fell asleep only to wake in the middle of the night miserably gnawed by the worm of conscience. He tried to pray, and found it did him no good; he turned his thoughts to Lucy, and burst into tears at the recollection of how he had treated her, imagining over and over twenty scenes in which he begged her forgiveness. He fell asleep at last, dreamed that she turned her back upon him, and refused to hear him, and woke in the morning with the resolution of going to see her that night, and confessing everything.

His father had come home after he went to bed, and it was with great trepidation that he went down to breakfast, expecting to find that he knew already of his relation to Lucy. But Richard Boxall was above that kind of thing, and Mr. Worboise was evidently free from any suspicion. He greeted his son frankly, and seemed in good spirits.

"Our friends are well down the channel by this time, with such a fair wind," he said. "Boxall's a lucky man to be able to get away from business like that. I wish you had taken a fancy to Mary, Tom. She's sure to get engaged before she comes back. Some hungry fellow on board, with a red coat and an empty breeches pocket, is sure to pick her up. You might have had her if you had liked. However, you may do as well yet, and you needn't be in a hurry now."

Tom laughed it off, went to his office, worked the weary day through, and ran down to Guild Court the moment he left business.

Lucy had waked in the night as well, but to the hope that there was a power working good, and upholding them that love it; to the hope that a heart of love and help was at the heart of things, and would show itself for her need. When, therefore, Tom knocked at the door, she met him with a strange light in her pale face, and a smile flickering about her trembling lips, in sympathy with her rain-clouded eyes. She held out her hand to him cordially, but neither one offered to embrace—Thomas from shame, and Lucy from a feeling that something between them that had to be removed before things could be as they were.

Thomas gazed for a moment full into Lucy's eyes, and then dropped his own, holding her still by the consenting hand.

"Will you forgive me, Lucy?" he said, in a voice partly choked by feeling.

"O Tom!" answered Lucy, with a gentle pressure on his hand.

Now, as all that Tom wanted was to be reinstated in her favor, he took the words as the seal of the desired reconciliation, and went no further with any confession. The cloud cleared from his brow, and, with a sudden reaction of spirits, he began to be merry. To this change, however, Lucy did not respond. The cloud seemed rather to fall more heavily over her countenance. She turned from him, and went to a chair. Tom followed, and sat down beside her. He was sympathetic enough to see that things were not right between them after all, but he referred it largely to her uneasiness at his parents' ignorance of their engagement.

Perhaps Lucy ought to have refused to see Thomas even once again till he made his parents aware of their relation to each other. But knowing how little sympathy and help he had from those parents, she felt that would be turning him out into a snowstorm to find his way home across a desolate moor, and that her success by persuasion would be a better thing for

Thomas than her success by compulsion. Yet, for the sake of both, she remained perfectly firm in her purpose that Thomas should do something.

"Your uncle has said nothing about that unfortunate encounter, Lucy," said Tom, hoping that what had relieved him would relieve her. "My father came home last night, and the paternal brow is all serene."

"Then I suppose you said something about it, Tom?" said Lucy, with a faint hope dawning in her heart.

"Oh! There's time enough for that. I've been thinking about it, you see, and I'll soon convince you," he added hurriedly, seeing the cloud grow deeper on Lucy's face. "I must tell you something which I would rather not have mentioned."

"Don't tell me, if you ought not to, Tom," said Lucy, whose conscience had grown more delicate than ever, both from the turning of her own face towards the light, and from the growing feeling that Tom was not to be trusted as a guide.

"There's no reason why I shouldn't," returned Tom. "It's only that my father is vexed with me because I wouldn't set my cap for your cousin Mary. So it's just the worst possible time to tell him anything unpleasant, for he's not in any mood for the news just now."

Lucy made no reply to this speech, uttered in the eagerness with which a man, seeking to defend a bad position, sends one weak word after another, as if the accumulation of poor arguments will make up for his lack of a good one.

"I tell you what, Lucy," he continued. "I give you my promise, that before another month is over—so to give my father time to get over his vexation—I will tell him all about it, and take the consequences."

Lucy sighed, and looked dissatisfied. But again it passed through her mind that if she were to insist further and refuse to see Thomas until he had complied with her just desire, she would take from him the only influence that might yet work on him for good, and expose him entirely to such influences as she most feared. Therefore she said no more, but she could not throw the weight off her, or behave to Thomas as in old times. They sat silent for some time, Thomas troubled before Lucy, and Lucy troubled about Thomas. Then with a sigh, Lucy rose and went to the piano. She had never done so before when

Thomas was with her, for he did not care much about her music. Now she thought of it as the only way of breaking the silence. Strange it is how often silence is a thing that must be broken.

As she sang and played an old hymn, her sweet tones and the earnest music all had their influence upon Tom. They made him feel—and with that, as usual, he was content. And Tom was astonished to find that her voice had such power over him, and began to wonder how it was that he had not experienced this before. He went home more solemn and thoughtful than he had ever been.

But still he did nothing, and things went on unchanged for the space of about three weeks. Tom went to see Lucy almost every night, and sometimes stayed late; for his mother was still away from home, and his father was careless about his hours so long as they were decent. Lucy's face continued grave but lost a little of its trouble, for Tom often asked her to sing to him now, and she thought she was gaining more of the influence which she so honestly wished to possess. As the month drew toward a close, however, the look of anxiety began to deepen upon her countenance.

On a still and sultry evening, they were together as usual. Lucy was sitting at the piano where she had just been singing, and Tom stood beside her. The evening had grown brown, and Mrs. Boxall was just going to light the candles when Tom interposed a request for continued twilight.

"Please, Grannie," he said, "do not light the candles yet. It is so sweet and dusky! Just like Lucy here."

"All very well for you," said Mrs. Boxall, "but what is to become of me? My wooing was over long ago, and I want to see what I'm about now. Ah! Young people, your time will come next. Make hay while the sun shines!"

"While the candle's out, you mean, Grannie," said Tom, stealing a kiss from Lucy.

"I hear more than you think," said the cheery old woman. "I'll give you just five minutes grace, and then I mean to have my own way. I am not so fond of darkness, I can tell you."

"How close it is!" said Lucy. "Will you open the window a little wider, Tom? Mind the flowers."

She came near the window, which looked down on the little

stony desert of Guild Court, and sank into a high-backed chair that stood beside it.

"I can hardly drag one foot after another," she said, "I feel so oppressed and weary."

"And I," said Tom, who had taken his place behind her, leaning on the back of her chair, "am as happy as if I were in Paradise."

"There must be thunder in the air," said Lucy. "I fancy I smell the lightning already."

"Are you afraid of lightning, then?" asked Thomas.

"I do not think I am exactly, but it shakes me so! It affects me like a false tone on the violin."

A fierce flash broke upon her words. Mrs. Boxall gave a scream, and Lucy sat trembling. In that one flash Lucy had seen through Mr. Molken's window where he and another man were seated at a table casting dice, with the eagerness of hungry fiends upon both their faces. When the second flash came, Lucy saw that the blind of Mr. Molken's window was drawn down.

Then the wind began to rise, and a flash followed flash, with less and less of an interval. The wind blew a hurricane, roaring in the chimney and through the archway as if it were a wild beast caged in Guild Court and wanting to get out. All night long the storm raved about London. Chimney pots clashed on the opposite pavements, and even the thieves and burglars retreated to their dens. But before it had reached its worst, Tom had gone home. He lay awake for some time listening to the tumult and rejoicing in it, for it roused his imagination and the delight that comes of beholding danger from a far-removed safety.

Lucy lay awake for hours. There was no more lightning, but the howling of the wind tortured her nerves. She reaped this benefit, however, that such winds always drove her to her prayers.

When at last she fell asleep, it was to dream that another flash of lightning revealed Thomas casting dice with Molken, and then left them lapt in the darkness of a godless world. She woke weeping, fell asleep again, and dreamed that she stood in the darkness once more, and that somewhere near Thomas was casting dice with the devil for his soul, but she could neither see him nor cry to him, for the darkness choked both voice and eyes. Then a hand was laid upon her head, and she heard the words in her heart, "Be of good cheer, my daughter."

It was not in London or the Empire only that the storm raged that night. From all points of the compass came reports of its havoc. On the next morning save one, a vessel passing one of the rocky islets near Cape Verde found the fragments of a wreck floating on the water. On sending a boat to the island, they found her stern lying on a reef, round which little innocent waves were talking to each other. On her stern they read her name, *Ningpo,* and on the narrow strand they found three bodies. There were no survivors to be found.

21. Mattie's Fight

That storm beat furiously against Mattie's window and made a dreadful tumult in her head. When her father went into her little room in the morning he found her lying awake but unaware with wide eyes. Her head and her hands were both hot, and her words spoke plainly that she was wandering. In great alarm, he sent for the doctor, and he went up the court to ask Lucy to come to see her.

Lucy was tossing in a troubled dream; she thought she was one of the ten virgins, but whether one of the wise or foolish she did not know. She had knocked at a door, and as it opened, her lamp went out. But Thomas' hand laid hold of hers in the dark, and would have drawn her to him. She clung to it, and would have drawn him to her, but she could not move him. She woke in an agony just as she was losing her hold of Thomas, and heard Mr. Kitely's knock. She was out of bed in a moment, put on her dressing gown and shoes, and ran downstairs.

On learning what was the matter, she made haste to dress, and in a few moments stood by Mattie's bedside. The child did not know her. When the doctor came, he shook his head, and after prescribing for her, said she must be watched with the greatest care, and gave Lucy urgent directions about her treatment. Lucy resolved that she would not leave her, and began at once to make preparations. Mattie took the medicine he sent. In a little while the big eyes began to close, sink and open again, to settle their long lashes at last on the pale cheek below them. Then Lucy wrote a note to Mrs. Morgenstern, and left her patient to run across to her grandmother to consult with her how she should send it. But when she opened the door into the court, there was Poppie, who flitted the moment she saw her—but only a little way off, like a bold bird.

"Poppie, dear Poppie!" cried Lucy, earnestly. "Do come here, I want you."

"Blowed if I go there again, Lady!" said Poppie, without moving.

"Come here, Poppie. I won't touch you—I promise you. I wouldn't tell you a lie, Poppie."

To judge by the way Poppie came a yard nearer, she did not seem at all satisfied by the assurance.

"Look here, Poppie. Mattie is lying very ill here, and I can't leave her. Will you take this letter for me to that big house in Wyvil Place to tell them I can't come today?"

"They'll wash me," said Poppie, decisively.

"Not again, Poppie. They know now that you don't like it. And you needn't go into the house at all. Just ring the bell, and give the letter to the servant."

Poppie came closer to Lucy. "I'm not afraid of *him,* Lady. *He* won't touch me again. If he do, I'll bite worser next time. But I won't run errands for nothink. You ain't forgotten what you guv me last time? Do it again, and I'm off."

"A good wash, Poppie—that's what I gave you last time."

"No, Miss," returned the child, looking up in her face beseechingly. "You knows as well as me." And she held up her pretty grimy mouth so that her meaning could not be mistaken.

For a moment Lucy hesitated. "I tell you what, Poppie, I will kiss you every time you come to me with a clean face, as often as you like."

Poppie's dirty face fell. She put out her hand, took the letter, turned, and went away slowly. Lucy could not bear it. She darted after her, caught her, and kissed her; the child, without looking round, instantly scudded.

Lucy could hardly believe her eyes when, going down at Mr. Kitely's call, some time after, she found Poppie in the shop.

"She say she wants to see you, Miss," said Kitely. "I don't

know what she wants. Begging, I suppose."

And so she was, but all her begging lay in the cleanness and brightness of her countenance. She might have been a little saint but for the fact that her halo was all in her face, and around it lay a border of darkness.

"Back already!" said Lucy, in astonishment.

"Yes, Lady. I didn't bite him. I throwed the letter at him, and he throwed it out again, and says I, pickin' of it up, 'You'll hear o' this tomorrow, Plush.' And says he, 'Give me that letter, you wagabones.' And I throwed it at him again, and he took it up and looked at it, and took it in. And here I am, Lady," added Poppie, making a display of her clean face.

Lucy kissed her once more and she was gone in a moment.

While Mattie was asleep Lucy did all she could to change the aspect of the place.

"She shan't think of Syne the first thing when she comes to herself," she said.

With the bookseller's concurrence, she removed all the old black volumes within sight of her bed, replaced them with the brightest bindings to be found in the shop, took down the dingy old chintz curtains from her tent bed, and replaced them with her own white dimity. These she drew close round the bed, and then set about cleaning the windows, inside and out. But she soon perceived that the light would be far too much for her little patient, especially as she had now only white curtains to screen her. So the next thing was to get a green blind for the window. Not before that was up did Mattie awake, and only then to stare about her, take her medicine, and fall again into some state resembling sleep.

Lucy scarcely left her side for a week. And it was a great help to her in her own trouble to have such a charge to fulfill. At length one morning, when the sun was shining clear and dewy through a gap between the houses of the court, the child opened her eyes and saw. Then she closed them again and Lucy heard her murmuring to herself.

"Yes, I thought so. I'm dead. And it is *so* nice! I've got white clouds to my bed. And there's Syne cutting away with all his men—just like a black cloud, away out of the world. Ah! I see you, Syne! You ought to be ashamed of yourself for worrying of me as you've been doing all this time. You see it's no use.

You ought really to give it up. *He's* too much for you, anyhow."

The whole week had been filled with visions of conflict with the enemy, and the Son of man was with her in those visions. The spiritual struggles of them that are whole are the same in kind as those of this brain-sick child. They are tempted and driven to faithlessness, to self-indulgence, to denial of God and of His Christ, to giving in—for the sake of peace. It was such a fight, perhaps, that brought the maniacs of old time to the feet of the Saviour who gave them back their right mind.

Lucy did not show herself for a little while, but at length she peeped within the curtain, and saw the child praying with folded hands. Ere she could withdraw, Mattie opened her eyes and saw her.

"I thought I was in heaven!" she said, "but I don't mind, if you're there, Miss. I've been seeing you all through it. But it's over now," she added, with a sigh of relief. And then she was asleep once more.

It was quite another fortnight before Lucy ventured to give up her place to her grandmother. During this time, she saw very little of Thomas—only for a few minutes every evening as he left his place—and somehow she found it a relief not to see more of him.

All the time of Mattie's illness, Mr. Spelt kept coming to inquire after her. He was in great concern about her, but he never asked to see her. He had a great gift in waiting, the little man. But perhaps his quietness might be partly attributed to another cause—namely, that since Mattie's illness he had brooded more upon his suspicions that his wife had once had a child.

Every day of those three weeks, Poppie was to be seen at one hour or other in Guild Court, prowling about with a clean face—the only part of her that was clean—for the chance of seeing Lucy. And as often as Lucy saw her, she gave her what she wanted.

But if Lucy did not see her sometimes, at least there was one who did see her from his nest in the rock: Mr. Spelt. He saw her and watched her, until at last, as he plied his needle, he began to wonder whether Poppie might not be his own lost child. The supposition had not lasted more than five minutes before he passionately believed it, or at least passionately desired to believe it, and began to devise how to prove it, or at least to act on it.

22. Fishing for a Daughter

Mr. Spelt sat in his watchtower wondering how to prove that Poppie was indeed his own child. He had missed his little Mattie much, and his childlike spirit was longing greatly for some childlike companionship. And the thought had come to him that perhaps Mattie was taken away from him to teach him that he ought not (as Mattie had said with regard to Mrs. Morgenstern) to cultivate friendship only where he got good from. The very possibility that he had a child somewhere in London seemed to make it his first duty to rescue some child or other from the abyss around him.

It was far better to think that Poppie was or might be his child, than to know that she was not. And, after all, what did it matter whether she was or was not? Was she not a child? What matter whether his own or someone else's? God must have made her all the same. And if he were to find his own child at last, neglected and ignorant and vicious, could he not pray better for her if he had helped the one he could help? Might he not then say, "O Lord, they took her from me, and I had no chance with *her*, but I did what I could—I caught a wild thing, and I tried to make something of her, and she's none the worse for it; do Thou help my poor child, for I could not, and Thou canst. I give Thee back Thine; help mine." He had resolved that he would try to get hold of Poppie, and do for her what he could. For whether or not he was her father, she was worth helping.

Tailors have time to think about things, and no circumstance is more favorable to true thought than work which employs the hands and leaves the head free. Before another day had passed, Mr. Spelt had devised his bait.

The next morning came, a lovely morning for such fishing as he contemplated. Poppie appeared in the court, prowling as usual in hope of seeing Lucy. But the tailor appeared to take no notice of her. Poppie's keen eyes went roving about as usual, wide awake to the chance of finding something. Suddenly she darted to a small object—a bull's-eye candy—lying near the gutter, picked it up, put it in her mouth, and sucked it with evident pleasure. The tailor only plied his needle and thread more busily, casting down sidelong glances in the drawing of the same. And there was no little triumph, for it was the triumph of confidence for the future, as well as of success for the present. Suddenly Poppie ran away.

The next morning she was there again, and returned to the spot where she had found the bull's-eye. There, to the astonishment even of Poppie, who was very seldom astonished at anything, lay another—a larger one than the one she had found yesterday. It was in her mouth in a moment, but she gave a hurried glance round the court, and scudded at once. Like the cherub that sat aloft and saw what was going to come of it all, the little tailor drew his shortening thread and smiled.

The next morning there again sat Mr. Spelt watching at his work. With the queerest look of inquiry and doubtful expectation, Poppie appeared from under the archway, with her head already turned toward El Dorado—namely, the flagstone on which the gifts of Providence had been set forth on other mornings. There—if she could believe her eyes—lay a splendid sweetmeat, the most melting compound of sugar and lemon juice ever devised. This time Poppie hesitated a little and glanced up and around. She saw nobody but the tailor, and he was too cunning even for her. Busy as a bee, he was earnestly toiling away. Then, as if the sweetmeat had been a bird for which she was laying snares, as her would-be father was laying them for her, she took two steps nearer on tiptoe, then stopped and gazed again. It was not that she thought of stealing, any more than do the birds who take what they find in the fields and on the hedges; it was only from a sort of fear that it was too good fortune for her, and that there must be something evanescent about it.

But the temptation soon overcame any suspicion she might have. She made one bound upon the prize and scudded as she never had before. Mr. Spelt ran his needle under the nail of his left thumb, and so overcame his delight in time to save his senses.

That evening Mr. Spelt drove two tiny staples of wire—one into the doorpost close to the ground, and the other into his own. The next morning, as soon as he arrived, he chose a thread the color of the flagstones, fastened one end with a plug of toffee into a hole he bored with his scissors in another splendor of rock, laid the bait in the usual place, drew the long thread through staples, and sat down in his lair with the end attached to the little finger of his left hand.

At length Poppie appeared peeping cautiously round the corner toward the trap. She saw the bait and was now so accustomed to it, that she saw it almost without surprise. She had begun to regard it as an operation of nature—namely, as that which always was so and always will be so. But this time, just as she stooped to snatch it to herself and make it her own, away it went as if in terror of her approaching fingers—but only to the distance of half a yard or so. Eager as the tailor was—far more eager to catch Poppie than Poppie was to catch the lollipop—he could scarcely keep his countenance when he saw the blank astonishment that came over Poppie's pretty brown face. Certainly she had never seen a living lollipop, yet motion is a chief sign of life, and the lollipop certainly moved. Perhaps it would have been wiser to doubt her senses first, but Poppie had never yet found her senses in the wrong, and therefore had not learned to doubt them. She pounced upon it again so suddenly that Mr. Spelt was unprepared. He gave his string a tug just as she seized it, and fortunately, the string came out of the plugged hole. Poppie held the bait, and the fisherman drew in his line before his fish saw it.

The motions of Poppie's mind were as impossible to analyze as those of a fieldmouse or hedgesparrow. This time she began at once to gnaw the sugar, staring about her as she did so, and apparently now in no hurry to go. Poppie never could be much surprised at anything. Why should anything be surprising? To such a child everything was interesting—nothing overwhelming. She seemed constantly shielded by the divine buckler of her own exposure and helplessness. Perhaps God had said to her as to His people of old, "Fear thou not, O Poppie," and she did not fear. It is a terrible doctrine that would confine the tender care of the Father to those who know and acknowledge it. He carries the lambs in His bosom, and who shall say when they cease to be innocent lambs and become naughty sheep? Even then He goes into the mountains, and searches till He finds.

Not yet would the father aspirant show his craft. When he saw her stand there gnawing his innocent bait, he was sorely tempted to call, in the gentlest voice, "Poppie, dear." But like a fearful and wise lover, who dreads startling the maiden he loves, he must yet approach with guile.

He tried the bait once more without the line. Poppie came the next morning, found the bull's-eye, took it, and sucked it leisurely to nothing upon the spot.

The next morning Mr. Spelt tried the string again, watched it better, and by a succession of jerks drew her step by step in the eagerness of wonder, as well as the love of sweets, to the very foot of his aerie. When she laid hold of the object desired at the doorpost, he released it by a final tug against the staple. Before she could look up from securing it, another lump of rock fell at her feet. Then she did look up, and saw the smiling face of the tailor looking out over the threshold of his elevated and stairless door. She gave back a genuine whole-faced smile, then turned and scudded. The tailor's right hand shuttled with increased vigor all the rest of the day.

23. Mr. Fuller

One evening Lucy was sitting with Mattie, who had gone to bed early. By this time Lucy had quite transformed the room—all the books out of it, a nice clean paper upon the walls, and a few colored prints from the *Illustrated London News* here and there.

"What shall I read tonight, Mattie?" she asked.

"Oh, read about the man that sat in his Sunday clothes," said Mattie.

"I don't know that story," returned Lucy.

"I wish dear Mother were here," said Mattie, with the pettishness of an invalid. "He would know what story I mean."

"Would you like to see Mr. Spelt?" suggested Lucy. "He was asking about you not an hour ago."

"Why didn't he come up, then? He never comes to see me."

"I was afraid you weren't strong enough for it, Mattie. But I will run and fetch him now, if he's not gone."

"Oh, yes—do, please."

Lucy went, and Mr. Spelt came gladly.

"Well, Mother," said Mattie, holding out a worn little cloud of a hand, "how do you do?"

Mr. Spelt could hardly answer for emotion. He took the little hand in his, and it seemed to melt away in his grasp.

"Don't cry, Mother. I am very happy. I do believe I've seen the last of old Syne. I feel just like the man that had got his Sunday clothes on, you know. You see what a pretty room Miss

Burton has made, instead of all those ugly books that Syne was so fond of; well, my poor head feels just like this room, and I'm ready to listen to anything about Somebody. Read about the man in his Sunday clothes."

But Mr. Spelt, no less than Lucy, was puzzled as to what the child meant.

"I wish that good clergyman that talked about Somebody's burden being easy to carry, would come to see me," she said. "I know he would tell me the story. He knows all about Somebody."

"Shall I ask Mr. Potter to come and see you?" said Spelt, who had never heard of Mr. Fuller by name.

"I don't mean Mr. Potter—you know well enough. He's always pottering," said the child, with a laugh. "I want to see the gentleman that really thinks it's all about something. Do you know where he lives, Miss Burton?"

"No," answered Lucy, "but I will find out tomorrow, and ask him to come and see you."

"Well, that will be nice," returned Mattie. "Read to me, Mr. Spelt, anything you like."

The little tailor was very shy of reading before Lucy, but Mattie would hear of nothing else, for she would neither allow Lucy to read nor yet to go away.

"Don't mind me, Mr. Spelt," said Lucy, beseechingly. "We are all friends, you know. If we all belong to the Somebody Mattie speaks about, we needn't be shy of each other."

Thus encouraged, Mr. Spelt could refuse no longer. He read about the daughter of Jairus being made alive again.

"Oh, dear me!" said Mattie. "And if I had gone dead when Syne was tormenting me, He could have come into the room and taken me by the hand and said, 'Daughter, get up.' How strange it would be if He said, 'Daughter' to me, for then He would be my Father, you know. And they say He's a King. I wonder if that's why Mr. Kitely calls me *princess*. To have Mr. Kitely and Somebody," she went on, musingly, "both for fathers is more than I can understand. I wish my father would go and hear what Mr. Fuller has got to say about it. Miss Burton, read us a hymn, and that'll do Mother good, and then I'll go to sleep."

The next day, after she came from Morgenstern's, Lucy

went to find Mr. Fuller. She had no idea where he lived, and the only way she could think of finding him was to ask at the warehouses about the church. She tried one after another, but nobody even knew that there was any service there. With its closed, tomblike doors, and the utter ignorance of its concerns manifested by the people of the neighborhood, the great ugly building stood like some mausoleum built in honor of a custom buried beneath it, a monument of the time when men could buy and sell and worship God.

How she wished she could take Thomas with her the next time she went to receive Mr. Fuller's teaching! She had seen very little of Thomas, and had been so much occupied with Mattie that she did not even know whether he had fulfilled his promise about telling his father. Perhaps she had been afraid to ask him, foreboding the truth that he had in fact let his promise lapse. And what likelihood was there of the good seed taking good root in a heart where there was so little earth?

Finding Mr. Kitely in his shop door, Lucy told him what she had been about, and her want of success.

"What does the child want a clergyman for?" asked Mr. Kitely, with some tone of dissatisfaction. "I'm sure you're better than the whole lot of them, Miss. Now I've listened to you outside the door, Miss Burton, when you was a-talking to Mattie inside."

"That wasn't fair, Mr. Kitely."

"No more it wasn't, but it's done me no harm, nor you either. But for them parsons, they're neither men nor women. I beg their pardons—they're old wives!"

"But are you sure that you know quite what you are talking about? I think there must be all sorts of them, as well as of other people. I wish you would come and hear Mr. Fuller some evening with Mattie and me when she's better. You would allow that he talks sense, anyhow."

"I ain't over hopeful, Miss. And to tell the truth, I don't much care. I don't think there can be much in it. It's all an affair of the priests. To get the upper hand of people, they work on their fears and superstitions. But I don't doubt some of them may succeed in taking themselves in, and so go on like the fox that had lost his tail, trying to make others cut theirs off too."

Lucy did not reply, because she had nothing to say. The bookseller feared he had hurt her. "And so you couldn't find this Mr. Fuller? Well, you leave it to me. I'll find him, and let you know in the afternoon."

"Thank you, Mr. Kitely. Just tell Mattie, will you? I must run home now, but I'll come back in the afternoon to hear how you have succeeded."

About six o'clock Lucy reentered Mr. Kitely's shop, received the necessary directions to find the parson, ran up to tell Mattie that she was going, and then set out.

Although the parsonage lay on the bank of one of the main torrents of city traffic, it was withdrawn and hidden behind shops, among offices, taverns, and warehouses. After missing the most direct way, she arrived at last, through lanes and courts, much to her surprise, at the border of a green lawn, on the opposite side of which rose a tree that spread fair branches across a blue sky filled with pearly light. The parsonage was a long, rather low, country-looking house. One side of the square yard was formed by a vague commonplace mass of dirty expressionless London houses. The other side was of much the same character, and the remaining side was formed by the long, barnlike wall of the church. The church was built of brick, nearly black below but retaining in the upper part of the square tower something of its original red. Lucy went up to the door of the parsonage, and was shown into Mr. Fuller's study. She told him her name, that she had been to his weeknight service with Mattie, and that the child was ill and wanted to see him.

"Thank you very much," said Mr. Fuller. "Some of the city clergymen have so little opportunity of being useful! I am truly grateful to you for coming to me. A child in my parish is quite a godsend to me—I do not use the word irreverently. You lighten my labor by the news. I am sorry she is ill, but I am very glad to be useful."

He promised to call the next day, and after a little more talk, Lucy took her leave.

Mr. Fuller was a middle-aged man, who all his conscious years had been trying to get nearer to his brethren, for the more anxious he was to come near to God, the more he felt that the high road to God lay through the forest of humanity.

He was only a curate still. But the incumbent of St. Amos—an old man with a grown-up family, almost unfit for duty, and greatly preferring his little estate in Kent to the city parsonage—left everything to him. He did not pay him enough to marry, but Mr. Fuller did not mind that, for the only lady he had loved was dead, and all his thoughts for this life were bent upon such realizing of divine theory about human beings, and their relation to God and to cach other, as might make life a truth and a gladness. It was therefore painful to him to think that he was but a *city* curate. Perhaps not one individual of the crowds that passed his church every hour in the week would be within miles of it on Sunday.

He seemed to himself to be greatly overpaid for the work he had in his power to do. His heart at times burned within him to speak the words he loved best, to such as he could hope had the ears to hear them. Among the twelve people that he said he preferred to the thousand, he could sometimes hardly believe that there was one who heard and understood.

Meantime, this visit of Lucy gave him pleasure, and hope of usefulness. The next morning he was in Mr. Kitely's shop as early as he thought the little invalid would be able to see him.

"Good morning, Sir," said Mr. Kitely, brusquely as usual. "What can I do for you this morning?"

"You have a little girl that's not well?" returned Mr. Fuller.

"Oh! You're the gentleman she wanted to see. She's been asking ever so often whether you wasn't come yet. She's quite impatient to see you, poor lamb."

While he spoke, Kitely had drawn nearer to the curate, regarding him with projecting and slightly flushed face, and eager eyes. "You won't put any nonsense into her head, will you, Sir?" he said, almost pleadingly.

"Not if I know it," answered Mr. Fuller, with a smile of kind humor. "I would rather take some out of it."

"That child never committed a sin in her life," Kitely went on. "It's all nonsense; and I won't have her talked to as if she was a little hellcat."

"But you see we must go partly by what she thinks herself, and I suspect she won't say she never did anything wrong."

"I don't exactly say that, you know," interposed Mr. Kitely. "I only said she hadn't committed any sins."

"And where's the difference?" asked Mr. Fuller quietly.

"Oh! Doing wrong—why, we all do wrong sometimes. But to commit a sin, that's something serious. That's about the Ten Commandments."

"I don't think your little girl would know the difference, but I do. I think she's very likely to know best. Children are wise in the affairs of their own kingdom."

"Well, I believe you're right, for she's the strangest child I ever saw. She knows more than anyone would think. Walk this way, Sir. You'll find her in the back room."

"Won't you come too, and see that I don't put any nonsense into her head?"

"I must mind the shop, Sir," objected Kitely, seeming a little ashamed of what he had said.

"Mr. Kitely," he said, "Suppose you were right about your little girl, or suppose even that she had never done anything wrong at all, she would want God all the same. And we must help each other to find Him."

If Mr. Kitely had any reply ready for this remark, Mr. Fuller did not give him time to make it, for he walked at once into the room, and found Mattie sitting alone in the half twilight of the cloudy day. Even the caged birds were oppressed, for not one of them was singing. A thrush hopped drearily about under his load of speckles, and a rose-ringed parrot with a very red nose looked ashamed of the quantity of port wine he had drunk.

The child was reading a little old hymnbook. She laid it down, and rose from the window seat to meet Mr. Fuller.

"Well, how do you do, Sir?" she said. "I am glad you are come."

Any other child of her age Mr. Fuller would have kissed, but there was something about Mattie that made him feel it an unfit proceeding. He shook hands with her, and offered her a white camellia.

"Thank you, Sir," said Mattie, and laid the little blossom on the table.

"Don't you like the beautiful flower?" asked Mr. Fuller, somewhat disappointed.

"Well, where's the good?" replied Mattie. "It will be ugly tomorrow."

"Oh, no, not if you put it in water directly."

"Will it live forever, then?" asked Mattie.

"No, only a few days."

"Well, tomorrow or next week—where's the difference? It *looks* dead now when you know it's dying."

"Ah!" thought Mr. Fuller, "I've got something here worth looking into." But what he said was, "You like the birds, though, don't you?"

"Well, yes. But they won't last forever. One of them is dead since I was taken ill. And Father meant it for Miss Burton."

"Do you like Miss Burton, then?"

"Yes, I *do.* But she'll live forever, you know. I'll tell you something else I like. There," and she held out the aged little volume, open at a hymn about blind Bartimaeus.

"Will this last forever, then?" he asked, turning the volume over in his hand, so that its withered condition was plain to Mattie.

"Now you puzzle me," answered Mattie. "You know it's not the book I mean; it's the poem. Now I have it. If I know that poem by heart, and I live forever, then the poem will live forever. There!"

"Then the book's the body, and the poem the soul," said Mr. Fuller.

"One of the souls, for some things have many souls. I have two, at least."

Mr. Fuller felt they were getting on rather dangerous ground. "Two souls! That must be something like what King David felt, when he asked God to join his heart into one. But you do like this poem?" he hastened to add. And he knew what he must bring her next time—not a camellia, but a poem. Still, how sad it was that a little child should not love flowers!

"When were you in the country last, Miss Kitely?"

"I never was in the country that I know of. And my name's Mattie."

"Wouldn't you like to go, Mattie?"

"No, I shouldn't, not at all. The country, by all I hear, is full of things that die, and I don't like that."

Mr. Fuller resolved that he would make Mattie like the country before he had done with her. But he would say no more now, because he was not sure whether Mattie as yet regarded him with a friendly eye, and he must be a friend before he would speak about religion. He rose, therefore, and held out his hand.

Mattie looked at him with dismay. "But I wanted you to tell me about the man that sat at Somebody's feet in his Sunday clothes."

Mr. Fuller guessed at once what she meant, and taking a New Testament from his pocket, read to her about the demoniac, who sat at the feet of Jesus, clothed, and in his right mind.

"Well, I was wrong. It wasn't his Sunday clothes," she said. "Or, perhaps, it was, and he had torn the rest all to pieces."

"That's very likely," responded Mr. Fuller.

"I know—it was Syne that told him, and he did it. But he wouldn't do it anymore, would he, after he saw Somebody?"

"I don't think he would," answered Mr. Fuller. "I will come and see you again tomorrow, and bring something that you will like."

"Thank you," answered the old-fashioned creature. "But don't be putting yourself to any expense about it, for I am not easy to please." And she lifted her hand to her head and gave a deep sigh, as if it was a very sad fact indeed. "I wish I were easier to please," she added to herself—but Mr. Fuller heard her as he left the room.

"She's a very remarkable child that, Mr. Kitely, too much so, I fear," he said, reentering the shop.

"I know that," returned the bookseller, curtly, almost angrily. "I wish she wasn't."

"I beg your pardon. I only wanted to ask you whether you do not think she had better go out of town for a while."

"I daresay. But how am I to send her? The child has no relation but me. She would fret herself to death without someone she cared about."

"Certainly it wouldn't do. But mightn't Miss Burton help? Is she any relation of yours?"

"None whatever. I believe she's a stray angel," answered Mr. Kitely, smiling, "for she ain't like anyone else I know of but that child's mother, and she's gone back to where she came from, many's the long year."

"I don't wonder at your thinking that of her, if she's as good as she looks," returned Mr. Fuller. And bidding the bookseller good- morning, he left the shop and walked home, thinking all the time.

Next morning he called earlier, and saw Lucy leaving the court just as he was going into the shop. He turned and spoke to her.

"Fancy a child, Miss Burton," he said, "that does not care about flowers—and her heart full of religion too! How is she to consider the lilies of the field? She knows only birds in cages, and has no idea of the birds of the air. The poor child has to lift everything out of that deep soul of hers, and the buckets of her brain can't stand such hard work."

"I know, I know," answered Lucy. "But what can I do?"

"Besides," Mr. Fuller continued, "what notion of the simple grandeur of God can she have when she never had more than a peep of the sky from between these wretched houses? How can the heavens declare the glory of God to her? You don't suppose David understood astronomy, and that it was from a scientific point of view that he spoke when he said that the firmament showed His handiwork?

"The little darling knows nothing of such an experience. We must get her into the open. She must love the wind that bloweth where it listeth, and the clouds that change and pass. She doesn't even like anything that does not last forever, but the mind needs a perishing bread sometimes as well as the body does—though it never perishes when once made use of. I beg your pardon, for I am preaching a sermon. What a thing it is to have the faults of a profession in addition to those of humanity! It all comes to this—you must get that child, with her big head and her big conscience, out of London, and give her heart a chance."

"Indeed, I wish I could," answered Lucy. "I will do what I can, and let you know. Are you going to see her now, Mr. Fuller?"

"Yes, I am. I took her a flower yesterday, but I have brought her a poem today. I am afraid, however, that it is not quite the thing for her. I thought I could easily find her one till I began to try, and then I found it very difficult indeed."

They parted—Lucy to Mrs. Morgenstern, Mr. Fuller to Mattie.

24. The Fate of the Ningpo

That very morning the last breath of the crew and passengers of the *Ningpo* had bubbled up in the newspapers. All the world who cared to know it read that the vessel had been dashed to pieces upon a rock of the Cape Verde Islands, and all hands and passengers lost.

Mr. Stopper's first feeling was one of dismay, for the articles of partnership had not been completed before Mr. Boxall sailed. Still, as he was the only person who understood the business, he trusted to make his position good, especially as old Mrs. Boxall must now be nearest of kin. Here, however, occurred the thought of Thomas, who had influence there—and that influence would be against Stopper, for had he not insulted Tom? This he could not help yet, so he would wait for what might turn up.

What Mr. Worboise's feelings were when first he read the paragraph in the paper cannot be known—whether he had an emotion of justice and an inclination to share the property with Mrs. Boxall. He did not seem to clearly recognize the existence of his friend's mother. In his mind her significance was thinned by age, little regard, and dependence into a thing of no account—a shadow living only in waste places of human disregard. He certainly knew nothing of her right to any property that had been in the possession of her son. But one result followed: he became more ambitious for his son.

Mrs. Boxall did not yet know anything of the matter. She did not read the newspapers and, accustomed to have sons at sea, had not even begun to look for news of the *Ningpo.*

Nor did Lucy know, for she was busy telling Mrs. Morgenstern all about the recent events with Mattie and Mr. Fuller.

"Well, Lucy," Mrs. Morgenstern said, "it is clear to me that the child will go out of her mind if she continues as she is. Now, Miriam has not been out of London since last August. Couldn't you take both Miriam and Mattie down to St. Leonards or Hastings? You can go on with your lessons there all the same."

"But what will become of my grandmother?" said Lucy.

"She can go with you, can't she? I could ask her to accompany you. It would be much better for you to have her, and it makes very little difference to me, you know."

"Thank you very much," returned Lucy, "but I fear my grandmother will not consent to it. I will try her, however, and see what can be done. Thank you a thousand times, dear Mrs. Morgenstern. Wouldn't you like to go to Hastings, Miriam?"

Miriam was delighted at the thought of it, and Lucy was not without hopes. She would be glad to be away from Thomas for a while; for until he had done as he ought, she could not be happy in his presence.

But as she was going out, she met Mr. Sargent who had come to see her.

"Ah, Miss Burton," said Mr. Sargent, "I am just in time. I thought perhaps you would not be gone yet. Will you come into the garden with me for a few minutes? I won't keep you long."

Lucy hesitated. Mr. Sargent had of late been more confidential in his manner than was quite pleasant to her. With the keenest dislike to false appearances, she yet could not take his intentions for granted, and tell him that she was engaged to Thomas. He saw her hesitation and hastened to remove it. "I only want to ask you about a matter of business," he said. "I assure you I won't detain you."

Mr. Sargent had learned all about Lucy's relations, and knew that her uncle and whole family had sailed on the *Ningpo.* Anxious to do what he could for her, and fearful lest, in their unprotected condition, some advantage should be taken of the two women, he had made haste to offer his services to Lucy, not without risk of putting himself in the false position of a fortune hunter. He heartily abused himself for not having made more definite advances before there was any danger of her becoming an heiress; for although a fortune was a most desirable thing, he was above marrying for money alone; and in the case of Lucy, he was especially jealous of being unjustly supposed to be in pursuit of her prospects.

"Have you heard the sad news?" he said, as soon as they were in the garden.

"No," answered Lucy, without concern, for she did not expect to hear anything about Thomas.

"The *Ningpo* is lost."

Lucy did not cry, but she turned very pale. Not a thought of the possible interest she might have in the matter crossed her mind, for she had never associated good to herself with her uncle or any of his family.

"How dreadful!" she murmured. "My poor cousins!"

"Are there any other relations but your grandmother and yourself?" he asked, for Lucy remained silent.

"I don't know of any," she answered.

"Then you must come in for the property."

"Oh, no. He would never leave it to us. He didn't like me, for one thing. But that was my fault, perhaps. He was not overly kind to my mother, and so I never liked him." And here at length she burst into tears and wept very quietly. Mr. Sargent went on.

"But you must be his next of kin. Will you allow me to make inquiry, to do anything that may be necessary, for you? Don't misunderstand me," he added, pleadingly. "It is only as a friend—what I have been for a long time now, Lucy."

Lucy scarcely hesitated before she answered, with a restraint that appeared like coldness, "Thank you, Mr. Sargent. The business cannot in any case be mine. It is my grandmother's; I can, and will, take no hand in it."

"Will you say to your grandmother that I am at her service?"

"If it were a business matter, there is no one I would more willingly ask to help us, but as you say it is a matter of friendship, and I must refuse your kindness."

Mr. Sargent was vexed with himself, and disappointed with Lucy, supposing that she had misinterpreted his motives. "Miss Burton," he said, "for God's sake, do not misunderstand me, and attribute to mercenary motives the offer I make only in the confidence that you will not do me such an injustice."

Lucy was greatly distressed. Her color went and came for a few minutes, and then she spoke. "Mr. Sargent, I am just as anxious that you should understand me: but I am in a great difficulty, and have to throw myself on your generosity. I refuse your kindness only because I am not free to lay myself under such obligation to you. Do not ask me to say more."

But he understood her perfectly, and honest disappointment was visible enough on his countenance.

"I understand you, Miss Burton," he said, in a calm voice which only trembled a little, "and I thank you. Please remember that if you ever need a friend, I am at your service." Without another word, he lifted his hat and went away.

Lucy hastened home full of distress at the thought of her grandmother's grief, and wondered how she should convey the news. But when she entered the room, she found Mrs. Boxall already in tears, and Mr. Stopper seated by her side comforting her with commonplaces.

25. The Waiting Game

During all this time Thomas had been doing gradually worse. His mother had been at home for a long time now, and Mr. Simon's visits had been resumed. But neither of these circumstances tended to draw him homeward.

Mrs. Worboise's health was so much improved by her sojourn at Folkestone that she now meditated more energetic measures for the conversion of her son. At length she resolved that, as he had been a good scholar when at school, she would ask him to bring his Greek Testament to her room, and help her to read through St. Paul's Epistle to the Romans with the fresh light which his scholarship would cast upon the page. It was not that she had the least difficulty about the apostle's meaning. She knew it as well almost as the apostle himself; but she would invent an innocent trap to catch a soul with, and put it in a safe cage, whose strong wires of exclusions should be wadded with the pleasant cotton of safety. Alas for St. Paul, his mighty soul and his laboring speech in such hands!

"Thomas," she said, one evening, "I want you to bring your Greek Testament, and help me out with something."

"O Mother, I have forgotten all about Greek. What is it you want to know?"

"I want you to read Romans with me."

"Oh! Really, Mother, I can't. It's such bad Greek, you know!"

"Thomas!" said his mother, sepulchrally, as if his hasty assertion with regard to St. Paul's scholarship had been a sin against the truth St. Paul spoke.

"Why don't you ask Mr. Simon? He's an Oxford man."

Thomas was breaking loose from his mother's authority, yet was not prepared to brave her and his father with a confession of his engagement to Lucy.

Since he could see so little of Lucy, he spent almost all his extra time with Molken. In consequence, he seldom reached home in anything like decent time. When his mother spoke to him on the subject, he shoved it aside with, "You were in bed, Mother," prefacing some story, part true, part false, arranged for the occasion. So long as his father took no notice of the matter, he did not much mind. Just so Tom was out of bed early enough in the morning, his father did not much care at what hour he went to it. He had had his own wild oats to sow in his time. The purity of his boy's mind and body did not trouble him much, provided that, when he came to take his position in the machine of things, he turned out a steady, respectable cog.

Thomas had sauntered more and more into the power of Mr. Molken. Although he had vowed to himself, after his first experience, that he would never play again, he had easily broken that vow. It was not that he had any very strong inclination to gamble—the demon of play had not yet quite entered into him; it was only that whatever lord asserted dominion over Thomas, to him Thomas was ready to yield that which he claimed. Molken said, "Come along," and Thomas went along.

Yet Mr. Molken found him rather harder to corrupt from his shilly-shally ways than he had expected. Above all, the love of woman, next to the love of God, is the power of God to a young man's salvation; everything, from first to last, is of our Father in heaven.

His gambling was a very trifle as far as money went, and an affair of all but life and death as far as principle was concerned. But for Thomas, the worst thing in the gambling was that it fell in so with his natural weakness. Gambling is the employment for the man without principles and without will, for as far as he is concerned, his whole being is but the roulette ball of chance. The wise man, on the contrary, does not believe in Fortune, yields nothing to her sway, but goes on his own fixed path regardless. Thomas got gradually weaker and weaker, and had it not been for Lucy, would soon have fallen utterly. But she, like the lady of an absent lord, still kept one fortress for him in a yielded and devastated country.

There was no newspaper taken in at Mr. Worboise' so, when Thomas reached the countinghouse, he had heard nothing about his late master and family. However, the moment he entered the place he felt the clouded atmosphere. Mr. Wither, whose face was as pale as death, rose from the desk where he had been sitting, caught up his hat, and went out. No one took any notice of Thomas, however, but a funereal gloom hung about all their faces. Mr. Stopper was sitting within the glass partition, whence he called for Thomas who obeyed with a bad grace, as anticipating something disagreeable.

"There!" said Mr. Stopper, handing him the newspaper, and watching him as he read.

Thomas read, returned the paper, murmured something, and went back with scared face to the outer room. There a conversation arose in a low voice, as if it had been in the presence of the dead. Various questions were asked and conjectures hazarded, but nobody knew anything. Thomas' place was opposite the glass, and he saw Mr. Stopper take the key of the door of communication from a drawer, unlock the door, and with the *Times* in his hand walk into Mrs. Boxall's house, closing the door behind him. Then first the thought struck Thomas that Lucy and her grandmother would come in for all the property. This sent a glow of pleasure through him, and he had enough ado to keep the funereal look which belonged to the occasion. Now he need not fear to tell his father the fact of his engagement—indeed he might delay the news as long as he liked, sure that it would be welcome whenever it came.

But Mr. Worboise was troubled about the property. With perfect law on his side, there was that yet against him which all his worldliness did not quite enable him to meet with coolness. But the longer the idea of the property rested upon his mind, the more, as if it had been the red-hot coin of the devil's gift, it burned and burrowed out a nest for itself, till it lay there stone-cold and immovably fixed, and not to be got rid of. Before many weeks had passed he not only knew that it was his by law, but felt that it was his by right—his own right of possession;

and the clinging of his heartstrings around it—his own because it was so good—was such that he could not part with it. Still, it was possible that something adverse might turn up, and there was no good in incurring odium until he was absolutely sure that the fortune would be his. Therefore, he was in no haste to propound the will.

At the same time he began to be more ambitious for his son, and desired an advantageous alliance. Therefore, he began to look about him, and speculate. He had not the slightest suspicion of Thomas being in love; indeed, there was nothing in his conduct or appearance that could have aroused such a suspicion in his mind. Mr. Worboise believed, on the contrary, that his son was leading a rather wild life.

There was one adverse intelligence, of whom Mr. Worboise knew nothing, ready to pounce upon him the moment he showed his game. This was Mr. Sargent. Smarting from the lingering suspicion that Lucy had altogether misinterpreted his motives, he watched for an opportunity of proving his disinterestedness; this was his only hope, for he saw that Lucy was lost to him. He well knew that in the position of Lucy and her grandmother, it would not be surprising if something with a forked tongue or a cloven foot should put its head out of a hole before very long, and begin to creep toward them; and therefore, he kept an indefinite but wide watch. He had no great difficulty in discovering that Mr. Worboise had been Mr. Boxall's man of business, but he had no right to communicate with him on the subject.

Mr. Stopper, who had taken the place of adviser in general to Mrs. Boxall, had already asked Mr. Worboise whether Mr. Boxall had left a will, to which he had received a reply only to the effect that it was early yet, that there was no proof of his death, and that he was prepared to give what evidence he possessed at the proper time—an answer Mrs. Boxall, with her fiery disposition, considered less than courteous. Of this Mr. Sargent, of course, was not aware, but as the only thing he could do at present, he entered a caveat in the Court of Probate.

Mr. Stopper did his best for the business in the hope of one day having not only the entire management as now, but an unquestionable as unquestioned right to the same. If he ever thought of anything further, since he had now a free entrance to Mrs. Boxall's region, he could not think an inch in that direction without encountering the idea of Thomas.

It was very disagreeable to Thomas that Mr. Stopper, whom he detested, should have this free admission. He felt as if the place were defiled by his presence, and to sit knowing that Mr. Stopper was overhead, was absolutely hateful. But Lucy was not at home, and that mitigated the matter very considerably. Mr. Stopper was on the whole more civil to Thomas than he had hitherto been, and appeared even to put a little more confidence in him than formerly. Because of his insecurity and the vulnerabilty of his position, he wished to be friendly on all sides, with a vague general feeling of strengthening his outworks.

Mr. Wither never opened his mouth to Thomas upon any occasion or necessity, and from several symptoms it appeared that his grief, or rather perhaps the antidotes to it, were dragging him downhill.

Amy Worboise was not at home. The mother had seen symptoms of love - and much as she valued Mr. Simon's ghostly ministrations, she did not wish him for her son-in-law. So Amy disappeared into the country for a season, upon a convenient invitation.

26. Mattie in the Country

Lucy did not intend, in the sad circumstances, to say a word to her grandmother about Mrs. Morgenstern's proposal. But it was brought about very naturally.

When the first burst of her grandmother's grief was over, and after Mr. Stopper had gone back to the countinghouse, Lucy ventured to speak.

"They're gone home, dear Grannie," she said.

"And I shan't stay long behind them, my dear," Grannie moaned.

"That's some comfort, isn't it, Grannie?" said Lucy, for her own heart was heavy, not for the dead, but for the living.

"Ah! You young people would be glad enough to have the old ones out of the way," returned Mrs. Boxall, in the petulance of grief. "Have patience, Lucy: it won't be long, and then you can do as you like."

"O Grannie!" cried Lucy, bursting into tears. "I do everything like I want now. I only wanted to comfort you," she sobbed. "I thought you would like to go too. I wish *I* were dead."

"*You,* Child!" exclaimed Mrs. Boxall. "Why should you wish you were dead? You don't know enough of life to wish for death." Then, as Lucy went on sobbing, Mrs. Boxall's tone changed, for she began to be concerned at Lucy's distress. "What is the matter with my darling?" she said.

Then Lucy went to her and kissed her, and knelt down, and

laid her head in the old woman's lap. And her grannie stroked her hair and spoke to her as if she had been one of her own babies; and, in seeking to comfort her, she forgot her own troubles for the moment.

"You've been doing too much for other people, Lucy," she said. "You should go to the seaside for a while. You shan't go about giving lessons anymore, my lamb. There is no need for that any more, for they say all the money will be ours now." And the old woman wept again at the thought of the source of their coming prosperity.

"I should like to go to the country very much, if you would go too, Grannie."

"No, no, Child, I don't want to go."

"But I don't like to leave you, Grannie," objected Lucy.

"Never mind me, my dear. I shall be better alone for a while. And I daresay there will be some business to attend to."

And so Lucy told her all about Mrs. Morgenstern's plan, and how ill poor Mattie looked, and that she would be glad to go away for a little while herself. Mrs. Boxall would not consent to go, but urged Lucy to accept the proposed arrangement.

Two days later, Lucy and Mattie met Mrs. Morgenstern and Miriam at the London Bridge railway station. Mattie looked quite dazed with the noise and bustle, but when they were once in motion, she heaved a deep sigh and looked comforted. She said nothing, however, for some time, and her countenance revealed no surprise. Whatever was out of the usual always oppressed Mattie, rather than excited her, and therefore the more surprising anything was, the less did it occasion any outward shape of surprise. But as they flashed into the first tunnel, Lucy saw her start and shudder ere they vanished from each other in the darkness. She reached out and took Mattie's hand. It was cold and trembling; but as she held it gently and warmly in her own, it grew quite still. By the time the light began to grow again, her face was peaceful, and when they emerged in the cutting beyond, she was calm enough to speak the thought that had come to her in the dark. "I knew the country wasn't nice," she said.

"But you don't know what the country is yet," answered Lucy.

"I know quite enough of it," returned Mattie. "I like London best. I wish I could see some shops."

Before they reached Hastings that evening, Mattie was fast asleep. She scarcely woke when they stopped for the last time. Lucy carried her from the carriage to a cab. When they arrived at the lodgings, Lucy made all haste to get her to bed and asleep.

Mattie woke early in the morning, and the first thing she was aware of was the crowing of a very clear-throated cock. She could not collect her thoughts for some time. Something certainly had happened. She was aware that her eyes were open, but she did not know that Lucy was in another bed in the same room watching her. The room was different from anything she had been used to. She crept out of bed and went to the window. There was no blind, only curtains drawn close in front.

When Mattie went to the window of her own room at home, she saw Guild Court; but this house was halfway up one side of a hill. Hence when Mattie went between the curtains she saw nothing but that lovely Hastings sea lying away out into the sky, piled up like a hill, vast and blue, and triumphant in sunlight—just a few white sails below, and a few white clouds above. She saw nothing of the earth on which she was upheld—only the sea and the sky. She started back with a feeling of terror, loneliness, and helplessness, and turned and flew to her bed. But instead of getting into it, she fell down on her knees, clutched the bedclothes, and wept aloud. Lucy was by her side in a moment, took her in her arms, carried her to her own bed, and comforted her in her bosom.

Mattie had all her life been sitting in her own microcosm, watching the shadows that went and came. All her doings had gone on in the world of her own imaginings; and although that big brain of hers contained a being greater than all that is seen, heard, or handled, yet the show of divine imagination which now met her eyes overpowered that world within her.

She needed just such a sight as this to take the conceit out of her. The whole show of the universe was well spent to take an atom of the self out of a child. And no human fault is overcome, save by the bringing on of true grand things. A sense of the infinite and the near, the far yet impending, rebuked the conceit of Mattie to the very core, and without her knowing why or how. She clung to Lucy as a child would cling.

Lucy held her peace, and in the silence of that waiting she became aware that a lark was singing somewhere out in the great blue vault.

"Listen to the lark," Lucy said.

And Mattie moved her head enough to show that she would listen. At length she said with a sob, "What is a lark? I never saw one, Miss Burton."

"A bird like a sparrow. You know what a sparrow is, don't you, Dear?"

"Yes. I have seen sparrows often in the court. They pick up dirt."

"Well, a lark is like a sparrow, only it doesn't pick up dirt, and sings as you hear it. And it flies so far up in the sky that you can't see it. You can only hear the song it scatters down upon the earth."

"Oh, how dreadful!" said Mattie, burying her head again. "To fly up into that awful place up there. Shall we have to do that when we die?"

"It is not an awful place, Dear. God is there, you know."

"But I am frightened. And if God is up there, I shall be frightened at Him too. It is so dreadful! I used to think God could see me when I was in London. But how is He to see me in this great place, with so many things about, roosters and larks and all, I can't think. I'm so little and hardly worth taking care of."

"But you remember, Mattie, what Somebody says—that God takes care of every sparrow."

"Yes, but that's the sparrows, and they're in the town, you know."

Lucy saw that it was time to stop. The child's fear was gone for the present, or she could not have talked such nonsense.

"Why don't you speak, Miss Burton?" asked Mattie at length, no doubt conscience-stricken by her silence.

"Because you are talking nonsense now, Mattie."

"I thought that was it. But why should that make you not speak? I need the more to hear sense."

"No, Mattie. Mr. Fuller says that when people begin to talk falsely, it is better to be quite silent, and let them say what they please, till the sound of their own nonsense makes them ashamed."

"As it did me, Miss Burton, as soon as you wouldn't speak any more."

"He says it does no good to contradict them then, for they are not only unworthy to hear the truth—if they would hear it, but they are not fit to hear it. They are not in a mood to get any good from it, for they are holding the door open for the devil to come in, and truth can't get in at the same door with the devil."

"Oh, how dreadful! To think of me talking like Syne!" said Mattie. "I won't do it again, Miss Burton. Do tell me what Somebody said about God and the sparrows. Didn't He say something about counting their feathers? I think I remember Mr. Spelt reading that to me one night."

"He said something about counting your hairs, Mattie."

"Mine?"

"Well, Jesus said it to all the people that would listen to Him. I daresay there were some that could not believe it, because they did not care to be told."

"That's me, Miss Burton. But I won't do it again."

"Mattie, if God knows how many hairs you have got on your head, you can't think you're too small for Him to look after you."

"I will try not to be frightened at the big sky anymore, dear Miss Burton."

In a few minutes she was fast asleep again.

Lucy's heart was nonetheless trustful that she had tried to increase Mattie's faith. He who cared for the sparrows would surely hear her cry for Thomas and look after him. In teaching Mattie she had taught herself. She had been awake long before her, turning over and over her troubled thoughts, but now she too fell fast asleep in her hope, and when she awoke, her thoughts were all knit up again in an even resolve to go on and do her duty, casting her care upon Him who cared for her.

And now Mattie's childhood commenced. She could not indulge her disputations in the presence of the great sky, which grew upon her till she felt that it was the great eye of God looking at her. She began to love the sky, and be sorry and oppressed upon cloudy days when she could no longer look up into it.

The next day they went down to the beach, in a quiet place

amongst great stones under cliff. Lucy sat down on one of them, and began to read a book Mr. Fuller had lent her. Miriam was at a little distance picking up shells, and Mattie on another stone nearer the sea. The tide was rising when suddenly Mattie came scrambling in great haste over all that lay between her and Lucy. Her face was pale, scared, and eager.

"I'm so frightened again!" she said. "The sea! What does it mean? It's roaring at me, and coming nearer and nearer, as if it wanted to swallow me up! I don't like it."

"You must not be afraid of it. God made it, you know."

"Why does He let it roar at me, then?"

"I don't know. Perhaps to teach you not to be afraid."

Mattie said no more, stood a little while by Lucy, and then scrambled back to her former place.

The next day, they climbed the East Hill. Mattie gazed at the sea below her, the sky over her head, the smooth grass under her feet, and gave one of her great sighs. Then she looked troubled.

"I feel as if I hadn't any clothes on," she said.

"How is that, Mattie?"

"Well, I don't know. I feel as if I couldn't stand steady—as if I hadn't anything to keep me up. In London, you know, the houses were always beside to hold a body up, and keep them steady. But here, if it weren't for Somebody, I should be so frightened for falling down—I don't know where!"

Lucy smiled. She did not see then how exactly the child symbolized those who think they have faith in God, yet when one of the swaddling bands of system or dogma to which they have been accustomed is removed, or even slackened, they immediately feel as if there were no God, as if the earth under their feet were a cloud, and there was nothing to trust in anywhere. They rest in their swaddling bands, not in God. The loosening of these is God's gift to them so that they may grow. But at first they are much afraid.

Wandering along the cliff, they came to a patch that was full of daisies. Miriam rushed among them with a cry of pleasure and began gathering them eagerly. Mattie stood by with a look of condescending contempt on her pale face.

"Wouldn't you like to gather some daisies too, Mattie?" suggested Lucy.

"Where's the use?" said Lucy. "The poor things will be withered in no time. It's almost a shame to gather them, I do think."

"Well, you needn't gather them if you don't want to," returned Lucy. "But I wonder you don't like them, they are so pretty."

"But they don't last. I don't like things that die. I had a little talk with Mr. Fuller about that."

Lucy thought for a moment, and then said, "Listen, Mattie. You don't dislike to hear me talk, do you?"

"No, indeed," answered Mattie.

"You like the words I say to you, then?"

"Yes, indeed," said Mattie, wondering what would come next.

"But my words die as soon as they are out of my mouth."

Mattie began to see a glimmering of something coming, and held her peace and listened. Lucy went on. "Well, the flowers are some of God's words, and they last longer then mine."

"But I understand your words. I know what you want to say to me. And I don't know the meaning of *them.*"

"That's because you haven't looked at them long enough. You must suppose them words in God's Book, and try to read them and understand them."

"I will try," said Mattie, and walked away soberly toward Miriam.

But she did not begin to gather daisies. Rather, she lay down in the grass to look at the daisies, and thus continued for some time.

Then she rose and came slowly back to Lucy. "I can't tell what they mean," she said. "I have been trying very hard too."

"I don't know whether I understand them either. But I fancy we get some good from what God shows us even when we don't understand it much."

"They are such little things!" said Mattie. "I can hardly fancy them worth making."

"God thinks them worth making though. He wouldn't do anything that He did not care about. There's the lark again—hear how glad he is! If he couldn't sing it would break his heart. Do you think God would have made his heart so glad if

He did not care for his gladness? And He must have made the song and taught it to the lark. And would He not have made the daisies so pretty if their prettiness was not worth something in His eyes? And if God cares for them, surely it is worth our while to care for them too."

Mattie listened very earnestly, went back to the daisies, and lay down again beside them. Miriam kept running about from one spot to another, gathering them. What Mattie said, or what Miriam replied, Lucy did not know, but in a little while Mattie came to Lucy with a red face—a rare show for her.

"I don't like Miss Miriam," she said. "She's not nice at all."

"Why, what's the matter?" asked Lucy, in some surprise, for the children had gotten on very well together as yet. What has she been doing?"

"She doesn't care a bit for Somebody."

"But Somebody likes her."

To this Mattie returned no answer, but stood thoughtful. The blood withdrew from her face, and she went back to the daisies once more.

The following day she began to gather flowers as other children do, even to search for them as hidden treasures. And she would gaze at some of them in a way that showed plainly enough that she felt their beauty. No person can be quite the same as before after having *loved* a new flower.

Thus, by degrees, Mattie's thoughts and feelings were drawn outward, and she grew younger and humbler. Every day her eyes were opened to some fresh beauty on the earth, some new shadowing of the sea, some passing loveliness in the heavens. She had hitherto refused the world as a thing she had not proved; now she began to feel herself at home in it, that is, to find that it was not a strange world to which she had come, but a home, full of the Father's presence, thoughts, and designs. Is it any wonder that a child should prosper better in such a world than in a catacomb filled with the coffined remains of thinking men, such as her father's bookshop? Here, God was ever before her in the living forms of His thought, a power and a blessing. Every wind that blew was His breath, and the type of His inner breathing upon the human soul. Every morning was filled with His light, the type of the growing of that Light which lighteth every man that cometh into the world. And there are no natural types that do not dimly work their own spiritual reality upon the open heart of the human being.

Before she left Hastings, Mattie was almost a child.

27. Poppie in Town

Within Guild Court there stood a narrow house occupied by different households. Mr. Spelt had for some time had his eye upon it, in the hope of a vacancy occurring in its top chambers. He would be nearer his work, and have a more convenient home in case he should some day succeed in taming Poppie. Things had been going well in every way with the little tailor, and he had had a good many more private customers for the last few months.

Likewise his fishing had prospered. Poppie came for her sweets as regularly as a robin for his crumbs in winter. Spelt, however, did not now confine his bait to sweets; a fresh roll or a currant bun would hang suspended by a string so that Poppie could easily reach it, and yet it should be under the protection of the tailor from chance marauders. And every morning as she took it, she sent a sweet smile of thanks to the upper regions whence came her aid. Though not very capable of conversation, she would occasionally answer a few questions about facts, as, for instance, where she had slept the last night, to which the answer would commonly be, "Mother Flanaghan's," but once, to the tailor's discomposure, it was, "The Jug." She did not seem to know exactly why she was incarcerated—there had been a crowd, somebody had stolen something, and there was a scurry, and she scudded as usual, and got took up.

Mr. Spelt was more anxious than ever to take her home after

this. But sometimes the moment he began to talk to her, she would run away, without the smallest appearance of rudeness, only of inexplicable oddity, and Mr. Spelt would fancy then that he was not a single step nearer to the desired result than when he first baited his hook. He regarded it as a good omen, however, when the topmost floor of the house in Guild Court became vacant, and he secured it at a weekly rental quite within the reach of his improved means. He did not imagine how soon he would be able to put the rooms to the use he most desired.

One evening, just as the light was fading, he heard the patter of Poppie's bare feet on the slabs. Looking down, he saw the child coming toward him, holding the bottom of her ragged frock up to her head. She stopped at the foot of the shop and looked up pale as death, with a dark streak of blood running through the paleness, and burst into a wail. The little man was down in a moment, but before his feet reached the ground Poppie had fallen upon it in a faint. He lifted the child in his arms, and sped up the three stairs to his own dwelling. There he laid her on his bed, struck a light, and proceeded to examine her. He found a large and deep cut in her head, from which the blood was still flowing. He rushed down again, sent the cobbler for a doctor, and returned like an arrow to his treasure. Having done all he could to stop the bleeding, he waited impatiently for the doctor's arrival. Before he came, the child began to revive; Mr. Spelt got some water and held it to her lips, and Poppie drank and opened her eyes. When she saw who was bending over her, the faintest ghost of a smile glimmered about her mouth, and she closed her eyes again, murmuring something about Mother Flanaghan.

Mr. Spelt finally determined that Mrs. Flanaghan had come home a little the worse for "the cream of the valley," and wanted more. She found her gin bottle empty and came to the hasty conclusion that poor Poppie was the thief. Just as an ill-trained child expends the rage of a hurt upon the first person within his reach, she broke the vile vessel upon Poppie's head, with the ensuing result.

The doctor came and dressed her wound, and gave directions for her treatment. And now Mr. Spelt was in the seventh heaven—he had someone of his own to take care of. He did not lie down all that night, but hovered about her bed, as if she might at any moment spread out great wings and fly away from him forever. Sometimes he had to soothe her with kind words, for she tossed a good deal, and would occasionally start up with wild looks, as if to fly once more from Mother Flanaghan with the gin-bottle bludgeon uplifted in her hand; then the sound of Mr. Spelt's voice would instantly soothe her, and she would lie down again and sleep.

When the light came, Mr. Spelt hurried downstairs to his shop, carried his work and all his implements upstairs, and sat with them on the floor where he could see Poppie's face. There he worked away busily, every now and then lifting his eyes from his seam to the bed, seeking Poppie's pale face. He found he could not get on so fast as usual, but he still made progress, and it was a comfort to think that by working thus early he was saving time for nursing his white little Poppie.

When at length she woke, she seemed more feverish, and he found that he must constantly watch her, for she was ready to spring out of bed at any moment. The father-heart grew dreadfully anxious before the doctor came, and all that day and the next he got very little work done, for the poor child was really in danger. Indeed, it was more than a week before he began to feel a little easy about her, and ten days passed before she was able to leave her bed.

And herein lay the greatest blessing both for Spelt and Poppie, for nothing else could have given him a reasonable chance of taming a wild animal. Her illness compelled her into such dependence that the idea of him had time to grow into her heart. And all her scudding propensities, which prevented her from making a quiet and thorough acquaintance with anybody, were not merely thwarted but utterly gone while she remained weak. The humanity of the child had therefore an opportunity of developing itself; the well of love belonging to her nature began to pulse and to flow, and she was (as it were) compelled to love Mr. Spelt.

28. St. Amos

Mr. Fuller's main thought was how to make his position in the church as far as possible from a sinecure. If the church was a reality at all, if it represented a vital body, every portion of it ought to be blossoming with life. Yet here was one of its cells all but inactive—a huge building of no use all the week, and on Sundays filled with organ sounds, a few responses from a sprinkling of indifferent worshipers, and his own voice reading prayers and trying to move those few to be better men and women than they were.

Mr. Fuller was ashamed of St. Amos, and was thinking day and night how to retrieve the character of his church.

"What is Sunday?" he asked himself. "A quiet hollow scooped out of the windy hill of the week. Must a man then go for six days shelterless ere he comes to the repose of the seventh? Are there to be no great rocks to shadow him between? No hiding places from the wind to let him take breath and heart for the next struggle? And if there ought to be, where should they be if not in our churches? But our churches stand absolute caverns of silence amidst the thunder of the busy city. Why should they not lift up their voices against the tumult of care? They may be caverns of peace but they are caverns without entrance, sealed fountains that mock of the thirst and confusion of men. Might there not be too much of a good thing on the Sunday, and too little of it on a weekday?

"And what is the priest?" he asked, going on with the same

catechism. "He is a man to keep the windows of heaven clean, that its light might shine through upon men below." Such was the calling of the clergyman, as Mr. Fuller saw it—a lofty one, and a true one. If the clergyman cannot rouse men to seek his God and their God, if he can only rest in his office, which becomes false the moment he rests in it, if he has no message from the Infinite to quicken the thoughts that cleave to the dust, then the sooner he takes to gravedigging or any other honest labor, the sooner he will get into the kingdom of heaven, and the higher he will stand in it.

Therefore, Mr. Fuller purposed that his church, instead of accumulating a weary length of service on one day, should be open every day, and that there he would be ready for any soul. So each day he set the church door wide against the wall, and got a youth to play the organ about one o'clock, when those who dined in the city began to go in search of their food, such music as might possibly waken the desire to see what was going on in the church.

Over the crowded street, over the roar of omnibuses, carts, wagons, cabs, and all kinds of noises, rose the ordered sounds of harmony. Day after day arose the music of hopes and prayer—but not a soul in the streets took notice. Why should they? The clergy had lost their hold of them, for they believed that the clergy, like all men, were given over to gain and pleasure. They were wrong, but who was to blame them for it? The blame lay with the clergy of the eighteenth century, because so many of them were neither Christians nor gentlemen; and with the clergy of the present century, because so many of them are nothing but gentlemen, and do not lift their voices to cry out against any wickedness anywhere.

But at last one day, about a quarter past one o'clock, a man came into the church. Mr. Fuller, who sat in the reading desk, listening to the music and praying to God, lifted up his eyes and saw Mr. Kitely.

The bookseller had been passing and had heard the organ. He thought he would just look in and see what was doing in the church, for it was a sort of link between him and his daughter, now that she was away.

Mr. Fuller began to read the collect for the day, in order that Mr. Kitely might pray with him. The organ ceased, and Mr.

Kitely knelt, partly out of regard for Mr. Fuller. The organist came down and knelt beside Mr. Kitely, and Mr. Fuller went on with the second and third collects. After this he read the Epistle and the Gospel for the foregoing Sunday, and then he opened his mouth and spoke—for not more than three minutes, and only to enforce the lesson. Then he knelt and let his small congregation depart with a blessing.

Mr. Kitely dropped in again before long, and again Mr. Fuller read the collect and went through the same form of worship. This he did every time anyone appeared in the church, and before many more weeks there were very few days indeed upon which two or three persons did not drop in. To these he always spoke for a few minutes, and then dismissed them with the blessing.

29. A Dreary Holiday

"Couldn't you get a holiday on Saturday, Tom?" asked Mr. Worboise. "I mean to have one, and I should like to take you with me."

"I don't know, Father," answered Tom, who did not regard the proposal as involving any great probability of enjoyment. "My holiday is coming so soon that I should not like to ask for it, especially as Mr. Stopper—"

"What about Mr. Stopper? Not overly friendly, eh? He is not a bad fellow, though, is Stopper. I'll ask for you, if you like that better."

"I would much rather you wouldn't, Father."

"Pooh, pooh! Nonsense, Man! It's quite a different thing if I ask, you know."

Thomas made no further objection, for he had nothing at hand upon which to ground a fresh one. He lived in constant dread of something coming to light about Lucy. He feared his father much more than he loved him—not that he had ever been hardly treated by him, or had ever seen him in a passion; it was the hardness and inflexibility read upon his face from earliest childhood that caused fear thus to overlay love.

Mr. Worboise had a country client, Sir Jonathan Hubbard, a decent man, jolly, companionable, with a husky laugh, and friendly unfinished countenance. On the day appointed, Mr. Worboise and Tom called upon him at his country home on some pretext of business, and were naturally invited to linger as friends.

There was no Mrs. Hubbard alive, but there was a Miss Hubbard at the head of the house, and hence Mr. Worboise's strategy. Sir Jonathan was pleased with Tom and would not allow him to wait companionless in the drawing room; he sent for his daughter, and insisted on the two guests staying to dinner.

Thomas was seated in the drawing room, which looked cold and rather cheerless. The door opened, and in came a fashionable girl, rather tall, handsome, and bright-eyed. She was well-dressed, though Thomas did not like the fashion. But she soon made him forget that, for she was clever, pleasant, and altogether amusing. He could not help being taken with her; and when his father and Sir Jonathan came into the room, the young people were talking away.

"Laura, my dear," said Sir Jonathan, "I have prevailed on Mr. Worboise to spend the day with us. You have no engagement, I believe?"

"Fortunately, I have not, Papa."

"Well, I'll just give orders about dinner, and then we'll take our friends about the place. I want to show them my new stable."

Laura put on her hat, and they went out into the grounds, and from the grounds to the stable, where her favorite horse ate apples out of her pocket; from the stable to the hothouses and kitchen garden; then out at a back door into the lane, shadowy with trees, in which other colors than green were now carrying the vote of the leaves. Great white clouds in a brilliant sky tempered the heat of the sun. What with the pure air, the fine light, and the handsome girl by his side, Thomas was in a lighter mood than he had been for many a long day. Miss Hubbard talked plentiously about balls and theatres and dinners; and although of all these Thomas knew very little, yet, being quick and sympathetic, he was able to satisfy the lady sufficiently to keep her going. He was fortunate enough besides to say one or two clever things with which she was pleased, and to make an excellent point once in a criticism upon a girl they both knew, which slighted her yet conveyed a compliment to Miss Hubbard. By the time they had reached this stage of acquaintanceship, they had left Sir Jonathan and Mr. Worboise far behind. Having nothing more amusing to do, she proposed they should go home by a rather longer road, which would lead them over a hill whence they could have a good view of the country.

"Do you like living in the country, Miss Hubbard?"

"Oh, dear, no! London for me. I can't tell what made Papa come to this dull place."

"The scenery is very lovely, though."

"People say so. I'm sure I don't know. Scenery wasn't taught when I went to school."

"Were you taught horses there?" asked Thomas.

"No. That comes by nature. Do you know I won this bracelet in a handicap last Derby?" she said, showing a very fine arm as well as the bracelet.

Miss Hubbard had no design upon Thomas. How could she have? She knew nothing about him. She would have done the same with any gentleman she liked well enough to chatter to. And if Thomas felt it, and thought that Laura Hubbard was more entertaining than sober Lucy Burton, he made up to Lucy for it by asserting to himself that, after all, she was far handsomer than Miss Hubbard.

Thomas was fool enough to mention Byron, and she soon made him ashamed of showing any liking for such a silly thing as poetry. That piqued him as well, however.

"You sing, I suppose?" he said.

"Oh, yes, when I can't help it—after dinner, sometimes."

"Well, you sing poetry, don't you?"

"I don't know. One must have some words or other just to make her open her mouth. I never know what they're about. Why should I? Nobody ever pays the least attention to them or to the music either, except it be somebody that wants to marry you."

They soon reached the house, and by the time he had heard her sing, and his father and he were on their way home again, Thomas had had nearly enough of her. He thought her voice loud and harsh in speech, showy and distressing in song, and her whole being *bravura*. The contrasts with Lucy had come back upon him with a gush of memorial loveliness, for she still held the fortress of his heart.

They were scarcely seated in the railway carriage before the elder Worboise threw a shot across the bows of the younger.

"Well, Tom, my boy," he said, rubbing his lawyer palms, "how do you like Miss Hubbard?"

"Oh, very well, Father," answered Thomas, indifferently. "She's a jolly sort of girl."

"She is worth a hundred thousand," said his father.

"Girls?" asked Thomas.

"Pounds!"

Tom was now convinced of his father's design in taking him out for a holiday. Even now he shrunk from confession, but he thought he was very brave indeed, and replied, "Why, Father, a fellow has no chance with a girl like that, except he could ride, and knew all the slang of the hunting field as well as the racecourse."

"A few children will cure her of that," said his father.

"What I say is," persisted Thomas, "that she would never look at a clerk."

"If I thought you had any chance, I would buy you a commission in the Blues."

"It wants blue blood for that," said Thomas, whose heart notwithstanding danced at the sound of *commission*. Then, afraid lest he should lose the least feather of such a chance, he added hastily, "But any regiment would do."

"I daresay," returned his father, at right angles. "When you have made a little progress it will be time enough. She knows nothing about what you are now. Her father asked me, and I said I had not made up my mind yet what to do with you."

"But as I said before," resumed Thomas, fighting somewhat feebly, "I haven't a chance with her. She likes better to talk about horses than anything else, and I never had my leg across a horse's back in my life—as you know, Father," he added, in a tone of reproach.

"You mean, Tom, that I have neglected your education. Well, no longer. You shall go to riding school on Monday night."

Thomas, wretched creature, dallied with his father's proposal. He did not intend adopting the project, but the very idea of marrying a rich, fashionable girl like that, with a knight for a father, flattered him. Still more was he excited at the very possibility of wearing a uniform. And what might he not do with so much money? Then, when the thought of Lucy came, he soothed his conscience by saying to himself, "See how much I must love her when I am giving up all this for her sake!" Still his thoughts hovered about what he had said he was giving up. He went to bed on Sunday night, after a very pathetic sermon from Mr. Simon, with one resolution, and only one—namely, to go to the riding school on Monday night.

But something different was awaiting him.

30. An Explosion

Lucy Burton had been enjoying a delightful time of rest by the seaside. Nevertheless, she saw more clearly than ever that things must not go on unchanged between her and Thomas. She would give him one more chance, and if he did not accept it, she would not see him again, let come of it what would. She had not written to him since she came; that was one thing she could avoid. Now she resolved that she would write to him just before her return, and tell him that the first thing she would ask him when she saw him was whether he had told his father; upon his answer depended their future.

But what address she was to put upon the letter? She was not willing to write either to his home or to the countinghouse, for evident reasons. But her grandmother's last letter referred to an expected absence of Mr. Stopper, and she concluded (hastily, perhaps) that Mr. Worboise was from home, and that she might without danger direct a letter to Highbury.

Through some official at the Court of Probate, Mr. Worboise had heard of a caveat having been entered with reference to the will of Mr. Richard Boxall, deceased. Something must have occurred to irritate him against those whom he, with the law on his side, was so sorely tempted to wrong. Though not equal to Miss Hubbard, Lucy would have been a very good match, even in Mr. Worboise's eyes. On the other hand, however, if he could but make up, not his mind, but his conscience, to take Boxall's money, his son would be so much more the likely to secure Miss Hubbard. Together with what he himself could leave him, that would amount to a fortune of over two hundred thousand—sufficient to make his son somebody. If Thomas had only spoken in time, that is, while his father's conscience still spoke, and before he had cast eyes of ambition towards Sir Jonathan's bankers!

All that was wanted on the devil's side now was some personal quarrel with the rightful heirs. And if Mr. Worboise had not already secured that by means of Mr. Sargent's caveat, he received it on Monday morning. Before Thomas came down to breakfast, the postman had delivered a letter to him, with the Hastings postmark upon it.

When Thomas entered, and had taken his seat with the usual cool good-morning, his father tossed the letter to him across the table, saying, more carelessly than he felt, "Who's your Hastings correspondent, Tom?"

The question, coming with the sight of Lucy's handwriting, made the blood surge into Tom's face. His father was not in the way of missing anything that there was to see, and he saw Tom's face.

"A friend of mine," stammered Tom. "Gone down for a holiday."

"One of your fellow clerks?" asked his father, with a dry significance that indicated the possible neighborhood of annoyance, or worse. "I thought the writing of doubtful gender."

"No," faltered Tom, "he's not a clerk. He's a—well, he's a—teacher of music."

"Hm!" remarked Mr. Worboise. "How did you come to make his acquaintance, Tom?"

And he looked at his son with awful eyes, lighted from behind with growing suspicion.

Tom felt his jaws growing paralyzed. His mouth was as dry as his hand, and it seemed as if his tongue would rattle in it like the clapper of a cracked bell if he tried to speak. But he had nothing to say. A strange tremor went through him from top to toe, making him conscious of every inch of his body at the very moment when his embarrassment might have been expected to make him forget it altogether. His father kept his eyes fixed on him, and Tom's perturbation increased every moment.

"I think, Tom, the best way out of your evident confusion will be to hand me over that letter," said his father, in a cool determined tone, holding out his hand.

Tom had strength to obey only because he had not strength to resist. But he rose from his seat and would have left the room.

"Sit down, Son," said Mr. Worboise, in a voice that revealed growing anger, though he could not yet have turned over the leaf to see the signature. In fact, he was more annoyed at his son's cowardice than at his attempted deception. "*You* make a soldier!" he added, in a tone of contempt that stung Tom—not to the heart but to the backbone. When he had turned the leaf and seen the signature, he rose slowly from his chair and walked to the window, unfolding the letter as he went. After a while he turned again to the table and sat down. It was not Mr. Worboise's way to go into a passion when he had anything like reasonable warning that his temper was in danger.

"Tom, you have been behaving like a fool. Believe me, it's not safe amusement to go trifling with girls this way."

With a great effort, a little encouraged by the quietness of his father's manner, Tom managed to say, "I wasn't trifling."

"Do you mean to tell me," said his father, with more sternness than Tom had ever known him assume, "that you have come under obligation to this girl?"

"Yes, I have, Father."

"You fool! A dressmaker is no fit match for you."

"She's not a dressmaker," said Tom, with some energy, for he was beginning to grow angry, and that alone could give a nature like his courage in such circumstances. "She's a lady, if ever there was one."

"Stuff and nonsense!" said his father. "Don't get on your high horse with me. She's a beggar, if ever there was one."

Tom smiled unbelievingly, for now his tremor, under the influence of his wholesome anger, had abated. A little more, and he would feel himself a hero, stoutly defending his lady-love, fearless of consequences to himself. But he said nothing more just yet.

"You know better than I do, you think, you puppy! I tell you she's not worth a penny—no, nor her old grandmother either. A pretty mess you've made of it! You just sit down and write the poor girl that you're sorry you've been such a confounded fool, but there's no help for it."

"Why should I say that?"

"Because it's true. By all that's sacred!" said Mr. Worboise, with solemn fierceness. "You give up that girl or you give up me! I swear, if you carry on with that girl, you shall not cross my door as long as you continue with her, and not a penny shall you have out of my pocket. You'll have to live on your salary, my fine fellow, and perhaps that'll bring down your proud stomach a bit. Come, my boy," he added with sudden gentleness, "don't be a fool."

Whether Mr. Worboise meant all he said, at least he meant Thomas to believe all he said. And Thomas did believe it. All the terrible contrast between a miserable clerkship with lodging as well as food to be provided, and a commission in the army with unlimited pocket money, and the very name of business forgotten, rose before him. A conflict began within him which sent all the blood to the surface of his body, and made him as hot now as he had been cold before. He again rose from his seat, and this time his father, who saw that he had aimed well, did not prevent him from leaving the room. He only added, as his son reached the door, "Mark what I say, Tom; *I mean it.* And when I mean a thing, it's not my fault if it's not done. You can go to the riding school tonight, or you can look for other lodging."

Thomas stood on the heel of one foot and the toes of the other, holding the handle of the door in his hand till his father had done speaking. He then left the room without reply, closed the door behind him, took his hat and went out.

He was halfway to London before he remembered that he had left Lucy's letter unread in his father's hands. This crowned his misery, and he *almost* made up his mind to never enter the house again. He then thought how Lucy must love him when he had given up everything for her sake, knowing quite well too, that she was not to have any fortune after all! But he did *not* make up his mind—he had never yet made up his mind. Or, if he had, he unmade it again upon meeting the least difficulty. And now his "whole state of man" was in confusion. He went into the countinghouse as if he had been walking in a dream, sat down to his desk mechanically, and droned through the day. When six o'clock arrived, he no more knew what he was going to do than when he started on the morning.

But that evening he neither went to the riding school nor to look for lodging. In his very absence of purpose, he strolled up Guild Court to call upon Molken, who welcomed him even more heartily than usual. After a few minutes of conversation they went out together; having no plan of his own, Thomas was in the hands of anyone who had a plan. They betook themselves to one of their usual haunts. It was too early yet for play, so they called for some refreshment, and Thomas drank more than he had ever drunk before—not with any definite idea of drowning the trouble in his mind, but sipping and sipping from mere restlessness and the fluttering motions of a will unable to act.

They talked, not about gaming, but about politics and poetry, about Goethe and Heine. Molken exerted all his wit and all his sympathy to make himself agreeable to his dejected friend, urging him to rise above his dejection by an effort of the will; using in fact much the same arguments as Lady Macbeth when she tried to persuade her husband that the whole significance of things depended on how he chose to regard them.

At length, between Molken's talk and the gin, a flame of excitement began to appear in Thomas's weary existence; and almost at the same instant a sound of voices and footsteps was heard below, and several fellows came up the stairs eager for the excitement of play as a drunkard for his drink, all talking, laughing, chaffing. A blast of wind laden with rain from a laboring cloud which had crept up from the west and darkened the place smote on the windows, and soft yet keen the drops pattered on the glass. All outside was a chaos of windy mist and falling rain. They called for lights, and each man ordered his favorite drink. Two dirty packs of cards were produced from the archives of the house; drawing round the table they began playing very gently—and fairly, no doubt—and for some time Thomas went on winning.

There was not even the pretense of much money among them. Probably a few gold pieces was the most any of them had. When one of them had made something at this sort of small private game, he would try his luck at one of the more public tables. As the game went on and they grew more excit ed, they increased their stakes a little. Thomas began to lose more rapidly than he had won. He had two or three pounds in his pocket when he began, but all went now. He borrowed of Molken—lost; borrowed and lost, still sipping his gin and water, till Molken declared he had himself lost everything. Thomas laid his watch on the table, for himself and Molken—it was not of great value—a gift of his mother only. He lost it. What was to be done? He had one thing left—a ring of some value which Lucy had given him to wear for her. It had belonged to her mother. He pulled it off his finger, showed that it was a rose diamond, and laid it on the table. It followed the rest. He rose, caught up his hat, and, as so many gamblers had done before, rushed out into the rain and darkness.

Through all the fumes of the gin, the thought gleamed upon his cloudy mind that he ought to have received his quarter's salary that very day. If he had had that, what might he not have done? It was his, and yet he could not have it. His mind was all in a confused despair, ready to grasp at anything that offered him a chance of winning back what he had lost, of which Lucy's ring was his chief misery. Something drove him toward Guild Court, and before he knew where he was going, he was at Mrs. Boxall's door. He found it ajar, and walked up the stair to the sitting room. That door too was open, and there was no one there. But he saw from the box on the floor and the shawl on the table that Lucy had returned, and he supposed that her grandmother had gone upstairs with her. The same moment his eyes sought the wall, and there hung two keys, to the door of the countinghouse and to the safe.

He knew that there were eleven pounds odd shillings in the cashbox, for he had seen one of the other clerks count it; he knew that the cashbox was in the safe; he knew that the firm owed him twenty-five pounds; and he knew that he could replace it again before morning. He soon found himself standing before the safe with the key already in the lock, and the cold handle of the door in his hand. It was dark all around and within him. In another moment the door was open, and the contents of the cashbox—gold, silver, copper—in his pocket. He left the safe open with the key in it, and sped from the house.

He reached the room where he had left his friends, but it

was dark, and empty. They had gone to try their luck in a more venturous manner. He knew their haunts, followed and found them. His watch and ring were gone, but he learned where they were, and obtained what he needed to reclaim them on the morrow. Meantime he would play. He staked and won, lost, won again; doubled his stakes, won still; and when he left the house it was with a hundred pounds in his pocket and a gray dawn of wretchedness in his heart.

31. Mrs. Boxall and Mr. Stopper

Lucy was not upstairs with her grandmother when Thomas went into the room. She had arrived some time before, and had run across to the bookseller's to put Mattie to bed, leaving the door just ajar that she might not trouble her grandmother to come down and open it for her. She had come home hoping against hope that Thomas had by this time complied with her request—that he must have written to his father, and would appear in Guild Court some time during the evening with a response to her earnest appeal. When she had put the child to bed, she lingered a few moments with the bookseller in his back parlor.

"And how have you been, Mr. Kitely?"

"Oh, among the middlins, Miss, thank you. How's yourself been?"

"Quite well, and no wonder."

"I don't know that, Miss, with two young things a-pullin'of you all ways at once. I hope Mattie wasn't over and above troublesome to you."

"She was no trouble at all. You must have missed her, though."

"I couldn't ha' believed how I'd miss her. Do you know the want of her to talk to made me do what I ain't done for twenty year?"

"What's that, Mr. Kitely. Go to church of a Sunday?"

"More than that, Miss," answered the bookseller, laughing a

little sheepishly. "I've been to church of a weekday more than once. But then it wasn't a long rigmarole—he didn't give us a Sundayful of it, you know. We had just a little prayer, and a little chapter, and a little sermon—good sense too, upon my word. I know I altered a price or two in my next catalog when I come home again. I don't know as I was right, but I did it, just to relieve my mind and make believe I was doin' as the minister told me. If they was all like Mr. Fuller, I don't know as I should ha' the heart to say much against them."

"So it's Mr. Fuller's church you've been going to? I'm so glad. How often has he a service, then?"

"Every day, Miss. Think o' that. It don't take long though, as I tell you. But why should it? If there is any good in talking at all, it comes more of being the right thing than the muchness of it, as my father used to say. Says he, 'It strikes me, Jacob, there's more for your money in some o' these pamphlets, if you could only read 'em, than in some o' them elephants. When a little man with a shabby coat brings in off the stall one o' them sixpenny books in Latin, that looks so barbarious to me, and pops it pleased like into the tail of his coat—as if he meant to have it out again the minute he was out of the shop—then I thinks there's something in that little book, and something in that little man,' says Father, Miss. I've been thinking about it since, and I think Mr. Fuller's right about the short prayers. They're much more after the manner of the Lord's Prayer, anyhow. I never heard of anybody getting tired before *that* was over. As you are fond of church, Miss, you'd better drop into Mr. Fuller's tomorrow mornin'. If you go once, you'll go again."

She went out by the side door into the archway. As she opened it, a figure sped past her, fleet and silent. She started back. Why should it remind her of Thomas? And she found the door not as she left it.

"Has Thomas been here, Grannie?" she asked, with an alarm she could not account for.

"No, indeed. He has favored us with little of his company this many a day," answered her grannie, speaking out of the feelings which had gradually grown from the seeds sown by Stopper. "The sooner you're off with him, my dear, the better for you!" she continued. "He's no good, I doubt."

With a terrible sinking at the heart, Lucy heard her grandmother's words. But she would fight Thomas's battles to the last.

"If ever that man dares to say a word against Thomas in my hearing," she said, "I'll - I'll - I'll leave the room."

A lame and impotent conclusion! But Lucy carried it further than her words; for when Mr. Stopper entered the next morning, with a face scared into the ludicrous, she, without even waiting to hear what he had to say, though she foreboded evil, rose at once and left the room. Mr. Stopper stood and looked after her in dismayed admiration, for Lucy's anger was of such an unselfish and unspiteful nature, that it gave her a sort of piquancy.

"I hope I haven't offended the young lady," said Mr. Stopper, with some concern.

"Never you mind, Mr. Stopper. I've been giving her a hint about Thomas, and she's not got over it yet. But it's me you've got to do with, and I ain't got no fancies."

"It's just as well, perhaps, that she did walk herself away," said Mr. Stopper.

"You've got some news, Mr. Stopper. Sit ye down. Will you have a cup o'tea?"

"No, thank you. Where's the keys, Mrs. Boxall?" The old lady looked up at the wall, then back at Mr. Stopper. "Why, go along! There they are in your own hand."

"Yes, but where do you think I found them? Hanging in the door of the safe, and all the money gone from the cashbox. I haven't got over the shock yet."

"Why, good heavens!" said the old lady, who was rather out of temper with both herself and Lucy, "Mr. Stopper, you don't think I've been a robbing of your cashbox, do you?"

Mr. Stopper laughed aloud. "Well, Ma'am, that would be a roundabout way of coming by your own. I don't think we could make out a case against you, if you had. But, seriously, who came into the house after I left it? I hung the keys on that wall with my own hands."

"And I saw them there when I went to bed," said Mrs. Boxall, making a general impression ground for an individual assertion.

"Then somebody must have come in after you had gone to

bed—someone that knew the place. Did you find the street door had been tampered with?"

"Lucy opened it this morning."

Mrs. Boxall went to the door and called her granddaughter. Lucy came, thinking Mr. Stopper must be gone. When she saw him there, she would have left the room again, but her grandmother interfered. "Come here, Child," she said, peremptorily. "Was the house door open when you went down this morning?"

Lucy felt the foreboding—but she kept her self-command. "No, Grannie. The door was shut as usual."

"Did nobody call last night?" asked Mr. Stopper, who had his suspicions, and longed to have them confirmed.

"Nobody," answered Mrs. Boxall.

"A most unaccountable thing," said Stopper, rubbing his forehead.

"Have you lost much money?" asked the old lady.

"Oh, the money's a fleabite. But justice—that's the point," said Mr. Stopper, with his face full of meaning.

"Do you suspect anyone, Mr. Stopper?"

"I do. If Mr. Worboise were come," he continued, looking hard at Lucy, "he might be able to help us out with it. But it's an hour past his time, and he's not made his appearance yet. I fear he's been taking to fast ways lately. I'll just go across the court to Mr. Molken, and see if he knows anything about him."

"You'll oblige me," said Lucy, cold to the very heart, "by doing nothing of the sort. I will not have his name mentioned in the matter. Does anyone but yourself know of the—the robbery, Mr. Stopper?"

"Not a soul, Miss. I wouldn't do anything till I had been to you. I was here first, as I generally am."

"Then if I am to have anything to say at all," she returned with dignity, "let the matter rest at least till you have some certainty. If you don't, you will make suspicion fall on the innocent."

"Hoity-toity, Lass!" said her grandmother. "We're on our high horse, I believe."

Before she could say more, however, Lucy left the room. She just managed to reach her bed and fell fainting upon it.

Money had evidently, even in the shadow it cast before it, wrought no good effect upon old Mrs. Boxall. The bond between her and her granddaughter was already weakened, for she had never spoken thus to her till now.

"Never you mind what the girl says," she went on to Stopper. "The money's none of hers, and shan't be except I please. You just do as you think proper, Mr. Stopper. If that young vagabond has taken the money, why you take him, and see what the law will say to it. The sooner our Lucy is shut off him the better for her—and maybe for you too, Mr. Stopper," added the old lady, looking insinuatingly at him.

But whether the head clerk had any design upon Lucy or not, he seemed to think that her favor was of as much consequence as that of her grandmother. He might have reasoned that he could not expose Thomas without making Lucy his enemy; and Mrs. Boxall was old, and Lucy might take her place any day in the course of nature. Whereas as long as he kept the secret and strengthened the conclusions against Thomas without divulging them, he had a hold over Lucy, even a claim upon her gratitude which he might employ as he saw occasion. Therefore, when the clerk downstairs opened the moneybox, he found in it only a ticket with Mr. Stopper's initials and the sum abstracted, by which it was implied that Mr. Stopper had taken the contents for his own use. So, although it seemed odd that he should have emptied it of the whole sum, even to the few coppers, there was nothing to be said, and hardly anything to be conjectured even.

As Thomas did not make his appearance all day, not a doubt remained upon Mr. Stopper's mind that he had committed the robbery. But he was so well acquainted with the minutest details of the business that he knew very well that the firm had lost only the small amount taken. He chuckled over his own good fortune in getting rid of him so opportunely, for Tom would no longer stand in his way, even if he were to make advances to Lucy; she could never have anything more to do with a fellow who *could* be tried for burglary.

Mr. Stopper went upstairs in the evening after the counting house was closed. Lucy was not there. She had not left her room since the morning, and the old woman's tenderness had revived a little.

"Perhaps you'd better not hang them keys up there, Mr. Stopper. I don't care to have the blame of them. There's Lucy, poor dear, lying on her bed like a dead thing, and neither bit nor sup passed her lips all day. Take your keys away with you, Mr. Stopper, and don't you go and take away the young man's character."

"Indeed, I should be very sorry to, Mrs. Boxall. He hasn't been here all day, but I haven't even made a remark on his absence to anyone."

"That's very right, Mr. Stopper. The young gentleman may be at home with a headache."

"Very likely," answered Mr. Stopper, dryly. "Good night, Mrs. Boxall. And I'll just put the keys in my pocket and take them home with me."

"Do that, Mr. Stopper, and good night to you. And if the young man comes back tomorrow, don't ye take no notice of what's come and gone. If you're sure he took it, you can keep it off his salary, with a wink for a warning, you know."

"All right, Ma'am," said Mr. Stopper, taking his departure in less good humor than he showed.

For some time Lucy was so stunned as to be past conscious suffering. For one half hour, she would be declaring him unworthy of occasioning her trouble; for the next she would be accusing his attachment to her, and her own want of decision, as the combined causes of his ruin—for as ruin she could not but regard such a fall as his. She had no answer to her letter—heard nothing of him all day, and in the evening her grandmother brought her the news that Thomas had not been seen that day. She turned her face away toward the wall, and her grandmother left her, grumbling at girls generally, and girls in love especially.

32. THE ELDER SISTER

Mattie had expected Lucy to call for her in the forenoon and take her out to Wyvil Place to see Miriam. When Lucy did not come, she ran up and knocked at her door. Hearing from Mrs. Boxall, however, that Miss Burton was too tired to go out with her, she turned in some disappointment and sought Mr. Spelt.

"Well, Mother, how do you do?" she asked, lifting up her little gray face toward the watch tower of the tailor.

"Quite well, Mattie. And you look well," answered Mr. Spelt.

"And I am well, I assure you; better than I ever expected to be in this world. I mean to come up beside you a bit. I want to tell you something."

"I don't know, Mattie," answered Mr. Spelt with some embarrassment. "Is it anything in particular?"

"In particular! Well, I should think so," returned Mattie, with a triumph just dashed with displeasure, for she had not been accustomed to any hesitation on the part of Mr. Spelt. Then lowering her voice to a keen whisper she added, "I've been to see God in His own house."

"Been to church, have you?" said Mr. Spelt.

"No, Mr. Spelt," she answered with dignity, "I've not been to church. You don't call that God's house, do you? It's nothing but a little shop like your own. But God's house! Take me up, I say. Don't make me shout such things in the open street."

Thus adjured, Mr. Spelt could stand out no longer. He stooped over his threshold and lifted Mattie towards him. But the moment her head reached the level of his floor, she understood it all—in her old place in the corner sat little Poppie.

"Well!" said Mattie. "Will you set me down again, if you please, Mr. Spelt?"

"I think, perhaps," said the tailor meekly, holding the child still suspended in the air, "I could find room for you both—try the corner opposite the door there, Mattie."

"Put me down," insisted Mattie, in such a tone that Mr. Spelt dared not keep her in suspense any longer, but lowered her gently to the ground. All the time Poppie had been staring with great black eyes, which seemed to have grown much larger during her illness, and, of course, saying nothing.

Instead of turning and walking away with her head high, Mattie began a parley with the offending Mr. Spelt. "I have heard, Mother—Mr. Spelt—that you should be off with the old love before you're on with the new. You never told me what you were about."

"But you was away from home, Mattie."

"You could have written. It would only have cost a penny."

"Well, Mattie, shall I turn Poppie out?"

"Oh! I don't want you to turn her out. You would say I drove her to the streets again."

"Do you remember, Mattie, that you wouldn't go to that good lady's house because she didn't ask Poppie too? Do you?"

A moment's delay in the child's answer revealed shame, but she was ready in a moment. "Hers is a big house. That's my very own corner."

"Don't you see how ill Poppie is?"

"Well!" said the hard little thing.

Mr. Spelt began to be a little vexed. She was turning to go away, when he spoke in a tone that stopped her. "Mattie, do you remember the story Somebody told us about the ragged boy that came home again, and how his brother, with the good clothes, was offended?"

"I don't know. There's some difference, I'm sure. I don't think you're telling the story right. I'll just go and look. I can read it for myself, Mr. Spelt."

Mattie walked away to her house, with various backward tosses of the head. Mr. Spelt drew his head into his shell, troubled at Mattie's naughtiness. Poppie stared at him, but said nothing, for she had nothing to say.

Mattie entered the bookshop and went to her own room, where she took hold of a huge family Bible and heaved it upon her bed. Somehow she found the place, and spelled the story to discover whether the tailor had garbled it to her condemnation. But the story itself laid hold upon her little heart, and she found a far deeper condemnation there than she had found in her friend's reproof. About half an hour after, she ran—Mattie seldom ran—past Mr. Spelt and Poppie and knocked at Mrs. Boxall's door.

Lucy was still lying on her bed when she heard little knuckles at her door, and next felt a tiny hand steal into hers. She opened her eyes, and saw Mattie by her bedside. Nor was she too much absorbed in her own griefs to note that the child had hers too.

"What is the matter with you, Mattie, my dear?" she asked in a faint voice.

Mattie burst into tears—a rare proceeding. "I've been so naughty, Miss Burton!"

Lucy raised herself and took the child's hand. "I'm sorry to hear that, Mattie. What have you done?"

"Poppie . . . far country . . . elder brother. . . . "

These were the only words Lucy could hear for the sobs of the poor child. Hence she could only guess at the cause of her grief, and her advice must be general. "If you have done wrong to Poppie, or anyone, you must go and tell her so, and try to make up for it."

"Yes, I will, for I can't bear it," answered Mattie, beginning to recover herself. "Think of doing the very same as the one I was so angry with when Mother read the story! I couldn't bear to see Poppie in my place in Mother's shop, and I was angry, and wouldn't go in. But I'll go now."

She walked right under Mr. Spelt's door, and called aloud, but with a wavering voice, "Mother, take me up. I'm very sorry." A pair of arms hoisted Mattie into the heaven of her repentant desire, and she crawled on her hands and knees towards Poppie.

"How do you do, Prodigal?" she said, putting her arms round the bewildered Poppie, who had no idea what she meant. "I'm very glad to see you home again. Put on this ring, and we'll both be good children to Mother there."

So saying, she took a penny ring from her finger with a bit of red and two bits of green glass in it and put it on Poppie, who submitted speechless, but was pleased with the glitter of the toy.

"Mother," Mattie went on, "I was behaving like—like—a wicked Pharisee and Sadducee. I beg your pardon, Mother. I will be good. May I sit in the corner by the door?"

The little tailor was greatly moved, believing more than ever before in the wind that blows where it will. "I think if I were to move a little, you could sit in the corner by the window, and then you would see into the court better."

So Mattie and Poppie sat side by side, and the heart of the tailor had a foretaste of heaven. Presently Mattie began to talk to Poppie, and before long had taken her in hand.

There was more hope for Poppie, and Spelt too, now that Mattie was in the work, for there is no teacher of a child like a child. All the tutors of Oxford and Cambridge will not bring on a baby as a baby a year older will. The childlike is as essential an element in the teacher as in the scholar.

When Mattie had left her, Lucy again threw herself down and turned her face to the wall as Mattie's words filled her troubled mind. For who was a prodigal son but her lost Thomas? Lost, yes, but *found* was in the parable as well. Thomas might be found again. And if the angels in heaven rejoiced over the finding of such a lost wanderer, why should she cut the cable of love and let him go adrift from her heart? Was he not more likely to come back someday if she went on loving him? The recent awakening of Lucy's spiritual nature—what would be called by some her conversion—had been interpenetrated with the image, the feeling, the subjective presence of Thomas. She thought so much of him that she could not leave him out now. If there were joy in heaven over him, she too might rejoice over him when he came back; and if the Father received the prodigal with all His heart, she too might receive him with all hers. But she would have no right to receive him thus if she did nothing to restore him. Her conscience began to reproach her that she had not before done all that she could to reclaim him, and if she only knew the way, she was now at least prepared to spend and be spent for him.

But she had already done all that she was, at this juncture of his history, to be allowed to do for the wretched trifler. God had taken the affair out of her hands, and had put it into those of somewhat harder teachers.

33. MR. SARGENT LABORS

When Mr. Worboise found that Thomas did not return that first night, he concluded at once that he had made up his mind to thwart him in his cherished plan, to refuse Laura Hubbard, and marry the girl whom his father disliked. He determined at once, even supposing he might be premature as regarded the property, to have the satisfaction of causing the Boxalls sharp uneasiness, at least. His son would not have dared to go against his wishes but for the enticements of "that minx," in the confidence that her uncle's property was about to be hers. He would teach both of them a lesson. He thought himself into a rage over her interference with his plans, and judged himself an injured person. He was now ready to push his rights to the uttermost, to exact the pound of flesh that the law awarded him. The second morning after Thomas' disappearance, he went and propounded the will.

In due time this came to the knowledge of Mr. Sargent. He wrote Mrs. Boxall a stiff business letter acquainting her with the fact, and then called upon Mr. Worboise to appeal for an arrangement. Having learned the nature of the will, he saw that almost any decent division of the property in justice would be better than a contest. Mr. Worboise received him with graciousness, talked lightly of the whole as a mere matter of business about which there was no room for disputing, smiled aside every attempt made by Mr. Sargent, and made him understand (without saying a word to that effect) that he was prepared to push matters to the extreme. He even allowed that he had reasons beyond the value of the money for setting about the matter in the coolest, most legal fashion in the world.

Mr. Sargent went away baffled, to ponder upon what grounds he could oppose the grant of probate.

While Mr. Sargent was having his interview, Mr. Stopper was awaiting his departure in the clerk's room. While Mr. Stopper came to plead the case of the widow and orphan, he must be especially careful for his own sake not to give offense. Him too, Mr. Worboise received with the greatest good humor, assured him that there was no mistake in the matter and no flaw in the will. He had drawn it up himself, and had, at his friend's request, entered his own name. His friend might have done it as a joke, but he had no intention of forgoing his rights, or turning out of Luck's way when she met him in the teeth. On the contrary, he meant to have the money and to use it, for it could not have been a joke that his friend had omitted his mother and his niece. He must have had some good reason for doing so, and he was not one to treat a dead friend's feelings with disrespect, and so on, all in pleasant words and with smiling delivery, ended by a hearty, "Good morning."

At the door Stopper turned and said, "I hope nothing is amiss with your son, Mr. Worboise. I hope he is not ill."

"Why do you ask?" returned Mr. Worboise, just a little staggered, for he was not prepared to hear that Thomas was missing from Bagot Street as well as from home. When he heard of Tom's absence, however, he merely nodded his head, saying, "Well, Mr. Stopper, he's too old for me to horsewhip him. I don't know what the young rascal is after. I leave him in your hands. I don't know that it wouldn't be the best thing to discharge him. It would be a lesson to him, the young scapegoat! He's really gone too far, though you and I can make allowances, eh, Stopper?"

Mr. Stopper was wise enough not to tell what even Mr. Worboise would have considered bad news, for the lawyer had a reverence for locks and money, and regarded any actionable tampering with either as disgraceful. "Besides," thought Stopper, "if it was only to spite the young jackanapes, I could almost marry that girl without a farthing. But I shouldn't have a chance if I were to tell about Tom."

Mr. Worboise was uneasy, though. He told his wife what had passed between Tom and himself, but enjoyed her discomfiture at the story. He said spitefully, as he left the room, "Shall I call on Mr. Simon as I go to town, and send him up, Mrs. Worboise?"

His wife buried her face in her pillow and made no reply. But he did call on Mr. Simon and sent him to his wife.

Mr. Simon inquired, and also discovered that Thomas had vanished from the countinghouse. Thereupon, a more real grief than she had ever known seized the mother's heart; her conscience reproached her as often as Mr. Simon hinted that it was a judgment upon her for having been worldly in her views concerning her son.

Mr. Worboise comforted himself by thinking, "The young rascal's old enough to take care of himself. He knows what he's about too. He thinks to force me to a surrender by starving me of his precious self. We'll see. I've no doubt he's harbored in that old woman's house. She'll find I'm not one to take liberties with!"

The best that Mr. Sargent could do was to resist probate on the ground of the uncertainty of the testator's death, delaying the execution of the will. He had little hope, however, of any ultimate success, except by shaming Mr. Worboise into such an arrangement.

Mrs. Boxall sent for Mr. Sargent and begged him to do his best for them, saying that if he were successful, she would gladly pay him whatever he demanded. He repudiated all idea of payment, however, and privately considered himself only too fortunate to be permitted to call as often as he pleased, for then he generally saw Lucy. But he never made the smallest attempt to renew even the slightest friendship which had formerly existed between them.

The first effect of her son's will upon Mrs. Boxall was rage and indignation against Mr. Worboise, who, she declared, must have falsified it. She would not believe that Richard could have omitted her name and put in that of his attorney. The moment she heard the evil tidings, she rose and went for her bonnet, with the full intention of giving the rascal a bit of her mind. If there was justice to be had on the earth she would have it, if she went to the Queen herself to get it. It was all that her granddaughter and Mr. Stopper could do to prevent her. However, the paroxysm of her present rage passed off in tears followed by gloomy fits, interspersed with outbreaks of temper against Lucy, although she spoke of her as a poor dear orphan reduced to beggary by the wickedness and greed of lawyers in general, who lived like cannibals upon the flesh and blood of innocents. In vain would Lucy try to persuade her that they were no worse now than they had been, reminding her that they were even happier together before the expectation of plenty came to trouble them.

On Lucy this change of prospect had little effect. Her heart was too much occupied with a far more serious affair to be moved about money. Had everything been right with Thomas, she would have built many a castle of things she would do; but till Thomas was restored to her by being brought to his right mind, no one thing seemed more worth doing than another. Sadness settled upon her, but she went about her work as before, and did what she could to keep sorrow from hurting others. She sought comfort in holding up her care to God, and what surer answer to such prayer could there be than that she had strength to do her work? We are saved by hope, and Lucy's hope never died. As often as she could, she went to Mr. Fuller's church, and she never returned without what was worth going for—fresh strength, and fresh resolution to do right. And the strength came chiefly as she believed more and more in God's care She believed that the power which made her a living soul was not, could not be, indifferent to her sorrows—however much she might have deserved them—because they were for her good. And if He cared that she suffered, if He knew that it was sad and hard to bear, she could bear it without a word.

Mr. Sargent was soon thoroughly acquainted with all Mrs. Boxall's affairs. And he had little hope of success in regard to the will when he found that she had no vouchers to produce for her own little property placed in her son's hands. He was prepared to offer to withdraw from the contest, provided the old lady's rights were acknowledged. With this view he called once more upon Mr. Worboise, who received him just as graciously as before.

"Mrs. Boxall informs me, Mr. Worboise, that her son, at the

time of his death, was, and had been for many years, in possession of some property of hers, amounting to somewhere between two and three thousand pounds. She does not know the amount exactly, but that could be easily calculated from the interest he was in the habit of paying her."

"But whatever acknowledgment she holds for the money will render the trouble unnecessary," said Mr. Worboise, who saw well enough to what Mr. Sargent was coming.

"It was very wrong of a man of business, or anybody, indeed, but unfortunately her son never gave her any acknowledgment in writing."

"Oh!" said Mr. Worboise with a smile. "Then I don't exactly see what can be done. It is very awkward."

"You can be easily satisfied of the truth of the statement."

"I am afraid not, Mr. Sargent."

"She is a straightforward lady, and—"

"I have reason to doubt it. At all events, seeing she considers the entire property hers by right, an opinion in which you sympathize with her, it will not be so surprising if I should be jealous of her making a statement for the sake of securing a part of those rights. Let her produce her vouchers, I say."

"Mr. Stopper may be able to prove it. There will be enough evidence of the interest paid."

"As interest, Mr. Sargent? I suspect it will turn out to be only an annuity that the good fellow allowed her, notwithstanding the reasons he must have had for omitting her name from his will."

"Our cause is so far from promising that I should advise Mrs. Boxall to be content with her own, and push the case no further."

"Quite right, Mr. Sargent. The most prudent advice you can give her."

"You will then admit the debt, and let the good woman have her own?"

"Admit the debt by no means, but certainly let her have her own as soon as she proves what is her own," answered Mr. Worboise with a smile.

"Mr. Worboise," said Mr. Sargent, doing his best to keep his temper, "I believe her statement to be perfectly true."

"I believe you, Mr. Sargent, but I do not believe the woman," returned Mr. Worboise, again smiling.

"But you know it will not matter much, because, coming into this property as you do, you can hardly avoid making some provision for those so nearly related to the testator, and who were dependent upon him during his lifetime. You cannot leave the old lady to starve."

"We can discuss that when my rights are acknowledged. Till then I decline to entertain the question."

There was something in Mr. Worboise's manner, and an irrepressible flash of his eye, that convinced Mr. Sargent that there was nothing to be got from him. He therefore left him, and started a new objection in opposing the probate of the will. He argued the probability of all or one of the daughters surviving the father; not of their being yet alive, but of having outlived him.

The property would come to Mr. Worboise only in the case of all those mentioned in the will dying before Mr. Boxall, for a man can only will that which is his own at the time of his death. If Mr. Boxall died before any of his family, Mr. Worboise had nothing to do with it, and it would go after the last survivor's death to her heirs. Hence, if any of the daughters survived the mother and father, if only for one provable moment, the property would be hers, and go to her heir, her grandmother. The whole affair then turned upon the question whether it was more likely that Richard Boxall or every one of his daughters died first.

Mr. Sargent was not in a good practice, and would scarcely have been able to meet the various expenses of the plea. But he had already told Mr. Morgenstern of the peculiar position in which Lucy and her grandmother found themselves. Now Mr. Morgenstern was not only rich, but he felt that he had something to spare. Lucy was a great favorite with him, and so was Mr. Sargent. He could not but see that Sargent was fond of Lucy, and that he was suffering from some measure of repulse. He therefore hoped to at least give the son of his old friend a chance of commending himself to the lady by putting it in his power to plead her cause. And it did not put Mr. Morgenstern to an expense that cost him two thoughts. Even if it had been serious, the pleasure with which his wife regarded his generosity would have been to him reward enough.

34. THOMAS

When Thomas left the gambling house, he had plenty of money and no home. On this raw morning when nature seemed to be nothing but a drizzle diluted with gray fog, he had nowhere to go, and indeed, he had a good many places where he must *not* go. Nor even now could he feel it much, for, weary and sick, all he wanted was some place to lay down his head and go to sleep. He was conscious of an inclination to dive into every courtyard he passed—of a proclivity toward darkness, as if the darkness within him had come at last to the outside and swathed all in its funereal folds.

As the light grew, his terror increased. There was no ground for immediate alarm, for no one yet knew what he had done. He felt safer where the streets were narrow and the houses rose high to shut out the dayspring. He hurried on, not yet knowing what he was, only seeing revelation at hand clothed in terror. And the end of it was that he buried his head in the public house where the mischief of the preceding night had begun, and was glad to lie down in a filthy bed.

When he woke, it was afternoon; he could not tell where he was, and the horror came and crushed his whole being. The morning had vanished, and with it his only chance to return the money unseen. All must be known now, and he would be a wanted man. For the first time in his life, his satisfaction with himself gave way utterly. Up to this point, he had never seen himself as contemptible. Even yet, it was the disgrace, and not the sin, that troubled him. But honor, although a poor substitute for honesty or religion, is yet something, and the fear of disgrace is a good sword to hang over the heads of those who need such reminders.

Thomas' heart burned with shame. In vain he tried to persuade himself that he was not himself when he took the money. He knew that no defense of that sort would have any influence in restoring him to the position he had lost. He was an outcast. He lay in moveless torture. Wide awake, he did not think of rising, for there was nothing for him to do and nowhere for him to go. At length he heard voices in the room below him—voices he knew, and was sick of, for he was lying over the scene of last night's temptation. He sprang from the bed, hurried on his clothes, crept down the stairs, paid for his lodging, and went into the street.

But he was too near his former haunts, and the officers of justice must already be after him. He turned from one narrow street into another, and wandered on till he came where the bowsprit of a vessel projected over a wall across a narrow lane near the Thames. The sun was going down, and the friendly darkness was at hand, but he could not rest. Since he knew nothing of the other side of the river, it seemed to him that he would be safer there. He would take a boat across. He passed several stairs, turned down the next opening, found a boat, and telling the waterman to take him across the river, sat down in the stern.

The sun was going down behind the dome of St. Paul's, and all the brown masts and spars of the vessels shone like a forest of gold-barked trees in winter. The dark river caught the light and threw it shimmering up on the great black hulls, which shone again in the water below. The Thames, with all its dirt and all its dead, looked radiant. What was it to him, despised in his own eyes, that the sun shone? He looked up at the sky only to wish for the night.

The boatman had been rowing up the quiet water as the tide hurried out, but now he was crossing. As they drew near the Surrey side, all at once Thomas found himself in a multitude of boats, flitting like waterflies on the surface of a quiet pool. What they were about he could not see. Now they would gather in dense masses, the air filled with shouting, expostulation, and good-humored chaff and abuse. Guns were firing, flags were flying, Thames liveries gleaming here and there. The boats were full of men, women and children. It was an aquatic crowd—a people exclusively living on and by the river—assembled to see a rowing match between two of their own class for a boat, probably given by the publicans of the neighborhood—who would reap ten times the advantage.

But Thomas did not see the race, because something else happened. In a boat a little way up was a large family party, and in it a woman who was more taken up with a baby in her arms than with all that was going on around her. In consequence of her absorption in the merry child who was springing with all the newly discovered delight of feet and legs, she was so dreadfully startled when the bows of another boat struck the gunwhale just at her back, that she sprang half up from her seat and the baby jerked from her arms into the river.

Thomas was gazing listlessly at the water when he saw the child swccp past him a foot or so below the surface. The next instant he was in the water. He caught the child, then let himself drift with the tide till he came upon the cable of a vessel that lay a hundred yards below. Boats came rushing about him. In a moment the child was taken from him and handed across half a dozen of them to its mother, and in another moment, he was in a boat. When he came to himself, a gin-faced, elderly woman, in a threadbare tartan shawl, was wiping his face with a handkerchief, and murmuring some feminine words over him, while a coarse-looking man was holding a broken cup with some spirit in it to his mouth.

"Go ashore with the gentleman, Jim," said the woman. "There's the India Arms. That's a respectable place. You must go to bed, my dear, till you gets your clothes dried."

"I haven't paid my man," said Tom feebly. He was now shivering with cold, for after the night and day he had spent, he was in no condition to resist the effects of the water.

"Oh, we'll pay 'im. Come along," cried several voices. He looked up and saw that they were alongside a great barge which was crowded with row after row of dirty little creatures. "Come this way—solid barges, Sir, all the way. Ketch hold of the gen'lm'n's 'and, Sammy. There. Now, Bill."

They hauled and lifted Thomas onto the barge, then conducted him along the side across to the next yawning wooden gulf, and so over about seven barges to a plank which led to the first floor of a public house. There his two ragged little conductors left him.

Through an empty bar he followed the man who had given him the gin. The man said to the woman who was pumping a pot of beer, "This gen'leman, Mrs. Cook, 'as been and just took a child out o' the water, Ma'am. 'e ain't got a change o' clothes in 'is wescut-pocket, so if you'll do what ye can for 'im, there's many on us'll be obliged to ye, ma'am."

"No! Whose child was it, Jim?"

"I don't know as you know 'er, Ma'am. The man's name's Potts—keeps a public down about Lime'us, someveres."

Thomas stood shivering—glad, however, that the man should represent his case for him.

"The gentleman 'ad better get to bed till we get 'is clothes dried for 'im," said the landlady. "I think that's the best we can do for 'im."

"Take a drop o' summat, Sir," said the man, turning to Thomas. "They keeps a good licker 'ere. Put a name upon it, Sir."

"Well, I'll have a small glass of pale brandy," said Thomas. It was served immediately; he drank it, and proceeded to put his hand in his pocket—no easy matter in the state of his garments.

"I'm a goin' to pay for this," interposed the man, in a determined tone, and Thomas was hardly in a condition to dispute it.

The landlady said, "Will you walk this way, Sir?" Thomas followed, and found himself in a neat room, where he was only too glad to undress and go to bed. As he pulled off his coat, it occurred to him to see that his money was safe. He had put it, mostly in sovereigns, into a pocketbook in his breastcoat pocket.

It was gone. His first conclusion was that the man had taken it. He rushed back into the bar, but he was not there. In the midst of his despair, a fresh pang at the loss of his money shot through Thomas' soul. But he soon came to the conclusion that the man had not taken it. It was far more likely to have slipped from his pocket as he went overboard. This was the reward of his first act of self-forgetfulness; yet sometimes the best thing that can happen to a man is to lose his money. God may regard it as the first step to the stair by which the man shall rise above it. Thomas began to feel that he had no ground under his feet—the one necessary condition before such a man could find a true foundation. Until he lost the money, he did not know how much, even in his misery, the paltry hundred pounds had been to him. Now it was gone, and things looked black indeed. He emptied his pockets of two or three sovereigns and some silver, put his clothes out at the door, and got into bed. There he fell to thinking.

Thomas was comforted in these moments of hopeless degradation suddenly to find himself, as the result of a noble deed, a sympathetic and admiring public. No matter that they were not of his class, nor yet that Thomas was not the man to do the human brotherhood justice; he could not help feeling the present power of humanity, the healing medicine of approbation in the faces of the common people who had witnessed and applauded his deed.

It had been given to him so that a touch of light might streak the dark cloud of his fate, that he might not despise himself utterly and act as unredeemable—kill himself or plunge into wickedness to drown his conscience. Any good deed partakes of the life whence it comes, and is a good to him who has done it. This act might be a beginning.

Poor weak Thomas, when he got his head on the pillow, began to cry. He pitied himself for the helplessness to which he was now reduced, and a new phase of despair filled his soul. He felt that his ill-gotten gain had turned to rubbish in his hands. What he was to do he could not tell. He was tolerably safe for the night, and worn and weary, soon fell into a sleep which not even a dream disturbed.

When he woke all was dark, and he welcomed the darkness as a friend to that soothed and comforted him. If it were only always dark! If he could find some cave to creep into where he might feed upon the friendly gloom! Thomas leaned on his elbow and saw that his clothes had been placed by him while he slept. He rose and put them on, opened the door of his room, saw a light somewhere, approached it softly, and found himself in a small room, with a large oriel window. The day had changed from gold to silver; the wide expanse of the great river lay before him, and up and across, it gleamed in the thoughtful radiance of the moon. Never was there a picture of lovelier peace. But Thomas could not feel this, for its very repose was a reproach to him. He was degraded to all eternity.

Then it struck him that all was strangely still. Not only was there no motion on the river, but there was no sound, and the silence laid sudden hold upon him. He found himself all alone with that white thing in the sky, and he turned from the glorious window to go down to the bar. But all the house was dark, and he alone was awake and wandering in the dead waste of the night. A horror seized him when he found that he was alone. Why should he fear? The night covered him, but there was God. Or rather, the fear of the unknown God, manifested in the face of a nature which was strange and unfriendly to the evildoer. It is to God alone that a man can flee from such terror, but to God Thomas dared not or could not flee.

Full of the horror of wakefulness in the midst of sleeping London, he felt his way back to the room he had just left, threw himself down, and closed his eyes to shut out everything. His own room at Highbury, even that of his mother with Mr. Simon talking in it, rose before him like a haven of refuge. But between him and that haven lay an impassable gulf. No more returning thither—he must leave the country. And Lucy? He must vanish from her eyes, that she might forget him and marry someone else. Was not that the only justice left him to do her?

A fresh billow of shame rushed over him. In the person of Lucy he condemned himself afresh to ineffaceable shame. The pale moon, the spectral masts, the dead houses on the opposite shore, the glitter of the river—all gleamed in upon him, and a fresh terror of loneliness in the presence of the incomprehensible overcame him. He fell upon his knees and sought to pray; doubtless to the ear that is keen with mercy it sounded as prayer, though to him that prayed it seemed that no winged thought arose to the Infinite from a heart as dry as dust. Mechanically, at length, all feeling gone, both of fear and of hope, he went back to his room and his bed.

When he woke in the morning his landlady's voice was in his ears. "Well, how do we find ourselves today, Sir? None the worse, I hope?"

He opened his eyes. She stood by his bedside, with her short arms set like handles of an urn. Hers was a common face, with eyes that stood out with fatness. Yet Thomas was glad to see them looking at him, for there was kindness in them.

"I am all right, thank you," he said.

"Where will you have your breakfast?" she asked.

"Where you please," answered Thomas.

"Will you come down to the parlor, then? Jim Salter's inquirin' after ye."

"Who?" said Thomas with a start.

"The man who brought you in last night, Sir. I told him to wait till I came up."

"I shall be down in one minute," said Thomas, a hope of his money darting to his mind.

He rose from bed, descended the stairs, and passed through the bar to the little room at the back. Against the counter leaned Jim, smoking a short pipe, with his hand upon a pot of beer. When Thomas entered, he touched his cap, saying, "Glad to see you lookin' middlin', Guv'nor. Is there anything I can do for you today?"

"Come into the room here," said Thomas, "and have something. I haven't had my breakfast yet."

Salter followed him with his pewter in his hand. Thomas disliked his appearance less than on the preceding evening. What was unpleasant in his face was chiefly owing to smallpox. He was dirty and looked like a beer drinker, but there seemed no harm in him. He sat down near the door, and put his pot on the windowsill.

"I was in hopes you had heard of something I lost, but I suppose it's at the bottom of the river," said Thomas.

"Not your watch?" asked Salter with some appearance of anxious interest.

"A great deal worse," answered Thomas. "My pocketbook."

"Much in it?" asked Jim with a genuine look of sympathetic discomfiture.

"More than I like to think of. Look," said Thomas, turning out the contents of his pocket. "That is all I have in the world."

"More than I ever had," returned Salter. "Keep me a

month."

Thomas relapsed into thought. This man was the only resemblance of a friend he had left. He did not like to let him go loose in the wilds of London without the possibility of finding him again. If this man vanished, the only link, Thomas felt, between him and the world of men would be broken.

"Where do you live?" he asked.

"Stepney way," answered Jim.

"I want to see that part of London. What do you work at?"

"Oh, nothin' perticlar, Guv'nor. Take a day at the docks now and then. Any job that turns up. I'm not perticlar. I like to be movin'. I had a month in Bermondsey last—in a tanyard, you know. I knows a bit of everything."

"Well, where are you going now?"

"Nowheres—anywheres you like, Gov'nor. If you want to see them parts, as you say, there's nobody knows 'em better than I do."

"Come then," said Thomas. But here a thought struck him. "Wouldn't it be better, though," he added, "if I put on workman's clothes?"

Jim looked at him. Thomas felt himself wince under his gaze, but was relieved when he said with a laugh, "You won't look much like a workman, put on what you like."

Jim had been observing him, and had associated this wish of Thomas' with the pocketbook, and his furtive troubled looks. But Jim was as little particular about his company as about anything else, and it was of no consequence to him whether Thomas had deeper reasons than curiosity for seeking to disguise himself.

"I tell you what," he said, "if you want to keep quiet for a day or two, I'm your man."

By this time Thomas had finished his breakfast. "Well," he said, rising, "if you've nothing particular to do, I'll give you a day's wage to go with me. Only let's get into Stepney, or away somewhere in that direction, a soon as possible."

Jim called the landlady, they settled Tom's very moderate bill, and together they went out into a London he had never seen before.

35. Poppie Chooses a Profession

When roses again bloomed on Poppie's cheeks, she began to grow restless, and the heart of the tailor grew anxious. It was very hard for a wild thing to be kept in a cage against her will. He therefore began to reason with himself as to what ought to be done with her. So soon as she was strong again all her wandering habits would return, and he must make some provision for them. The streets were her home, and they made life pleasant to her. And yet it would not do to let her run idle.

In a manner undefinable by Mr. Spelt, his love had broken down a silent barrier within Poppie; where she had not spoken, and seemed as if she would never speak, now she spoke, and seemed as if she had always spoken. Meantime the influence of Mattie had grown upon Poppie. Remembering her own childhood, Mattie sought to interest her pupil in her dolls, proceeding to dress one (which she called Poppie) in a gorgeous scarlet cloth. And Poppie was interested. The color drew her to the process. By degrees, she took a part—first only in waiting on Mattie, then in sewing on a button or string, at which she was very awkward.

A certain amount of self-consciousness began to dawn during the doll dressing, and Poppie's redemption first showed itself in a desire to be dressed. The tailor detected this interest as a most hopeful sign, and made a dress ready for her. The result was altogether admirable in Poppie's eyes, though somewhat strange in those of others—a scarlet jacket of fine cloth trimmed with black, and a black skirt.

This dress Mr. Spelt readied in view of a contemplated walk with Poppie. He was going to take her to Highgate on a Sunday morning, with his Bible in his pocket. Mr. Spelt was an apparent anomaly, loving his New Testament, yet having no fancy for going to church. The Spirit of God teaches men in a thousand ways, and Mr. Spelt knew some of the highest truths better than nine of ten clergymen. Yet Mr. Spelt was inwardly reproached that he did not go to church, and made the attempt several times, with the result that he doubted the truth of the whole thing for half the week after.

It was a bright frosty morning, full of life and spirit, when the father and daughter set out for Highgate. Poppie was full of spirit, and once she darted a hundred yards in advance upon another little girl who was listlessly standing at a crossing, took the broom from her hand, and began to sweep vigorously. Nor did she cease sweeping till she had made the crossing clean, and her father had come up. She held out her hand to him, received in it a ready penny, and tossed it to the girl. Then she put her hand in his again, and trotted along with him, excited and sedate both at once.

"Would you like to sweep a crossing, Poppie?" asked he.

"Wouldn't I just, Daddie? I should get no end o' ha'pence."

"What would you do with them when you got them?"

"Give them to poor girls. I don't want them, you see, now I'm a lady."

"What makes a lady of you, then?"

"I've got a father of my own, all to myself. And look at my jacket."

Perhaps Mr. Spelt thought that her contempt of money (or rather, want of faith in it) went a good way to make her a very peculiar lady indeed, but he did think that he would buy her a broom if the attraction of the streets grew too strong for Guild Court.

This day things did not go quite to the tailor's mind. He took Poppie to an arbor behind an old favored public house, sat down with her, pulled out his Bible, and began to read to her. But he could not get her to mind him. Every other moment she was up and out of the arbor, now after one thing or another—a spider busy with a fly, a chicken escaped from the henhouse, or a passing sparrow.

"Come along, Poppie," said her father. "I want you to listen."

"Yes, Daddie," Poppie would answer, returning instantly. But in a moment, ere a sentence was finished, she would be half across the garden. He gave up in despair.

"Why ain't you reading, Daddie?" she said.

"Because you won't listen to a word of it, Poppie."

"Oh, yes. Here I am," she said.

"Come then, and I will teach you to read."

But Poppie was off after another sparrow.

"Do you know that God sees you, Poppie?" asked Mr. Spelt.

"I don't mind," answered Poppie.

He sighed and closed his book, drank the last of his half-pint of beer, and rose to go. Poppie seemed to feel that she had displeased him, for she followed without a word across the fields to the road. In passing an old church, the deep notes of the organ reached their ears.

"There," said Poppie. "I suppose that's God making His thunder. Ain't it, Daddie? I've heard it coming out many a time."

"Were you never in a church?" asked her father.

"No," answered Poppie.

"Would you like to go?" he asked again, with the hope that something might take a hold of her.

"If you go with me," she said.

Now Mr. Spelt had heard of Mr. Fuller from Mr. Kitely, and had been once to hear him preach. They got on an omnibus, to Poppie's great delight, and rode back into the city. After tea they went to the evening service, where they saw Lucy, and Mattie with her father. Mattie was very devout, and listened even when she could not understand. Poppie only stared, and showed by her restlessness that she wanted to be out again. When they were again in the street she asked just one question: "Why did Jesus put on that ugly black thing?"

"That wasn't Jesus," said Mattie with a little pharisaical horror.

"Oh? Wasn't it?" said Poppie in a tone of disappointment. "I thought it was."

"O Poppie, Poppie!" said poor Mr. Spelt. "Haven't I told

you twenty times that Jesus is the Son of God?"

But he might have told her a thousand times, for she could not conceive it. What was Mr. Spelt to do? He had tried and tried, but he had put no idea into her yet.

Her restlessness increased, and her father bought her a broom—the best he could find—and told her she might, if she pleased, go sweep a crossing. Poppie caught at the broom, and vanished without a word. Not till she was gone beyond recall did her father think that the style of her dress was scarcely accordant with the profession she was about to assume. He remembered too, that crossing sweepers are exceedingly tenacious of their rights, and she might get into trouble.

At the dinner hour Poppie came home, but with her brilliant jacket nearly as dirty as her broom.

"O Poppie! What a mess you've made of yourself!"

"Tain't me, Daddie," she answered. "It's them nasty boys that threw dirt at me. Twasn't their crossing I took—they hadn't no call to chide me. But I gave it to them!"

"What do you mean, Poppie?" asked her father, a little anxiously.

"I looks up at St. Paul's and says, 'Please Jesus, help me give it to 'em.' And then I flies at 'em with my broom, and I knocks one o' 'em down, and a cart went over his leg, and he's took to the 'ospittle. I b'lieve his leg's broke."

"O Poppie! I wonder they didn't take you up!"

"They couldn't find me. I thought Jesus would help me, and He did."

Mr. Spelt had nothing to say to that, and therefore changed the subject. "Didn't you get any ha'pence?" he asked.

"Yes. I gave 'em all to the boy. I wouldn't if the cart hadn't gone over him, though. Catch me!"

"Why did you give it to him?"

"I wanted to."

"Did he take them?"

"Course he did. Why shouldn't he? I'd ha' took 'em."

Mr. Spelt later told Mr. Fuller all about Poppie. To his surprise, however, when he came to her onset with the broom, Mr. Fuller burst into a fit of the heartiest laughter.

"You don't think it was very wicked of your poor child to pray to God and shoulder her broom, do you?" he said, still laughing.

"We're told to forgive our enemies, Sir. And Poppie prayed against hers."

"Yes, yes. You and I have heard that and learned it, I hope. But Poppie, if she has heard it, certainly does not understand it yet. Do you ever read the Psalms? You will remember then how David prayed against his enemies."

"Yes, Sir. It's rather awful sometimes."

"What do you make of it? Was it wicked of David to do so?"

"I daren't say that, Sir."

"Then why should you think it was in Poppie?"

"Perhaps David didn't know better."

"And you think Poppie ought to know better than David?"

"Why, David lived before our Saviour came into the world to teach us better."

"And so you think Poppie more responsible than a man like David, who loved God as not one Christian in a million has learned to love him yet? A man may love God, and pray against his enemies. Mind you, I'm not sure that David hated them. I know he did not love them, but I am not sure that he hated them. And I'm sure Poppie did not hate hers, for she gave the little rascal her coppers, you know."

"Thank you, Sir," said Mr. Spelt, grateful to his heart's core that Mr. Fuller stood up for Poppie.

"Do you think God heard David's prayer against his enemies?" resumed Mr. Fuller.

"He gave him victory over them, anyhow."

"And God gave Poppie the victory too. I think God heard Poppie's prayer, and Poppie will be the better for it. She'll pray for a different sort of thing before she is done praying. It is a good thing to pray to God for anything. It is a grand thing to begin to pray."

"I wish you would try to teach her something, Sir. I've tried and tried, and I don't know what more to do. I don't seem to get anything into her."

"You're quite wrong, Mr. Spelt. You have taught her. She prayed to God before she fell upon her enemies with her broom."

"But I do want her to believe. I confess to you, Sir, I've never been much of a churchgoer, but I do believe in Christ."

"Tell me how you came to hear or know about Him without going to church."

"My wife was a splendid woman, Sir—Poppie's mother, but—well, she was a bit of a disappointment to me."

"Yes. And what then?"

"Bein' unhappy, and knowin' no way out of it, I took to the Bible, Sir. And when I began to read, I began to think about it. And from then I began to think about everything that came my way, tryin' to get things all square in my own head, you know, Sir."

Mr. Fuller was delighted with the man, and promised to think about what he could do for Poppie. Spelt rarely missed a Sunday morning at Mr. Fuller's church after that, for he had found a fellowman who could teach him.

Mr. Fuller set about making Poppie's acquaintance, and presented his friendship's offering in the shape of the finest kaleidoscope he could purchase. It was some time before she could be taught to shut one eye and look with the other; but when she succeeded in getting a true vision of the wonders inside, she danced and shouted for joy. This confirmed Mr. Fuller's opinion that it was through her eyes, and not through her ears, that he must approach Poppie's heart.

He must get her to ask questions by showing her things that might suggest them. He therefore began searching the print shops, till he got together about a dozen engravings, mostly from old masters, that he thought would represent our Lord in a lovable aspect, and make the child want to have them explained. For Poppie had had no big family Bible with pictures to pore over in her homeless childhood, and now she had to go back to such a beginning.

By this time she was pleased to accompany Mattie to tea with the vicar, and then the pictures made their appearance. This took place again and again, till the pictures came to be looked upon as a regular part of the entertainment.

Meantime Poppie went out crossing-sweeping by fits and starts. Her father neither encouraged nor prevented her, though he ensured that she did not again wear her bright outfit.

One cold afternoon they were walking hand in hand. Poppie did not feel the cold so much as her father, but she did blow upon the fingers of her disengaged hand now and then.

"Have a potato to warm you, Poppie," said her father, as they came up to one of those little steam engines for cooking potatoes, which stand here and there on the edges of the pavement, blowing a fierce cloud of steam from their little funnels.

"Jolly!" cried Poppie, running up to the man, and laying her hand on the greasy sleeve of his coat.

"I say, Jim, give us a ha'porth," she said.

"Why 'taint never you, Poppie," returned the man.

"Why ain't it?" said Poppie. "Here's my father. I've found one, and a good 'un, Jim."

The man looked at Poppie's dress, then at Mr. Spelt, touched the front of his cap and said, "Good evenin', Guv'nor." Then in an undertone he added, "I say, Guv'nor, you never did better in your life than takin' that 'ere creeter off the streets. You look well arter her. She's a right good 'un, I know. Bless you, she ain't no knowledge what wickedness means."

His heart warmed, Mr. Spelt seized the man's hand, and gave it a squeeze of gratitude.

"Come Jim, ain't your taters done yet?" said Poppie.

"Bustin' o' mealiness," answered Jim, throwing back the lid, and laying a potato in the hollow of his left hand. Then he caught up an old (and dirty) knife, split the potato lengthwise, laid a piece of butter into the cleft as if it had been a trowelful of mortar, gave it a top dressing of salt and a shake of pepper, and handed it to Poppie.

"Same for you, Sir?" he said.

"Well, I don't mind if I do."

Spelt paid for the potatoes, and they moved away.

"I say, ain't it jolly?" remarked Poppie. "I call that a good trade now."

"Would you like to have one o' them things and sell hot potatoes?" asked her father.

"Just wouldn't I!"

"As well as sweeping a crossing?"

"A deal better, Daddie," answered Poppie. "You see, it's more respectable. It takes money to buy a thing like that. And I could wear my red jacket then. The thing would be my own, and a crossing belongs to everyone."

Mr. Spelt thought it might be a good plan for giving Poppie some liberty, and yet keeping her from roving about everywhere without object or end. So in the course of a fortnight, he managed to buy her one.

Great was Poppie's delight. She went out regularly in the dusk to the corner of Bagot Street. Her father carried the machine for her, and was one of her chief customers. Except for the paternal consumption, Poppie was soon paying all the expense of the cooking apparatus. Mr. and Miss Kitely were good customers too, and everything looked well for father and daughter.

Every night at half past nine, her father carried the "murphy buster" up the three flights of stairs to Poppie's own room. There they finished the remainder of the potatoes "with butter, with pepper, and with salt," as Poppie would exclaim.

If there were none left, they set out to buy their supper. At one time it was a slice of beef or ham that was resolved upon, at another a bit of pudding, sometimes a couple of mutton pies, or sausages with bread. Then came the delight of buying it, always left to Poppie; of carrying it home, still left to Poppie; of eating it, not left to Poppie alone, but shared by her father. Then came a chapter in the Bible, the Lord's Prayer, bed, and dreams of Mrs. Flanaghan and her gin bottle, or perhaps, of Lucy and her first kiss.

36. NEW TROUBLE

Meantime Mrs. Worboise had taken to her bed, and not even Mr. Simon could comfort her. The mother's heart now spoke louder than her theology.

Mrs. Worboise did not begin to see her sins as such when the desolation of Thomas's disappearance fell upon her, but the atmosphere of her mind began to change, and a spring season of mother's feelings came by the revival of a long-suppressed motherhood. Her husband's hardness and want of sympathy with her sufferings had driven her into the arms of exclusive Christians, whose brotherhood consisted chiefly in denying the greater brotherhood, and refusing the hand of those who would not follow with them. All that was worst in poor Mrs. Worboise was cherished by her spiritual companions, whose chief anxiety was to save their own souls, and who thus ran the great risk of losing them. They treated the words of the Bible like talismans or spells, the virtue of which lay in the words and the assent given to them, or at most, in the feelings that could be conjured up by them, and not in the doing of the things they presupposed or commanded. But there was one thing that did something to keep her fresh and prevent her from withering into a dry tree of supposed orthodoxy—her anxiety to get her son within the "garden walled around," and the continual disappointment of her efforts to that end.

Now her imagination continually presented to her the form of her darling prodigal, his handsome face worn with hunger and wretchedness, or with dissipation and disease. She began to accuse herself bitterly for having alienated his affections from herself by forcing upon him that which was distasteful. She said to herself that it was easy for an old woman like her, who had been disappointed in everything, and whose life and health were a wreck, to turn from the vanities of the world—but how could her young Thomas, in the glory of youth, be expected to see things as she did? How could he flee from the wrath to come when he had as yet felt no breath of that wrath on his cheek? She ought to have loved him and borne with him and smiled upon him, and never let him fancy that his presence was a pain to her because he could not take her ways for his.

Everything tended to turn the waters of her heart back into the old channel with the flow of a spring tide toward her son. She wept and prayed better tears and better prayers, because her love was stronger. She humbled her heart, proud of its acceptance with God, before a higher idea of that God. She began to doubt whether she was more acceptable in His sight than other people. There must be some who were, but she could not be one of them. Instead of striving after assurance, as they called it, she began to shrink from every feeling that lessened her humility, for she found that when she was most humble, then she could best pray for her son. She lay thus praying for him, and dreaming about him, and hoping that he would return before she died.

But Mr. Worboise's heart was full of money, and the love of it. How to get money, how *not* to spend it, how to make it grow—these were the chief cares that filled his heart. It was not what he needed that filled his mind with care, but what he did not need, and never would need—what other people needed, and what was not his to take, whatever the law might say.

But the heart occupied by the love of money will be only too ready to fall prey to other evils, for selfishness soon branches out in hatred and injustice. The continued absence of his son, which he still attributed to the Boxalls, irritated more than alarmed him, but it roused his worst feelings against Lucy and her grandmother. He vowed that, if favored by fortune, he would make them feel in bitterness how deeply they had injured him. To the same account he entered all the annoyance given him by the well-meaning Mr. Sargent, who had as yet succeeded in irritating him without gaining the least advantage over him. Mr. Sargent's every effort in resistance of probate failed. The decision of the court was that Mr. Boxall, a strong, healthy, well-seasoned middle-aged man, was far more likely to have outlived all his daughters than any one of them to have outlived him. Therefore, Mr. Worboise obtained probate and entered into possession.

Although Mr. Sargent could not but have doubted the result, he was greatly discomfited. He went straight to Mr. Morgenstern's office to communicate his failure and the foiling of the liberality which had made the attempt possible. Mr. Morgenstern wrote him a check for costs, and then asked, "What is to be done for those good people, Sargent?"

"We must wait to see. The old lady has a claim upon the estate, which, most unfortunately, she cannot establish. Now perhaps he will be inclined to be generous, for justice must be allowed in this case to put on the garb of generosity, else she will not appear in public. I mean to make one more attempt, though I confess to considerable misgivings. Tomorrow, before his satisfaction has evaporated, I will make it, and let you know the result."

Mr. Sargent's next application to Mr. Worboise shared the fate of all his preceding attempts—Mr. Worboise smiled it off inexorably. The very next morning Mrs. Boxall was served with notice to vacate her rooms; she had no agreement and paid no rent, and was consequently tenant only on sufferance. And now Mr. Stopper's behavior toward them underwent a considerable change, though he was not in the smallest degree rude. The door between the house and office was once more carefully locked, and the key put in his drawer. Having found how hostile his new master was to the inhabitants of the house, he took care to avoid every suspicion of intimacy with them.

Mrs. Boxall's indignant rage when she received the notice to leave was as impotent as the bursting of a shell in a mountain of mud. However, the volume of her anger had this effect, that everybody in Guild Court heard all the phases of her oppression and injury. Lucy never said a word about it, save to Mr. and Mrs. Morgenstern, whose offer of shelter for herself and her grandmother she gratefully declined, knowing that her grandmother would rather die than accept such a position.

"There's nothing left for me in my old age but the workhouse," said Mrs. Boxall, exhausted by one of her outbursts.

"Grannie, Grannie," said Lucy, "don't talk like that. You have been a mother to me. See if I cannot be a daughter to you. I am quite able to keep both of us as comfortably as ever."

"Nonsense, Child. It will be all that you can do to keep yourself, and I am not going to sit on the neck of a young thing like you, like a nightmare, and have you wishing me gone from morning to night."

"With Mrs. Morgenstern's recommendation I can get as much teaching as I can undertake. It will only be paying you back a very little of your own, Grannie."

Before Mrs. Boxall could reply there was a tap at the door, and Mr. Kitely entered.

"Begging your pardon, Ladies, and taking the liberty of a neighbor, I made bold not to trouble you by ringing the bell. I've something to speak about in the way of business."

"Do sit down, Mr. Kitely," said Lucy. "We're glad to see you, though you know we're in a little trouble just at present."

"I know all about it, and I don't believe there's a creature in the court that isn't ready to fly at that devil's limb of a lawyer. But you see, Ma'am, if we was to murder him it wouldn't be no better for you. And what I come to say to you is this—I've got a deal more room on my premises than I want, and it would be a wonderful accommodation to me, not to speak of the honor of it, if you would take charge of my little woman for me. If you would come and live there, you could get things for yourselves all the same as you does here, only you wouldn't have nothing to be out of the pocket for houseroom, you know. It would be the making of my poor motherless Mattie."

"Oh! We're not going to be so very poor as Grannie thinks, Mr. Kitely," said Lucy, trying to laugh, while the old lady sat rocking herself to and fro and wiping her eyes. "But I should like to move into your house, for there's nowhere I should be so much at home."

"Lucy!" warned her grandmother.

"Grannie, Mr. Kitely's a real friend in need. It only comes to this, Mr. Kitely, that I have got to work a little harder, and not lead such an idle life."

"You idle, Miss!" interrupted the bookseller. "I never see anyone more like the busy bee than yourself."

"But it would be a shame for me to go and live in just anybody's house, seeing I am quite able to pay for it. Now, if you have room in your house—"

"Miles of it!" cried the bookseller.

"I don't know where, then, for it's full of books from the ground to the garret."

"Don't you purtend to know more about my house, Miss, than I do myself. Just you say the word, and you'll find two rooms fit for your use, and at your service. What I owe you in regard to my little one, nothing I can do can ever repay. They're a bad lot, them Worboises—son *and* father! And that I saw, leastways in the young one."

This stung Lucy's heart. She kept hoping and hoping, and praying to God, yet her little patch of blue sky was so easily overclouded! But she kept to the matter before her.

"Very well, Mr. Kitely. You ought to know best. Now for my side of the bargain. I told you already I would rather be in your house than anywhere else, if I must leave this dear old place. And if you will let me pay a reasonable sum, as lodgings go in this court, we'll regard the matter settled. And then I can teach Mattie a little, you know."

Mrs. Boxall did not put in a word. She was weary of everything, and for the first time in her life began to allow her affairs to be meddled with.

Mr. Kitely scratched his head and looked a little annoyed. "Well, Miss," he said, pausing between every few words, a most unusual thing with him, "that's not what I meant when I came up here. But that's better than nothing—for Mattie and me I mean. So if you'll be reasonable about the rent, we'll easily manage all the rest. Mind you, Miss, it'll be a clear profit to me."

"It'll cost you a good deal to get the rooms put in order as you say, you know, Mr. Kitely."

"Not much. I know how to set about things better than most people. Bless you, I can buy wallpaper for half of what you'd pay. I know the trade, for I've been almost everything in my day. Why, Miss, I lived at one time such a close shave with dying of hunger, that after I was married, I used to make picture frames, and then pawn my tools to get glass to put into them, and then carry them about to sell, and when I had sold them I bought more gold beading and redeemed my tools, and did it all over again. Bless you! I know what it is to be hard up, if anybody ever did."

The matter was arranged, and the bookseller proceeded to get his rooms ready, which involved chiefly a little closer packing, and disposing of a good deal of rubbish.

Meantime another trial was gathering for poor Lucy. Mr. Sargent had met Mr. Wither, and had learned from him all he knew about Thomas. Mr. Wither was certain that everything was broken off between Lucy and Tom. Mr. Sargent resolved to see if he could get anything out of Molken, and called upon him for that purpose. But the German soon convinced him that, although he had been intimate with Thomas, he knew nothing about him now. The last information he could give him was that Thomas had staked and lost his watch and a lady's ring that he wore; that he had gone away and returned with money; and having gained considerably, had disappeared and never been heard of again.

Mr. Sargent soon persuaded himself that Lucy, having come to know Tom's worthlessness, had dismissed him forever, and that she would very soon become indifferent to a person so unworthy of her affection. He was urged yet more from the desire of convincing her that his motives had not been so selfish as accident had made them appear, and that his feelings toward her had not changed with the change of her prospects. He therefore kept up his visits.

For some time, however, so absorbed were Lucy's thoughts that his attentions gave her no uneasiness. But one day she was suddenly undeceived, when her grandmother left her alone with Mr. Sargent for a moment.

"Miss Burton," said Mr. Sargent, "I venture to think circumstances may be sufficiently altered to justify me in once more expressing a hope that I may be permitted to regard a nearer friendship as possible between us."

Lucy started as if she had been hurt, and looked all around her like a person suddenly awaking in a strange place. Then her grandmother reentered, and Mr. Sargent went away without any conviction that Lucy's behavior indicated repugnance to his proposal.

But Mrs. Morgenstern had easily divined Mr. Sargent's feelings, and the very next day began to talk about him to Lucy.

"I think at least, Lucy, you might show a little kindness to the poor fellow, if only from gratitude. A girl may acknowledge that feeling without compromising herself. Mr. Sargent has been wearing himself out for you, lying awake at night, and running about all day, without hope of reward, and you are so taken up with your own troubles that you haven't a thought for the man who has done all in his power to turn them aside."

Lucy could not help comparing his conduct with that of Thomas. And she could as little help her suspicion that Thomas had forsaken her that he might keep well with his father—the man who was driving them into the abyss of poverty—and that this disappearance was the only plan he dared to adopt for freeing himself. Doubtless his cowardice would be at least as great in doing her wrong as it had been in refusing to do her right.

And she did feel that there was some justice in Mrs. Morgenstern's reproach. For if poor Mr. Sargent was really in love with her, she ought to pity him for the very reason that she could not grant him what he desired. She could not hear Mrs. Morgenstern's reproaches without bursting into tears. And then her friend began to comfort her, but all the time supposing that her troubles were only those connected with her reverse of fortune. As Lucy went home, however, a very different and terrible thought darted into her head: "What if it is my duty to listen to Mr. Sargent?"

The thought was indeed a terrible one. All the rest of that day her soul was like a drowning creature—now getting one breath of hope, now with all the billows and waves of despair going over it. The evening passed in constant terror lest Mr. Sargent should appear, and a poor paltry little hope grew as the hands of the clock went round. At length she went to bed without annoying her grandmother, who, by various little hints, gave her clearly to understand that she was expected to make a good match before long.

She went to bed, and fell asleep from weariness of emotion. But presently she started awake again, and it was a resolution formed in her sleep that brought her awake—she would go to

Mr. Fuller, and consult him on the subject that distressed her. After that she slept till morning.

She had no lesson to give that day, so as soon as Mr. Fuller's churchbell began to ring, she put on her bonnet. Her grandmother asked her where she was going, and Lucy told her she was going to church.

"I don't like this going to church of a weekday—at least in the middle of the day, when people ought to be at their work."

Lucy made no reply, for Mrs. Boxall was one of those who would turn from any good thing done by those whose opinions differed from her own.

There were twenty or thirty people present when she entered St. Amos'—a grand assembly. It was a curious psalm they were singing, quaint and old-fashioned. During the psalm she listened to Mr. Fuller singing, and reasoned to herself from his joy—"He is glad in God, not because he thinks himself a favorite with God, but because God is what He is, a faithful God. He is not one thing to Mr. Fuller and another to me. He is the same, and though I am sorrowful, I will praise Him too. He will help me to be and do right, and that can never be anything unworthy of me." So, with a trembling voice, Lucy joined in the end of the song of praise. And when Mr. Fuller's voice arose in prayer—"O God, whose nature and property is ever to have mercy and to forgive, receive our humble petitions; and though we be tied and bound with the chain of our sins, yet let the pitifulness of Thy great mercy loose us; for the honor of Jesus Christ, our Mediator and Advocate. Amen"—she joined in it with all her heart, both for herself and Thomas.

Then, without the formality of a text, Mr. Fuller addressed his little congregation. When the worship ended, and the congregation retired, Lucy bent her trembling steps toward the vestry. Her troubled heart beat very fast as she opened the door in answer to Mr. Fuller's cheerful, "Come in." He came forward holding out his hand.

"How do you do, Miss Burton? I am delighted to see you. I suppose there is something I can do for you. Let me hear all about it. Sit down."

So saying, he gave her a chair, and seated himself on the only remaining one. With due regard to his time and her own dignity, she proceeded at once to explain to him the difficulty in which she found herself. It was a lovely boldness in the young woman that enabled her to set forth in a few plain words her situation—that she had been engaged for many months to a youth who seemed to have forsaken her, but whom she did not know to have done so, though his conduct had been worse than doubtful. And there was a gentleman—and here she faltered more—to whom she was under very great obligation, and who said he loved her; and she wanted much to know whether it was her duty to yield to his entreaties.

When Lucy had finished setting forth her case, Mr. Fuller said, "Now you must allow me, Miss Burton, to ask you one or two questions."

"Certainly, Sir. Ask me whatever you please. I will answer honestly."

"That I have no doubt about. Do you love this man to whom you say you are obliged?"

"Indeed I do not, though I am grateful to him."

"I understand you. It seems to me that whatever he may desire at the time, it is doing any man a grevious wrong to marry him without loving him. The kindest thing is to refuse. This is what seems to me the truth."

While Mr. Fuller spoke, Lucy heaved a deep sigh of relief. After a little pause he went on. "Now, one question more. Do you still love the other?"

"I do," said Lucy, bursting at last into a passion of tears. "But, perhaps," she sobbed, "I ought to give him up altogether. I am afraid he has not behaved well at all."

"To you?"

"I didn't mean that. I wasn't thinking about myself just then."

"Has he let you understand that he has forsaken you?"

"No, no. He hasn't said a word. Only I haven't seen him for so long."

"Then there is some room for hope. If you were to resolve upon anything now, you would be doing so without knowing what you were doing, because you do not know what he is doing. It may be a healthy shame that is keeping him away from you. It may become your duty to give him up, but I think when it is so, it will be clearly so."

"It seems to me that he has not been well brought up. His father is a dreadfully hard and worldly man, as my poor grandmother knows too well, and his mother is very religious, but her religion seems to me to have done Thomas more harm than his father's worldliness."

"That is quite possible. When you do see him again, try to get him to come and see me. Or I will go and see him. I shall not overwhelm him with a torrent of religion which he cannot understand, and which would only harden him."

"There is nothing I should wish more. But tell me one thing, Mr. Fuller. Would it be right to marry him? I want to understand. Nothing looks further off, but I want to know what is right."

"While you love him, it is clear to me that you must not accept the attentions of anyone else. While he is unrepentant, that is, as long as he does not change his ways, you would be doing very wrong to marry him. I do not say when, or that ever, you are bound to stop loving him—but that is a very different thing than to consent to marry him. Any influence for good that a woman has over such a man, she may exercise as much before marriage as after it. Indeed, if the man is of a poor and selfish nature, she is almost certain to lose her influence after marrying him."

"I am sure you are right, Mr. Fuller. It would be dreadful to marry a bad man, or a right man who had not strength even for love of a wife to turn from bad ways."

Lucy rose. "Good morning, Mr. Fuller. I do not know how to thank you. I only wanted leave to go on loving him. Thank you a thousand times."

"Do not thank me, as if I could give you leave to do this or that. I only tell you what seems to me the truth of the matter."

"But is not that the best thing to give or to receive?"

"Yes, it is," answered Mr. Fuller, as Lucy left the vestry.

It was with a heart wonderfully lightened that she went home to her grandmother. This new cloud of terror had almost passed away, only darkened a little on the horizon when she thought of having again to hear what Mr. Sargent wanted to say.

That same evening he came. Lucy never lifted her eyes to his face, even when she held out her hand to him. Then she drew it away and took the lead. "I am very sorry if I have led you into any mistake, Mr. Sargent, over what you said the other evening. I wish to remove any misapprehension, and remind you that I considered the subject you resumed then as quite settled."

"I too considered it settled, but circumstances having altered so entirely—"

"Because I had lost the phantom of fortune which I never possessed?"

"No. You gave me reason for refusing my attentions then, which I have the best ground for believing no longer exists."

"Which was?"

"That you loved another."

"And what ground have I given you for supposing that such has ceased to be the case?"

"You have not given me any. He has."

Lucy started. The blood rushed to her face, and then back to her heart. "Where is he?" she cried, clasping her hands. "For God's sake, tell me!"

"That, at least, is answer enough to my presumptuous hope," returned Mr. Sargent with some bitterness.

"Mr. Sargent," said Lucy trembling, "I beg your pardon for any pain I may have occasioned you. But by surprising the truth, you have saved me the repetition of what I told you before. Tell me what you know about Mr. Worboise."

Mr. Sargent felt it wrong that such a woman should pass him by for the sake of such a man as Thomas, and he answered in the heat of injury.

"For the sake of his game amongst low gamblers, he staked and lost a diamond ring—a rose diamond, which one of his companions seemed to know as the gift of a lady. That is the man for whom Lucy Burton is proud to express her devotion!"

Lucy had grown very pale. Still she *would* say one word for Thomas. "Your evidence is hardly of the most trustworthy kind, Mr. Sargent. Good evening."

"It is of *his* kind, anyhow," he retorted, and left the room.

Lucy left the room as well. She had not been long in her own chamber, however, before, with the ingenuity of a lover, she contrived to draw a little weak comfort even out of what Mr.

Sargent had told her. She believed that he had done worse than part with her ring; but when the thought struck her that it must have been for the sake of redeeming that ring that he had robbed his employer, the offenses appeared mutually to mitigate each other. And when she thought the whole matter over in the relief of knowing that she was free of Mr. Sargent, she quite believed that she had discovered fresh ground for taking courage.

37. A Companion in Misfortune

Lucy and her grandmother prepared to move into the bookseller's house. Mr. Kitely, Mr. Spelt, and Mr. Dolman all bore a hand in the moving, and in the course of a couple of hours, all the heavier articles were in their new places. It did not appear that, save for the diminution of space, they had had such a terrible downcome, and Lucy was heartily satisfied with their quarters.

Mattie was delighted at the thought of having Miss Burton live with them, and she presided at a little supper which Mr. Kitely had procured in honor of the occasion. Though Mr. Dolman would not stay, Mr. Spelt and Poppie came, and brought with them the unsold remains from their steamer, and so completed the feast.

"Mr. Spelt, you be Parson, and say grace," said Kitely, in his usual peremptory tone.

Mr. Spelt said grace so devoutly that nobody could hear him.

"Why do you say grace as if you was ashamed of it, Spelt? If I was to do it, I would let you hear me."

"I didn't know you cared about such things," evaded Spelt.

"Well," said Kitely, "I'm afraid that Mr. Fuller will get me into bad habits before he has done with me. He's a good man, and he's almost made me hold my tongue against the rest of the cloth. It seems a shame, with him in St Amo's, to say a word against Mr. Potter in St. Jacob's. I never thought I should take to the church in my old age."

As the others were so talking upstairs, Mr. Dolman was trudging along a wide and rather crowded thoroughfare with a pair of workman's boots in his hands.

"Well, Dolly, how do?" said a man in a long velveteen coat, with a short pipe in his mouth and a greasy cloth cap on his head. "You're late tonight, ain't you?"

"Them lawyers, them lawyers, Jim!" returned Dolman, enigmatically.

"What the blazes do you have to do with lawyers?" exclaimed Jim Salter.

"Not much for my own part," returned Dolman, feeling important from having assisted his neighbors move. "But there's good people in our court could tell you another story."

"Come and 'ave a drop of beer," said Jim, "And tell us all about it."

No greater temptation could have been held out to Dolman, but he had a certain sense of duty that must first be satisfied.

"No, Jim. I never touch a drop till I've taken my work home."

"I can't think, Dolly, why you roost so far from your work. Now, it's different with me. My work's 'ere and there and everywhere, but yours is allus in the same place."

"It gives me a walk, Jim. Besides, it's respectable. It's 'aving two places of one's own. My landlady, Mrs. Dobbs, knows that my shop's in a fashionable part, and she's rather proud of me for a lodger in consequence. And my landlord, that's Mr. Spelt, a well-to-do tailor—'ow's 'e to know that I ain't got a house in the suburbs?" answered Dolman, laughing.

The moment the boots were delivered, the two men took themselves to a public house in the neighborhood, where Dolman conveyed to Jim, with very tolerable correctness, the whole story of Mrs. Boxall's misfortunes. Before he reached the end of it, however, Jim, who had already "had a drop" with two of his acquaintances that night, got rather misty, and took his leave of Dolman with the idea that Lucy and her grandmother had been turned out, furniture and all, into the street, without a place to go, and had been taken up by the police.

Much as she had dreaded leaving her own house (as she had always considered it) Mrs. Boxall had a better night in her new abode than she had had for many months, and rose in the morning with a surprising sense of freshness. Finding that Lucy was not yet dressed, she went down alone to the back parlor, and having nothing else to do, began to look at Mr. Kitely's birds.

"Good morning, Sir," screamed a huge gray parrot the moment she entered. The bookseller had bought him of a sailor somewhere about the docks a day or two before, and its fame had not yet spread through the neighborhood; consequently, Mrs. Boxall was considerably startled by the salutation. "Have you spliced the main brace this morning, Sir?" continued the parrot, and burst into the song, "There's a sweet little cherub," and stopping suddenly, followed it with the inquiry, "How's your mother?" The next moment the unprincipled animal poured forth its innocent soul in a torrent of imprecations which reached the ears of Mr. Kitely. He entered in a moment and silenced the animal with prompt rebuke, and the descent of an artificial night in the shape of a green cloth over his cage. The creature exploded worse than ever for a while, and then subsided.

Meantime the bookseller turned to Mrs. Boxall to apologize. "I haven't had him long, Ma'am—only a day or two. He's been ill brought up, as you see, poor bird! I shall have a world of trouble to cure him of his bad language. If I can't cure him I'll wring his neck."

"The poor creature doesn't know better," said Mrs. Boxall. "Wouldn't it be rather hard to kill him for it?"

"But I can't have such words running in and out my Mattie's ears all day!"

"But you could sell him, or give him away."

"A pretty present he would be, the rascal! And for selling him, it would be wickedness to put the money in my pocket. If I was to sell that bird, Ma'am—how should I look Mr. Fuller in the face next Sunday? No, if I can't cure him, I must twist his neck."

But before Mr. Kitely had done talking, Mrs. Boxall's attention was entirely taken up with another bird, of the perroquet species. It had a green head, with a collar of red round the back of it, while white feathers came down on each side of its huge beak like the gray whiskers of a retired military man. This head looked enormous for the rest of the body, for from the nape of the neck to the tail, except for a few long blue feathers on the shoulders of its wings, there was not another feather on its body: it was as bare as if it had been plucked for roasting. A more desolate, poverty-stricken, wretched object can hardly be conceived. But the creature was absolutely, perfectly self-satisfied, without a notion of shame or even discomfort. He hopped from place to place, and turned himself round with such an absence of discomposure, that one could not help admiring his perfect self-possession.

Mr. Kitely said, "You're wondering at poor Widdles. Widdles was an old friend of mine I named the bird after before he lost his overcoat—all but the collar. Widdles! Widdles!"

The bird came close up to the end of his perch, and setting his head on one side, looked at his master with one round, yellow eye.

"He's the strangest bird I ever saw," said Mrs. Boxall. "If you talked of wringing *his* neck, now, I shouldn't wonder, Mr. Kitely."

"Wring Widdles's neck! His is the very last neck I should ever think of wringing. See how bravely he bears misfortune. Nobody could well lose more than Widdles, and nobody could well take it lighter. He's a sermon, is that bird. His whole worldly wealth consists in his wig. They was a fine pair once, only his mate used to peck him for he was the smaller of the two. They always reminded me of Spelt and his wife. But when they were took ill, both of them, she gave in, and he wouldn't. Death took his feathers, and left him jolly without them. Bless him, old Widdles! Try him with a bit of sugar," he continued, handing her a piece.

The friendly bird accepted it, taking it in one curious foot, and nibbling it with his more curious mouth. Mrs. Boxall was pleased with him now as well as with herself, and before long a firm friendship was established between the two. She even attempted, with the help of bear's grease smeared on his skin, to grow his feathers back. Before many days had passed she had become so much attached to the bird that his company helped shield her from the inroads of regret, mortification, and resentment.

And through Mrs. Morgenstern's influence and exertions,

Lucy soon had much to do in the way of teaching, and her grandmother knew no difference in her way of living from what she had been accustomed to.

38. Thomas on Ratcliffe

When Thomas left with Jim Salter, he had no idea in his head but to get away somewhere. But wherever he went, there were people, even policemen, about, and not one of the places they went through was a likely shelter. They walked all about the lower docks the whole day till Thomas was very tired. They had some dinner at an eating house, where Thomas made yet a further acquaintance with dirt and disorder.

At night Jim led him onto Ratcliffe highway—the paradise of sailors at sea, and the hell of sailors on shore. Light blazed from innumerable public houses, through the open doors of which he looked into back parlors, where sailors and women sat drinking and gambling, or down long passages to great rooms with curtained doorways, whence came the sounds of music and dancing. Had the weather been warmer, the gaily bedizened but vulgar girls inside would have been hanging about the street doors, chaffing the passers-by.

As Jim turned in the direction of the Mermaid, he asked, "Where will you sleep tonight, Gov'nor?"

"I don't know," answered Thomas. "I must leave you to find me a place. But can you think of anything I can turn to? My money won't last very long."

"Turn to!" echoed Jim. "Why, a man needs to turn to everything by turns to make a livin' nowadays. You ain't been used to 'ard work, by your 'ands. Do you know your bible well?"

"Pretty well," said Tom, "but I don't know what that has to do with making a living."

"Oh, don't you, Gov'nor? Yer bible means pips and pictures."

"You mean cards. No, I've had enough of that."

"Hum! Bitten!" said Jim.

"Not very badly. In the pocketbook I told you I lost, I had a hundred pounds, won at cards the night before."

"My eye!" exclaimed Jim. "What a devil of a pity!" He devoted a few moments of melancholy to the memory of the money.

"Look here, Jim. I don't know where to go to sleep. I have a comfortable room that I dare not go near, and a rich father who would turn me out—and in short, I've ruined myself forever with card-playing."

"Sorry for you, Gov'nor. I know a fellow that makes a good thing of the thimble."

"I've no turn for tailoring, I'm afraid."

"Beggin' your pardon, Gov'nor, but you *are* a muff! I meant the thimble and peas at fairs and such like. You tell 'em they don't know where the pea is, and they don't. A friend of mine'll put you up to it for five or six bob."

Thomas could hardly be indignant with Jim, but it stung him to the heart to think any magistrate would now regard him as quite capable of taking to the profession of thimblerigging.

They had gone a good way before Jim called out joyfully, " 'ere's the fishy one, at last! Come along."

He pushed the swinging door aside and entered a bar—served by a big, fat man, with an apron crusted with several strata of dirt, a nose like a half-ripe mulberry, and little round watery eyes.

Jim went straight up to the man and stared at him. "You don't appear to know me, Mr. Potts? And you don't remember this gen'leman neither? Do'ee now, Gov'nor? On yer honor?"

"Can't say I do."

"How's your young mermaid, as took to the water so nat'ral the other day?" continued Jim, leaning his elbows on the counter.

"Jolly," answered the landlord. "Was you by?"

"Wasn't I! And here's a gov'nor was nearer than I—the very

gen'leman as went a 'eader into the water and saved 'er, Mr. Potts."

"You don't mean it!" said the landlord.

"Ask the Mis'ess, then," said Jim.

"Come, Jim—don't make a fool of me," said Thomas. "I wish I had known you were bringing me here. Come along."

Then a woman entered from behind the shop.

"There, Mis'ess," said her husband, "can *you* tell who that gentleman is?"

"Bless my soul! It's the gentleman that took our Bessie out of the water! How do you do, Sir?" she continued with pleasure and respect, as she advanced and curtsied to Thomas.

"None the worse for my ducking, thank you," said Thomas, in the delight brought by a word of real friendship.

"Oh! Isn't he, then!" muttered Jim.

"Won't you come in, Sir?" she asked, turning to lead the way.

"Thank you," said Thomas. "I have been walking about all day, and I am very tired. If you would let me sit down for a while—and if it wouldn't be too much trouble to ask for a cup of tea?"

"With pleasure, I'm sure."

Thomas followed her into a dingy back room, where she made him lie down on a sofa from which he would have recoiled three days ago, but for which he was very grateful now. She then bustled about to get some tea and little delicacies. She had a true regard for inward comforts, if not for those outward luxuries of neatness and cleanliness.

The moment Thomas was out of the shop, Jim began to talk with Mr. Potts. "None the worse, said 'e? Oh, no. That's the way your true blue takes the loss of a few banknotes. Nothing but a 'undred pounds the worse."

"You don't mean it?" said Mr. Potts, his eyes round as sixpence.

The account Jim gave of Thomas's position was this: when Thomas went overboard, he had in his coat a hundred pounds of his master's money—that he dared not go home without it, that the police were after him, and in short, that he was in a terrible fix.

Mr. Potts listened with a general stare, and made no reply.

"You'll give 'im a bed tonight, won't you, Gov'nor?" asked Jim. "I'll come back in the morning and see what can be done for 'im."

Mr. Potts replied, in a voice a little huskier than usual, "All right."

Jim went out of the beershop, and Mr. Potts went to talk to his wife. He told her Jim's story, and she proceeded to get the best room ready for Thomas. He accepted her hospitality with gratitude, and was glad to go to bed.

Meantime, Mr. Potts went out to find his brother-in-law, the captain of a collier trading between Newcastle and London.

The next morning, when Thomas came downstairs, he found more than his breakfast waiting for him: a huge seafaring man, with short neck and square shoulders, was seated in the room. He rose when Thomas entered, and greeted him with a bow of kindness and patronage.

Mrs. Potts came in and said, "This is my brother, Captain Smith of the *Raven,* come to thank you for what you did for 'is little pet niece, Bessie."

"Well, I donnow," said the Captain, with gruff breeziness. "I came to ask the gentleman if, bein' on the loose, 'e wouldn't like a trip to Newcastle, and share my little cabin with me."

It was the first glimmer of gladness that had lightened Thomas' horizon for an age. "Thank you!" he said. "It is the very thing for me!" And as he spoke, the awful London wilderness vanished, and open sea and sky filled the world of his imaginings. "When do you sail?" he asked.

"Tonight, with the ebb—but you'd better come with me after breakfast, and we'll go on board at once. You needn't mind about your chest. I can lend you a jersey that'll do better than your 'longshore togs."

Thomas applied himself to his breakfast with vigor, for hope made him hungry. How true it is that we live by hope! Before he had swallowed his last mouthful, he started from his seat.

"You needn't be in such a hurry," said the captain.

"I must see Mr. Potts for a minute." He went to the bar and asked the landlord to change a sovereign for him, and to give half to Jim as his promised day's wages.

"It's too much," said Mr. Potts. "Five shillings is over enough."

But Thomas insisted, for he felt he owed him far more than that. In pulling out the small remains of his money, Thomas brought out two bits of pasteboard, the sight of which shot a pang to his heart: they were the pawntickets for his watch and Lucy's ring, which he had bought back from the holder on that same terrible night on which he had lost almost everything worth having. It was well he had only thrust them into the pocket of his trousers, instead of putting them into his pocketbook.

He *must* get at least the ring back. But if he went after it now, even if he had the money to redeem it, he might run into the arms of the searching Law, and he and it too would be gone. The cold dew broke out on his face.

But Mr. Potts had been watching, and he knew the look of those tickets. "I beg your pardon, Sir," he said, "but a long experience in them things makes me able to give you good advice. Now I ain't no witch, but I can see with 'alf an eye that you've got summat at your uncle's you don't like to leave there. Have you got the money?"

"No!" cried Thomas.

"Come now," said Potts kindly, "Tell me all about it, and I'll see what I can do—or can't do, it may be."

Thomas told him that the tickets were for a watch and a diamond ring. He didn't care about the watch, but he would give his life to get the ring again.

"You give 'em to me," said Potts. "Here, Bessie! I'm going out for an hour. Tell the captain not to go till I come back." He removed his white apron, put on a black frock coat and hat, and went out with the tickets.

He returned an hour later and laid a small screw of paper before Thomas, saying, "There's your ring, Sir. You won't want your watch this voyage. I've got it, but I'm forced to keep it, in case I should be behind with my rent. Any time you look in, I shall have it, or know where it is."

Thomas did what he could to express his gratitude, and took the ring with a wonderful feeling of relief. It seemed like a pledge of further deliverance. He begged Mr. Potts to do what he pleased with the watch, and hoped it would be worth more to him than what it had cost him to redeem them both. Then, after many kind farewells, he left with the captain. As they walked along, he could not help looking round every few yards; but after his new friend had bought him a blue jersey and a glazed hat, and tied his coat up in a handkerchief, he felt more comfortable. And soon they were on the board the *Raven.* They set sail the same evening, but not till they were well away did Thomas begin to feel safe from pursuit.

Thomas was left mainly to his own company—which, though far from agreeable, was the very best for him under the circumstances. For it was his real self that he looked in the face—the self that told him what he was, what he had lost, how he had been wasting his life. And he began to see not only his faults, but the weakness of his character which had brought him to this pass.

And his behavior to Lucy was the bitterest thought of all. She looked ten times more lovely to him now that he had lost her. How she had entreated him to do her justice! And he saw now that she had done so even more for his sake than for her own. He had not yet any true idea of Lucy's worth—did not know how she had grown since she had first listened to his protestations. While he had been going down the hill, she had been going up. He did see that she was infinitely beyond him, and it was the first necessity of a nature like his to be taught to look down on himself. Therefore, it was well for him that the worthlessness of his character should break out in some plainly worthless deed, that he might no longer be able to hide himself from the conviction and condemnation of his own conscience. Hell had come at last, and he burned in its fire.

He was very weary and went to bed in a berth in the cabin. But he was woken while it was still dark by the violent rolling and pitching of the vessel, and running to and fro overhead. He dressed in haste and clambered up the ladder. A wild storm was blowing hard. The brig was under reefed sails, but she was a good boat, and rode the seas well. There was just light enough for him to see the water by the white rents in its darkness.

And that storm came to him as a wonderful gift from the Father who had not forgotten his erring child. New strength and hope invaded his weary heart from the hiss of the wind through the cordage on the masts, and his soul rejoiced in the heave of the wave under the bows and its swift rush astern.

Even though life seemed to him now a worthless thing—for he saw no way of recovering his lost honor, and avoiding eternal disgrace, even if God and man forgave him—the wild refreshing fury of the storm bore a new and genuine hope to him.

Although he had to hold hard by the weather shrouds, not a shadow of fear crossed his mind. Thomas feared nothing that merely involved bodily danger to himself, for he possessed a fine physical courage. He was deficient in moral courage—the power of looking human anger and contempt in the face, and holding to his own way. He could look a storm in the face, but a storm in a face he could not endure. The storm thus wrought along with all that was best in him. In the fiercest of that night, he often kissed Lucy's ring, which he had ventured to draw once more upon his hand.

The wind increased as the sun rose. He wanted to help the men staggering to and fro, but he did not know one rope from the other. Then one of two men at the wheel was called away aloft, and Thomas sprang to his place.

"I will do whatever you tell me," he called out, "only let me set a man free."

The captain himself gave a nod and a squirt of tobacco juice, as cool as if he had been steering with a light gale over a rippling sea. Thomas did his best, and in five minutes he had learned enough to obey the captain's word. In an hour the wind began to moderate, and before long the captain gave the helm to the mate, saying to Thomas, "We'll go and have some breakfast—you've earned your rations, anyhow. Your father should have sent you to sea. It would have made a man of you."

This was not very complimentary, but Thomas had only a suppressed sigh to return for answer. He did not feel himself worth defending any more.

39. Return to London

Thomas made rapid progress in the favor of Captain Smith, who had looked upon him as a landlubber, but now saw that, clerk as he was, he was yet capable at sea. He soon found that Thomas' education, though not first-rate, enabled him to ask more questions concerning wind and water and ships than he was quite able to solve. Before the voyage ended, Thomas could bear a hand in taking a reef in the fore-topsail, and could steer a course with tolerable steadiness. As he presumed upon nothing, the sailors warmed to him and gave him what help they could—though not without a few jokes at his expense, during which he did his best to laugh with them. The captain soon began to order him about like the rest, which was the best kindness he could have shown him.

"Do you think you could ever make a sailor of me?" asked Tom one day.

"Not a doubt of it," answered the captain. "A few voyages more, and you'll go aloft like a monkey."

"Where is your next voyage, Sir?"

"I did think of Dundee."

"Would you take me with you?"

"To be sure, if you can't do better."

"I can't. I don't want anything but my rations, you know."

"We're one hand short this voyage, and you've done something to fill the gap."

"I'm very glad, I'm sure. But what would you advise me to

do when we reach Newcastle? It will be some time before you get off again."

"Not long. If you like to help loading cargo, you can make wages by that—but it's dirty work."

"There's plenty of water about," answered Thomas.

At Newcastle, Thomas worked as hard as any of them. He had never known what it was to *work* before, and although it tired him dreadfully at first, it did him good.

Among the men was one whom he liked more than the rest, who had sailed to India and other places. Thomas chiefly consorted with this man, Robins, when their day's work was over. He made the best of the company he had, knowing it was far better than he deserved, and far better than the company he had recently quitted.

One evening they went into a public house to get a bit of bread and cheese and ale. They sat down in a little room with colored prints of ships in full sail on the walls. On the other side of a thin partition, more customers sat and drank their grog and talked a full gale of words and stories.

Thomas, half listening, heard the name *Ningpo.* Now he knew nothing of the unusual fate of the property Mr. Boxall left behind him, thinking that Mrs. Boxall would inherit it.

"Did you hear someone in the next room mention the *Ningpo?*" asked Thomas.

"Yes. She was a barque in the China trade."

"Lost last summer on the Cape Verdes. I knew of the captain, and knew his brother and family. They were all on board, and all hands lost."

"Ah!" said Robins. "That's the way of it. People oughtn't to go to sea but them as has business there. Did you say the crew was lost as well?"

"So the papers said."

Robins rose and went into the next room, thinking the voice had sounded familiar. He returned in a few minutes with a sailor—rough, hairy, brown, and hard.

"Here's the gentleman," said Robins, "as knew your captain, Jack."

"Do, Sir?" said Jack, touching an imaginary cap.

"What'll you have?" asked Tom. This important point settled, they had a talk together. Jack's story indicated that he had been on the *Ningpo* when she went to pieces—that he had drifted ashore on a spar, after sitting through the night on the stern, and seeing every soul lost but himself. "But I almost wasn't the only one," he concluded. "There was poor little Julia, the captain's niece! How she did stick to me through the night! But she died long afore the starn broke up. Then from the island, that same day it was, I was picked up by a brigantine bound from Portingale to the Sambusy. And that's the bitter end of the *Ningpo,* and I'm the only man alive to tell her tale."

They parted soon after, and the friends went on to their next voyage. They made good sailing to Dundee, returned to Newcastle, and were bound back to London again.

"If you would rather not go back to London," said the captain to Tom, "there's a friend of mine who will take you on Aberdeen."

But Tom's heart was burning to see Lucy once more—if only to see her and restore her ring. He thought that with his tanning and the change of his clothes, he was not likely to be recognized. So he worked his way to London on the *Raven.*

It was a bright, cold, frosty morning in March when they went ashore. Tom's first glimpse of the turrets of the Tower of London brought strange feelings; danger and exposure lay before him, but he thought only of Lucy, not of the shame now.

Tom wandered northward, lost in his own thoughts, until he found himself by the gray timeworn tower of the old church of Hackney. This sent a strange pang to his heart, for close by had once lived that family whose bones now whitened among the rocky islands of the Atlantic. He went into the churchyard and sat down on a gravestone. Now that thc fiction of his own worth had vanished, he was not able to conceal from himself that his behavior to Mary Boxall had helped cause the loss of the whole family. He saw the mischief that had come of his own weakness and and lack of courage and principle. If he had but defended his own conduct where it was blameless, or at least allowed it to be open to the daylight and the anger of those whom it might not please, he might have prevented a host of tragedies.

Self-abased, he rose from the gravestone and walked slowly past the former Boxall house, where merry faces of unknown children looked from the upper windows. Then he went away westward toward Highbury to pass his father's door. There was no fear of being seen, for his father would be at his office and his mother could not leave her room.

And how he had behaved to his mother! A new torrent of self-reproach rushed over his soul. If he could only distinguish himself in any way, he would go and beg her forgiveness. But what chance was there of doing anything now? Thomas did not yet see that his duty was to confess his sin, waiting for no means of covering its enormity. He walked on past the silent door, and down the long walk with the lime trees on one side. Just as he reached the gates, he met Amy and Mr. Simon coming from the other side. They were talking and laughing merrily, and looking in each other's face. Tom and never seen Mr. Simon look so pleasant before. But no sooner did Mr. Simon see the "sailor" than the clerical mask came over his face. Amy did not see him at all. "It is clear," he said to himself, "that they don't much care what has become of me."

He wandered again for a while, and had some dinner. He wrote a note to Lucy, though he did not call her by name or use any term of endearment:

"My heart is dying to see you once more. I wish to return your mother's ring, which, though it has comforted me often in my despair, I no longer have any right to retain. I am working honestly for my bread—I am a sailor now, and am quite clear of all my bad companions. Dare I ask you to meet me once more—tomorrow night, or any night soon, as I am not safe in London? I will tell you all when I see you. Send one line by the bearer of this note to say where you will meet me. Do not, for the sake of your former love to me, refuse me this. I want to beg your forgiveness, that I may go away less miserable than I am. God bless you."

He started out for Guild Court, looking for a messenger to carry his note to Lucy. Thomas walked through Hampstead, and by Haverstock Hill, Tottenham Court Road, and Holborn to the City. By this time the moon was up. Then he turned off to the left, and at the further end of Bagot Street was Poppie with her "murphy-buster." Seeing her face only by the street lamp, he recollected only that he had seen the girl about Guild Court, and had no suspicion that she would know him.

"Do you know Guild Court, my girl?" he asked. "Would

you take this letter for me, and give it to Miss Burton, who lives there, and wait for an answer? If she's not at home bring it back to me. I will take care of your potatoes, and give you a shilling when you come back."

Poppie scudded. While she was gone he sold three or four of her potatoes. He knew how to deliver them, but he didn't know the price, and just took what they gave him. He stood trembling with hope.

Suddenly he was seized by the arm from behind, and a gruff voice said, "Here he is! Come along, Mr. Worboise. You're wanted."

Thomas turned. There were four men but no policemen—a comfort. Two of them were little men. Tom twisted his arm from the man's grasp, and was just throwing his fist at this head, when he was pinioned by two arms cast round him from behind.

"Don't strike," said the first man, "or it'll be the worse for you. I'll call the police. Come along, and I swear nothing but good will come of it—to you as well as to other people. I'm not the man to get you into trouble. Don't you know me? Kitely, the bookseller. Come along. I've been in a fix myself before now."

Thomas yielded, and they led him away through streets and lanes until they bustled him in at a church door. In the vestibule Thomas saw that here were but two with him—Mr. Kitely and Mr. Spelt. The other two had disappeared, for neither Mr. Salter nor Mr. Dolman cared to tempt Providence by coming further. Mr. Kitely made way for Thomas to enter first. Fearful of any commotion, and with the fear of the police still before his eyes, Thomas followed Mr. Kitely up the church while the little tailor brought up the rear. Mr. Kitely popped his head into Mr. Fuller's study and said, with ill-suppressed triumph, "Here he is, Sir! I've got him!"

"Whom do you mean?" said Mr. Fuller, surprised.

"Young Worboise. The lawyer-chap, you know, Sir," he added, seeing that the name conveyed no idea.

"Oh!" said Mr. Fuller, prolongedly. "Show him in, then."

Thomas entered, bewildered. Nor was Mr. Fuller quite at ease at first, when the handsome brown sailor-lad stepped into the vestry. But he shook hands with him, and asked him to take a chair. Thomas obeyed. Seeing his conductors lingered, Mr. Fuller then said, "You must leave us alone now, Mr. Kitely, Mr. Spelt."

Those two retired, consulted together, and went home.

Now Jim Salter had not failed to revisit The Mermaid on the day of Tom's departure, but he was rather late, and Tom was gone. As to what had become of him, Mr. Potts thought it more prudent to profess ignorance. He likewise took another procedure upon Jim, which, although well-meant, was not honest. Regardless of Tom's desire that Jim should have a half-sovereign for the trouble of the preceding day, Mr. Potts, weighing the value of Jim's time, and the obligation he himself was under to Tom, resolved to take Tom's interests in his own hands, and therefore very solemnly handed a half-crown and a florin, as what Thomas had left for him, across the counter to Jim. Jim took the amount in severe dudgeon.

"Four and sixpence!" said Jim, in a tone of injury, in which there certainly was no pretence. "After a-riskin' of my life, not to mention a-wastin' of my precious time for the ungrateful young snob. Four and sixpence!"

Mr. Potts told him with equal solemnity and righteous indignation, while looking over the top of his red nose, to hold his jaw, or go out of his tavern. Whereupon Jim gave a final sniff, and was silent.

From that day, although he continued to call occasionally at the Mermaid, he lost all interest in his late client, never referred to him, and always talked of Bessie Potts as if he himself had taken her out of the water.

The acquaintance between Dolman and Jim began about this time to grow a little more intimate, and Mr. Dolman communicated to him such little facts as transpired about "them lawyers"—namely Mr. Worboise's proceedings, including the suspicious disappearance of the son. Mr. Salter, already suspicious of his man, requested a description of the missing youth, and concluded that it was the same in whom he had been so grievously disappointed, for the odd sixpence represented any conceivable amount of meanness, not to say wickedness.

Dolman would occasionally share a jug of beer with Jim in his shop. There was barely room for two, and Dolman stitched away while Jim did the chief part of the drinking and talking—

not so low but that Spelt above could hear enough to set him thinking. It was pretty clear that young Worboise was afraid to show himself, and this and other points Spelt communicated to his friend Kitely. This same evening they had been together thus when they heard a hurried step come up and stop before the window, and the voice of Mr. Kitely, well known to Dolman, called to the tailor overhead.

"Spelt, I say. Spelt!"

Mr. Spelt looked out of his door. "Yes, Mr. Kitely?"

"Here's that young devil's limb, Worboise, been and sent a letter to Miss Burton by your Poppie, and he's a-waitin' an answer. Come along, and we'll take him alive."

"But what do you want to do with him?" asked Spelt.

"Take him to Mr. Fuller."

"But what if he won't come?"

"We can threaten him with the police, as if we knew all about it. Come along. There's no time to be lost."

Spelt came down, and the two below issued from their station as well—Mr. Dolman anxious to assist in the capture, and Mr. Salter wishing to enjoy his disgrace, for the odd sixpence rankled. But when they had conducted him to the door of the church, the latter two turned and departed. They knew nothing about churches, and were unwilling to enter; they did not know what they might be in for. Neither had they any idea for what object Thomas was taken there. Dolman went away with some vague notion about the ecclesiastical court. Dolman went back to his work, hoping to hear about it when Spelt came home. Jim wandered eastward, and conveyed a somewhat incorrect narrative to the inhabitants of the Mermaid. In great perplexity and greater uneasiness, Captain Smith and Mr. Potts came to find out the truth of the matter. Jim conducted them to the church door and retired round the corner.

40. Confession

As soon as the door closed behind them, Mr. Fuller turned to Tom, saying, as he took a chair near him, "I'm very glad to see you, Mr. Worboise. I have long wanted to have a little talk with you."

"Will you tell me," said Tom, with considerable uneasiness, "why those people have made me come to you? I was afraid of making a row in the street, and so I thought it better to give in. But I have no idea why I am here."

"It certainly was a most unwarrantable proceeding if they used any compulsion. But I have no intention of using any—nor should I have much chance," he added, laughing, "if it came to a tussle with a young fellow like you, Mr. Worboise."

This answer restored Tom a little. "Perhaps you know my father," he said, finding that Mr. Fuller was silent. In fact, Mr. Fuller was quite puzzled how to proceed. He cared little for the business part; and for the other, he must not compromise Lucy.

"I have not the pleasure of knowing your father. I wish I had. But after all, it is better I should have a chat with you first."

"Most willingly," said Tom, with courtesy.

"It is a very unconventional thing I am about to do. But very likely you will give me such information as may enable me to set the minds of some of my friends at rest. You will understand that sometimes a clergyman is compelled to meddle with matters which he would gladly leave alone."

"I have too much need of forbearance myself not to grant it, Sir—although I do not believe any will be necessary in your case."

Mr. Fuller proceeded to business at once. "I am told that a certain near relative of yours is in possession of a large property which ought by right, if not by law, to belong to an old lady who is otherwise destitute. I wish to employ your mediation to procure a settlement upon her of such small portion of the property at least as will make her independent. I am certainly explicit enough now," concluded Mr. Fuller, with a considerable feeling of relief.

"I am as much in the dark as ever, Sir," returned Thomas. "If you mean my father, I am the last one to know anything of his affairs. I have not seen him or heard from him for months."

"But you cannot surely be ignorant of the case. It seems that your father has come in for all the property of the late Richard Boxall—"

"By Jove!" cried Thomas, starting to his feet in a rage, then sinking back on his chair in conscious helplessness. "He *did* make the will," he muttered.

"Leaving," Mr. Fuller went on, "the testator's mother and niece utterly unprovided for."

"But Grannie had money of her own in the business. I have heard her say so a thousand times."

"She has nothing now."

"My father is a villain!" exclaimed Thomas, starting once more to his feet, and pacing up and down like a wild beast in a cage. "And what am I?" he added, after a pause. "I have brought all this upon her." He could say no more. He sat down, hid his face in his hands, and sobbed.

"As to Miss Burton," Mr. Fuller said, "I happen to know that she has another grief, much too great to allow her to think about money. She never told me who he was, but she confessed to me that she was in great trouble."

"Oh, Sir, what shall I do?" cried Thomas. "I love her with all my heart, but I can never dare to think of her more. I came up to London at the risk of—of—I came up to London only to see her and give her back this ring, and beg her to forgive me, and go away forever. And now I have not only given her pain—"

"Pain!" echoed Mr. Fuller. "If she weren't so good, her heart would have broken before now."

Thomas turned his face away from Mr. Fuller, and stood miserably by the wall. Mr. Fuller put his hand on his shoulder kindly, and said, "My dear boy, I suspect you have got into some terrible scrape, or you would not have disappeared. And your behavior seems to confirm the suspicion. Tell me all about it, and I have very little doubt that I can help you out of it. But you must tell me everything."

"I will, Sir. I will."

"Mind, no half-confessions. I have no right to ask you to confess but on the ground of helping you. But if I am to help you, I must know all."

Tom turned round and looked Mr. Fuller calmly in the face. The light shone in his eyes—the very offer of someone hearing all his sin and misery gave him hope.

"I hate myself so, Sir," he said, "that I do not feel it worthwhile to hide anything. I will speak the truth. When you wish to know more than I tell, ask me any questions you please, and I will answer them."

At this moment a tap was heard at the vestry door, and it opened, revealing two scared faces—Captain Smith and Mr. Potts.

"Don't be be too 'ard on the young gentleman, Sir," said Mr. Potts, in the soothing tone of one who would patch up a family quarrel. "He won't do it again, I'll go bail. You don't know, Sir, what a good sort 'e is. Don't 'e get 'im into no trouble. He lost 'is life—all but—a reskewing of my Bessie, 'e did. True as the Bible, Sir."

"You just let me take him off again, Sir," put in Captain Smith.

"Are these men friends of yours, Mr. Worboise?" asked Mr. Fuller.

"Indeed they are," answered Thomas. "I think I must have killed myself before now, if it hadn't been for those two." Turning to the captain, he said, "Thank you, Captain, Mr. Potts, but I am quite safe with this gentleman. I will come and see you tomorrow."

"He shall sleep at my house tonight," said Mr. Fuller, "and no harm shall happen to him, I promise you."

"Thank you, Sir," and "Good night, Gentlemen," said both, and went through the silent wide church with a kind of awe that rarely visited either of them.

Without further preface than just the words, "Now, I will tell you all about it, Sir," Thomas began his story. When he had finished it, and had answered a few questions, Mr. Fuller was satisfied that he did know all about it, and that if ever there was case in which he ought to give all the help he could, here was one. He did not utter a word of reproof. Thomas's condition of mind was such that it was not only unnecessary, but might have done harm; he had now only to be met with the same simplicity which he had himself shown. The help must match the confession.

"Well, we must get you out of this scrape, somehow," he said, heartily.

"I don't see how you can, Sir."

"It rests with yourself chiefly. Another can only help. The feet that walked into the mire must turn and walk out of it again. I don't mean to reproach you—only to encourage you to effort."

"What effort?" said Tom. "I have scarcely heart for anything. I have disgraced myself forever. Suppose all the consequences were to disappear: I have a blot upon me to all eternity, that nothing can wash out. Is it worthwhile to do anything?"

"It is true that the deed is done, and cannot be obliterated," returned Mr. Fuller. "but a living soul may outgrow all stain and all reproach. I do not mean in the judgment of men merely, but in the judgment of God, which is always founded on the actual fact, and always calls things by their right names, and covers no man's sin, although He forgives it and takes it away. But, Thomas Worboise, if the stain of it were to cleave to you to all eternity, that would be infinitely better than that you should have continued capable of doing the thing. You are more honorable now than you were before. Then you were capable of the crime; now, I trust, you are not. It is the kindest thing God can do for His children, sometimes, to let them fall in the mire. You would not hold by your Father's hand; you struggled to pull it away; He let it go, and there you lay. Now that you stretch forth the hand to Him again, He will take you, and clean not only your garments, but your heart and soul and consciousness. Pray to your Father, my boy. He will change your humiliation into humility, your shame into purity."

"Oh, if He were called anything else than Father! I am afraid I hate my father."

"I don't wonder. But that is your own fault too."

"How is that, Sir? Surely you are making even me out worse than I am."

"No. You are afraid of him. As soon as you have ceased to be afraid of him, you will no longer be in danger of hating him."

"I can't help being afraid of him."

"You must break the bonds of that slavery. No slave can be God's servant, for His servants are all free men. You must not try to call God your Father till *father* means something very different to you from what it seems to mean now. Think of the grandest human being you can imagine—the tenderest, the most gracious, whose severity is boundless, but hurts himself most—all against evil, all for the evildoer. Even I, if you will but do your duty in regard to this thing, will not only love, but honor you far more than if I had known you only as a respectable youth."

"I will think God is like you, Sir. Tell me what I am to do."

"I am going to set you the hardest of tasks, one after the other. They will be like the pinch of death, but they must be done. And after that—peace. Who is at the head of the late Mr. Boxall's business now?"

"I suppose Mr. Stopper. He was head clerk."

"You must go to him and take him the money you stole."

Thomas turned ashy pale. "I haven't got it, Sir. It was eleven pounds—nearly twelve."

"I will lend you the money."

"Thank you, Sir. I will repay you. But—"

"Yes, now come the buts," said Mr. Fuller, with a smile of kindness. "What is the first but?"

"Stopper is a hard man, and never liked me. He will give me up to the law."

"I can't help it. It must be done. But I do not believe he will do that. I will help you so far as to promise you to do all that lies in my power to prevent it. And there is your father—his word will be law with him now."

"So much the worse, Sir. He is ten times as hard as Stopper."

"He will not be willing to disgrace his own family, though."

"He will make it a condition that I shall give up Lucy. But I will go to prison before I will do that. Not that it will make any difference in the end, for Lucy won't have a word to say to me now. She bore all that a woman could bear. She has given me up, of course, but I will never give her up that way."

"That's right, my boy. Well, what do you say to it?"

With a sudden resolve he said, "I will, Sir." With a new light in his face he added, "What next?"

"Then you must go to your father."

"That is far worse. Am I to tell him everything?"

"If he had been a true father to you, I should have said 'Of course.' But there is no denying the fact that such he has not been."

"What ought I to tell him, then?"

"I think you will know that best when you see him. We cannot tell how much he knows."

"Yes," said Thomas, thoughtfully. "I will tell him that I am sorry I went away as I did, and ask him to forgive me. Will that do?"

"I must leave all that to your own conscience, heart, and honesty. Of course, if he receives you at all, you must see what you can do for Mrs. Boxall."

"Alas! That will be useless, and it will only enrage him the more at them. He may offer to put it all right, though, if I promise to give Lucy up. Must I do that, Sir?"

Knowing Lucy, Mr. Fuller answered, "On no account whatever."

"And what must I do next?" he asked, more cheerfully.

"There's your mother."

"Ah! You needn't remind me of her."

"Then you must not forget Miss Burton. You have some apology to make to her too, I suppose."

"I had just sent her that note, when the bookseller laid hold of me. But how am I to see Lucy now? She will not know where I am. Perhaps she will not want to see me."

Here Tom looked very miserable again. Anxious to give him courage, Mr. Fuller said, "Come home with me now. In the morning, after you have seen Mr. Stopper, and your father and mother, come back to my house. I am sure she will see you then."

With more thanks in his heart than on his tongue, Tom followed Mr. Fuller from the church. When they stepped into the street, they found the bookseller, the seaman, and the publican talking together on the pavement.

"It's all right," said Mr. Fuller to them. "Good night." Then, turning again to Mr. Kitely, he added in a low voice, "He knew nothing of his father's behavior, Kitely. You'll be glad to hear that."

"I ought to be glad to hear it for his own sake, I suppose," returned the bookseller. "But I don't know as I am, for all that."

"Have patience," said the parson, and walked on, taking Thomas by the arm.

When Lucy came home, she found her grandmother sitting by the fire, gazing reproachfully at the coals. The immediate occasion of her present mood was Thomas' note on the mantlepiece. She regarded him with the same feelings with which she regarded his father, but she knew Lucy did not share in these feelings. And forgetting that she was now under Lucy's protection, she was actually vowing with herself that if Lucy had one word of other than repudiation to say to Thomas, she would turn her out of the house. *She* was not going to encourage such lack of principle. Lucy entered, saw and took the note with a trembling hand, and hurried from the room.

Then Mrs. Boxall burst into a blaze. "Where are you off to now, you minx?"

"I am going to take my bonnet off, Grannie," answered Lucy, understanding well enough, and waiting no further parley. Her hands trembled so much she could hardly open the note. Before she had read it through she fell to her knees. She had nothing to say but, "Thank God!" And she had nothing to do but weep. She wished to reply, but Mr. Kitely came and told her that young Worboise had gone to see Mr. Fuller in his vestry. He did not tell her how he came to be there. And the next thing was a note from Mr. Fuller, telling her that Thomas was at his house, bidding her to be of good cheer, and saying that she should hear from him again the next evening.

In the meantime, she had a good deal of questioning and complaining yet to bear from her grandmother, though the spiteful utterances of an ill-used woman did not go very deep into Lucy.

41. Reparations

Thomas did not sleep much that night, and was up early in the morning. Mr. Fuller had risen before him, however, and Thomas found him in his study reading. He received him very heartily, looking at him anxiously, as if to see whether he could read action there. Apparently he was encouraged, for his own face brightened up, and they were soon talking together earnestly. But knowing Mr. Stopper's habit of being first at the countinghouse, Thomas was anxious about the time, and Mr. Fuller hastened breakfast. That and prayers over, he put twelve pounds into Thomas' hand, which he had been out that morning already to borrow from a friend. Then, with a quaking heart but determined will, Thomas set out and walked straight toward the countinghouse, and there was the bookseller arranging his stall outside the window. Mr. Kitely regarded him with doubtful eyes, vouchsafing him a "Good morning" of the gruffest.

"Mr. Kitely," said Thomas, "I am more obliged to you than I can tell for what you did last night."

"Perhaps you ought to be—but it wasn't for your sake, Mr. Worboise, that I did it."

"I am quite aware of that. Still, if you will allow me to say so, I am as much obliged to you as if it had been."

Mr. Kitely grumbled something, for he was not prepared to be friendly.

"Will you let me wait in your shop till Mr. Stopper comes?"

"There he is."

Thomas delayed to give Mr. Stopper time to enter the more private part of the countinghouse, and then he hurried to the door and went in.

Mr. Stopper was standing with his back to the glass partition, and took Tom's step for that of one of his clerks. Thomas tapped at the glass door, but not till he had opened it and said, "Mr. Stopper," did he take any notice. He started, turned, and regarded him for a moment, gave a rather constrained smile, and, to Tom's surprise, held out his hand.

"It is very good of you to speak to me at all, Mr. Stopper," said Thomas, touched with gratitude already. "I don't deserve it."

"Well, I must say you have behaved rather strangely, to say the least. It might have been a serious thing for you, Mr. Thomas, if I hadn't been more friendly than you would have given me credit for. Look here."

And he showed him the sum of eleven pounds thirteen shillings and eightpence halfpenny put down to Mr. Stopper's debit in the petty cash book.

"You understand that, I presume, Mr. Thomas? You ran the risk of prison there."

"I know I did, Mr. Stopper. Listen to me for a moment, and you will be able to forgive me, I think. I had been drinking and gambling, losing all night—and I believe I was really drunk when I did that. Not that I didn't know I was doing wrong, and I know it doesn't clear me at all, but I want to tell you the truth. I've been wretched ever since, and daren't show myself. I have been bitterly punished. I haven't touched cards or dice since. Here's the money," he concluded, offering the notes and gold.

Mr. Stopper did not heed the action at first. He was regarding Thomas rather curiously. Thomas perceived it, and said, "Yes, I am a sailor. It's an honest way of living, and I like it."

"You'll come back now, won't you?"

"That depends," answered Thomas. "Would you take me now, Mr. Stopper?" he added with a feeble experimental smile. "But there's the money. Do take it out of my hands."

"It lies with your father now, Mr. Thomas. Have you been to Highbury? Of course, I took care not to let him know."

"Thank you heartily. I'm just going there. Do take the horrid money, and let me feel as if I weren't a thief after all."

"As for the money, eleven pound, odd," said Mr. Stopper without looking at it, "that's neither here nor there. It was a burglary, there can be no doubt, under the circumstances. But I owe you a quarter's salary, though I should not be bound to pay it, seeing you left as you did. Still, you worked very fairly for it. I will hand you over the difference."

Stopper took out the checkbook, and proceeded to write a check for thirteen pounds six shillings and threepence halfpenny. He handed Thomas the check with the words, "Now we're clear, Mr. Thomas. But don't do it again. It won't pass twice. I've saved you this time."

"Do it again!" cried Thomas, seizing Mr. Stopper's hand. "I would sooner cut my own throat! Thank you, thank you a thousand times, Mr. Stopper," he added, his heart brimful at this beginning of his day of horror.

Mr. Stopper very quietly withdrew his hand, turned round on his stool, replaced his checkbook in the drawer, and proceeded to arrange his writing materials, as if nobody were there but himself. He knew well enough that it was not for Thomas' sake that he had done it. There was therefore something rudely imposing in the way in which he behaved to Thomas, and Thomas felt it, but did not resent it, for he had no right to be indignant; he was glad of any terms he could make.

Thomas left the countinghouse a free man. He bounded back to Mr. Fuller, returned the money, showed him the check, and told him all.

"There's the beginning for you, my boy!" said Mr. Fuller, almost as delighted as Thomas himself. "Now for the next."

Tom's countenance fell. He was afraid, and Mr. Fuller saw it.

"You daren't go near Lucy till you have been to your father. It would be to insult her, Thomas."

Tom caught up his cap from the table and left the house, once more resolved. It would be useless to go to Highbury at this hour; he would find his father at his office in the city. And he had not far to go to find him—unfortunately, thought Tom.

When Tom was shown into his father's office, he was writing a letter. Looking up and seeing Tom, he gave a grin—that is, a laugh without the smile in it—handed him a few of his fingers, pointed to a chair, and went on with his letter. This reception irritated Tom, and put an edge on his sheepishness. Before his father he did not feel that he appeared exactly as a culprit. He had told him either to give up Lucy, or not to show his face at home again. He had lost Lucy, it might be, but he would not give her up. So he sat, more composed than he had expected to be, waiting for what should follow. In a few minutes his father looked up again, methodically folded his letter and cast a sneering glance at his son's garb.

"What's the meaning of this masquerade, Tom?"

"I'm dressed for my work," answered Tom, surprised at his own coolness, now that the ice was broken.

"What's your work then, pray?"

"I'm a sailor."

"You a sailor!"

"I've made five coasting voyages since you turned me out," said Tom.

"I turned you out! You turned yourself out. Why the devil did you come back, then? Why don't you stick to your new trade?"

"You told me either to give up Lucy Burton, or to take lodgings elsewhere. I won't give up Lucy Burton."

"Take her to hell, if you like. What do you come back here for, with your cursed impudence? There's nobody I want less."

This was far from true—he had been very uneasy about his son. Now that he saw him, his tyrannical disposition maddened by Thomas's resistance, and the consequent frustration of his money—making plans broke out against him in this fierce, cold, blasting wrath.

"I came here," said Thomas—and he said it merely to discharge himself of a duty, for he had not the thinnest shadow of a hope that it would be of service—"I came here to protest against the extreme to which you are driving your legal rights—of which I have only just learned—against Mrs. Boxall."

"And her granddaughter. But I am not aware that I am driving my *rights,* as you say," said Mr. Worboise, relapsing into his former manner, so cold that it stung. "I *have* driven them already as far as my knowledge of affairs allows me to consider prudent. I have turned those people out of the house."

"You have!" cried Thomas, starting to his feet. "Father! You are worse than ever I thought you. It is cruel! It is wicked!"

"Don't discompose yourself about it. It is all your own fault, my son."

"I am no son of yours. From this moment I renounce you, and call you *father* no more," cried Thomas, in mingled wrath and horror and consternation.

"Very well. Then I beg again to inform you that it is your own fault. Give up that girl, and I will provide for the lovely siren and her harridan grandmother for life, and take you home to wealth and a career which you shall choose for yourself."

"I will not."

"Then take yourself off, and be—" Thomas rose and left the room without waiting for him to finish. As he went down the stairs, his father shouted after him in a tone of fury, "You're not to go near your mother, mind."

"I'm going straight to her," answered Tom, as quietly as he could.

"If you do, I'll murder her."

Tom came up the stair again to the door next to his father's, where the clerks sat. He opened this and said aloud, "Gentlemen, you heard what Mr. Worboise has just said. There may be occasion to refer to it again." Then returning to his father's door, he said in a low tone, "My mother may die any moment, as you very well know, Sir. It may be awkward after what you have just said."

Having said this, he left his father a little abashed. As his wrath ebbed, Mr. Worboise began to admire his son's presence of mind, and even to take some credit for it. "A chip off the old block!" he muttered to himself. "Who would have thought there was so much in the rascal? Seafaring must agree with the young beggar!"

Thomas hailed the first hansom, jumped in, and drove straight to Highbury. Was it strange that notwithstanding the dreadful interview he had just had he should feel such a gladness in his being as he had never known before? The second and more awful load of duty was now lifted from his mind.

When the maid opened the door to Thomas, she stared like an idiot. Yet she was in truth a woman of sense, for before he had reached the foot of the stairs she ran after him.

"Mr. Thomas! Mr. Thomas! You mustn't go up to Mis'ess all of a sudden. You'll kill her if you do."

Thomas paused at once. "Run up and tell her then. Make haste."

She sped up the stairs. Thomas followed, and remained outside his mother's door. He had to wait a little while, for the maid was imparting the news with circumspection. He heard the low tone of his mother's voice, but could not hear what she said. At last came a little cry, and then he could hear her sob. A minute or two passed, which seemed endless to Thomas, and then the maid came to the door and asked him to go in.

His mother looked much worse than before. She stretched out her arms to him, kissed him, and held his head to her bosom. He had never before had such an embrace from her.

"My boy! My boy!" she cried, weeping. "Thank God, I have you again. You'll tell me all about it, won't you?"

She went on weeping and murmuring words of endearment and gratitude for some time. Then she released him, holding one of his hands only. "There's a chair there. Sit down and tell me about it. I am afraid your poor father has been hard upon you."

"We won't talk about him," said Thomas. "I have faults enough of my own to confess, Mother. But I won't tell you all about them now. I have been very wicked—gambling and worse, but I will never do so anymore. I am ashamed and sorry, and I think God will forgive me for it. Will you forgive me, Mother?"

"With all my heart, my boy. And you know that God forgives everyone that believes in Jesus. I hope you have given your heart to Him at last. Then I shall die happy."

"I don't know, Mother, whether I have or not, but I want to do what's right."

"That won't save you, my poor child. You'll have a talk with Mr. Simon about it, won't you? I'm not able to argue anything now."

"Mother, I will listen to anything you choose to say, but I won't talk about such things with a man whom I cannot respect."

Mrs. Worboise gave a slight sigh, but perhaps partly because her own respect for Mr. Simon had been shaken a little of late, she said nothing.

Thomas resumed. "If I hadn't been taken by the hand by a very different man from him, Mother, I shouldn't have been here today. Thank God! Mr. Fuller is a real clergyman!"

"Who is he, Thomas? I think I have heard the name."

"He is the clergyman of St. Amos' in the city."

"Ah! I thought so. A ritualist, I'm afraid, Thomas. They lay their snares for young people."

"Nonsense, Mother!" said Thomas irreverently. "Mr. Fuller would not feel flattered to be told that he belonged to any party whatever but that of Jesus Christ Himself."

"I'm sadly afraid, Thomas, you've been reading the wrong books."

"A sailor hasn't much time for reading, Mother."

"A sailor, Thomas! What do you mean? Where have you been all this time?" she asked, examining his appearance anxiously.

"At sea, Mother."

"My boy! My boy! That is a godless calling. However—"

Thomas interrupted her. "They that go down to the sea in ships were supposed to see wonders of the Lord, Mother."

"Yes, but when will you be reasonable? That was in David's time."

"The sea is much the same, and man's heart is much the same. Anyhow, I'm a sailor, and a sailor I must be. I have nothing else to do."

"Mr. Boxall's business is all your father's now, though I cannot understand it. Whatever you've done, you can go back to the countinghouse, you know."

"I can't, Mother. My father and I have parted forever."

"Why is that? What have you been doing?"

"Refusing to give up Lucy Burton."

"O Tom, Tom! Why do you set yourself up against your father?"

"Well, Mother, I don't want to be impertinent, but it seems to me that it's no more than you have been doing all your life."

"For conscience' sake, Tom. But in matters indifferent we ought to yield, you know."

"Is it an indifferent matter to keep one's engagements, Mother, to be true to one's word?"

"But you had no right to make them."

"They are made, anyhow, and I must bear the consequences of keeping them."

Mrs. Worboise was nearly worn out. Tom saw it, and rose to go.

"Am I never to see you again, Tom?" she asked, despairingly.

"Every time I come to London—so long as my father doesn't make you shut the door against me, Mother."

"That shall never be, my boy. Are you really are going on that sea again?"

"Yes, Mother. It's an honest calling. And believe me, Mother, it's often easier to pray to God on shipboard than it is sitting at a desk."

"Well, well, my boy!" said his mother with a great sigh of weariness. "If I only knew that you were possessed of saving faith, I could bear even to hear that you had been drowned. It may happen any day, you know, Thomas."

"Not till God pleases."

His mother gave him another tearful embrace. Thomas' heart was miserable at leaving her thus fearful, almost helpless about him. How terrible it would be for her in the windy nights! He searched eagerly for something that might comfort her.

"Mother, dear," he said, "Jesus said, 'Come unto Me, all ye that are weary and heavy-laden, and I will give you rest.' I will go to Him. I will promise you that, if you like. That is all I can say, and I think that ought to be enough. If He gives me rest, shall I not be safe? And whoever says that He will not if I go to Him—"

"In the appointed way, my dear."

"He says nothing more than *go to Him.* And I will go to Him, the only way that a man can, when He is in heaven and I am on the earth. And if Mr. Simon or anybody says that He will not give me rest, he is a liar. If that doesn't satisfy you, Mother, I don't believe you have any faith in Him yourself."

With this outburst Thomas again kissed his mother, and left the room. Nor did his last words displease her. Such a blunt utterance was far more calculated to carry some hope into his mother's mind than any amount of arguing upon the points of difference between them.

As he reached the landing, his sister, Amy, came rushing up the stairs, with her hair in disorder and a blushing face.

"Why, Tom!" she said, as he took her in his arms. "How handsome you have grown, Tom!" She broke from him and ran up to her mother's room.

Downstairs, Tom saw Mr. Simon looking into the fire. Unknown to Tom, he had just made Amy an offer of marriage. Tom let him stand and hurried back on foot to his friend Mr. Fuller, his heart full and his thoughts in confusion.

Mr. Fuller rose eagerly to meet him. " 'Now see I by thine eyes that this is done,' " he said, quoting King Arthur.

They sat down and Tom told him all.

"I wish you had managed a little better with your father," he said.

"I wish I had, Sir. But it is done, and there is no help for it now."

"No, I suppose not—at present, at least. But you have earned your dinner anyhow, and here comes Mrs. Jones to say it is ready. Come along."

Thomas' face fell. "I thought I should have gone to see Lucy now, Sir."

"I do not believe she will be at home."

"She was always home from Mrs. Morgenstern's before now."

"Yes, but she has to work much harder now, and has more lessons to give. You see her grandmother is dependent on her now."

"And where are they? My father told me himself that he had turned them out of the house in Guild Court."

"Yes. But they are no further off than that; they have been lodging with Mr. Kitely. I think you had better go and see your friends the sailor and publican after dinner, and by the time you come back, I shall have arranged for your seeing her. You would hardly like to take your chance, and find her with her grandmother and Mattie."

"Who is Mattie? Oh, I know—that dreadful little imp of Kitely's."

"I daresay she can make herself unpleasant enough," laughed Mr. Fuller, "but she is a most remarkable and very interesting child. I could hardly have believed in such a child if I had not known her. She was in great danger, I allow, of turning out to be a little prig, but your friend Lucy has saved her from that."

"God bless her," said Thomas. "She has saved me too, even if she refuses to have anything more to do with me. How shall I tell her everything? Since I have had it over with my father and Stopper, I feel as if I were whitewashed; and to have to tell her what a sepulchre I am is dreadful—and she so white outside and in!"

"Yes, it's hard to do, but it must be done."

They were now seated at dinner, and nothing more of importance was said until that was over. Then they returned to the study, where Mr. Fuller said, "Now, Thomas, it is time that I should talk to you a little more about yourself. There is only One who can absolve you in the grand sense of the word. If God Himself were to say to you, 'Let bygones be bygones, nothing more shall be said about them'—if He only said that, it would be a poor thing to meet our human need. But He is infinitely kinder than that. He says, 'I, even I, am He that taketh away thine iniquities.' He alone can make us clean—put our hearts so right that nothing of the kind will happen again.

"You must give yourself up to the obedience of His Son entirely and utterly, leaving your salvation to Him, troubling yourself nothing about that, but ever seeking to see things done as He sees them, and to do things as He would have them done. And for this purpose you must study your New Testament in particular, that you may see the glory of God in the face of Jesus Christ. Receiving Him as your Master, your Teacher, your Saviour, you may open your heart to the entrance of His Spirit, the mind that was in Him, so that He may save you. Every word of His, if you will but try to obey it, you will find precious beyond what words can say. And He has promised without reserve the Holy Spirit of God to them that ask it."

"I believe you, Sir, though I cannot quite see into everything yet. All I can say is that I want to be good. Pray for me, Sir, if you think there is any good in one man's praying for another."

"I do indeed—just in proportion to the love that is in it. Come then, we will kneel together, and I will pray with you."

Thomas felt more solemn by far, when he rose from that prayer, than he had ever felt in his life.

"Now," said Mr. Fuller, "go and see your friends. When you think of it, my boy, you will see how God has been looking after you, giving you friend after friend of such different sorts to make up for the want of a father, and so driving you home to Himself. He had to drive you, but He will lead you now. You will be home by half-past six?"

Thomas assented. He could not speak, but could only return the grasp of Mr. Fuller's hand. Then he took his cap and went.

He did not see the captain, who had gone down to his brig. Mrs. Potts (and Bessie too, after a fashion) welcomed him heartily, but Mr. Potts was a little aggrieved that he would drink nothing but a glass of bitter ale. He had the watch safe, and brought it out gladly when Thomas produced his check to reclaim it.

Jim Salter dropped in. When he saw Tom, he came up to him, holding out his hand, but speaking as with a sense of wrong. " 'ow de do, Gov'nor? Who'd a-thought to see you 'ere! 'Ain't you got ne'er another sixpence to put a name upon it? You're fond o' sixpences, *you* are, Gov'nor."

"What do you mean, Jim?" asked the bewildered Thomas.

"To think o' treatin' a man and a brother as you've treated me, after I'd been and devoted my life, leastways a good part of it, to save you from the pellice! Four *and* sixpence!"

Still bewildered, Thomas appealed to Mr. Potts, whose face looked as like a caricature of the moon as ever, although he had just worked out a very neat little problem in diplomacy.

"Don't you see, Jim?" he said. "You wouldn't have liked to rob a gentleman like that by takin' of half a suvering for loafin' about for a day with him when he was hard up. But as he's come by his own again, why there's no use in keeping it from you any longer. So there's your five and sixpence. But it's a devil of a shame. Now get out of my house."

"Whew!" whistled Jim. "Two words to that, Gov'nor o' the Marmaid. You've been and kep' me all this many a day out of my inheritance. What do you say to that, Sir? What do you think of yerself, Sir?"

While he spoke, Jim pocketed the money. Receiving no reply except a sniff of Mr. Potts' red nose, he broke out again. "I tell 'e what, Gov'nor, I don't go out o' your 'ouse till I've put a name upon it."

Quite defeated, and rather dejected, Mr. Potts took down his best brandy and poured out a bumper. Jim tossed it off, and set down the glass. Then, and not till then, he turned to Thomas, who had been looking on, half-vexed with Mr. Potts, and half-amused with Jim.

"Well, I *am* glad, Mr. Wurbus, as you've turned out a honest man arter all. I assure you, Sir, at one time I 'ad my doubts." And without another word, Jim Salter turned and left the Mermaid.

42. THOMAS AND LUCY

Mr. Fuller was so delighted with the result of his efforts with Thomas that he could hardly wait till the evening. Still, he had no intention of taking the office of a mediator between them, for that, he felt, would be to intrude for the sake of making himself important; and he had learned that one of the virtues of holy and true service is to get out of the way as soon as possible.

About six o'clock he was shown into the bookseller's back parlor, where he found both Lucy and her grandmother.

"Will you come out with me, Miss Burton, for an hour or so?" he said.

"I wonder at you, Mr. Fuller," interposed Mrs. Boxall. "A clergyman too!"

Mr. Fuller was considerably astonished, but did not lose self-possession. "Surely you are not afraid to trust her with me, Mrs. Boxall?" he said, merrily.

"I don't know that, Sir. I hear of very strange goings-on at your church. Service every day, the church always open, and all that! As if folk had nothing to do but say their prayers."

"I don't think you would talk like that, Mrs. Boxall," said Mr. Fuller pleasantly, "if you had been saying your prayers lately."

"You have nothing to do with my prayers, Sir."

"Nor you with my church, Mrs. Boxall. But come, don't let us quarrel. I don't wonder at your being put out sometimes;

you've had so much to vex you. But it hasn't been Lucy's fault, and I'm sure I would gladly give you your rights if I could."

"I don't doubt it, Sir," said the old lady, mollified. "Don't be long, Lucy."

Lucy hastened to get her bonnet and cloak. Mr. Fuller took her straight to his own house. She asked him no questions, content to be led toward what was awaiting her. It was a dark and cloudy night, but a cool west wind full of spring came down Bagot Street, blowing away the winter and all its miseries. Away with it went all thought of Thomas's past behavior. The prodigal had turned to go home, and she would walk with him and help his homeward steps. She loved him more than ever. Her heart beat so violently as she crossed Mr. Fuller's threshold, that she could hardly breathe. He took her into the sitting room where a most friendly fire was blazing, and left her.

Still she had no answers. She knew that she was going to see Thomas. She could sit there, she thought, for years waiting for him, but at length she fell into a dreamy study of the fire. The door opened, and she thought it was Mr. Fuller, so she sat still. A moment more, and Thomas was kneeling at her feet. He only said in a choked voice, "Lucy," and bowed his head before her. She put her hands on his head, drew it softly to her knees, gave one long, gentle, but irrepressible wail like a child, and burst into a quiet passion of tears. Thomas drew his head from her hands, sank on the floor, and lay sobbing. She could not move to make him cease. But when she recovered herself a little, after a measureless time to both of them, she stooped, put her hands round his face, and drew him upwards. He rose, but only to his knees.

"Lucy, Lucy," he sobbed, "will you forgive me?" He could say no more yet. She bent forward and kissed his forehead. "I have been very wicked," he continued. "I will tell you all about it—everything."

"No, no, Thomas. Only love me."

"I love you with all my heart and soul. I don't even ask you to love me one little bit. If you will only let me love you!"

"Thomas," said Lucy slowly, struggling, "my heart is so full of love and gladness that it is like to break."

By degrees they grew calmer, but Thomas could not rest till

she knew all. "Lucy," he said, "I can't be sure that all you give me is really mine till I've told you everything. Perhaps you won't love me—not so much—when you know all. So I must tell you."

"I don't care what it is, Thomas, for I am sure you won't again."

"I will not," said Thomas solemnly. "But please, Lucy darling, listen to me—for my sake, not for your own, for it will hurt you so."

"If it will make you easier, Thomas tell me everything."

"I will." And he did. But Lucy cried so much that when he came to the part describing his adventures in London, he yielded to the temptation to try to give her the comical side as well. And at the very first hint of fun in the description he gave of Jim Salter, Lucy burst into a fit of laughter. Thomas was quite frightened, for it seemed as if she would never stop; between her laughing and crying, Thomas was afraid to say anything. But at length the story was told, and Lucy laughed and cried at every new turn of the story.

When he came to the point of his father offering to provide for them if he would give up Lucy, he hesitated, and said, "Ought I to have done it, Lucy, for your sake?"

"For my sake, Tom! If you had said for Grannie's—she would starve rather than accept a penny from him, except as her right. Besides, I can make more money in a year than he would give her, I am sure. So if you will keep me, Tom, I will keep her."

Here Lucy discovered that she had said something very improper, and hid her face in her hands. But a knock came to the door, and Mr. Fuller put his head in and said, "Have you two young people made up yet?"

"Have we, Tom?" said Lucy.

"I don't know," said Tom.

Mr. Fuller laughed heartily, came near and put a hand on the head of each, and said, "God bless you. I too am glad at my very heart. Now you must come to supper."

But at supper Thomas had a good many questions to ask. And he kept on asking, for he wanted to understand the state of the case between Mrs. Boxall and his father. All at once, at one reply, he jumped from his seat looking very strange.

"I must be off, Lucy. You won't hear from me for a day or two. Good-bye, Mr. Fuller. Something may be done yet, though it may all come to nothing. Don't ask me any questions. There's no time to lose."

He rushed from the room, and left Mr. Fuller and Lucy staring at each other. Mr. Fuller started up and ran to the door, but only to hear the outer door banging, and Thomas shouting, "Cab ahoy!" in the street.

So there was nothing for it but to take Lucy home again. He left her at Mr. Kitely's door.

"Well, Miss, what have you been about?" said her grandmother.

"Having a long talk with Thomas, Grannie," answered Lucy.

"You have!" exclaimed Mrs. Boxall, rising slowly from her seat with the air of one about to pronounce a solemn malediction.

"Yes, Grannie, but he knew nothing till this very night about the way his father has behaved to us."

"He has made you believe that, did he? Then you're a fool, and you'll never see him again. He comes of a breed bad enough to believe anything of. You give him up, or I give you up."

"No, I won't, Grannie," said Lucy, smiling in her face.

"You or I leave this house, then."

"*I* won't, Grannie."

"Then *I* will."

"Very well, Grannie," answered Lucy, putting her arms round her and kissing her. "Shall I fetch your bonnet?"

Grannie vouchsafed no reply, but took up her candle and went—to bed.

Thomas drove to the Mermaid, and came upon Captain Smith.

"I say, Captain, you must let Robins off this voyage. I want him to go to Newcastle with me."

"What's up now? Ain't he going to Newcastle? And you can go with him if you like."

"I want him at once. It's of the greatest importance."

He sat down and told the captain what he was after—to find Robins' friend Jack for evidence he could give upon the question of the order of decease in the family of Richard Boxall. He explained the point of Julia's delayed death to the captain.

Then Mr. Potts joined them and they sat talking it over. At last Tom said, "There's one thing I shall be more easy when I've told you—that lawyer is my father."

"God bless my soul!" said Mr. Potts while Captain Smith said something decidedly different.

"So you'll oblige me," Tom went on, "if you'll say nothing very hard of him, for I hope he will live to be horribly ashamed of himself."

"Here's long life to him!" said Captain Smith.

"And no success this bout!" added Mr. Potts.

"Amen to both, and thank you," said Tom.

The captain soon found Robins, and in a few hours Robins and Tom were off to Newcastle.

43. PATIENCE

The Saturday following Tom's sudden departure Lucy had a whole holiday, and she resolved to enjoy it—an easy task, for everything was now beautiful, and not even Grannie's intermittent fits of ill-humor could destroy her serenity. The saddest thing was to see how the prospect of wealth, and the loss of that prospect, had worked for the temperamental ruin of the otherwise worthy old woman. Her goodness had had little foundation in principle; therefore, when the floods came and the winds blew, it could not stand against them. The last thing Mrs. Boxall said to Lucy as she went out that morning, rousing herself from a dark-hued reverie over the fire, was "Lucy, if you marry that man I'll go to the workhouse."

"But they won't take you in, Grannie, when you've got a granddaughter to work for you."

"I won't take a farthing of my own property, but as my own right."

"Thomas won't have a farthing of it to offer you. He quarreled with his father about just that, and he's turned Tom out."

"Then I *must* go to the workhouse."

"And I'll bring you packets of tea and snuff," said Lucy, merrily.

"Go along with you. You never had any heart but for your beaux."

"There's a little left for you yet, Grannie. And for beaux,

you know I never had but one." So saying, she ran up the court to Mr. Spelt's shop.

"Where's Poppie, Mr. Spelt?" she asked. "Will you let her come with me to the Zoological Gardens today?"

"With all my heart. Shall I fetch her from the house?"

"On no account! I'll go up myself." She found Poppie actually washing cups and saucers, with her sleeves tucked up, and looking a very lovely and orderly maiden. With her father and Mattie and Mr. Fuller and Lucy around her, it was no wonder that the real woman in her should have begun to grow. Lucy had had a great deal to do with the change, for she had been giving her and Mattie regular lessons for the last few months. The difficulty was to get Poppie to open her mental eyes to any information that did not come by sight of her bodily eyes. Conveying facts to her was almost an impossibility. For a long time she only stared and looked around her, as if she would be glad to scud if she dared. But she loved Lucy, who watched long and anxiously for some sign of dawning interest. It came at last in Poppie's most innocent remark: "Was Jesus a man? I sposed he wor a clergyman!" But having once got a glimpse of light, her eyes, if they opened slowly, strengthened rapidly. She learned to think with an amount of reality which showed that, while she retained many of the defects of childhood, she retained also some of its most valuable characteristics.

Poppie was older than Mattie, but while Mattie talked like an old woman, Poppie talked like a baby. A double exchange was happening between them: Poppie was getting wiser, and Mattie was getting merrier. Sometimes, to Mr. Kitely's delight, they would frolic about his house like kittens. However, such a burst would seldom last long, for Mrs. Boxall resented it as unfeeling toward her misfortunes, and generally put a stop to it. This did not please Mr. Kitely at all, but he intimated to Mattie that it was better to give in to her.

"The old lady is very cranky today. She don't feel comfortable in her inside," he would say, and Mattie would repeat the remark to Poppie. "The old lady don't feel over comfittable in her inside today. We must drop it, or she'll be worse." The tumult would be heard no more—at least for an hour, when it might break out again.

Lucy addressed Poppie. "Will you come with me today to see

the wild beasts?"

"But they'll eat us, won't they?"

"They would if they could, but they can't, so they won't."

"Do they pull their teeth out, then?"

"You come and see. I'll take care of you."

"Is Mattie going? Then I'll come." She threw down the saucer she was washing, dried her hands in her apron, and stood ready to follow.

"No, Poppie, that won't do. You must finish washing first, and put on your cloak and hat, and make yourself look nice and tidy, before I can take you."

"It's only the beasts, Miss! They ain't particler."

"It's not for the beasts, but because you ought always to be tidy. There will be people there, of course, and it's disrespectful to other people to be untidy."

"I didn't know, Miss. Would they give I to the bears?"

"Poppie, you're a goose. Make haste."

The children had never seen any but domestic animals before, and their wonder and pleasure in these strange new forms of life were boundless. Mattie caught the explosive affection from Poppie, and Lucy had her reward in the outbursts of interest that rose on each side of her, which were as varied in kind as the animals themselves. Poppie shrieked with laughter at the monkeys, while Mattie turned away, pale with dislike. Lucy found Mattie standing outside the door, waiting for them.

"I can't make it out," she said putting her hand into Lucy's.

"What can't you make out. Mattie?"

"I can't make out why God made monkeys."

Lucy had no answer to give her for she did not fancy it part of a teacher's duty to tell lies, pretending acquaintance with what she did not know anything about. Poppie had no difficulty about the monkeys, but the lions and tigers, and all the tearing creatures were a horror to her.

Poppie shouted with delight to see the seals tumble into the water, dive deep, then turn on their backs and look up at her. But their large, round yet pathetic, doglike eyes, fixed upon her, made the tears come in Mattie's eyes.

They came to the camel's house, and they got upon his back. After a short and not comfortable ride, they got down again. Poppie took hold of Lucy's sleeve, and with solemn face asked,

"Is it alive, Miss?" She was not sure that he did not go by machinery.

However, Lucy's private share of the day's enjoyment lay outside the Gardens. There the buds were bursting everywhere. Out of the black bark all begrimed with London smoke and London dirt, flowed the purest green. Verily there is One that can bring a clean thing out of an unclean. Reviving nature was all in harmony with Lucy's feelings this day—it was the most simply happy day she had ever had. The gentle wind with its cold and its soft streaks fading and reviving, the blue sky with its few flying undefined masses of whiteness, the shadow of green all around—for when she looked through the trees, it was like looking through a thin green cloud or shadow. All this made her more happy than she had ever been before, even in a dream.

She was walking southward through the park, for she wanted to take the two children to see Mrs. Morgenstern. They were frolicking about her, running hither and thither when she saw Mr. Sargent coming towards her. She would not have avoided him if she could, for her heart was so free that it was strong as well. He lifted his hat. She offered her hand. He took it, saying, "This is more than I deserve, Miss Burton, after the abominable way I behaved to you last time I saw you. I see you have forgiven me. But I dare hardly accept your forgiveness: it is so much more than I deserve."

"I know what it is to suffer, Mr. Sargent, and there is no excuse I could not make for you. Perhaps the best proof I can give is that I wish to forget all that passed on that dreadful evening is to be quite open with you still. I have seen Mr. Worboise since then," she went on, regardless of her own blushes. "He had been led astray, but not so much as you thought. He brought me back the ring you mentioned."

If Mr. Sargent did not place much confidence in the reformation Lucy hinted at, it is not very surprising. No doubt the fact would destroy any possibly lingering hope he yet cherished, but this was not all: he was quite justified in regarding with great distrust any such change as her words implied. He had known many causes of a man's having, to all appearance, entirely abjured his wicked ways for the sake of a woman, only to return after marriage, like the sow that was washed, to wallowing in the mire. There was nothing to be said at present on the subject, however, and after a few more words they parted.

Now had it not been for Thomas's foolish half-romantic way of doing things, no evil could have come of his sudden departure. If he had fully explained to his friends what his object was when he left them so suddenly, all would have been accounted for. He liked importance, and surprises, and secrecy. But this was self-indulgence, when it involved the possibility of so much anxiety as a lengthened absence must occasion both Lucy and Mr. Fuller. They had a right, besides, to know everything that he was about, after all that they had done for him, and still more from the fact that they must keep thinking about him.

When a month had passed, bringing no news of Thomas and when yet another month had passed and still he neither came nor wrote, hope deferred began to work its own work and make Lucy's heart sick. But she kept up bravely, through the help of her daily labor. Those who think it hard to have to work hard, as well as endure other sore trials, little know how much those other trials are rendered endurable by the work that accompanies them. They regard the work as an additional burden, instead of as the prop which keeps their burdens from crushing them to the earth. The same is true of pain—sometimes of grief, sometimes of fear. And all of these keep us in some measure from putting our trust in that which is weak and bad, even when they do but little to make us trust in God.

Nor did this season of trial to Lucy pass by without bringing some little measure of good to the poor, disappointed, fretful soul of her grandmother. She grew calmer, and began to turn her thoughts a little away from what she fancied might have been if things had not gone wrong so perversely, and to reflect on the fact—which she had often expressed in words, but never really thought about before—that it would be all the same a hundred years after—a saying which, however far from true, yet has wrapt up in it, after a clumsy fashion, a very great and important truth. By slow degrees her former cheerfulness began to show a little over her hitherto gloomy horizon. She would smile occasionally, and the communications with Widdles grew more airy.

"Ah, Widdles, Widdles!" she would say as she rubbed the unavailing balm on his blue back, "you and I know what trouble is, don't we, old bird?"

She began to have a respect for her own misfortunes, which indicated that they had begun to recede a little from the point of her vision. To have had misfortunes is the only distinction some can claim; but the heart that knows its own bitterness too often forgets that there is more bitterness in the world than that.

Widdles would cock his magnificent head and whiskers on one side, and wink with one eye, as much as to say, "I believe you, old girl." Then he would turn his denuded, featherless back upon her, as much as to add with more solemnity, "Contemplate my condition, Madam. Behold me. Imagine what I once was, that you may understand the spite of fortune which has reduced me to my present bareness. Am I not a spectacle to men and angels? But what the worse am I? Who cares, so long as you don't. Let's turn about once more. My dancing days are over, but life is life, even without feathers."

Mrs. Boxall began to recover her equanimity, and at length even her benevolence toward men in general—with one class exception, that of lawyers, and two individual exceptions, those of old Worboise and young Worboise. She had a vague conviction that it was one of that malignant class that had plucked Widdles. "Ah, my poor Widdles! Them lawyers!" she would say. "You would have been a very different person, indeed, Widdles, if it hadn't been for them. But it'll be all the same in a hundred years, Widdles. Keep up heart, old bird. It'll all be over soon. If you die before me, I'll put you on a winding-sheet that'll be a deal more comfortable than dead feathers, and I'll bury you with my own hands. But what'll you do for me, if I die first, you little scarecrow? You'll look about for me, won't you? And you'll miss the bits of sugar. Mattie, my dear, mind that Widdles has his sugar and everything, after I'm dead and gone."

44. Guild Court Again

One sultry evening in summer, Grannie left the rooms to visit a neighbor. Lucy was seated at her piano in Mr. Kitely's back parlor. She was not playing, but had just been singing.

Two arms came round her from behind, but she did not start. She was taken by (but not with) surprise. She was always with him in mood, if not in thought, and his bodily presence therefore overcame her only as a summer cloud. She leaned back into his embrace, and burst into tears. Then she rose to look at him, and he let her go. She saw him rather ragged, rather dirty, quite of a doubtful exterior to the eye of the man who lives to be respectable, but her eye saw deeper. She looked into his face and was satisfied. Truth shone there from the true light and fire within. He did not fall at her feet as once before; the redeemed soul stood and looked her in the face. He put out his arms once more, and she did not draw back. She knew that he was a man, that he was true, and she was his.

And he knew that the last low-brooding rims of the cloud of his shame had vanished from his heaven, and that a man may have sinned and yet be glad. He could give God thanks for the shame, whose oppression had led him to understand and hate the sin.

After a while, when their feelings were a little composed, Thomas began to tell Lucy all his adventures. In the middle, however, they heard Mrs. Boxall's voice in the shop.

"Don't tell Grannie anything about it yet," said Lucy. "She's much quieter in her mind now, and if we were to get her off again; it would only do her harm. Anything certain she has a right to know, but I don't think she has a right to know all that you are trying to do for her. That is your business. But you mustn't mind how she behaves to you, Tom dear. She thinks you and your father are all in the affair."

When the old lady entered she saw at a glance how things were going, but she merely gave a very marked sniff and retreated to her chair by the window. But she could not keep silent very long, and the beginning of speech as well as of strife is like the letting out of water.

"Thomas," she said, "is this room mine or yours?"

"Grannie," said Lucy, "Thomas had nothing to do with it. He was away from home, I assure you, when things went wrong."

"Very convenient, no doubt, for both of you! It's nothing to you, so long as you marry him, of course. But you might have waited. The money would have been yours. But you'll have it all the sooner for marrying the man that turned your grandmother into the street. Well, well! Only I won't sit here and see that scoundrel in my room."

She rose as she spoke, though what she would or could have done she did not know herself. It was on Lucy's lips to say to her, "The room's mine, Grannie, if you come to that, and I won't have my friend turned out of it." But she thought better of it, and led Thomas into the shop.

Thereupon Grannie turned to Widdles for refuge from the shame of her own behavior, took him out of his cage, and handled him so roughly that one of the three wing feathers left on one side came off in her hand. The half of our ill-temper is often occasioned by annoyance at the other half.

Thomas and Lucy finished their talk in a low voice in the leafy forest of books. Thomas told her all about it now—how he wanted to find the man Jack, and how Robins and he had worked their way to Lisbon and found him there and brought him home. But if the representation she and Mr. Fuller had given him of the state of the case was correct, there could be no doubt but Jack's testimony would reverse the previous decision, and Grannie would have her own.

"I can't help being rather sorry for it," concluded Tom,

"for it'll come to you then, Lucy, I suppose, and you will hardly be able to believe that it was not for my own sake that I went after Jack. I've got him safe, and Robins too, at the Mermaid. But I can't be grand and give you up—though I should almost like to, when I think of the money and my father."

"Don't give me up, Tom, or I'll give you up, and that would be a bad job for me."

Then they made it clear to each other that nothing was further from their intentions.

"But what am I to do next, Lucy? You must tell me the lawyers who conducted your side of the case."

"I am afraid I can't ask him to do anything more."

"Who, Lucy?"

"Mr. Sargent."

"Sargent—Sargent—I think I have heard the name. If you are not satisfied with him, the firm you employed will speak to another."

"He did everything, Thomas. But I will go and consult Mr. Morgenstern."

"There is no time to lose."

"Come with me to his office then. It is not far to Old Broad Street."

They went out instantly, found Mr. Morgenstern, and put him in possession of the discovered evidence. He was delighted with the news. "We must find Sargent at once," he said.

Lucy began to stammer out some objection.

"Oh! I know all about it, Lucy," he said. "But this is no time for nonsense. In fact you would be doing the honest fellow a great wrong if you deprived him of the pleasure of gaining his case after all. Indeed, he would feel that far more than your refusal of him. And quite right too. Sargent will be delighted. It will go far to console him, poor fellow."

"But will it be right of me to consent to it?" asked Thomas with hesitation.

"It is a mere act of justice to him," said Mr. Morgenstern, "and, excuse me, but I don't see that you have any right to bring your feelings into the matter. Besides, it will give Mrs. Boxall the opportunity of making him what return she ought. It will be a great thing for him—give him quite a start in his profession. I will go to him at once," concluded Mr.

Morgenstern, taking his hat.

Mr. Sargent was delighted at the turn affairs had taken from a business point of view, but his delight was greatly tempered by other considerations. He went into the matter mind and soul, if not heart and soul, and obtained a fresh trial on the ground of new evidence. The former judgment was rescinded and the property was declared Mrs. Boxall's.

Mr. Worboise and Mr. Sargent met afterward in the lobby. The latter, in very unlawyerlike fashion, could not help saying, "You would have done better to listen to reason, Mr. Worboise."

"I've fought fair, and lost, Mr. Sargent, and there's an end of it."

The chief consolation Mr. Worboise now had was that his son had come out so much more of a man than he had expected, having indeed foiled him at his own game, though not with his own weapons. To this was added the expectation of the property, after all, reverting to his son; while, to tell the truth, his mind was a little easier after he was rid of it, although he did not part with it one moment before he was compelled to do so. He made no advances toward a reconciliation with Thomas. Probably he thought that lay with Thomas, or at least would wait to give him an opportunity of taking the first step. Some might have expected that he would vow endless alienation from the son who had thus defeated his dearest plans, first in one direction, then in another; but somehow his heart took a turn short of that final bitterness.

Mrs. Boxall knew nothing yet of her happy reverse of fortune. They had judged it better to keep the fresh attempt from her, so that if by any chance it should fail, she might not suffer by it, and might be protected from anxiety and suspense.

"Let's give Grannie a surprise, Lucy," said Thomas.

"How do you mean, Thomas? We must be careful how we break it to her. Poor dear! She can't stand much now."

"Well, my plan will just do for that. Get her neighbor friend over the way to ask her to tea this evening. While she's away, Kitely, Spelt, and I will get all the things back into the old place. There's nobody there, is there?"

"No, I believe not. I don't see why we shouldn't. I'll run across to the old lady, and tell her we want Grannie out of the way for an hour or two."

Before Mrs. Boxall's visit was over, the whole of her household property had been replaced—each piece in the exact position it used to occupy when they had not yet dreamed of fortune or misfortune. Just as they were getting anxious lest she should come upon the last of it, Lucy suddenly thought of something.

"Mr. Kitely, you must lend us Widdles. Grannie can't exist without him."

"I wish you hadn't proposed it, Miss, for I did mean to have all the credit of that one stroke myself. But Widdles is yours, or hers rather, for you won't care much about the scaramouch."

"Not care about him! He's the noblest bird in creation! He doesn't mind being bald even, and that's the highest summit of disregard for appearances that I know of. I'm afraid I shouldn't take it so quietly."

Widdles followed the furniture, and when Grannie came home she found that her things were gone. She stared. Nobody was to be seen, but all were watching from behind Mr. Kitely's bookshelves.

"Mr. Kitely," she called at last, in a voice that revealed consternation.

The bookseller obeyed the summons.

"I didn't expect it of you, Mr. Kitely," she said, and burst into tears.

"We thought we could do a little better for you, Ma'am. This was a confined space for the likes of you, so Miss Lucy and I made bold to move your things up to a place in the court where you'll have more room."

She said nothing, but went upstairs. Both rooms were utterly empty.

Mr. Kitely followed her. "There's not a stick left, you see, Ma'am. Come, and I'll take you home."

"I didn't think you'd have turned me out in my old age, Mr. Kitely. But I suppose I must go."

It was with considerable self-denial that the bookseller refrained from telling her the truth. He led her up to the door of her own house.

"No, Mr. Kitely. I'll never set foot in that place again. I won't accept it from no one—not even rent-free."

"But it's your own," said Kitely, almost despairing of persuasion.

"That's just why I won't go in. It is mine, I know, but I won't have my own in charity."

"Thomas," whispered Lucy, for they were following behind, "*you* must tell her. Old people are hard to change, you know."

"Mrs. Boxall," said Thomas, going up to her, "this house is your own."

"Go away," returned Mrs. Boxall energetically. "Isn't it enough that you have robbed me? Will you offer me my own in charity? Call a cab, Lucy. We'll drive to the nearest workhouse."

Lucy saw it was time to interfere. "What Thomas says is true, Grannie, if you would only listen to him. Everything's changed. Thomas has been over the seas to find a man who was in Uncle's ship when it went down. He has given new evidence before the court, and the property is yours now."

"I don't care—it's all a trick. I don't believe he went over the seas. I won't take anything from the villain's hand."

"Villains don't usually plot to give away what they've got," said Lucy.

"But it's Thomas Worboise you mean."

"Yes; but he had nothing to do with it, as I've told you a hundred times, Grannie. He's gone and slaved for you, and that's all the thanks you give him—to stand there on the stones, refusing to take what's your very own."

The light was slowly dawning on Grannie's confused mind. "Then you mean," she said, "that all my son Richard's money—"

"Is yours, Grannie," said Lucy and Thomas in one breath.

"Only," added Lucy, smiling, "you've spoiled all our bit of fun by being so obstinate."

For sole answer the old woman gave a hand to each of them, and led them into the house, up the wide oak staircase, and along the passage to the old room, where a fire was burning cheerfully just as in the old time, and every article of furniture, bookcase, piano, and all, stood in its old place, as if it had never been moved.

Mrs. Boxall sat down in her own chair, and looked round. On the edge of the little table which had always been by her easy chair, stood Widdles.

"Poor Widdles!" said the old woman, and burst into tears.

45. Wound Up or Run Down

Thomas resumed his place in the office, occupying his old stool and drawing his old salary, upon which he now supported himself in comfort and decency. He took a simple lodging in the neighborhood, and went twice a week in the evening to see his mother and neither sought nor avoided his father.

His mother now lived on these visits and the expectation of them; she began not only to love her son more and more for himself, but to respect him, which respect only increased her love. If he was not converted, there must be something besides conversion that was yet good, if not so good. And she thought she might be excused if she found some pleasure even in that. It might be a weakness—it might be wrong, she thought, seeing that nothing short of absolute conversion was in the smallest degree pleasing in the sight of God; but as he was her own son, perhaps she would be excused, though certainly not justified. As Thomas' perception of truth grew, however, the conversations he had with her modified her judgment, although she never yielded one point of her creed as far as words were concerned.

The chief aid which Thomas had in his spiritual growth, next to an honest endeavor to do the work of the day and hour, and his love for Lucy, was the instruction of Mr. Fuller. Never, when he could help it, did he fail to be present at daily prayers in St. Amos'. Thomas did his work far more thoroughly and happily because of this daily worship and doctrine—a word never used by St. Paul except as meaning instruction in duty, in that which is right to do and that which is right not to do, including mental action as well as outward behavior.

It was impossible under the influence of such instruction that Tom should ever forget the friends who had upheld him in the time of his trouble. He often saw Captain Smith, and on one holiday he went on a voyage to Jersey with the Captain, working his passage as before, but with a very different heart inside his blue jacket. The Potts, too, he called on now and then, and even the unamiable Jim Salter came round to confess his respect for him, when he found that Tom never forgot his old mates.

As soon as Thomas resumed his stool in the countinghouse, Mr. Wither resigned his and went abroad.

Mrs. Boxall recovered her cheerfulness, but her whole character was more subdued. A certain tenderness toward Lucy appeared, which, notwithstanding all her former kindness, was entirely new. A great part of her time was spent in offices of goodwill toward Widdles. However, she always kept her behavior to Mr. Stopper somewhat stately and distant. He continued to do his best for the business, for it was the best for himself.

Mr. Spelt and Mr. Kitely each were happy in a daughter, with Mattie and Poppie growing away at their own history.

One evening, when Tom was seated with his mother, his father came into the room and said, without any greeting, "Keep a lookout on that Stopper, Tom. Don't let him have too much of his own way."

"But I have no authority over him, Father."

"Then the sooner you marry and take the business into your own hands the better."

"I'm going to be married next week."

"That's right. Make Stopper junior partner, and don't give him too large a share. Come to me to draw up the articles for you."

"Thank you, Father, I will. I believe Mrs. Boxall does mean to make the business over to me."

"Of course. Good night," returned Mr. Worboise, and left the room.

From that time Tom and his father met much as before their quarrel. Tom returned to the house for the week before his marriage, and his father made him a present of an outfit for the occasion.

Their wedding day came and went, and after their wedding journey they went back to newly fitted rooms in the old house in Guild Court.

"O Tom! I can hardly believe any of our good fortune," said Lucy, when they opened the door together.

"I don't deserve any of it," was all Tom's answer—in words, at least.